POINT BLANK

"DeWitt, are you and your men in the green?"

"Yeah, we're out, probably still downstream from you. We're getting ready to move. We took some return fire, and I don't know when it happened, but we've got one man shot up pretty bad . . . How deep are you in the brush?"

"Fifty yards. Work the road. We haven't seen any kind of resistance. We'll get close to the road and wait."

Murdock moved his squad back so they could see the road and offer defensive fire if needed.

Three minutes later, Lam lifted his head and turned his head so his ear was toward the trail. "Coming," Lam said. "Not sure who. Somebody. Making too much noise."

"DeWitt, are you on the road?"

"No, having trouble getting Ostercamp moved. He's worse than we thought. We're just past the road in the edge of the jungle."

"Still coming," Lam said. "My guess is about twenty armed men with all their equipment jingling."

In the soft Philippine moonlight, Murdock soon saw the men approaching. They were soldiers in a column of fours with their weapons at port and ready. They were less than forty yards away.

"Open fire," Murdock said. He had no idea what a 20mm round would do at point-blank range, but he was going to find out.

SEAL TEAM SEVEN
AMBUSH

KEITH DOUGLASS

BERKLEY BOOKS, NEW YORK

Special thanks to Chet Cunningham for his contribution to this book.

SEAL TEAM SEVEN: AMBUSH

A Berkley Book / published by arrangement with
the author

PRINTING HISTORY
Berkley edition / November 2001

Visit our website at
www.penguinputnam.com

ISBN: 0-425-18219-3

BERKLEY®
Berkley Books are published by The Berkley Publishing Group,
a division of Penguin Putnam Inc.,
375 Hudson Street,
New York, New York 10014.
BERKLEY and the "B" design
are trademarks belonging to Penguin Putnam Inc.

PRINTED IN THE UNITED STATES OF AMERICA

10 9 8 7 6 5 4 3 2 1

*This SEALs book
is gratefully dedicated to
those grunts, those drafted GIs,
who froze and roasted in Korea and
who put up with the trauma
of combat and came
home without a
deluge of self-pity and
harangue about how shabbily
they had been
treated by
the rest of the
country.*

Dear Reader,

Hey, help me out here, could you? I'm having a long-range fight with my editor about who reads the *SEAL Team Seven* books. I keep telling her we have a sizable number of women readers. She says it can't be true. These are *men's action* books. Why would a woman want to read them?

I'm not winning my argument. I know there are a lot of women readers who dig into the SEAL books. Maybe they are second-hand readers, getting it after their husbands or boyfriends read it. So? A woman reader is a woman reader.

I'd really like to get about a hundred letters or cards from you women readers out there. You guys write too. Let my good old editor know that you're out there and alive and reading. Thanks, I'd appreciate it. Send those cards and letters right here to:

Keith Douglass
SEAL TEAM SEVEN
8431 Beaver Lake Drive
San Diego, CA 92119

Thanks a lot, and I'll answer every letter I get. So, see if we can swamp my editor. Yeah!

Keith Douglass

Rear Admiral (L) Richard Kenner. Commander of all SEALs.

Commander Dean Masciareli. 47, 5'11", 220 pounds. Annapolis graduate. Commanding officer of Navy Special Warfare Group One in Coronado, including SEAL Teams One, Three, Five, and Seven, and its 965 men.

Master Chief Petty Officer Gordon MacKenzie. 47, 5'10", 180 pounds. Administrator and head enlisted man of all of SEAL Team Seven.

Lieutenant Commander Blake Murdock. Platoon Leader. 32, 6'2", 210 pounds. Annapolis graduate. Six years in SEALs. Father important congressman from Virginia. Single. Apartment in Coronado. Has a car and a motorcycle, loves to fish. Weapon: Alliant Bull Pup duo 5.56mm & 20mm explosive round. Alternate: H & K MP-5SD submachine gun.

ALPHA SQUAD

Timothy F. Sadler. Senior Chief Petty Officer. Top EM in platoon. Third in command. 32, 6'2", 220 pounds. Married to Sylvia, no children. Been in the Navy for fifteen years, a SEAL for last eight. Expert fisherman. Plays trumpet in any Dixieland combo he can find. Weapon: Alliant Bull Pup duo 5.56mm & 20mm explosive round. Good with the men.

*Third Platoon assigned exclusively to the Central Intelligence Agency to perform any needed tasks on a covert basis anywhere in the world. All are top-secret assignments. Goes around Navy chain of command. Direct orders from the CIA.

David "Jaybird" Sterling. Machinist's Mate Second Class, Lead petty officer. 24, 5'10", 170 pounds. Quick mind, fine tactician. Single. Drinks too much sometimes. Crack shot with all arms. Grew up in Oregon. Helps plan attack operations. Weapon: H & K MP-5SD submachine gun.

Luke "Mountain" Howard. Gunner's Mate Second Class. 28, 6'4", 250 pounds. Black man. Football at Oregon State. Tryout with Oakland Raiders six years ago. In Navy six years, SEAL for four. Single. Rides a motorcycle. A skiing and windsurfing nut. Squad sniper. Weapon: H & K PSG1 7.62 NATO sniper rifle. Or McMillan M-87R .50-caliber long-range gun.

Bill Bradford. Quartermaster's Mate First Class. 24, 6'2", 215 pounds. An artist in spare time. Paints oils. He sells his marine paintings. Single. Quiet. Reads a lot. Has two years of college. Platoon radio operator. Carries a SATCOM on most missions. Weapon: Alliant Bull Pup duo 5.56mm & 20mm explosive round.

Joe "Ricochet" Lampedusa. Operations Specialist Third Class. 21, 5'11", 175 pounds. Good tracker, quick thinker. Had a year of college. Loves motorcycles. Wants a Hog. Pot smoker on the sly. Picks up plain girls. Platoon scout. Weapon: Colt M-4A1 rifle with grenade launcher. Alternate: Alliant Bull Pup duo 5.56mm & 20mm explosive round.

Kenneth Ching. Quartermaster's Mate First Class. 25, 6' even, 180 pounds. Full-blooded Chinese. Platoon translator. Speaks Mandarin Chinese, Japanese, Russian, and Spanish. Bicycling nut. Paid $1,200 for off-road bike. Is trying for Officer Candidate School. Weapon: Colt M-4A1 rifle with grenade launcher.

Vincent "Vinnie" Van Dyke. Electrician's Mate Second Class. 24, 6'2", 220 pounds. Enlisted out of high school. Played varsity basketball. Wants to be a commercial fisherman after his current hitch. Good with his hands. Squad machine gunner. Weapon: H & K 21-E 7.62 NATO round machine gun.

Bravo Squad

Lieutenant (j.g.) Ed DeWitt. Leader Bravo Squad. Second in command of the platoon. 30, 6'1", 175 pounds. Wiry. SEAL for four years. From Seattle. Married to Milly. Annapolis graduate. A career man. Plays a good game of chess on traveling board. Weapon: Alliant Bull Pup duo 5.56mm & 20mm explosive round. Alternate: H & K G-11 submachine gun.

George Canzoneri. Torpedoman's Mate First Class. 27, 5'11", 190 pounds. Married to Navy wife, Phyllis. No kids. Nine years in Navy. Expert on explosives. Nicknamed "Petard" for almost hoisting himself one time. Top pick in platoon for explosive work. Weapon: Alliant Bull Pup duo 5.56mm & 20mm explosive round.

Miguel Fernandez. Gunner's Mate First Class. 26, 6'1", 180 pounds. Wife, Maria; daughter, Linda, 7, in Coronado. Spends his off time with them. Highly family-oriented. He has relatives in San Diego. Speaks Spanish and Portuguese. Squad sniper. Weapon: H & K PSG1 7.62 NATO sniper rifle.

Colt "Guns" Franklin. Yeoman Second Class. 24, 5'10", 175 pounds. A former gymnast. Powerful arms and shoulders. Expert mountain climber. Has a motorcycle and does hang gliding. Speaks Farsi and Arabic. Weapon: Colt M-4A1 with grenade launcher.

Tran "Train" Khai. Torpedoman Second Class. 23, 6'1", 180 pounds. U.S.-born Vietnamese. A whiz at languages and computers. Speaks Vietnamese, French, German, Spanish, and Arabic. Specialist in electronics. Understands the new 20mm Bull Pup weapon. Can repair the electronics in it. Plans on becoming an electronics engineer. Joined the Navy for $40,000 college funding. Entranced by SEALs. First hitch up in four months. Weapon: H & K G-11 with caseless rounds, 4.7mm submachine gun with 50-round magazine.

Jack Mahanani. Hospital Corpsman First Class. 25, 6'4", 240 pounds. Platoon medic. Tahitian/Hawaiian. Expert swimmer. Bench-presses 400 pounds. Once married, divorced. Top surfer. Weapon: Alliant Bull Pup duo 5.56 & 20mm explosive round. Alternate: Colt M-4A1 rifle with grenade launcher.

Anthony "Tony" Ostercamp. Machinist's Mate First Class. 24, 6'1", 210 pounds. Races stock cars in nearby El Cajon weekends. Top auto mechanic. Platoon driver. Weapon: H & K 21-E 7.62 NATO round machine gun. Second radio operator.

Paul "Jeff" Jefferson. Engineman Second Class. 23, 6'1", 200 pounds. Black man. Expert in small arms. Can tear apart most weapons and reassemble, repair, and innovate them. A chess player to match Ed DeWitt. Weapon: Alliant Bull Pup duo 5.56mm & 20mm explosive round.

1

The Mediterranean Sea
Near the Libyan coast

Lieutenant Commander Blake Murdock stared into blackness of night as rain wind-whipped into his face. He had been uneasy about this mission from the start. First, it had taken them ten minutes longer than planned to launch the two rubber ducks from the submarine deck. Now, as the two small craft powered toward the Libyan coast three miles away, his unease grew.

All sixteen SEALs from Third Platoon of SEAL Team Seven were crouched in the two fifteen-foot-long Zodiac-type IBSs (Inflatable Boat Small), each IBS powered by a fifty-five-horsepower outboard. In decent weather they could make eighteen knots. Not with the current four-foot seas and gusting wind.

The two craft were tied together by a thirty-foot line, and they had trouble staying that close to each other. Murdock, in his boat, and Lieutenant (j.g.) Ed DeWitt, in his, both had their Motorola personal radios out. The rest of the platoon kept their radios in the usual watertight compartments.

Murdock's radio sputtered.

"Skipper, we've got some trouble coming up on the port side. Sounds like a coastal patrol craft. No idea how big. He might miss us. He has a searchlight probing around."

"Roger that, Ed. Keep watching him. Yeah, I see him now. Unless he turns, we should be okay."

As soon as Murdock said it, the ghostly lighted craft, not

1

more than seventy-five yards off, turned and headed directly toward them.

"Lam, get the EAR out now," Murdock whispered just loud enough so his lead scout could hear. Joe Lampedusa, Operations Specialist Third Class, lifted a strange-looking weapon from under his poncho.

"Fully charged, Skipper," Lam said. He raised the Enhanced Audio Rifle, and aimed it at the oncoming patrol craft.

"If he spots us, give him two shots," Murdock whispered. Lam nodded in the darkness.

They watched the sweep of the powerful searchlight as it skipped across the whitecaps of the Mediterranean Sea. It almost touched them once, then rotated back the other way. The next time it came around, the craft itself was not more than twenty-five yards shoreward, and the light touched DeWitt's boat first.

"Fire," Murdock said. Lam aimed and pulled the trigger. The sound that came from the EAR was not an explosion; it was more like a whooshing of air. Half a second later the audio blast hit the patrol boat and the three crewmen on the small bridge had no time to react. They slumped over and fell to the deck. The craft's engines kept going at the set speed, but with no one on the wheel, it cut a slow-arc course away from land.

Lam spotted two more sailors rushing toward the bridge. He fired again. The EAR weapon had had the required ten seconds between shots to recharge itself. The second blast hit the patrol ship and the last two men on board fell as if sleeping. They would be unconscious for four to six hours, and wake up with no physical harm. Their only problem would be explaining to their commanding officer what had happened.

"Good shooting, Lam," Murdock said. He stared toward the shore now, and could see that the lights they had been keying on were closer. "Steady as she goes, Mr. DeWitt. We should still be on course. Let's move the throttles up so we can make ten knots. Nobody is going to hear us in this storm."

Murdock mulled over the mission. Every man in the pla-

toon knew the details. That was the way the SEALs operated. They were to land on what was supposed to be a
deserted stretch of beach near the small town of Al Hamim,
which was west of Tubruq. If matters went to the worst
scenario, the friendly border of Egypt was only sixty miles
to the east.

First they would land, then hide the boats and move
seven miles inland to a village called Bani Qatrun. Murdock
watched the lights. They appeared to be closer. The small
boats fought an outgoing tide as well as the weather. The
rain kept falling. It would help shield their entry and, hopefully, their exit. The submarine would hold just off the east
coast of Libya, and surface for a five A.M. pickup. If all
went well.

Murdock had argued about this mission. He felt that risk-
ing the lives of sixteen men to recover one man was not
good strategy. Then they'd explained who the one man was,
a top CIA field agent who had been compromised and captured. He had been in custody only two days, and might
not have leaked any of the vast amounts of special knowl-
edge that he had. Clive Ambrose Cullhagen was not an
ordinary CIA agent. He'd been instrumental in establishing
the CIA's newest world-events-evaluation center. He was
a living storehouse of U.S. plans and secrets and those of
half of our allies who used the center.

He had to come out.

The CIA director had emphasized that Cullhagen had to
come out dead or alive. A top-security phone call had involved four men on a conference call. Murdock had been
one; the CIA director, the Secretary of State, and the President of the United States had been the others. They had
talked it over for almost an hour; then the CIA director
had called the Chief of Naval Operations and the wheels
had turned.

"I can hear the surf ahead," the Motorola speaker in Murdock's ear reported.

"Yes, I've got it," Murdock said. "With the first breaker
we cut the tie rope."

"Roger that, Skipper," DeWitt said.

Murdock took the tiller then and directed the small craft

exactly where he wanted it, angling the motor, adjusting the direction. The breakers were not as severe as they could be. He heard the crash of the water against sand. Then they were there. Jaybird cut the tie line, and Murdock rammed the throttle forward to catch the surge of water that would develop into a breaker. He wanted to surf along the top and at the last minute race down the slope of the wall of water.

It didn't happen that way.

A larger swell came in at a forty-five-degree angle and ate up Murdock's surge. It battered the rubber duck, threatened to flip it over, then slammed it sideways toward the beach and the sand that came up suddenly. The rubber duck danced on the second surge for a moment, then righted itself and slid down the front of the breaker like a surfer avoiding the crashing water.

When the small craft nosed inward and then glided on shallow water toward the beach, Luke Howard, Gunner's Mate Second Class, and Machinist's Mate Second Class Jaybird Sterling jumped out, grabbed the pull ropes, and tugged the rubber craft higher on the beach on the thin flow of the receding breaker.

Four SEALs ran up the twenty yards of sand to the dry area and dropped to a prone position with their weapons covering the shoreline ahead of them. The rest of the SEALs crouched in the boats until they saw a signal from the scouts onshore. Then they left the rubber ducks and charged inland forty yards to a brushy area. They quickly secured the spot, posted lookouts; then men picked up the 265-pound rubber boats and ran with them to the brush, where the boats were hidden and camouflaged with branches.

Murdock stared out of the copse of stunted juniper and lentisk trees. They were growing only because of the moist influences of the Mediterranean Sea. He knew that the rest of Libya was dry; ninety-nine percent of the nation was classified as a desert with less than six inches of rainfall a year.

Murdock went over the images in his mind of the maps he had memorized. The village they needed was inland about seven miles, in a desert resort where water percolated up through the sand to create a true oasis. He checked his watch: ten minutes after midnight. If they stole a truck, they could be discovered. They had to stay as silent and unseen as possible until the attack on the house. The decision had been made to hike through the desert to the site. The men were traveling comparatively light with about sixty pounds of gear, weapons, ammo, and explosives. They wore their desert cammies and most had floppy hats, kerchiefs, or watch caps for headgear.

The men quickly took out their Motorolas and attached them with the lip mikes. Murdock called for a platoon radio check, and the seven men in his squad reported in the correct order. Then Bravo Squad came on. All accounted for.

"We have a fringe of developed land along the coast, maybe three miles deep," Murdock said into his mike. "We get through that into the increasingly dry desert, until within five miles we're in the heart of the Sahara with sand built on sand. We find a highway to the site and follow it. This time we hike. We don't want to ring an alarm by stealing a vehicle. Maybe on the way back. It's only seven miles. About an hour out. Let's chogie."

Joe "Ricochet" Lampedusa took the point as scout as usual, moving out fifty yards as the others waited in the brush. Lam crossed a blacktopped road and scurried to a ditch on the other side as two cars whipped past. Ahead lay the outskirts of the coastal village. Two houses and a pair of sheds. Lam worked around them, saw no lights on, and waved the platoon forward.

Murdock took his Alpha Squad out first. Here they were in a single-file combat mode, five yards apart. They jogged across the road when it was clear, and then moved silently past the houses into an irrigated field. It had been harvested, and Murdock figured the crop was a grain of some kind. The coastal plain here was irrigated from wells and some small oasis spots where water bubbled up from the underground water table. His intelligence reports said that at this spot along the coast the arable land extended only three miles inland.

Once across the irrigated field, Lam angled to the west, where he heard traffic. The reports said there would be little vehicular use of the roadway into the maximum-security facility.

For once Murdock had been given exacting information about their target. It was a former European-owned estate house, with a fenced compound, guards outside and in the main house. There were two other buildings on the site, one a barracks for the military guards, and another that was formerly a garage, now used for supply and storage. No dogs were reported inside the wire. The SEALs had worked out an attack plan, but situations often changed when the platoon came to the actual target.

The irrigated fields lasted for three miles inland, with an occasional house and a few buildings where the owner of the land lived. Background on the area advised Murdock that most of the parcels were small, some only five or six acres, and they were highly prized because of the shortage of arable land.

Sand and clumps of saltwort and spurge flax began to invade the area as the SEALs moved south toward the desert. The clump grasses would soon take over the land in the area that couldn't be irrigated.

Up front, Lam had located the roadway south and had paralleled it three hundred yards off. There had been some truck traffic, and now there was a sedan or two, all painted military dull-green. Once past the cultivated fields, Lam found what he figured were off-road vehicle trails. Some had metal tracks; others had low-pressure tires to bigfoot on the softer sandy areas. He stopped and listened, but heard only one sedan on the highway. He moved ahead.

"Some strange tracks, Skipper," Lam reported on the radio. "Not sure what they are, but they ain't here now."

"Roger that. Keep your ears open."

They moved ahead. Five minutes later the third platoon went to ground as a roaring, clattering armored personnel carrier stormed out of a wadi to the left and charged into the center of their line of march.

The desert-cammy-clad men dove into the sand and watched the machine storm toward them. It had no forward lights, but the Libyan moon was full, giving reasonable night vision. Tran Khai, Torpedoman Second Class, and

Jack Mahanani, Hospital Corpsman First Class, had to surge up from the sand and sprint ten yards to get out of the direct path of the growling giant.

There was no reaction from the men in the armored carrier. Either they didn't see any of the SEALs, or they discounted them as a friendly patrol. The rig continued in a straight line to the highway, then turned and headed south along the road.

"Radio check, Bravo," the JG whispered into his mike. All seven men responded. "Okay here, Skipper," DeWitt reported.

"The driver wasn't using night vision goggles or he would have spotted those two runners. We lucked out on that one. But it could mean tighter security around this special facility than we figured."

A half-mile march farther into the desert, they came to shifting sand and dunes twenty feet high. Lam moved the men closer to the road, but kept a hundred yards away.

Murdock figured they were still two miles from the facility when Lam called.

"Skip, we've got some trouble. Better come up and take a gander. I'd guess it's a blocking force up front."

Five minutes later, Murdock and Lam bellied up the side of a sand dune and peered over the top. They had heard voices, metal on metal, and even Murdock could smell the spicy aroma of food.

"Lunchtime for a twelve-hour shift," Lam said.

In a small wadi near the road, a field kitchen had been set up, complete with mess tent and a cook tent. Still in line at the serving table were a dozen troops in field gear and with weapons slung over their shoulders. They all wore steel helmets.

"How many?" Murdock asked.

Both men stared through their NVGs, which turned the night into a green dusk.

"Thirty, maybe thirty-five, depending how many are in the mess tent," Lam said.

"Agreed. If they're eating, they won't be on patrol. Might be a good time for us to move."

As he said it, an armored personnel carrier roared up

thirty yards downwind from the kitchen, and a dozen men poured out of the rig. They yelled and shouted and raced each other to the chow line. None carried mess kits. They would eat off metal trays.

On the way back to the rest of the troops, Lam and Murdock worked out their plan. They would move a half mile to the side of the eatery, and pound past as quickly as they could, then swing back toward the highway.

It took twenty minutes for the maneuver; then they worked south again five hundred yards off the highway. They were in their usual field formation, a diamond for each squad, with Lam out in front of Alpha Squad.

There was no warning. They were marching along, knowing they were coming closer, when three white flares burst over their heads turning the black night into midday bright. At once rifle fire stuttered from the darkness in front of them.

2

At the first crack of the flares high overhead, the SEALs dove for the ground hunting any cover they could find. There was none. No orders were needed. The SEALs automatically returned fire. Four men with Bull Pups aimed the 20mm lasered airburst rounds at the muzzle flashes in the darkness. Four seconds after the first rifle fire aimed at them, the SEALs had returned the first shots. Two seconds later four more 20mm airbursts thundered into the dark of the Libyan desert. Only one enemy rifle fired after that. The flare continued to burn for thirty seconds, which seemed to be a lifetime.

The SEALs had stopped firing when the enemy guns went silent.

"Hold for the flare, then we move up to where those guns fired from," Murdock ordered in his mike.

The flares fizzled out and glorious darkness reigned again.

"Let's go check our work," Murdock said. The SEALs lifted off the sand, formed into a line of skirmishers, and with weapons trained to the front, walked forward. The squad of Libyan soldiers lay sprawled in a wadi only two feet deep, but usually enough to offer total cover for the men. They didn't count on the airbursts.

One Libyan was still alive. Colt Franklin, Yeoman Second Class, grabbed the man and spoke gently to him in Arabic. Murdock hurried up. "Ask him why all the security."

Franklin did, and the man shook his head. "Said he has

no idea. He just does what the officers tell him."

"Ask if he knows what is in the large house a few miles south."

Again the Libyan shook his head. "He says some important people but he doesn't know who."

They went on questioning the man, who was badly wounded. He told them about the defenses, where the most troops were, and how the fence was electrified in some sections.

The man cried out in sudden pain; then his whole body shook for a moment before his head rolled back and both hands fell to his sides.

"He's gone," Murdock said. "Check the weapons, bring along anything that might help us. Should be some Kalashnikovs here. Sounded like them when they were firing. Then we haul ass before somebody else shows up."

They looked around in the darkness, found six rifles that looked new enough to take—they were the older AK47, but potent and with a better range than the MP-5's some of the SEALs carried.

Murdock put the men on a jog for a mile on south from the point of contact, and they soon heard a chopper swing over the area of the fight and land.

"A chopper out here means trouble," DeWitt said on the radio.

"True, and we'll see if we can give it some trouble as soon as we see it up close," Murdock said.

Another half mile through the sand along the roadway, and Lam called a halt and showed Murdock the lights ahead.

"Must be it," Lam said. "Lit up like a call girl's switchboard."

"Lights we can turn off," Murdock said. "They already know somebody is coming to visit. Hope they didn't kill the prisoner when they heard the firefight."

"We'll do it the way we laid it out," Murdock told the net. "Bravo will be the main assault force on the west side. Alpha will do the diversionary attack on the east side and hopefully draw off the firepower that way. We need to get close enough to blow the gate on the west side, or the fence nearby for access. Any questions?"

"How do the twenties come in?" Lam asked. They were all in a line, looking over the top of a sand dune a quarter of a mile from the compound.

Ed DeWitt spoke up. "Bravo will take out the gate guards and the gate itself with the twenties from two hundred yards. Then we move up half our squad, with the other half working the twenties on any force that appears to challenge us. Once we're inside, the twenty-shooters charge forward and join us."

"On the other side of the compound, Alpha Squad will be shooting up the fence and that side of the big house," Murdock said. "We'll use our twenties on anything that moves over there. Probably can't get through the fence with the twenties, but we'll use charges and blow a hole big enough for ingress."

"Questions?" DeWitt asked the radio net.

"How do we find the guy once we're inside?" Fernandez asked.

"We have two Arabic speakers," DeWitt said. "They will question anyone we find alive. He's in the big house somewhere. It can't have more than twenty rooms according to the blueprints we saw. Two stories, no basement."

"We don't use the EARs?" Jaybird asked.

"No, we don't want to knock out our CIA man and have to carry him back to the water," DeWitt said.

"Let's do it," Murdock said. "Alpha on me. We have fifteen minutes to get into position and start our diversion. Five minutes after our first shot, Bravo will attack. Let's move."

It took Alpha twenty minutes to get to the other side of the fortified house and to set up for their ambush. They settled in ten yards apart. They had three of the Bull Pups for this mission, and Bravo had four. Murdock checked the perimeter fence with his NVGs and then gave the word to fire. They hit the fence and caught one interior guard walking his post. The twenties boomed in the night and exploded on contact. Murdock's first shot blew the side door off the house. A jeep rolled around the corner, then retreated behind the safety of the house. The SEALs didn't aim at any windows to keep from hitting the prisoner inside.

Half a dozen rifles began returning fire, but the SEALs had set up in a gully three feet deep for top protection. The jeep driver decided to try to get from the house to the storage shed. It was halfway there when a 20mm round blew the vehicle off its wheels and dumped it upside down against the building.

A moment later Ed DeWitt opened fire on the main gate. The first round knocked out the guard post there; the next three hit the rollback electrically operated gate and closed a circuit somewhere. The heavy gate rolled open and stayed there. A squad of six men ran around the barracks, and was cut down by shrapnel from a pair of exploding twenties on the front of the barracks itself. One man limped away, but was dumped into the dirt by a sniper rifle shot. For a moment all was quiet at the front of the place. DeWitt could hear firing at the other side.

Then an engine roared and an armored personnel carrier stormed around the barracks, headed for the main gate. It slued to a stop, then straightened itself until its big automatic cannon swung out toward the gun flashes.

"Kill the lights," DeWitt told his radio mike. Miguel Fernandez, Gunner's Mate First Class, swung his H & K 7.62 sniper rifle around and began taking down the searchlights one by one.

"Franklin, put enough WP in front of that tank to blind him. Now. Six, eight rounds, and let's hope there isn't a lot of wind."

The first 40mm grenade from the Colt M-4A1 landed beside the tank, exploded with a spray of white phosphorus that turned into a dense smoke. The second and third rounds hit in front of the armored personnel carrier. It was like the heavy hitter had gone away, until they heard the sound of the cannon going off and three rounds slammed into the ground twenty feet behind them, spraying deadly shrapnel the wrong way to hurt the SEALs.

DeWitt used his 5.56mm rounds from his Bull Pup to

kill two more lights, and the whole front of the compound went dark.

"Let's move up," DeWitt said on his mike. "Split and half go up on each side of the gate. Leave forty yards between us for the big gun to shoot into. Move it. Now."

They went forward at a trot, weapons on their hips ready to fire. Sporadic shots came through the front gate aimed where the SEALs used to be. They didn't fire now so they wouldn't give away their location. They went a hundred yards; then the smoke eased away from the armored personnel carrier.

"More smoke," DeWitt said on the net. "Both of you, three rounds each."

Franklin and Ostercamp both fired, and the personnel carrier rapidly vanished again. The SEALs were running now, flat out for the front gate.

"Assault fire," DeWitt called, and the eight weapons opened up. The twenties fired, the sniper rifle, the G-11 with caseless rounds, and then the 5.56's on the Bull Pups chattered. There was little return fire. No SEAL was hit.

They stormed toward the gate with the smoke covering it, and jolted through. DeWitt had been making a bomb with a quarter pound of TNAZ as he ran. He inserted a timer and set it for five seconds. The armored machine leaped out of the smoke at them suddenly, and DeWitt raced the twenty feet to the side. He pushed the bomb into the tread of the machine and pressed the activator on the five-second timer. Then he ran forward.

Five seconds on these timers could be tricky. Sometimes they went off at four and even three, sometimes seven or eight. This one blasted on four seconds, and the last of the SEALs through the gate had just cleared the machine when the TNAZ exploded. It blew the tread all the way off the vehicle and dumped it on its side.

A squad of three Libyan soldiers surged around the far end of the house, their rifles up. Tran Khai, Torpedoman Second Class, splattered the trio with a dozen rounds from his G-11 submachine gun, and they spun away dead before they hit the ground.

"Front door," DeWitt said on the radio.

Canzoneri got there first. He had two TNAZ bombs ready, and pasted one on each side of the door lock, activated ten-second timers, and rushed away to the side of the building.

The explosion blasted large sections of the door inward, leaving a gaping hole where it had been, and also blew away two feet of the front wall.

As planned, DeWitt went in first, diving to the left. Fernandez dove in to the right a moment later. Lights were still on in the house.

"Clear, right," Fernandez said.

"Here too," DeWitt said.

Two more SEALs charged through the door and down the hall they knew was there. Two enemy riflemen came into the far end of the corridor, only to be met with a hail of SEAL lead that put them down and crawling back around the corner. DeWitt guessed that the prisoner would be held on the second floor. The stairs were in the center of the house off the hallway. He and Fernandez rushed past doors the others would clear, made it to the stairs, and started up. A stutter of a submachine gun came from the top of the steps.

DeWitt took a round to his left arm, and jerked back out of sight. Fernandez hadn't started up the steps yet; now he undid a fragger hand grenade from his webbing, pulled the pin, and leaned around the wall far enough to throw the bomb to the top of the steps. It hit, bounced once against the top wall, and exploded.

The two SEALS stormed up the stairs, their weapons aimed ahead and fingers on triggers. There was no response. At the top of the steps they found two soldiers dying of their wounds. They kicked away their weapons and charged to the first door along a hall that had four. DeWitt kicked in the door. The room was empty.

Fernandez took the next room, tried the doorknob. Locked. He rapped on the door, standing to the side against the wall. Four rounds blasted through the light door. Fernandez stepped back, unpinned a grenade, and held it ready. Then he kicked in the door and threw in the grenade in one move, and dodged behind the hall wall again.

When the shrapnel from the grenade stopped flying, DeWitt charged into the room. His Bull Pup chattered off two three-round bursts; then Fernandez ran into the room and found it clear, with two officers who must have just been getting up from their beds. They wouldn't have to worry about sleeping ever again.

The two SEALs rushed out of the room and to the next door. Before they could try for it, a dozen rounds blasted through the door. "Might be our man inside," DeWitt said. "No grenade." The door was locked. DeWitt kicked in the door and leaped to the safety of the wall. Twenty rounds whistled through the opening and into the wall opposite it. DeWitt checked around the door jamb from the floor level. Just one man in the small room. He had his officer's jacket neatly hung on a chair back with the gold star on the shoulder boards polished bright.

DeWitt flipped in a grenade and when it exploded, the two SEALs moved to the last door on the hallway. It was double and had a nameplate on it they couldn't read.

No response from inside. Fernandez kicked in the door and barely got out of the way to the wall, but no gunfire came from the room. Fernandez checked the room from the floor level. He grunted, stood, and walked into the room.

There were three civilians standing there, all holding their hands in the air. On a chair facing them sat a man in a rumpled business suit. On the dresser lay a medical kit with six syringes and a dozen small vials of fluid.

The man in a white doctor's coat said something, and indicated the man sitting in the chair.

"Franklin, get your ass up to the second floor, last room, we need your Arabic," DeWitt said on the radio.

DeWitt stepped forward and looked at the man in the chair. It was Cullhagen; he'd seen the man's picture. He was a bear, almost six feet four and 250 pounds. Dark curly hair spilled down into his eyes and he had a three-day beard. He seemed to be dazed, probably drugged. Franklin ran in a few moments later before DeWitt could talk to the man.

"Ask them what they've done to this man," DeWitt said. The doctor looked up at the Arabic question and responded briefly. "He says questioning him, that's all."

"What drugs did they use?"

In response to that question, the doctor hesitated, then pointed to the tray and showed them one vial. Franklin looked at the label, and shook his head. "No idea what it is."

"Ask him how long for the man to recover from the drug."

The doctor held up his hands and said he didn't know. DeWitt hit the man in the jaw with his fist, jolting him backward against the wall. "Ask him again."

Franklin did. The doctor cowered back and mumbled an answer.

"He said about four more hours."

"We don't have four hours. There will be choppers and troops all over this place within an hour." DeWitt looked at the vials on the dresser. "Ask him which one of these drugs will bring him out of the other drug state."

Franklin did, and the doctor lifted his brows.

"Tell him if he tries to use the wrong one to kill the prisoner, I'll tear his tongue off, gouge out his eyes, rip off his balls, and make him eat them. Tell him that exactly."

As Franklin repeated the words to the Libyan doctor, the man's frozen smile faded and a look of stark terror replaced it. He began to tremble, then sagged against the wall.

"Search all three," DeWitt bellowed. They found a small automatic, three small knives, and two pills.

The doctor motioned to the box of drugs. "He says the one with the blue label will bring the prisoner around in ten minutes, and leave no harmful effects."

"DeWitt, you have the subject, can he travel?" Murdock asked on the radio.

"Not yet, maybe in ten minutes. Your situation?"

"We're through the fence, mopping up. Found half a dozen more guards. Most of the others seem to be out in blocking positions. We control the area. You really smashed that personnel carrier."

"Good old TNAZ."

DeWitt looked back at the doctor. "Tell him to do it now.

Any problem and he's a dead man, very slowly and painfully a dead man."

Fernandez had tied the other two civilians' arms behind them with plastic strips and sat them down along the far wall. The doctor picked up the medication, put it in a syringe, and went toward Cullhagen. DeWitt grabbed his hand.

"Do it right or you're dead." He put the Bull Pup muzzle against his head and said, "Bang." The doctor almost fainted. He nodded, pushed the needle into Cullhagen's arm, and injected the drug.

Two minutes later the CIA man began to recover. Five minutes and he looked around, scowled, and started talking, but they couldn't understand him.

DeWitt frowned and called Murdock to come up. They watched Cullhagen and whispered to each other.

"Is he going to be lucid enough to travel with us?" DeWitt asked.

"Or do we put him down?" Murdock asked.

"I didn't want to make that decision myself," DeWitt said.

Twelve minutes after the injection, Cullhagen coughed, looked up, and blinked. He rubbed one hand over his face and stared at the doctor standing in front of him.

"Like I told you, you sonofabitch, I'm not going to tell you a damn thing. I don't know anything. I'm a fucking driver who got pulled into this assignment because our regular guy got the—do you believed it—mumps." He looked around, grinned when he saw the SEALs. "Well, different uniforms. Our side, I hope." He held out his hand to DeWitt. "Cullhagen here. When the hell does the chopper get here to take us out of this pigsty of a rat fucking hole?"

"Sir, as soon as you can walk and carry an AK47 rifle and forty rounds."

Cullhagen blinked, shook his head. "Damn glad to see you guys. Let me walk around a little. Don't hurt these guys, they weren't half bad. They had an Army interrogator coming in. He'd have pulled my asshole right out my nose before he was done with me. Let's get moving."

"It's seven miles through the sand," Murdock said.

"Hell, I did two tours in Nam. I can hike fifty miles with a fifty-pound pack. Let's go."

They went down the stairs and out to the front of the house. Half a dozen soldiers lay on the ground where they had been tied up after capture. They would live. Jaybird ran up waving his arms. "Found a truck at the side of the barracks. Old, but it runs. Might beat walking."

Murdock had watched Cullhagen walk down the stairs and then out of the house. There was no chance that he could do seven miles even without a rifle.

"Can we all get inside?" DeWitt asked.

"It's a flatbed with stakes on the sides and back. Room for everyone."

"Get it over here," Murdock said. "We run into the patrols this way and any blocking force, we use the EAR on them so they don't warn anyone ahead we're coming. Let's do it."

Ten minutes later they left the front gate. They had to nudge the toppled personnel carrier out of the way, then rolled down the gravel road. The old truck would do thirty miles an hour top speed. That was five times what they could do walking.

A mile down the road they saw lights and slowed. The two men with the EAR weapons aimed them over the top of the cab and waited. It was a blocking force of troops, about fifty, Murdock decided. Two vehicles lit up the sides of the road. Two men stood in the road waving for them to stop. At two hundred yards, the pair of EAR weapons fired. The effect was immediate. Almost all of the men in the roadway collapsed unconscious. The EARs fired again ten seconds later, one at each side of the road. Most of the rest of the surprised soldiers went down unconscious. Half a dozen men survived the effects of the enhanced audio and ran into the desert.

At the block itself, the truck stopped, SEALs jumped out, and dragged enough unconscious soldiers out of the way so the truck could drive through without crushing anyone.

"One of our more humane days," Murdock told Cullhagen. "Don't count on that happening too often."

The CIA man was fascinated by the EAR weapon.

"Heard we had something like that on the shelf. Didn't know it was operational."

"It isn't yet, but we snagged a few for field testing," Murdock said. "Works damn well for silent attacks."

Once in the truck, Mahanani heard about DeWitt's shot arm, and peeled up his shirt sleeve and checked it. "An in-and-out, j.g. No big deal. Might slow down your left-handed drinking, but that's about all." He sterilized the areas with alcohol wipe pads, then put some medication on the two wounds, and wrapped them securely to stop any more bleeding. "Good as new, j.g., but no Purple Heart, since we were never here and this mission never happened."

Five minutes later, a pair of headlights showed down the road coming at them. They let it come, and crouched down in the truck bed, hoping not to attract the attention of those in the oncoming rig. It turned out to be a sedan that slammed past them at maximum speed and continued on without backward glance from the driver.

Jaybird turned the rig right when they came to the paved road along the beach, and a half mile down he turned toward the coast. It was less than two hundred yards away.

"Let's find our little bunch of trees and get out of here," Murdock said. Lampedusa found the right trees, and the rubber boats were still there.

"Good," DeWitt told Cullhagen. "You won't have to swim out."

Cullhagen was showing signs of exhaustion. "No sleep or food or water for three days," he said. The SEALs gave him water, then some of their emergency food bars.

"So damn hungry I can't even taste them," he said.

Ten minutes later the rubber ducks were in the water and the SEALs and Cullhagen loaded on board. The storm was over, and the Mediterranean Sea looked like a big pond, it was so calm. The time was almost 0400. Two hours of darkness left if they were lucky.

Murdock made a call with the Motorola, but got no response. He kept trying as they motored slowly due north. The submarine was supposed to be on the surface from 0400 to 0600. When they were a mile offshore, the sub answered on a Motorola the SEALs had left on board. The sub was waiting. Murdock stood high in the IBS and waved three light sticks. His radio spoke again.

"Floaters, I have your signal. Red light sticks. You're dead ahead and we'll make contact."

"Oh, yeah," Vinnie Van Dyke said. "A whole fucking mission and we didn't even get wet."

Twenty minutes later they made a safe transfer to the sub, collapsed the IBS craft as far as they would go, and pushed them into the boat. Once inside the submarine, Cullhagen asked for an encrypted radio and sent a message to Washington.

The SEALs found bunks and sacked out. Murdock didn't sleep much. He still had to integrate totally two new men in the platoon into the operation. That would take some doing.

3

NAVSPECWARGRUP-ONE
Coronado, California
Lieutenant Commander Blake Murdock leaned back in his
chair in his office in Third Platoon, SEAL Team Seven,
and played it over in his mind again. Yes, it should work.
He needed a good test for his new men in the squad. They
had performed well in the mission to Libya, but that had
been fairly routine. There had been no real test for either
Luke Howard or the new Senior Chief Timothy Sadler.

The training exercise he had in mind would help glue
the new men into the squad, and help Sadler begin to earn
the respect and loyalty of all the men in the platoon.

It was 0630, and Murdock was the only man in the platoon area. He liked it that way. It would give him time to
sort things out without any interruptions.

By 0730 Murdock had his desk cleaned up, his after-
action report on the Libya affair finished on the computer
and e-mailed to Master Chief MacKenzie, who would
download it and print up the number of copies needed for
distribution.

Senior Chief Sadler came in and showed surprise.

"Sorry, sir, just can't get used to you being in so early.
In my other platoon I was always the first one across the
quarterdeck. My PL usually wandered in about 0900."

"Old habit, Senior Chief. This way I get my desk cleaned
for the day's training. I have a new routine for us for today.
Give you a chance to work the men and get to know them
a little better."

"Good, Commander. I've needed that. Taking me a while to get settled in here. Some of your men have been together for three years?"

"Going on that, Sadler. We're a combat outfit. We get a lot of action and the men tend to build strong bonds when they're saving each other's skins. Sometimes they think one of them should be Senior Chief, but they don't have the rate, so it can't happen. Coffee?"

They both had cups, and the Senior Chief looked up. "Commander, what's the training sked for today?"

"In the field. We'll go out east on Highway Eight a little past Boulevard, where we have a handshake arrangement with a landowner. We can do some live firing up in his hills as long as we pick up our brass and don't start any fires. Some rugged hills up in there that make good training grounds, and a lot closer than going all the way out to Niland and the desert site there."

"Live firing?"

"You bet, and some tricky work that will take some concentration by all the troops. I'll brief you on the way up. First call is for 0800 as usual. The six-by will be here by that time, and all we have to do is pick up our ammo, equipment, and gear and we'll be off. I want you to final-check each man before we leave. Oh, I hope you're working on names. I want you to know each man's name and be able to identify him from looking at the back of his head."

"Working on that, sir. Have our squad down, but not all of Bravo."

Later Murdock watched as Sadler checked out the equipment on each of the thirteen other EM SEALs. He caught a few minor problems and smoothed over the corrections. Murdock had never doubted Sadler's ability as a SEAL. He had interviewed four men before he picked Sadler for the top spot here. But as with any new man, the personalities had to mix just right for the top man to be the true EM leader of the platoon. So far Sadler was looking good.

The ride in the six-by truck out to the shooting grounds always took longer than Murdock wanted it to.

By 1030 they were on the ground hiking toward a pair of peaks off the highway by eight miles.

Senior Chief Sadler had given the troops the news. "Men, we're going on a short hike, about six miles; then we'll go into combat mode and attack the hill to the left. There are some steep spots and we may have a little rock-climbing work to do to get there. It's going to take some teamwork and roping. You all have the 600-strength nylon rope. We'll probably need it. I'll set the pace at five miles an hour; it'll help us get the kinks out."

There were a few grumbles, but nothing Sadler could pick up on. He grinned and led out toward the mountains over the San Diego back country's dry hills, which received under ten inches of rain a year and grew mostly some low grass and sage. Here and there a splash of green showed in canyons where runoff helped nourish a few live oak trees.

Murdock nodded at the pace. It was strong. The average good walker can do a mile in fifteen minutes, about four minutes to the mile. Five miles is pushing it. Race walkers, who always have one foot on the ground at all times, can do seven to eight miles an hour.

An hour later the sweating SEALs eyed the sharp cliffs and rises in front of them.

"We going up that mutha?" Paul Jefferson, Engineman Second Class, asked. Then he laughed. "Shit, I can do that one blindfolded with one hand."

Senior Chief Sadler smiled. "Good, Jefferson. You can take the lead. You won't need any pitons here, but some roping will help. I want you to go up to that first ledge, tie off a rope, and let it down to help anyone up who needs it. I'd just as soon see that rope left untouched by the rest of you."

Jefferson grinned as he looked at the rock. He'd done some free climbs and quite a bit on rock. He picked his route up the thirty feet to the ledge, and went up it almost without stopping. He kicked loose some rock on one of the footholds. Jefferson tied off his line to a solid upthrust and tossed it down the side.

"Hey, you tenderfeet, you'all can come up now," Jefferson said.

"Bravo Squad, up the side in combat order. Jefferson, you go up to the next level and wait."

The climb to the first ledge wasn't difficult. It took a little care and balance, but the first six men in Bravo made it fine. Only Khai had to grab the rope to keep from falling and power up the last two handholds to the ledge.

Senior Chief Sadler went up the rocks right behind j.g. DeWitt, and then passed the rest on the ledge and worked up thirty-five feet to the second ledge, where Jefferson sat whistling.

"Hey, Senior Chief, about time you got up here. What a view. Look out there, you can see the highway."

"Yeah, Jefferson, nice view. Now let's get a rope tied off and down to the first level just in case."

"Watch Howard, the new guy. Told me he hated rock climbing."

"Okay, Bravo, send up the squad," Sadler barked. "Weapons over your backs as usual. Let's move it."

The Bravo Squad worked up the next slope, while Alpha came up the first one. The second slope was tougher, with no easy path, and two or three ways that would get you to the top. Fernandez made it with ease; then Franklin went a different route and slipped and skidded four feet back to the ledge. Three SEALs caught him and he tried again. This time he made it.

As the men came to the top of the second shelf, Sadler told Jefferson to lead them off to the left where the ledge bled into a gentle slope toward the top of the mountain.

Ostercamp had some trouble on the second slope, grabbed the rope and saved himself, and went on to the top. From there it went smoothly until Howard started up the second climb. He went up partway, then climbed down and tried another way. On the third try he slipped and fell ten feet down the rocks. Bradford and Lampedusa saw him sliding and broke his fall. All three slammed to the rocky ground, but no bones were broken.

Bradford pointed to the far left route. "That's the best one, man. Do that one and it'll be a piece of cake."

Howard took a deep breath and started up the climb. At the branch to the left route he hesitated, then went that direction and, with only one small slip, gained the top.

Ten minutes later all sixteen SEALs sat in a group on the flank of the mountain looking at the top. Sadler stood and pointed up where they were all looking.

"Nope, we're not going all the way up. Fact is, it's time for a short lunch break, twenty minutes to devour those gourmet lunches you brought in your small packs, the ever-loving MREs. So take twenty."

Meals Ready to Eat were not the favorite of the SEALs, but they had kept them alive more than once on long missions. The SEALs ate what they wanted, and trashed the rest, then carefully picked up every plastic bit and envelope and package, and stuffed it all back in their packs.

Sadler checked his watch, and at precisely twenty minutes after the lunch break started, it ended. "Men, look over to your right. See that snag of a live oak? How far are we from it?"

"A thousand yards," Ching said.

"More like twelve hundred," Jaybird chirped.

"Not a chance, it's not more than nine hundred," Lampedusa said.

"The scout is right, it's nine hundred yards. We're going to capture it. From here to there we have a ravine, a slab of rock an acre wide, and some sagebrush. We'll go on twenty-yard surges. The rear man gives covering fire as his partner races up twenty yards, goes prone, and when the man behind him stops firing, he opens up as his buddy runs past him and up twenty yards.

"The important points here are two. I want a straight-string line across those men advancing and going prone. Any man more than two feet out of line gets a hundred push-ups on the spot. Second, be sure you don't gun down your buddy running up beside and then out in front of you.

"Pair off in your combat sequence. We want an eight-man front across here, ten yards apart. Get paired up. I'm with Van Dyke at the end of the line, but I'll be watching your progress. Any questions?"

"If my partner shoots and kills me, can I have a different partner next time?" Jaybird asked.

"Not a chance, Jaybird, because we'll be using you for

our target in the Shoot the Naked SEAL Runner game."

The platoon howled in laughter. The Senior Chief had a quick wit to match Jaybird.

"Let's line up and do it," Sadler bellowed. They each paired off beginning with the first two men in the combat order, and looked at Sadler.

"This isn't a race. Keep in line on the run forward. Let's go. As soon as the first man takes off, his partner should be live-firing five yards to his left. Watch where you're shooting. Go."

The eight men ran forward. As soon as they left, the prone eight men began firing. Then all stopped as their partners dove to the ground in the prone and began firing. The backup men ran forward, past their partners, and kept running for twenty yards.

"Keep the fucking line straight," Sadler brayed as he ran in his turn advancing with the others. They straightened the line, then hit the ground and began firing.

After five rotations of the teams, they had covered two hundred yards, and Sadler blew a whistle. All firing stopped, all men paused in place. Third Platoon hadn't heard a whistle since most of them were in BUD/S.

"Hold it in place," Sadler shouted. He went up to the front. "Enough. You have the idea. We don't need to waste any more ammo. This drill is called teamwork. If you don't do your job exactly right, precisely the way you're supposed to, one of you could get shot up and be dead on the spot."

He looked around. "You guys done good. That's all of my part in this little showcase. I think the j.g. has something to say."

Ed DeWitt stood, pulled the Bull Pup off his back, and held it in front of him with both hands. A bulge on his left forearm showed where the bandage was that covered his in-and-out bullet wound.

"We're back from a quick mission. Sometimes I like them. They give us some action, let us get shot at, and then we're home where we can take it easy for a while. The trouble is, we never know how long a little while will be. Right now we have no orders. I don't even know of any hot spots around the world where we might be called to participate.

"So, we're going back to basics. In a combat situation, we must be sharp mentally and physically. Not much we can do to change our mental ability other than to stay focused and stay alert during a mission. On the physical side we can always get better. You can do a hundred push-ups? Fine, how about five hundred? You can run a mile in six minutes? Fine, can you do it in five minutes flat? Top mile runners can do the mile now under four minutes.

"Starting tomorrow we'll have light packs and weapons on a seven-minutes-to-the-mile run. We do ten miles. In the afternoon we will go to the ups schedule: pull-ups, sit-ups, and push-ups. The man who wins each category gets a free case of Bud."

That brought a cheer.

"For now we're out here for live firing. I want Senior Chief Sadler and Howard to run some rounds through on the Bull Pup, and the EAR. The commander will work with the rest of you on firing yours and the rest of the weapons for all-around familiarity. We don't use the fifty much anymore. Our Bull Pups have replaced it with gratifying results. We'll move up a hundred yards so we're five hundred from the old live oak snag over there, and spread out for firing."

Senior Chief Sadler had fired his Bull Pup on the mission, but never quite understood the range and damage the weapon was capable of. Now, in the daylight, he fired at the snag, and marveled at the way the rounds either hit close to it or did an airburst with the laser sighting.

"You were right, j.g., this damn weapon will revolutionize the ground soldier's job. He won't have to wait for mortars to come up, or for artillery to wipe out something, and he can shoot over the fucking reverse slope of hills, into bunkers and in back of buildings. I love this gun!"

Howard took his turn with the Bull Pup. He winced at the kick the 20mm round gave off. "Hey, like a shotgun," he said. Then he watched the burst over the snag and laughed. "Keriest in a fucking bucket, look at that thing. I want to buy one of these to go duck hunting with. Hell, have my limit with the first flight."

They both fired the EAR weapon, and asked about the range.

"We're not sure, from two hundred to three hundred yards. Howard, would you walk out there four hundred yards and see if we can knock you off your feet?"

Howard stood automatically, then frowned. "You pullin' my leg, j.g. Don't think I'll take that walk."

They all laughed. "We've used it at two hundred yards, but I can't remember anything much longer than that," DeWitt said. "They must be working on a more powerful model that will reach out longer and have more of a punch, and a larger battery in the stock."

Murdock worked the men on the weapons until he was sure that each man had fired all the types of weapons they had brought. It was essential that every man could fire effectively every rifle and machine gun that they used. If the machine gunner went down, another man had to be as good with it as the first man was, and grab it and use it at once.

By 1600 they were finished. It took them another half hour to police up the brass from the firing. They dumped the shell casings in their packs and then began the hike back to the truck. They moved mostly downhill and Sadler led them, sometimes running, sometimes walking fast. They were sweating and tired when they came to the truck after the six-mile trip. The men climbed on board at once, eager to get back to the base and a good meal later on.

Sadler looked at the Navy man who was their driver for the day. He had stayed with the truck and eaten his MRE. He had dumped the envelopes and papers and packaging in a circle around where he had sat for his lunch in the shade of the truck.

"Ready to go, Senior Chief?" the driver asked.

"Sailor, you have a name?" Sadler asked.

"Yeah, Senior Chief, I'm Rawlings."

"Rawlings, I hope you enjoyed your lunch."

"No way, Chief. Not a chance. It was an MRE."

"I should make you eat the wrappings, Rawlings. Now down on your knees and pick up every spot of paper and plastic you see for ten yards and cram it all into your pockets. Don't you ever leave a litter like that again on a SEALs trip."

Rawlings's eyes went wide; then he saw the Senior Chief wasn't kidding, and he dropped to his knees and began picking up the green plastic wrappings and the envelopes and wrappings from the MRE.

The SEALs in the truck burst out cheering. Sadler went around the truck and crawled into the cab. Murdock slid in beside him.

"Good play, Senior Chief," he said, and the two men slapped hands in a low five.

"It's a start, Skipper. Now we have to keep these guys in tip-top condition. That's going to take some work."

4

Back at the platoon equipment room, Bill Bradford changed into his civvies and hurried across the quarterdeck and out to the parking lot. His four-year-old Honda Civic started on the first try, and he buzzed into Coronado and across the bridge into San Diego. Down on India Street, he parked in the alley, and walked into a storefront that had a sign over the door that said: "San Diego's Artist Colony."

The front held a five-wall design with paintings hung on every available space. Each wall had a person's name on it. Bradford went to the side and looked at his display. His paintings. All marines: some fishing boats at the embarcadero, some with breakers smashing into the rocks down at Sunset Cliffs. There were eight oils there, all marked with prices from $65 to $245. All were framed and ready to hang.

"Hey, man, you made it," a man said. He wore faded jeans and a paint-smudged white T-shirt. He held a pallet and two brushes.

"Yeah, Rollo. Late workday. Anybody else here?"

"Yeah, Xenia rolled in a half hour ago. She's in a funk of some kind. Went into her room upstairs and banged the door. Don't see why she's got her tit in a wringer. She's selling more than anybody."

Bradford chuckled. "She's the sensitive type."

A woman walked in wearing a see-through blouse, no bra, and a short skirt. She was barefoot, and her dark hair had been piled on top of her head, probably to get it out of the way of the fresh paint. "Who is the sensitive type? Rollo here? That's painful to think about."

"I meant you, Xenia; is there something bugging you?" Bradford asked.

"Yeah, life, death, art, salesmen, the percentage they take, every fucking thing is bothering me."

Bradford grinned. "Hey, same old Xenia. Everything about the same. How is that portrait coming along?"

"It sucks, but I can probably sell it. Isn't this wine-and-cheese night? Where's the damn food and drink?"

"Jeffrey's turn to bring it tonight," Rollo said. "I told him two bottles would be enough. We never have more than half a dozen people stop by."

"Mostly our friends for the free wine," Xenia said. She shrugged. "Hell, they told me this wouldn't be easy when I started. It still ain't." She motioned to Bradford. "You started yet, or can you take a look at my non-progress?"

"Happy to."

"You can't look, Rollo. You're too fucking critical."

"Yeah, my life story." He took his brushes and went around to the wall on the far side, where his easel and a high stool were set up, and went to work on a still life.

Xenia lifted her brows and shook her head. She was a tiny woman, five feet tall if she went on tiptoe. Her long black hair framed her face when it was down, and fell halfway down her back. She had brown eyes that snapped and daggered, and a thin nose over strangely full lips and a delicate chin. She looked like a caricature of a little china doll, but with the temper of a coiled rattler.

They went up steps to the loft where generous street and side windows let in painter's light. She turned on more fluorescent bulbs and pointed to an oil she was working on, a twelve-by-fourteen, on a piece of canvas that looked like it came over on the Mayflower.

"Why the ratty old canvas?" asked Bradford. "I thought this was going to be one of your good ones."

"Look at it, weirdo."

"It *is* one of your good ones. Reminds me of some of those other small portraits you did. This one of your relatives or just a good face?"

"What do you think?"

"Not a relative, for damn sure. I like it. Why are you bitching?"

"I'm always bitching." She pushed up against him and rested her breasts on his chest, then reached up and pulled his head down and kissed him. Then he kissed her back, picked her up, and carried her to the sofa where she slept. He sat down easily and she stayed on his lap.

"You don't feel a bit bitchy to me," he said. "Now what's the trouble?"

"Oh, nothing I can tell you. I thought I had four paintings like this one sold, a kind of set, different faces, same background, same general look, only different people. At the last minute the guy changed his mind and said he could sell only two of them. There go two sales. That's enough to make me into a wild, clawing hellcat."

"Ouch, X, I know how that hurts. Hey, I only sold three of my cheapies last month. Didn't make enough to pay my share of the rent. Hey, I know hurt."

She stared hard at him, her brown eyes going soft. She pecked a kiss on his cheek. "Hell, you're only here half the time. We should cut your share of the rent on this place."

"No way. I'm in, I can make the fee." He lifted her off his lap, pushed her to her feet, and stood. "Hey, I need to get some work done. I saw some wild ocean lately and this small boat on it almost in trouble, just one man in it fighting for his life."

"Go," she said. Xenia sat back down on the cot and looked at her painting. Then she sighed, got up, and went to work on it.

"I'll be next door when you want coffee," Bradford said. He went across the hall and into another room with the same front view, and turned on the soft fluorescent lights. There were three partly finished oils. One on an easel, two leaning against the wall. He went to work on the oil of a fishing boat tied at the dock down near Seaport Village.

A half hour later, Xenia knocked on his door and came in. She had on the same clothes, see-through blouse and all.

"Some people came in downstairs. Rollo must be out on

the sidewalk dragging them inside. Let's take a look."

There were six people in the small showroom. Three men soon surrounded Xenia at her paintings, looking mostly at Xenia's breasts, and only now and then at the six paintings on display.

Bradford found a thin man with a scar on his right cheek and flaming red hair who stared pointedly at one of the moonlight-on-waves oils on display that Bradford had done over a year ago.

"I like it," the redhead said. "Gives you the idea that there's a lot more there we can't see, just what the moonlight shows us in the streamer of light across the whole painting."

He moved to the side six feet and stared at it again. "I like the waves. You have them down perfectly. Have I seen your work before?"

"This is the only place I show," Bradford said.

"A shame. I like this one. How big is it?"

"Thirteen by twenty, a rather strange size, but I liked it."

"Yes, the proportions are exactly right. I'll take it. How much is it?"

"One ninety-five, but if—"

The man held up his hand and stopped him. "Young man, never cut your prices. Never. Your work is worth more than that, but I'll pay what you ask. I may be back to look for another. I'm putting in a new restaurant bar with a marine theme. I'm trying to patronize only San Diego artists, but I can't find everything I want. Do you have any more marines in the back room?"

"Yes, two, but they aren't framed. One is of—"

"Bring them out. Let me take a look. Framing is no problem."

Bradford hurried up the stairs, and took two oils he had done six months ago and never had framed. One was of a fishing boat just casting off from Seaforth sport fishing pier with twenty eager fishermen on board getting their gear ready. The other was of a wave crashing into the rocks out on the Mission Beach jetty. He took them down and held them.

The redhead nodded. "Yes, the jetty. Good. I'll take that one too. How much do I owe you?"

Bradford was stunned. "This jetty is a hundred and fifty, so that makes three hundred and forty-five."

The redheaded man nodded. "You shouldn't take checks, since you have no way to clear them. I have enough cash." He took a roll of bills from his pocket and peeled off three one hundreds, then dug a fifty out of the inside of the roll. "Here, that's close enough. Can you wrap them up? I don't want to get them gouged before I hang them."

Ten minutes later the customer was gone. Only two lookers were still in the showroom, and half the wine and all of the cheese and crackers were gone. One man was talking with Xenia. He looked at her paintings and then at her breasts. She moved her shoulders so her breasts rolled, and the man laughed.

"You do a self-portrait in that blouse and I'll buy it," he said.

She slapped him gently. "You are bad, bad. But I kind of like it. How 'bout this nude on velvet? She's got bigger tits than I do."

They both laughed, and the man shook his head and walked away.

"Zippo. I struck out again," she said. "Maybe I should cover up the boobs. They seem to draw all the attention. Maybe that blouse, the green one that shows about an inch of cleavage."

"That might be better, but just for the shows."

"You're bad too. Did I see you score?"

Bradford held out the four bills for her to see.

"You lie, Brad, you lie in your teeth."

"No lie. Two of my marines. He's opening a new bar somewhere with a marine theme. Hope he comes back."

Another artist, Hoya, came around from his display. He was darkly Mexican, and his paintings were almost primitive with wild blacks and oranges. "Not tonight," he said, smiling. "Maybe next week. I'm out of here."

At ten they shut off the lights. Rollo went home. Xenia was the only one of the six artists who lived upstairs.

"Come on up," she said to Bradford. "Want a beer?"

They popped the tops and sat and looked at the paintings. Bradford kept looking at her work in progress. "I like it," he said. "It has that Rembrandt feeling without being so stodgy. The colors are muted and faded almost. Yes, I like it. How much do you charge for a near-master like that?"

"Twenty thousand," she said, her eyes sparkling.

"Sure, and I just sold two for fifty grand each. Sorry, I had no right to ask."

"Hey, big-selling painter. What's the chances of my getting laid tonight?"

"I'd say pretty fucking good."

Twice that week the SEALs had a four-thirty end of the day, and both times Bradford took Xenia out to dinner. Once at Marie Callender's Restaurant, the other time at Denny's. They talked painting. Bradford almost wished he was out of the SEALs and painting full time. He had a knack for it, and with more experience he should be able to make a living at it. But he knew he didn't have the deft touch that Xenia had.

"How do you get such shadings in your work?" he asked.

"Practice, amigo. I've been painting for fifteen years, every day, all day. For the first five years I almost starved. I shared an apartment with another painter. I slept with him and he fed me. It was a good arrangement. When I sold enough paintings to go on my own, I moved out."

"You're good. You should be able to get more for your work than two or three hundred."

"Hey, I pay the bills, meet the rent on time, and eat more or less regularly."

That night they had another wine-and-cheese showing. They had distributed handbills: "Six starving artists showing their work tonight from six to ten." They draped a hundred of them on cars parked along India and in one big parking lot. Xenia wore a modest blouse and sold a painting. Bradford came up empty, but one woman nearly bought one until her husband pulled her away. Bradford almost slugged him.

Upstairs, after the lights went off on the displays, Xenia pulled off her blouse and threw it against the wall. "Hate clothes. Why do we have to wear them?" She grabbed her brushes, which she had left in water so they wouldn't go dry, and wiped them off, then went to work on the second of the two portraits of older men. Bradford watched her.

"You often paint in the nude?" he asked. She said she did, and slipped out of her skirt and underpants.

"Yes, that's more like it," Bradford said. He let her paint for another half hour, and then grabbed her and carried her to her cot.

"All right, but a quickie. I've got to have that painting ready to ship in two weeks, and it takes more than a week to dry. Stay with me and we'll both work until midnight."

They did.

The next night Bradford moved his easel into her room and painted and watched her. She was good. He was curious about the portrait. It vaguely reminded him of something. Bradford concentrated on the painting, and the only thing he could think of was a Rembrandt-type work. Not Rembrandt but of that era, back when paintings were commissioned by wealthy patrons who always wanted portraits of them and their families.

Xenia went downstairs to the bathroom, and he looked at her desk. Her checkbook lay there. He flipped it open to the last check written. The balance slammed up at him and he was astonished. Xenia had over fifteen thousand dollars in her checking account.

He put it back and went to his painting. He made three mistakes in a row, and took his pallet knife, scraped off the oil, and did it again. Nice thing about oil. Make a mistake, take it off and do it again. Her bank balance worried him. The old-master-style paintings worried him. She never exhibited any of them downstairs. He wondered why not. Slowly he began to get an idea, and he didn't like it.

She had said she sold her portrait paintings for twenty thousand dollars. Maybe she wasn't kidding. She came back, and he made an excuse about a hard day the next day. She frowned.

"Something I said?"

"No. I just have to leave. See you in a couple of days.

We have a night problem tomorrow." She knew he was a SEAL, she would buy that.

The next night, as soon as he was off work, he drove to the main library on Eighth Street downtown. He went to the reference room and found three huge books on Rembrandt and his fellow painters in the 1600's in Holland. There were hundreds of pictures, and at last he found what he was looking for. A school of painters who did works that looked much like the portraits that Xenia did. He studied them for an hour, and when he was almost ready to give up, he found a series of four portraits that looked almost identical to the type that she was doing.

He read the name. Roycen Van Dyke. He'd died in 1673. The article about him said that he was a perfectionist, that he did few paintings, and that he sold even fewer. The archives recorded only twelve of his works, but experts figured there were probably a hundred or more that had been lost or destroyed, or maybe were sitting on dusty shelves in some studio storage rooms in Europe or the United States.

What a perfect cover. More of the Van Dykes could be "found" and sold at a good price. Not for millions, but for maybe a hundred thousand. He had to confront her about it. No way around it.

The next night he worked hard on his oil, and was pleased with the two hours of effort. Then Xenia came in and he knew he had to talk to her about his suspicions, to find out for sure. She invited him for a beer, and they went into her room. At once he went to her painting and stared at it. Then he was sure. The shadings, the tones, the size of the bust in the picture. He turned to Xenia, who came with two bottles of beer.

"Roycen Van Dyke," he said.

Xenia closed her eyes and wilted. She put the beer on a table and sank onto the cot.

"Why did you have to find out? Why? Things were going so well. I sell two of them a year and then I can paint what I want to."

"Where?"

"A man in Santa Barbara specializes in 'recovered' old masters and not-quite old masters."

"And you do get twenty thousand each for them?"

"Yes. I don't know how much he sells them for. I picked Van Dyke because he's almost unknown in this country. But he has enough of a name that some private collector will look him up and buy. For fifty or sixty thousand that collector has what looks exactly like an old master and he can show it off to his friends."

"It's called forgery and fraud."

Her voice was small. "I know. Damnit, I know. I'm better than this. I should be getting five thousand for a painting, maybe ten or fifteen thousand for my own work. But I'm stuck here showing off my tits and hoping for a three-hundred-dollar sale of a nude."

"You could stop doing Van Dyke."

"Sure, and really starve. I tried that. Who do you suppose pays for the rent when the other four can't get up their share? Who pays for all of the lights and heat? Yeah, you're being kept by the goodness of Van Dyke, whether you know it or not."

"You've got to walk away from it, Xenia. If they nail you, it could mean ten years in prison. Then how would you paint?"

"I can't leave it yet. Right now I don't have the studio contacts to show my work where I can get enough money. Maybe in a year. I have one who shows me. I need three or four more. They are hard to find, and they take forty percent. I'm jacking my prices up to three thousand for my big works, instead of three hundred. So far I've sold one up in Laguna Beach of all places. I need more time. Maybe these two Van Dykes and two more and I'll be set."

"Do you sign them?"

"Oh, God, no. That would be a sure giveaway. These are supposed to be old ones he wasn't too proud of and they got lost somewhere. So he didn't sign them."

"If this dealer in Santa Barbara gets arrested, would he give you up?"

"Charlie? Sure, if it would save him a couple of years

off his sentence. He'd give up his mother and his brother. Who also are both in the forgery business."

They sat there looking at each other.

"X, I don't know how to help you."

"Nobody can help me. I do it on my own. I always have. Always will. Now get the hell out of here and let me have a long cry. Maybe I'll speak to you again, and maybe the fuck I won't."

5

Training the next two weeks was the hardest Murdock could remember. He made sure it stayed that way. Men could die in the field if they couldn't run fast enough, if they couldn't shoot straight, and for a dozen other reasons that could be prevented or at least made less likely by tough, realistic training.

For the past two days they had been at Niland, near the Chocolate Mountains in the desert just east of the Salton Sea. Today they had split into squads for training in tactics, and each unit went in a different direction. They were to meet at a certain flat-topped mountain at 1400 for some joint operations.

The Navy bus they arrived in was loaded heavily with ammo. Each day they fired their weapons until they ran out of rounds, then worked the rest of the daylight with simulated firing drills and attacks on various gullies, sand dunes, and giant cacti.

The platoon marched back to the bus shouting the age-old Army chant: "You had a good home and you left. You're right. You had a good home and you left. You're right. Sound off. One, two. Sound off. Three, four. Cadence count. One, two, three, four—one, two . . ."

They went through twenty different verses to the ditty, some of them not fit for a family audience, and were marching with style when they came to the bus and stopped. The bus had pulled along the cool waters of the Coachella Canal of the massive irrigation network from the Colorado River that made the whole Imperial Valley green and areas to the west and north blossom with farm crops.

Senior Chief Sadler stared at the men. It had been a tough training day. "That water looks good, doesn't it? I'm not saying you can take a swim and cool off, but I'm not saying you can't. Fact is, I'm going to get my boots off and get my feet wet right now. Platoon dismissed."

There was a shout from thirteen throats as the men dropped their packs, weapons, and combat vests, and dashed for the swiftly running waters of the canal. Every summer people drowned in the canal when they misjudged its swiftness. The SEALs didn't mind. They had trained in this powerful flowing water and knew what it could do. They splashed into it with their desert cammies on. They could wash them and cool off at the same time.

Murdock, Sadler, and DeWitt watched the men.

"Good job, Senior Chief," Murdock said. "I think you might work out in this job."

"Thanks, Skipper. We've got a good team here. It's pulling together like no outfit I've ever worked with before."

"When their asses are on the line, the men know they have to work together, or they'll die alone," Murdock said. He dropped his weapon, pack, and pants, which had his billfold in them. "You guys going to let the men have all the fun?" He ran for the canal and did a surface dive, then floated downstream with the current.

It was almost 1800 when the men straggled out of the canal, dug out dry cammies, and changed clothes. They spread their wet clothes in the sun to dry.

Senior Chief Sadler blew three short blasts on his whistle. "Listen up. We have just been attacked by a group of twenty infantry from across the canal. Form up now in a line of skirmishers and return fire."

They were all out of ammunition so they dry-fired a few times, then went bang-bang. Two minutes into the exercise the whistle blasted once. "End of alert," Sadler said. "Get dressed and on the old pony. We'll eat our last MREs on the way back and then stop at Jack in the Box."

The men cheered.

"About time," Jaybird called. "I got myself killed twice back there by hand grenades."

"We noticed," Sadler cracked. "Your service will be in ten minutes." The rest of the SEALs hooted in delight. At last they had a mouth that could match Jaybird's.

The trip back was routine, but it would take three hours. Bill Bradford sat on the bus dozing, trying to figure out what to say to Xenia when he saw her again. They were in the same little building, right next to each other. He knew her secret and he didn't know what to do about it. He certainly wasn't going to turn her in. She must know that. Was there any way he could help her? Maybe find some more outlets to hang her work? That would take time, and luck. Good painters were everywhere. You had to be distinctive to stand out and get noticed. He didn't know what to do.

It was after ten o'clock when he pushed in the dark doorway at the gallery on India Street. He'd seen lights upstairs, so Xenia must be there. Bradford went up the steps, making some noise so she would hear him coming. She leaned against her doorway as he came down the short hall.

"Well, at least you didn't bring the cops," she said. "I'm almost clean here. I force-dried one to get some small cracks in the oil. Then sent it to Santa B. The other one is done, but I can't force-dry it for three more days. You still talking to me?"

"Damn right. Trying to figure out how I can help you."

"Hey, God couldn't help any, what chance do you have?"

"God?"

"Sure. I used to go to church. They said pray. I prayed. They said put your troubles on Jesus. I heaped them all on his shoulders. None of it helped a fucking damn bit. So, if those two didn't make a dent in my problems, why in hell do you think you can?"

"Hey, with a SEAL all things are possible. Let's get our heads together and see what we can work out."

"Oh, God, but I've been hoping you would say something like that. I've been fucking scared to death you would cut and run. Yeah, let's get together, but first come in here,

I'm in a real need. I've just got to have somebody about six foot two spread out on top of me and socking it to me hard and fast."

It was nearly an hour later before they both came down from their highs and their breathing and heartbeats had returned to near normal. They sat on the side of the cot sipping at cold beers.

"Great," she said. "Perfect." She sighed. "I wish the rest of it was so easy. Once I get this last portrait out of here, I'll breathe a lot easier."

"Your last one?"

"Going to try. Going to work like a schizophrenic nymphomaniac and try to get a gallery in La Jolla to represent me. I'm going into the fifteen-hundred-to-five-thousand-dollar class and see where the goddamn chips fall."

"Sounds good for a start. What about Laguna Beach?"

"Too much competition. There are a hundred forty galleries up there. Would you believe it? Probably twice that many good artists. No, I'm going to hit Long Beach, and LA and Beverly Hills. I'll do good theater, dressing the part for each different location. If I try for a spot in redneck Santee, I'll go nude."

"So how do you force-dry an oil painting?"

"Some say it can't be done. I set it in the direct sun for three hours at a time, then put it in my refrigerator for an hour, then back in the direct sun. Hardens the outside, but not all the way through. Then when the inside hardens completely in about three weeks, the outside will develop what I call my aging cracks. Looks pretty damn good."

"Three more days?"

"Yep, if I can hold out and if the damn fraud squad doesn't run right up my ass."

"You keep the wet one hidden?"

"Oh, yeah. A sliding panel I built in the wall. Take a fucking magician to find it. Only you, I, and Rollo know where it is. If he ever gave me up, I'd slice his balls off."

"Let's see what you're working on now," Bradford said. It was a seascape off a windy hill with a huge house in the background and a woman sitting on the cliff watching the sea. Xenia had it about half done.

"Yes, I like it. What is it, three by four feet? Big enough to get a lot in there. Just don't try to get in too much."

"Yes, old master." She poked him in the ribs. Then she kissed his cheek. "Damn, I like having sex with you."

The next day, the SEALs training went wet. They swam ten miles with flippers and in wet suits, then jogged for four miles, and wound up with rubber ducks surfing in on the crashing Pacific waves. They went in and out three times, and the eight men in each boat made the surfing each time without dumping the boat in a breaker.

Bill Bradford gave a long sigh as he changed into his civilian clothes and headed over the quarterdeck to the parking lot. He turned on the local news station as he always did. It was just past five o'clock, the national five minutes were over, and the local news came on.

"The weather has turned sultry again, and the weatherman says there's a chance of some southern flow moisture coming to us out of Baja California if the onshore flow will hold off a little and not blow all of the rain into Arizona.

"San Diego Police and the FBI arrested a local artist today on charges of fraud in a complicated scheme to paint and then sell copies of seventeenth-century old Dutch masters as originals. The charges are fraud, conspiracy, and interstate transfer of the fraudulent paintings. Santa Barbara Police cooperated in the arrest. They say the dealer there was selling the 'just found' lost old-master paintings for as much as a hundred thousand dollars to private collectors. The name of the local artist has not been revealed pending the search for more members of the conspiracy.

"In other news, another water main broke this morning—"

Bradford snapped off the radio and pulled to the side of a Coronado street. He shook his head in surprise and denial. He suddenly felt cold and shivered. How? It had to be Xenia. Why didn't they give her name? Were they hunting *him*? He thought it through, and decided that the police would only want to talk to him. They couldn't charge him with anything. He wasn't that good a painter. He started the Honda and drove on to the co-op studio on India Street. Two men in suits and holding hats sat in the small display area. Rollo stood there talking to them. He turned.

"Oh, Bradford. Didn't know if you'd be in today or not. These men from the FBI want to talk to you."

"Why? They want to buy a painting of mine? Hell, they can talk as I paint. I haven't done any good work now in three days, and that has to stop. Upstairs, gentlemen, and you'll see how a starving artist works."

One of them started to protest, but the other shook his head and they all went up the stairs. At the door to the studio, Bradford stopped and held up his hand.

"Yes, I heard about the arrest of an artist for fraud. It can't be me. However, I'm allowing you into my studio, but not authorizing you to search the place or to remove anything. Are we agreed on that?"

"Yes, we agree. We just want to talk to you," said the taller FBI man Bradford mentally named Jeff.

They talked. It was what Bradford had expected. Yes, they had Xenia in custody.

"I'd seen some of the portraits she did and was blown away at the quality of her work. She's a gifted artist. I liked the modern work she does better, like the marine she's working on now."

"Did you know that she was painting copies of old masters?" Mutt, the shorter of the FBI duo, asked.

"I've had some art training. Anyone who has had art history courses can recognize the style and type of painting of the seventeenth-century artists. Every artist born copies old masters for practice, to see if he or she can get the light just right, get the tone and feel of the painting."

"Did you know she was selling them?" Jeff asked.

"Of course. We try to sell everything we paint. That's why we have a gallery downstairs. Would either of you be interested in a nice marine for your office? I specialize in marines." He picked up a finished and dry oil from a table. It was oil on canvas and not yet framed. "How about this one? I can have it hanging on your wall for only a hundred and forty-nine dollars. Plus tax, of course."

The FBI men looked at each other and shook their heads.

"Mr. Bradford. Did you know to whom she was selling the copies and how much she was getting for them?"

"Hey, her business. We try not to pry. If Rollo sells a nude to a grade-school teacher, I'm supposed to report him? Hell, this is a co-op so we can pay the rent, not so we can baby-sit each other. Of course I didn't ask her how much she sold her paintings for. I knew the prices downstairs. We don't snoop on each other. There are six of us here. Have you talked to everyone?"

"You're the last," the Mutt FBI clone said.

"Good. Now if you're not going to buy a painting, I'm going to have to ask you to leave. I've been working on this windswept tree on the cliff for two days, and I still can't get it right. If you can't help me there, then I'd appreciate it if you leave."

"So far, Mr. Bradford, you haven't been charged with anything. We understand you're in the Navy. It would be in your best interest not to leave town for the next few days."

"I'll try to remember that." He pointed to the door. The feds took one last look around and went out the door and down the steps. When he figured they should be out of sight, he started down. Rollo was halfway up.

"You heard," Rollo said. "She must have been getting big bucks for those old master copies."

"How did they get onto her?"

"The FBI said they couldn't tell me, but that they had been watching her for a month or more. Watching all of us. They came early this morning when I arrived. Xenia was still sleeping. They rousted her out. Had a search and arrest warrant, searched her room, found an old master copy, and took her and the painting downtown."

"You talked to them first?"

"Well, yeah."

"You knew she was doing the copy work?"

"Yeah, I did."

"And you spilled your guts to the feds, didn't you, you slimeball. Without you they probably couldn't have arrested her. Did she have the fraudulent painting hidden?"

"Yes."

"And you told them where it was. You little fucking bastard."

Bradford hit him with a punch that came so fast, Rollo didn't have time to dodge it. The blow caught him on the side of his head and slammed him to the floor. He looked up with surprise and anger.

"So what did you tell them about me, you traitor?" Bradford said.

"You? Nothing." He scooted backward on the floor toward the door. "Nothing about you. You don't do copies."

"So you're the one who's been searching through my studio when I'm not there."

"Hey, just once. I needed some good canvas and you usually had more than you needed."

"Yeah, sure. What's important now is how can we help Xenia."

Rollo stood cautiously. "You're not going to hit me again?"

"No. If I did, I'd probably keep right on hitting you until your face was a bloody mush and your brains were spilling out a big crack in your lousy fucking skull. How can we help Xenia?"

"Bail? I couldn't help her there. They want ten percent of the bail price for a bond. Not a chance with me."

"You tell them I was sleeping with her?"

"Yes, but I said I did too. So that cooled that down."

"You're a real bastard, Rollo. And a fucking bad painter. You should stick to living rooms, one-story apartments, and fences."

Bradford turned, put his brushes back in the jar of water, and at the door, turned off the lights.

"Stay out of my way, Rollo. Then I won't have to kill you." Bradford pushed past the startled artist and hurried down the stairs. He wondered if the FBI had had a search warrant and raided his apartment. When he drove home to the second-floor, three-room apartment in Coronado, he found that the FBI had been there. The landlady met him.

"Nothing I could do," Mrs. Chalmers said. She was about

forty, round and plump, with thick glasses and a limp. "They had a warrant, so I opened the door for them so they didn't break it down."

Inside, he found they had been neat. Everything had been moved, then replaced. Even the pictures on the wall had been lifted and checked behind. Most were not rehung straight. Mrs. Chalmers stood in the doorway.

"I watched them. I told them if they weren't neat about the search, I'd find out where they lived and phone their mothers. One laughed, the other shut him up. They were neat."

"Did they take away anything?"

"Not that I saw. Anything missing?"

"Not that I can tell so far. There was nothing here that would interest them. It just makes me mad."

"I read the warrant. It said there was just cause to think that you may be involved in some criminal activity."

"That's what they think, but they're wrong." He hesitated. "Thanks, Mrs. Chalmers, for your help. I better get some sleep."

Bradford went over the quarterdeck the next morning at 0745 as usual, waved at the Master Chief MacKenzie, and hurried to Third Platoon of SEAL Team Seven. Half the platoon was already there and the men were working on their gear.

"Bradford," Senior Chief Sadler called. "We're on a four-hour alert. Something is cracking wide open in the Philippines. We'll probably be out of here by noon."

By 0815 all members of the platoon had reported in and were working on their tropical-weather duffel. They would take three sets of forest cammies, two pairs of boots, and other clothing for an extended stay.

"This is a tropical nation and we'll be near the equator, maybe four hundred miles away," said Sadler. "Daytime temperatures can go to a hundred degrees with humidity close to that as well. We'll be there in January, the best time of the year climate-wise. Sometimes the daytime temperatures will get up only to sixty degrees. So think warm, wet, and humid. Lots of times it rains every day over there in January. Think wet. Carry on."

In the small office, Murdock looked over at Ed DeWitt. "The chain-of-command edict has ruptured in places. I took a call from Don Stroh this morning at home. He said to gear up. The official word won't come for three hours and then we'll have only an hour to get ready. He's arranged transport out of the North Island Air Station for us. The Master Chief knows the score."

"What's the problem in the Philippines?" DeWitt asked.

"Not sure. Stroh said he'd meet us in Davao in Mindanao. That's near the bottom of the batch of islands. As I remember, they've been having a lot of trouble with Muslim guerrillas down there. The whole Island is Muslim, not Catholic like the rest of the country."

"As hot as Nam?"

"Closer to the equator, so hotter, more humid. Not a fun vacation. Jungle on jungle. Won't be a walk in the park."

A tenseness filled the equipment room. The SEALs took multiple weapons; every man had two. All seven of the Bull Pups were slotted as well as both the EAR weapons. They had a good mix this time, with MP-5's for close-in work and the MGs and sniper rifles. Since they wouldn't be stopping at any U.S. military bases, they took as much ammo as they thought they might need. They went heavy on the 20mm rounds, and had six extra batteries for the EARs.

By 1100 they were ready.

Murdock took a call and scowled. "I'm sorry, that man is not available."

"This isn't routine, Commander. I'm with the San Diego Police Department and we have a warrant for your man's arrest. I just want to make certain that you will have him available and not out on a training exercise somewhere when I get there. We're talking about a felony here, Commander."

"Do you know who we are and what we do, Sergeant?"

"Somewhat. SEALs."

"Our platoon has just been alerted by the Chief of Naval Operations in Washington, D.C. He's the top dog in the Navy. We're out of here in a little less than half an hour to fly to Manila, on direct orders from the CNO and the President of the United States. You'll have to tell your captain that the PD has been outgunned and outranked. Anything that has happened with this man will have to wait until we return. Of course you can always go through channels, starting with Admiral Kenner in Little Creek, Virginia. That's Rear Admiral, lower, Richard Kenner. I'm sure he'd be glad to talk to you."

There was a long pause.

"Sergeant, what's the charge against Bradford?"

"Conspiracy to paint and sell copies of old masters. A felony."

"Sounds a little vague to me, Sergeant. I'll give you a call when we get back from the Philippines in two or three weeks."

"You do that, Commander. I'll talk to your commanding officer. This is a civilian crime and the Navy has no jurisdiction whatsoever."

"Good, tell that to the admiral."

They hung up and Murdock frowned. What in hell had Bradford been doing in his spare time? He'd seen some of his marine paintings. Murdock had one in his apartment. They were good, but not in the class of an old master. There had to be some mistake. Murdock would get it sorted out as soon as they came back from Mindanao.

6

Davao Air Base
Davao, Mindanao, Philippines

Murdock felt like a quarter horse had been galloping through the inside of his head. They had taken a long series of flights, but even in the sleek Gulfstream II business jet the Navy called the VC-11, it had been an exhausting day and a half. The men were bunked down in temporary quarters there at the air base at Davao while the briefing continued. The American ambassador was on hand, as well as two top Philippine generals and the nation's Vice President, Rosales Domingo. A colonel in charge of the Mindanao province continued the briefing.

"As of today there seems to be no change. The rebels have demanded a hundred thousand U.S. dollars for each hostage. Our best count is that they have sixty-four hostages: two Filipino guides and two Filipino drivers, and sixty nationals from sixteen different foreign countries.

"Our government has urged the governments of those nations not to allow any ransom money to be sent to these criminal outlaws. This offshoot of the Moro Islamic Liberation Front is notorious for supporting itself by kidnapping. Usually it's a Chinese businessman or visiting merchant who is kidnapped; a ransom demand is made, it's quickly paid, and business continues as usual. This is a flagrant expansion of that operation, and we want it stopped and crushed for all time.

"That is why we have asked for help. The kidnappings are now two days old. Yesterday we sent in a well-armed

Army force to rout out one of the strongholds of the rebels where we suspected they might have the hostages. Our force of twenty-five men suffered eighty percent casualties including nine dead. The team did not reach the strong point, or even see it, and barely saw the dug-in guerrillas. They knew we were coming."

Murdock's forehead pounded like a Chinese gong on New Year's Eve. It was his version of a headache produced by too much caffeine and too little sleep and too much tension. DeWitt and Senior Chief Sadler didn't look in much better shape, he decided.

Murdock jerked his attention back to the colonel talking.

"So, we come to you for help. This small force you have sent us seems woefully inadequate. Sixteen men? We understand that there are more than two hundred and fifty rebels in this group holding the hostages. We can give you what intelligence we have on them. We know of two camps they use in the jungle. One is the one we tried to attack yesterday. The other is deeper into the jungle and would require a helicopter trip, which we can provide." He paused and then looked at Murdock.

"Commander, what can you suggest for this operation?"

"Nothing at the moment, Colonel. My planning team will go over your data and information, then come up with an attack plan and consult with you for possible use of your choppers and a possible backup squad of your Marines. The planning will not take long. The time now is 1235. We should be able to stage an attack with first dark tonight. What helicopters do you use, Colonel?"

"We have the ones you are used to, Commander, the CH-46."

"Good. Keep one on standby here. I'll meet with my men and consult with you in two hours about our plan. We'll want any input from you, the attachment of two guides who know the area we'll move to, and the location of the two targets."

"Commander, we'll have that information and personnel all assigned as soon as you're ready."

The three SEALs went back to the quarters they had been assigned to and stared at the oversized map of Mindanao.

It was an irregular island 350 miles wide and almost that long top to bottom. The two targets the Philippine Army colonel had designated were about fifty miles from Davao in the middle of the mountains. There were no roads or trails within twenty miles of the camps.

Murdock pulled in Jaybird and Lampedusa to help on the planning. Jaybird shook his head.

"Damn, they aren't asking us for much. We go in and out by chopper, for fucking sure. How good is their intel?"

"Nobody knows. They got their asses kicked at Site A yesterday. There probably is a mole in the top echelons of the military feeding the rebels information."

"So let's try Camp B," Lam said.

"We can't blast the place with twenties; it would put the hostages in peril," DeWitt said.

"How close can we land to Camp B?" Murdock asked. "If we get close enough to save our legs, the rebels will know we're coming."

"So we go in, land, recon the place, and wait twelve hours before we attack," Jaybird said. "We catch them off stride, tire them out just waiting, while we sack out."

"Weapons?" Murdock asked.

"Every goddamn thing we've got," Jaybird said. "Maybe easy on the EAR so we don't have to carry out the unconscious hostages."

"So we'll need three more forty-sixes on standby at Davao to pack out the hostages when we rescue them," DeWitt said. "Do they have them available?"

"Good idea, we'll check," Sadler said. "I didn't see a lot of aircraft at this air base. We'll ask the colonel."

"Is there a double canopy of trees here like in Nam where the tops reach up sixty, seventy feet?" Lam asked. "If there is, will we be able to find a chopper LZ anywhere near the camp?"

"Have to find out," Murdock said. "We've got more questions than plans. Let's go see the colonel and the two locals he's providing us with. Then do the rest of our prelim plans there."

At the conference a half hour later they had questions answered. Yes, there were landing areas within five hundred yards of either camp along a river. Yes, lots of double canopy in places, single in others. They had six CH-46's at Davao. That was all but one that the Philippine Air Force owned. They were ready to go when needed. Each had a door gunner with a mounted machine gun.

"We've picked Camp B to attack first," Murdock told the group. "It's more remote; they could be less ready for an attack there. Are there trails along the river to the camp?"

"Yes, trails that will be defended," Philippine Army Master Sergeant Pedro Estrada said. He was about thirty, short and sturdy, and looked competent to Murdock. He had been introduced as one of the two men who would be their local guides and advisors.

"We can deal with that. What type weapons do they have?"

Army First Lieutenant Juan Ejercito, the other local now on the SEALs' team, responded. "I was on the attack yesterday. They had machine guns and submachine guns. I heard some AK-47's as well. They are well armed. I was one of four men in my section who didn't get hit. They ambushed us on a trail. Complete surprise. They have never been that sophisticated before in their tactics."

"They are getting outside help?" Murdock asked.

"Possible," the officer said.

Murdock looked at Jaybird. "Speed of the forty-six and how long to travel the sixty miles to the target?"

"Cruises at about a hundred and fifty, so that would be two-point-five miles a minute. Put that into sixty miles and we get exactly twenty-four minutes flying time."

"When is it dark here, Sergeant?" DeWitt asked.

"Sir, about 1800 this time of year."

"Can we land and deplane at that site in the dark?" Sadler asked the lieutenant.

"We went in during the day. It might be safer to fly in so we land just before dusk, say at 1745, even 1730. We don't want to crash on landing."

"I agree since we don't know the terrain," Murdock said.

"Communications?" Lam asked.

The colonel frowned. "We'll have our regular radio net

with the pilot. It's good, reliable. Distance no problem."

"We could supply the pilot or his gunner with one of our Motorolas," Jaybird said. "Then we could contact them for possible exfiltration and the pilot could bring in rescue birds if we free any hostages at this camp."

"Done," Murdock said. He looked around. "Anything else? Any questions?"

"You have adequate ammunition?" the colonel asked. "We have NATO rounds in most sizes and forty-millimeter grenades, fraggers, flares."

"We should be good for this mission," Sadler said. "Downstream we may need some resupply. I'll keep our liaison with you up to date."

"That's a wrap then, gentlemen," Murdock said. "We'll be ready to leave here at 1700. We'd prefer the lieutenant and sergeant to bring their gear and weapons to our quarters soon so we can integrate them. This is a combat situation."

Back at their quarters, the SEALs worked out weapons assignments, went over final preparations on their gear, and loaded ammo into their vests and pockets.

In the mess, the cooks worked up a steak dinner for the SEALs and their two friends.

"Damn, I feel like a fatted hog ready for slaughter," Jaybird yelped.

"Stupid, wasn't no fatted hog, it was a fatted calf, butchered for the Prodigal Son's return," Fernandez said.

"Right now I'd settle for a roasted Jaybird," Mahanani brayed, and they all roared with laughter and finished the meal.

The SEALs were on the tarmac ready to load the chopper at 1700. Murdock had given the bird a quick inspection. It seemed to be in good repair, and the machine gun in the door was up and ready to fire. The Filipino pilot, Captain Pepe Gonzalez, was on hand early and shook hands with Murdock.

"Checked out the bird and she looks solid, Commander," said Gonzalez. "I've flown this one every day for the past month and she's sound and ready."

"Have you been over the area where this river goes?" Murdock asked.

"Some of it, not up that high. A real wilderness back in there. No roads. A few trails an off-road motorcycle might cover."

"We'll need an LZ as close to the target as possible. You've done night landings?"

"Lots of them, and we have a new strobe searchlight I can use to be sure where the ground is. No sweat on that."

Murdock gave him a Motorola.

"Our person-to-person radio," Murdock said. "It's good for about five miles. We'll use it to call you in when we're ready to leave or to have you call in the rescue choppers. You can clip the transceiver on your belt and put the earplug in and use a lip mike, or just hold it all in one hand."

"Try it," Captain Gonzalez said.

They walked apart a dozen yards and Murdock called the captain. It worked perfectly, and Gonzales called Murdock back.

Then it was time to load. The eighteen men stepped into the side doors of the forty-six and settled down.

Murdock had assigned Lieutenant Ejercito to stay with Bravo Squad, and Sergeant Estrada would be with him and Alpha.

"Call me Pedro," the short sergeant said. "It's quicker and I know you're talking to me."

"Good, call me Murdock. Out here we don't have any rate or rank. We're all fighters. We're a team. We fight together and we win together or we die together. It's that tight. I expect you to blend right in. Every SEAL helps every other SEAL. We support, we protect, and we make the enemy pay."

Pedro grinned as the big bird lifted off. "Good to be with you, Murdock. I've chased these bastards for ten years."

Just after they'd arrived at the base, they'd had a briefing. The Island of Mindanao had for many years been settled mainly by Muslims. First there had been the Moro Islamic Liberation Front fighting for freedom for Mindanao as a separate nation. Later there was a Separatist Islamic Liberation Front that came to terms with the Philippine government and accepted many of the programs from the national groups to help train the people on the big island and lift them out of poverty.

Just when things began to go better for the people on the big island, the Rebel Separatist Islamic Liberation Front mobilized and squeezed away from the traditional group that was cooperating with the federal government, and began attacking and kidnapping and agitating for more local control and eventual freedom. This had spawned the Chinese merchant kidnappings, and now the group was out for the pot of gold, six million dollars in ransom.

Twenty of the twenty-four minutes slanted past quickly, and the crew chief turned on a red light over the rear hatch. "Gentlemen," he shouted over the roar of the engines and the whine of the blades. "We have four minutes to touch-down. The pilot will be searching for a good LZ, so it could be two or three minutes longer. Suggest you get up, check your gear, and be sure to take everything with you."

"And thank you for flying Hedgehopping Hazardous Air-lines," Jaybird cracked.

Most of the men were too busy to laugh. Another mission, another step into the unknown.

"Just hope he finds a good LZ that won't come alive with rifle fire," Murdock said.

Pedro grinned. "Good man, the captain. I've ridden with him before. He'll set us down at the best spot."

They could see the ship coming in lower; then it stopped, moving forward, hovered, and settled gently to the ground. The red light turned to green.

"Go, go, go," Murdock shouted. One squad went out each side door, ran out of the rotor wash, and hit the ground in a defense parameter. Pedro was at Murdock's elbow.

"We go upstream," the sergeant said. "So far, so good." Murdock led off with his squad, Lam out in front by twenty yards in the thick jungle growth. Pedro had run ahead and guided Lam into an animal trail next to the river, and now they moved ahead at a slow walk, testing the air as they went for any enemy activity.

Lam went down after four hundred yards. "Skipper, best to come up here with Pedro. Damn peculiar."

Murdock and Pedro ran up to where Lam stretched out behind a two-foot-thick log. They looked over the top. Murdock saw a village. It looked totally and completely deserted. One chicken scratched in the moonlight where it streamed through sixty-foot high lauan, or Philippine mahogany trees.

The place had the feel of being recently inhabited. Lam made a dash for the first building, a hut made of native materials woven together. He went in and out and shook his head. Murdock used his NVG and watched the rest of the place. He saw no sign of life. In the middle of the set of twenty huts was a tree that had been stripped of its branches and leaves. Only one strong branch stretched out at right angles to the trunk. Hanging on the branch Murdock saw two bodies.

"Let's go in," Murdock said. "Everyone move up, the place looks deserted."

He and Pedro hurried to the hanging tree. A man and a woman hung there. Their bodies could not have been dead more than a day. Each had a sign nailed into the chest. One read: "I was a spy for the President." The other said, "I cooperated with the misdirected Moro Liberation Front."

"Nobody home," Lam said on the Motorola.

"Everyone up here. Search this place. See if you can find anything that might show where they went."

Lam vanished into the brush and trees.

After twenty minutes, the SEALs had found nothing of value, nothing to indicate where the inhabitants went, or even if the hostages had been held here. Then Ostercamp saw something gleaming in the dust. He picked it up and frowned.

Murdock looked at it and grinned. "The hostages were here, I'd bet my booty on it. This is a PEO pin. A half-inch-high five-pointed gold star with the black letters. My mother had one and I used to hide it, and then be a hero when I could find it just before she went to the meeting. It's a Christian-related sorority of some kind. The meaning of the letters is a big secret. Chances are it was dropped by one of the American hostages."

Lam came back and talked to Murdock, Ejercito, and

DeWitt. "I found their trail heading upstream. Looks like four or five off-road motorcycles and a bunch of wheeled carts and a whole bunch of footprints. Lots of bare feet, also a lot of shoe prints. No spike heels, but some low heels on women's prints, and a number of men's shoe prints. I'd say the hostages were hoofing it north."

Murdock tried to call the chopper, but had no response. "Gonzales said he would make ten-mile circles south of our LZ. Bradford, try to contact the chopper every five minutes." He looked at the two bodies hanging in the moonlight.

"Should we cut them down and bury them?"

Juan shook his head. "No, then their relatives would never find them. Leave them up there. In two or three weeks the relatives will come back and do what they need to do for a Muslim funeral."

"Time to move," Murdock said. "Lam, head us back downstream toward that LZ. We've got a chopper to catch."

They were halfway there when Bradford made contact with the bird.

"Big Bird. Our mission is finished. Looking for a ride at the same LZ."

"Read you loud and clear. I'm five miles from the former LZ. See you there."

Thirty-two minutes later the forty-six chopper landed back at Davao. Murdock, Estrada, Ejercito, DeWitt, Sadler, and Lam all went into a debriefing.

"Is there a woman's organization called the PEO here in the Philippines?" Murdock asked the colonel.

The man shook his head. "Never heard of it. I'll ask our G-2 to check it out. What kind of a group is it?"

"A Protestant woman's group," Murdock said. "Since this is a mostly Muslim country, the chances are low it would have chapters here. One of my men found this PEO pin in the deserted village. It's our only evidence that the hostages were there."

There was a knock on the door; it opened, an aide came in, and gave the colonel a message. He read it and shook his head.

"It's an ultimatum from the rebels. They say they have

already shot one of the hostages, an American woman. One more will be shot every day until the ransom is delivered to the point that was previously communicated to the Army. Also, they say the presence of United States Navy SEALs in the Philippines is unacceptable and they must be withdrawn at once."

Murdock scowled. "We've only been here twelve hours. How in hell do they know that we're here?"

7

Colonel Alvarez shook his head. "We must have a leak in our organization somewhere."

Murdock scowled. "Colonel, no disrespect, but our lives are on the line here. I suggest that we work with only you and one man from your staff, Estrada and Ejercito, and my people. Nothing on paper, nothing on e-mail, no radio use, nothing over a phone line. Our missions and targets are top secret. If the rebels know in advance where we're going, we'll never find them."

"Agreed. I will be the only one from the Army besides your two liaison men. We have one more lead. They are calling themselves the Rebel Separatist Islamic Liberation Front, and they have been asking local villages to support them. We have heard about their calls. We have an area closer to us here where we think there may be one of the two GHQs of the rebels. How do you want to play it?"

Jaybird spoke up first. "My suggestion, Colonel, is that we do the chopper assault again, only do it in the daytime, and bring one chopper in from both directions along the river. They'll think we're attacking from both ends, only we'll have all our firepower in one chopper and take them out."

The colonel laughed and shook his head. "Good, yes, a good idea. I'm amazed that it comes from an enlisted man. If I suggested to my staff that we include corporals on our strategy planning sessions, they would hoot me out of the room."

"Several of my men have had three years of combat and

actions like this on a nearly monthly basis, Colonel. We learn from experience, and rank has nothing to do with intelligence. Some of my men have been on thirty bloody combat missions similar to this one. Experience pays off."

Colonel Alvarez nodded. "I wholeheartedly agree. What about timing?"

"We can get in a good sleep period and be ready to go at noon tomorrow."

Senior Chief Sadler frowned. "Skipper, what would you think about sending out a false signal. Say we were planning a night mission tomorrow at the first camp that was hit by the Lieutenant Ejercito and his group yesterday."

"A little misinformation," Murdock said. "Colonel?"

"Yes, good. I can have some memos written up and sent to you and to some other staffers, also one to Flight Ops and to Supply for a possible need for ammunition. It could help."

"With the colonel's permission, it's almost lights out for my troops."

"Yes. Dismissed. We'll try to keep everything under wraps. I'll send a messenger to alert the two chopper pilots and tell them not to tell anyone what they are doing or who they are flying or anything. If they get pinned down, they'll say it's a training flight."

"Thank you, Colonel."

The SEALs and the two Filipino Army men left the room.

Murdock called to the two locals. "Gentlemen, not that I doubt your loyalty, but I want you both restricted to our SEAL quarters until we take off tomorrow noon."

DeWitt agreed. The Filipinos said that would be no problem. DeWitt still frowned. "Chow," he said. "If we get special chow before we go it could tip off somebody. Let's eat normal chow for breakfast, then draw some MREs, if they have any, to eat on the chopper for lunch."

"Done," Sadler said. "I'll do a walk-by at the mess tomorrow morning and bring back the goodies." He turned to Lieutenant Ejercito. "You do have some kind of emergency field rations, don't you."

"We do. We buy MREs from the States." They all laughed.

In the morning, mess call came at 0730 and all the SEALs made it. They heaped extra food on their trays and ate it all. One of the local Filipinos assigned to the SEALs walked in front and one behind them to smooth out any problems in the mess line. Murdock and DeWitt ate along with the rest of the men.

Back in their quarters, all of the SEALs gathered and went over what intel the colonel had given them. It was another small village on a different river. They guessed at about twenty reed houses and maybe a hundred people. If the rebels were there, there might be fifty men and some or all of the hostages. It was a big if, but it was all they had right then.

"We need to develop some information on these rebels on our own," Murdock said. "But I don't see how that's possible."

"What we need to do is to spot two men in the field, track the rebels, send out word where they are and what they're doing," DeWitt said.

"Highly dangerous," Lieutenant Ejercito said. "You saw what they did with the two spies they caught."

"Still, if we rely on the colonel's intel, we might be here a year chasing our tails around in circles," Murdock said.

"Sounds like my meat," Lampedusa said. "Only how would I get the intel out?"

"SATCOM," Bradford said. "You can use mine and we'll get another one. Didn't we bring a backup SAT-COM?"

"That we did, oh, wise one," Sadler said.

"Lam, you don't know the turf," Murdock said.

"So send along somebody who does."

"I'll go," Ejercito said. "I've been going crazy sitting around here. I'm better in the field."

Murdock scowled and stared at the two men. "Two problems. Would it work? Could you get close enough to them to do any good? Could you even find them? From what I hear they could be anywhere over there within a fifty-square-mile area."

Ejercito nodded. "Yes, Commander. If they are at this village we're going to tomorrow, Lam and I simply stay behind after we hit them. We track them and dig out intel, grab a prisoner and question him for more intel, get everything we can and zap it out to you every night on the SAT-COM. I've seen them work. We have something similar on different frequencies."

Murdock looked at Lam.

"Hell, yes, with a local native guide we should be able to ace them right up their assholes and they'll never know we're there," Lam said. "Packing the damn SATCOM will be a pain, but no way we can keep within five miles of a chopper with a Motorola. Yeah, we can do it."

Murdock put a big X on a sheet of paper. "Okay, let's say it's workable, you can do the job. The next big problem as I see it is can you stay alive and get back out without getting your heads turned into worm buckets and your hearts roasted over a campfire."

The Filipino Army lieutenant smiled. "I don't think it will come to that, Commander. I've seen Lam working. He slipped up on me once when I was watching for him and I never saw or heard him. With his guts and skills, and my understanding of the local jungle and the people, we should survive."

Murdock looked at Lam. "This is above and beyond."

"Oh, hell, yes, way up there above. I like it out there. I won't have Senior Chief Sadler yelling at me all the time." He grinned. "Just kidding, Senior Chief. Yeah, Skipper. I want to go. Without it we're fucking ourselves in public."

DeWitt walked across the room and came back. Everyone watched him, waiting. He was thinking. He'd done this many times before. "So, do we tell the colonel?" DeWitt asked. He answered himself. "Hell, no, not until he misses the lieutenant. I'm not overjoyed with the colonel and his security."

They looked at Lieutenant Ejercito. "You're probably right," he said. "I have no responsibility to tell him. I don't report to him. I'd say go on our own. He'll miss me sooner or later. Then maybe you'll have to tell him. He's going to wonder where we get new intel if you make strikes we set up for you from the field."

"We'll tell him when we have to, probably before the first hit you zero us in on," DeWitt said.

"Okay, let's do it," Murdock said. "You two will need extra ammo and a duffel filled with ammo and emergency rations and clothes. You'll need a cache somewhere. Senior Chief, work it out. The rest of you get some rest. We have a liftoff tomorrow at 1200."

The next morning, preparations for the hit on the village went on schedule. Senior Chief Sadler arranged for extra emergency food and uniforms to be supplied by the Filipinos to be in the duffel for the two recon men. The pair decided to take only the H & K MP-5's for close-in work. They wouldn't do any attacking, and would use the weapons for defense if they were seen or chased.

Both Lam and the lieutenant were checked out on the SATCOM, and a new battery was put in the one Lam would carry. Both men decided that they would stash their combat vests with the cache on site, and travel light and fast, keeping their MP-5's across their backs. Lam figured out how to strap down the SATCOM on his back.

"Damn, this is still a light load," he said when he tested the setup without the usual heavily loaded combat vest. They crawled on the chopper promptly at 1150 and dug into their favorite MREs. Both birds took off exactly at 1200. The flight time to target was thirty-two minutes. All eighteen men were in one chopper; the other one was empty. It would make the run from upstream from the camp, then down toward it, loiter in the area for five minutes, then return to the airfield. The first chopper would stay on the ground downstream at the LZ and wait for a possible return of the SEALs. If there was a need for evac birds for the hostages, the helicopter pilot on the ground would radio the field for the number of craft needed.

Murdock stayed near the cabin as they came up to the river.

"River Run Two, this is One, making my turn down the

river from ten miles upstream your position," the speaker radio said.

"Roger that, One. We are about two miles from our LZ. Your timing is good. Continue run, then do it again, then bug out."

"That's understood, Two. Continuing run. Good luck."

Murdock could see the landing zone ahead. It was a three-acre plot that had been cleared of brush and trees at a level spot near the river. It probably flooded each wet season, and now had been harvested. Probably rice. The area held a foot-high dike around it so it could be flooded to help the growing crop. The land was dry now as the bird settled down, the green lights came on at the open doors, and the SEALs darted out and charged to the cover of the trees at the edge of the river.

Under the shade of the trees, Murdock took a radio check. All men reported in. "Upstream," he said. "Lam out front by twenty. Regular patrol string but single file. Let's move at a trot. We have about six hundred yards to the village. Any surprise we might have had is gone, and we hope they have panicked."

Five hundred yards later, Ejercito, Lam, and Murdock stared at the edges of the village past a heavy growth of trees. This one was not deserted.

"Looks like a normal village," Lam said. Murdock glanced at the Filipino. Ejercito shook his head. "No, it's too normal. The choppers would alert them and they should be tense, afraid, wondering who would attack. And it gave time for any rebels to hide and wait for us."

"We circle around it," Murdock said. "We keep half of our men on this side. Lam, you take Bravo around at ninety degrees to us. We don't want to be shooting each other. Then we'll fire some rounds into the trees. We don't want to kill the civilians."

"The rebels will use them as human shields," Ejercito said. "I've seen them do it."

"We won't kill civilians," Murdock said. "If they use them as shields to run, let them go. We'll chase them as well as we can, then examine the village for any hostages or clues where they might be going."

Murdock called DeWitt and told him the plan. He moved his men where Lam directed, and called Murdock on the Motorola when they were in position.

Alpha Squad had come up, and Murdock spaced them out ten yards apart from the river into the jungle so they had cover and could see the village.

"Alpha only. Each man, ten rounds into the trees. Don't hit any civilians. We think the rebels are hiding somewhere in the village. Fire, now."

The nine weapons chattered and cracked as the rounds riddled the tops and trunks of a dozen trees in the compound. The villagers in the open dove to the ground; some ran for huts, others dropped where they were and covered their heads.

In the sudden silence, Lieutenant Ejercito shouted out his demands.

"All villagers stay clam. We have no fight with you. The criminal outlaw rebels now in your village must come out with their hands up. We know you are hiding there. Surrender now and receive a fair trial for any criminal activity. Surrender now."

Two machine guns and a rifle answered Ejercito, ripping the rounds into the area where he was protected behind a huge mahogany tree. Each of the SEALs had a tree to hide behind during the return fire.

"Take any sure shots you have, Bravo," Murdock said on the Motorola. Two shots came almost at once, then one more. They heard a scream from the village. A man in white pants ran into the yard. "They are dead. All three of the rebels are dead."

"Easy, careful," Murdock said. "DeWitt, what can you see?"

"We nailed two of them. They had no protection from this angle. Shot the third and he crawled off somewhere. We think that was all of them."

"See if you can find the wounded one and capture him. Don't take any risks. If he still has a weapon, and uses it, waste him. Go."

Without waiting, Ejercito sprinted from his cover to the

closest house thirty yards across the opening. He drew no fire.

"Lieutenant, take it easy. Careful," Murdock said on the radio.

They waited.

Three minutes later, the earpieces spoke again.

"We've got him, Skipper," DeWitt said. "He's alive and has two rounds in his legs. Doing a lot of blubbering in the native language."

"Ejercito, find them and talk to the man. Pump him for everything you can. We need information. Any hostages here? Where are they? What's the next rebel camp in this area? Everything he'll talk about."

"Yes, sir. I see them. I'll be busy for a few minutes."

"DeWitt, search the houses and huts, tell those who speak English that the fighting is all over. Have them come out of their huts. See if there are any hostages kept here."

Murdock kept his men covering the village. When it was cleared, the civilians came out cheering and shaking hands. The SEALs took it easy in the shade. Murdock went to the hut where the prisoner was being questioned. He had been tired to a wooden chair. He was naked. DeWitt stood in the background.

Ejercito asked the man a question in Filipino, the other official language of the island nation in addition to English. The man shook his head. Ejercito put a four-inch slice across the man's shoulder. He wailed in pain. Ejercito slapped him twice. The small man looked up, hatred and fear showing on his face. At last he nodded.

"You speak English, don't you?"

"Yes."

"Good. You said there is another rebel camp nearby. How close?"

"Ten miles upstream."

"This is an outpost?"

"Yes, we report by radio. We smashed the radio when you attacked."

"How many rebels in the next camp?"

"Twenty, thirty, maybe forty. It changes every day."

"Is that where they hold the sixty hostages?"

The man's eyes went wide. "Hostages? I don't know about any hostages."

"How long have you been posted here?"

"For three months. Nobody said anything about hostages."

Ejercito stared hard at the prisoner, who didn't change his expression. At last the lieutenant nodded and stepped back.

"I think he's telling the truth. The next step is ten miles. Do we take it now or do Lam and I recon it?"

"We do it now," Murdock said. "Bradford. Call the chopper on the Motorola and tell him we're moving ten miles upstream. He should wait two hours, then follow us and find an LZ in that immediate area. Better at nine miles than ten. Do it."

Murdock motioned to the captive. "What about him?"

"He's got both legs shot up," the lieutenant said. "One broken. We can leave him here. The locals will take care of him. Many of them sympathize with the rebels. He can't hurt us. No way he can run up and warn them ahead."

"Good, cut him free." The captive was grinning and nodding.

"DeWitt, any casualties?"

"None. We're ready to move."

"Lam, let's find the trail upstream and we'll get the men lined up. Single file and keep locked and loaded. Let's move, SEALs."

Bradford used the Motorola then and contacted the chopper.

Five minutes later they were on the trail. "It's a little after 1330. We have two hours to do ten miles. We'll start with a jog and then speed it up if we have to. Lam, stay ahead twenty. Moving out."

It was two hours and twenty minutes before they saw Lam give the down signal. The SEALs hit the jungle floor. Murdock and DeWitt checked in with Lam, who stood behind a big tree and pointed ahead. It was a crudely camouflaged outpost built along the trail behind a huge Philippine mahogany tree.

"I've seen two men," Lam whispered. "Neither one looks over twenty. Both are smoking. I'd swear I could smell pot smoke a few minutes ago."

Murdock drew his KA-BAR and touched the sharp edge. Lam nodded and drew his. Murdock motioned for Lam to go left and he would go right. Silence was understood.

DeWitt slipped back to the rest of the troops to caution them for absolute quiet. He told the Filipino lieutenant about the outpost.

"Good," he whispered. "There might be two of them. There almost always are."

Murdock slid into the brush and jungle growth for fifteen yards directly away from the river and the two rebels. Then he went to his stomach and did a hard right and worked forward, careful not to rustle any leaves or move any branches. He figured he was fifteen yards from the outpost on the trail. He worked that far upstream, then turned at a ninety-degree angle and wormed his way under most of the growth in the fifteen yards he had to go toward the river. After five yards he stopped to listen. He could hear faint voices, then a laugh. Five more yards and he could hear the words plainly. He stared hard through the growth, but it was too thick. He worked forward again. Suddenly the underbrush vanished. It looked as if it had been chopped down to give security to the sentries.

Murdock stopped just inside the fringe and behind a tree. He eased his face around it. There, ten feet away, sat two guards inside the crude outpost. Both had automatic rifles, and wore Army shirts but civilian white pants. Both were smoking, and Murdock recognized the pot smoke at once. No way to tell how high they might be. He snicked the Motorola send button once. He was ready.

He waited. A minute later, he received a return snick in his earpiece. Ten seconds after the second snick they both would charge. Eight, nine, ten, Murdock counted slowly to himself. Then he lifted up soundlessly. Both rebels looked out a small window and along the trail downstream, their backs to Murdock. He took three steps without a sound, saw Lam come out of some brush and take three steps.

They nodded, then charged with their KA-BARs held straight in front of them like lances.

One of the guards sensed something behind him and began to turn. Before he could even see Murdock, the commander's KA-BAR drove into his back. Murdock turned the blade and twisted it sideways into the man's spinal column.

As Murdock hit the first man, Lam came at the second. His man turned more, and the six-inch blade of the KA-BAR sliced through the uniform, plunged into the man's side. It tore through part of his lung and daggered deep into his heart, killing him before he could make a sound.

Murdock's man spilled off the stool to the ground, where he thrashed for a moment; then his cut spinal cord refused to send messages to his body, and his heart and lungs closed down and he gushed out a long, final breath.

"Clear front," Murdock whispered in his Motorola. Lam moved along the trail upstream.

"Murdock, Ejercito says there often will be two outposts in front of any good-sized rebel force," radioed DeWitt. "Lam, you copy?"

"Lam. I copy."

Far off, Murdock thought he could hear a helicopter, but then the sound faded. He wiped his blade on the dead man's pants and put it back in its sheath. A few moments later the rest of the platoon hiked up and they moved forward on the trail.

Murdock had checked the outpost. There were no phone lines and no radios present. The SEALs should have the element of surprise.

Ten minutes later, Lam called up the officers. Lieutenant Ejercito went along. The four of them watched ahead as four men replaced four men in another guard position. It was not done in a military manner, but they finished the transfer and the four replaced men hiked upstream. All of these men had new Army-type uniforms of dark green.

Murdock heard the rebel radio transmission that came at once. It was in Filipino, and Ejercito held up his hand as he concentrated. Then he nodded.

"The new guards are checking in. All is quiet. They expect no trouble. There has been no word of any new developments on the money payments on the hostages."

"That's just dandy," Ed DeWitt whispered. "But how in hell are we going to take down this guard post without alerting the rest of the rebels that they have some serious trouble coming right at them?"

8

Jungle near Davao
Mindanao, Philippines

"Easy to silence the outpost," Tran Khai said. "We use the EAR. Ain't that why I've been carrying it all this way?"

"Didn't think we brought one," DeWitt said.

"Get up here, Khai," Murdock said. "Your friends and neighbors need your help."

"We find the radio the rebels have and take it," Ejercito said. "Then I can answer any calls in either language before we hit the main camp." Lieutenant Ejercito looked to Murdock for approval. Lieutenant Commander Murdock nodded. "Your men told me about the EAR. I still can't believe it," said Ejercito.

"You will," Lam said.

Khai came up a moment later and saw the outpost guardhouse. It was made of woven reeds and branches and blended into the surroundings.

"Blow the house down?" Khai said. He looked at Murdock.

"Fire when ready."

Khai sighted in and pulled the trigger. The familiar whooshing sound came from the weapon; then the reed walls of the hut ahead shivered and wavered. Lam and Murdock sprinted for the guard shack thirty yards away. By the time they got there, none of the four rebels was moving. The SEALs bound them hand and foot and gagged them, then found the radio and waved the troops forward.

Ejercito shook his head in amazement. "And in four to

six hours they wake up with no more damage than a slight headache. What a great weapon."

Lam had moved out ahead, and he reported they were at least a half mile from the main camp.

"How can you tell?" Murdock asked.

"I hear people singing and shouting."

"Give us plenty of time to catch up before you take on the whole damn rebel camp," Murdock said.

"Will do."

Twenty minutes later, they found Lam waiting for them. There was a forty-five-degree bend in the river, which had dwindled down to a stream only twenty feet across and somewhere less than a foot deep. Lam pointed ahead.

"Took a gander round the bend. The camp is there, big sucker. Looks like a village of maybe two hundred huts and some wooden houses. Saw a few of the green-shirted rebels but not that many. Like trying to attack Hometown, Philippines, with all those civilians."

"We'll get out of sight," Murdock said. "You and the lieutenant take a recon. Go all the way around it and get back here in an hour."

"Hour and a half," Lam said. "It's a big place."

Murdock put one squad on each side of the trail. They were fifty feet back in brush and jungle that was now showing some pines. The SEALs settled into places where nobody could see them unless they stepped on them.

"We wait," Murdock said on the Motorola.

Waiting was always the hardest part. Murdock filled in the time remembering the last time Ardith Jane Manchester stayed with him at his apartment. It had felt so damn good, so wonderfully comfortable, so . . . right, that he'd almost asked her to marry him. Almost, but not quite. It hadn't been a special day. He'd worked with the training routine, come home filthy and tired. Had a shower and then some thin-cut pork chops Ardith had fixed the way he liked them, with mashed potatoes and brown gravy and frozen corn and a mixed green salad with the best Roquefort dressing he'd ever tasted. She wouldn't tell him where she'd bought it.

Just a nice normal-type middle-class day. Nobody was

killed, nobody jumped out of an airplane or dove deep into the sea, or blew up a ship or anything like that. A fine, normal day and evening. Then they made love in the king-sized bed and drifted into a great night's sleep.

A nice normal day for them was exceptional, and 180 degrees from the usual day for both of them. The next morning he got a call from Don Stroh. They had four hours to be on a plane to God only knows where, and Ardith had a call from the Senate Armed Services Committee. It summoned her to testify early the next day in Washington about some research she had been doing. She had to fly out at noon, only she was heading east, while Murdock and the SEALs were moving west.

Murdock came back to reality suddenly. He frowned. A strange sound. It came again. He grinned, found a rock, and threw it over ten feet and hit Bradford. He was snoring.

The big guy snorted, roused, and stopped snoring. That made Murdock wonder about the call he'd had just before they left, about a warrant for Bradford's arrest. He hadn't told the big SEAL about it. No reason to worry him. Maybe it would be all ironed out by the time they got back. Maybe not. He knew that Bradford was in a small group of artists who rented a little gallery down on India Street. Bradford certainly wasn't counterfeiting old masters, that was for sure. He didn't do that kind of art. Murdock had taken Ardith down to look at his paintings one weekend.

His earpiece clicked twice. "Yes?"

"Halfway around, Skip. We've seen about fifteen green shirts. None in a group, scattered all over the place. No GHQ that we can tell. Have seen nothing that looks like what the lieutenant thinks would be a lockup for the hostages. Where could they escape to? Not too wild about taking on this place without a hell of a lot more data."

"Yeah, Lam, I hear you. Do the rest of the circuit and then we'll decide. Out."

"Bummer," DeWitt said on the radio.

"Worse than that. Bradford, have you made contact with that chopper pilot lately?"

"Twice, Skipper. He has an LZ about a mile behind the

big angled turn in the river. A mile downstream. Best he can do. He's ready when we're ready."

"Thanks, Bradford. How's the artwork selling?"

"Hey, just sold two before we left for three hundred and fifty bucks. I can help pay the rent."

"Good, Bradford, that's good."

The net went quiet for another ten minutes; then Lam came on. "Jackpot, Skipper. We've just found a pair of old wooden buildings set back a ways from the rest of the village. Must be twenty, maybe thirty of the green shirts going and coming. No sign of any hostages. We're about a quarter of the way around the right-hand side of the camp. Best to cross the creek and come up through the brush. Should we take them out?"

"We're moving, Lam. We'll take one more look and check it out. I'd say a good chance we get some target practice in before the day is over."

The SEALs moved across the creek and worked into the jungle brush for fifty yards, then moved upstream. Lam caught them before they passed him. He, DeWitt, and Murdock went for one more look.

A short time later the Motorolas sounded off. "Squads move up. Lam will check you out. Alpha to the upstream, Bravo to the downstream side. Set up where Lam shows you and get a good field of fire. Range will be about seventy-five yards."

Murdock had whistled softly when he saw the target. The two buildings were old, the traffic heavy. He saw two off-road motorcycles parked nearby. "We'll use the twenties, three rounds each to start, then switch to 5.56 for the stragglers. Somebody be sure to get those motorcycles with a twenty. Everyone fire your weapon. Not a chance any hostages are in there. Lam says no sign of any hostages anywhere. We take what we can get. Anyone not in position, sound off." He heard nothing. The men were spread out five yards apart along the far side of the stream across a small clearing.

Murdock sighted down on the open door to the first building. "Fire when ready," he said, and pulled the trigger. The impact of the 20mm round exploding inside the place came immediately, followed by six more rounds of the twenties, and soon hundreds of rounds from the machine gun, the sniper rifle, and the M-4A1 rifles.

Three men tried to run out the door. They died in a heap just outside. Men crawled out windows on the ground floor, but were splattered with rounds. A fire broke out in one of the buildings. Men screamed and tried to return fire, but they didn't have a chance. As targets died, the volume of fire fell off.

"Cease fire," Murdock said. One man staggered out the door of the building not burning, stumbled, and collapsed on the ground outside. Green-clad men pushed forward toward the buildings, then, when they saw the carnage, dodged behind the buildings or ran the other way.

"Fire at any green shirts you see alive," Murdock said. The sniper rifle replied at once. A man trying to run from one of the buildings to the other made it only halfway before a round took him high in the chest and he fell, slamming hard into the dirt and grass, not to move again.

More shots drilled into the afternoon as rebels tried to get to the back of the buildings.

"Bravo, with DeWitt, move out double time back to the trail and downstream," Murdock called on the Motorola.

A minute later he ordered Alpha Squad to move in the same direction.

"Bradford, use the Motorola and tell the chopper we'll be down there in ten minutes."

There was no return fire or any pursuit. The rebels were in total disarray; those who were left alive were still in hiding.

It took the SEALs ten minutes to jog the mile down the trail to the clearing where the forty-six waited, its rotor turning slowly. The SEALs crashed on board. Murdock counted heads. He came up with eighteen and ordered the chopper to fly.

"Casualty report," Murdock said into his Motorola so the men could hear him over the chopper noise.

"Checked, Skipper," Mahanani said. "Only one is the j.g. with his old one, the shot arm. It busted loose, but I did some ointment and a new bandage and he can do the rope climb again."

"Nothing else?"

"We don't count scratches and sprains. We're in good shape."

"Don't forget Lam and me," Lieutenant Ejercito said. "We'd like to be dropped off between these two camps. Anywhere along here."

"Right." Murdock went up to talk to the pilot. Two minutes later he set down on a small harvested field beside the stream.

Lam and the Filipino Army lieutenant jumped out of the chopper and took their duffel bag. Lam already had the SATCOM strapped to his back. "Keep in touch," Murdock called. "Use that SATCOM every night at midnight. We'll be listening for your call. Tac One." Lam waved and headed for the brush and concealment.

Murdock waved at them, and the pilot jolted the big bird back into the sky. They had a start. They had reduced the rebel garrison by what he figured was at least thirty men, and demolished one of their headquarters.

As the CH-46 clattered its way over the jungle and ridges back toward Davao, Murdock began to work up his after-action report for Colonel Alvarez. He still wasn't certain about the man. He wasn't Muslim, so how could he have any connection with the rebels? He might have spent a lot of his time in this Muslim province, but he was most likely Catholic. There would be no report about Lieutenant Juan Ejercito and Lam being left behind to do advanced recon work. Not a word about that. There had been no sign of the hostages in the large village. Where could the rebels be keeping them?

The briefing was a total surprise for the colonel, and he couldn't contain his shock.

"You say you captured the one small village, but there were only three rebels there?"

"That's right, Colonel. We questioned the survivor and he told us about another village only ten miles upstream."

"Yes, good. Now we know where another one is. We'll have to plan to hit that one. Maybe the hostages are there."

"They aren't, Colonel. We hit that village this afternoon."

Murdock and DeWitt gave him the report on the attack on the large settlement.

The colonel began to sweat. He mopped his forehead and scowled. "So, you attacked the village and think that you killed thirty of the rebels. Yes, good news. I'll relay that on to the President. He's interested in this hostage situation. Says it makes our whole nation look bad." The colonel fiddled with an unlit cigar that he had been holding.

"This brings up a chain-of-command problem, Commander," he said. "We follow the chain strictly here in the Philippines. No subordinate takes independent action. All operations must be cleared by my office or by me personally. This is to maintain a balance in the operation and to be sure that you don't attack villages full of innocent civilians."

"Yes, sir. I understand. However, in the field, there must be a certain amount of flexibility in any army or fighting force. When a target of opportunity presents itself, there is no time to call back to headquarters for permission to attack."

The colonel smiled. Murdock figured he knew he was in command here and held all the trump cards. "I can see your point, Commander. However, in this situation you're in a sovereign nation, and you must be guided by our rules and laws. I'm sure your senior officers would agree with that."

"Understood. We'll make every effort to plan our operations with your guidance and intel about the rebels."

There was a commotion at the door; then it opened and a man in civilian clothes backed in talking to someone in the other room. He turned around, and Murdock grinned.

"Hey, Murdock and DeWitt. Hi, you guys." Don Stroh, their CIA contact, turned to the colonel. "You must be Colonel Alvarez. Heard about you. Tough assignment out here in the boonies with all these Muslims shooting up the place. But we have the help that you need. Sorry I'm late, men, but I had a holdup in Manila. I still don't know why. Some kind of official intelligence agency problem. But now I'm here to get to work."

"Colonel Alvarez, I'd like to introduce you to CIA Agent Don Stroh," Murdock said. "He's our control and advisor and contact with the CIA director, the Chief of Naval Operations, and the President of the United States."

Colonel Alvarez nodded and after a pause, reached out and took Stroh's hand.

"Welcome to my country, Mr. Stroh. We're just getting started on this operation. Looks like it could take a while."

"Colonel, with the SEALs on board, the whole thing could come to a head faster than you could hope for."

"We were just finished with our briefing after today's set-to, Stroh," Murdock said. "Could I buy you a cup of coffee and get you up to date?"

"Sounds good. The officers club looked interesting."

They were dismissed by the colonel and headed for the club. Murdock derailed them back to the SEAL quarters.

"Stroh, this place seems to be so full of leaks it would make a sieve jealous. My guess is that the rebels know everything we're going to do, as soon as we get it planned out. We're not too sure about the colonel. I'm not saying he's feeding us to the rebels, but he sent us on two missions. The first one showed us a deserted village and two hung spies with messages. The second one we found three rebels."

He told Don the rest of the story, and Stroh was surprised by the colonel's reaction.

"You sure he wasn't mad that he wasn't in on the hit? That he couldn't take any of the credit? Some top brass get feeling hurt that way. Might be worse over here."

"So, anything new on the hostages?" DeWitt asked.

"Figured you'd know. Two Dutch hostages were ransomed out this morning. Some of the other countries are caving in. We think there are still about fifty-five hostages."

"If there is a problem with Alvarez, is there a general somewhere we can appeal to for cooperation?" Murdock asked. "We need the choppers for our attacks. Alvarez authorizes them."

"I'll see what I can find out. Must be a general out here somewhere. Anybody hurt?"

"DeWitt picked up an in-and-out in his arm couple of weeks ago, but nothing else."

They entered the SEALs building, and found the men had finished cleaning and oiling their weapons and had all their gear ready for another attack.

Inside the big room a voice cranked up.

"Well, if it isn't the D.C. society set's favorite boy toy, Don Stroh," Jaybird cracked.

Stroh grinned. "Jaybird, those ladies really know how to take good care of a guy. Not that I'm bragging, but would you believe eight times in one night?"

"Wouldn't believe two, Stroh," Ching yelped, and everyone cheered.

"Good to see you guys in such good spirits," Stroh said. "This one could get ugly. The President wants those American hostages back yesterday."

"We're working at it."

"Where's Lam? He off his feed?"

Murdock told the CIA man where Lam and the Filipino officer were.

"Yes, I love it. Spy work right here on the ground. I'd guess you didn't tell your favorite colonel."

"Not yet. Not until we have to. We'll make contact with Lam tonight at midnight, see what they've found."

Stroh frowned, then rubbed one hand over his freshly shaved face. "Think that I should make a call to Manila. I met a general there who is a good friend of our resident field agent here. See what I can find out about the command in this region. There may even be a general hiding out somewhere on this base. I'll find a secure phone somewhere and make some calls."

Murdock checked with the Senior Chief. All was well. The men were ready and waiting.

"Figure some sack time tonight and maybe no mission tomorrow," Sadler said. "We've got to give Lam some time to come up with something out there in the boondocks."

"I'm betting they do," Murdock said.

After chow, the men sat around their quarters talking. Murdock came in, and DeWitt slid over and got into the play. They were talking about the security.

"Don't seem like they got shit for security here," Oster-camp said.

"Maybe they want it that way," Sadler said. "They bring us in, then give us bad intel, and if we get some good shit they leak it to the rebels, who are long gone by the time we get there."

DeWitt joined in. "Look at their record so far. They sent us on a mission to an empty village. Then the next day we hit a small village with the great big total of three rebels in it. So far they have shown us next to nothing. If it wasn't for that prisoner talking today, we'd be zippo out of two. As it is, our only success is when we did it ourselves, and without telling anyone in the Philippine establishment."

"I'm with the j.g. on this one," Vinnie Van Dyke said. "Hell, the top brass must have brought us in. The local brass doesn't like getting stepped on, so he shits all over us and we get pulled out and it ain't no skin off his chin."

"Fuck 'em all," Franklin said. "Hell, if they don't want us here, I'd just as soon be back in Coronado cruising for some hot redhead who is just crazy to get laid."

There were a few huzzahs and shouts.

Murdock chuckled. "Hey, Franklin may have the right idea, but for now we're stuck here, so we do what we can. Say Lam gets a hot prospect for us, a big camp or even where the hostages are. How do we go to Colonel Alvarez and tell him we want six choppers to go in and bring out the hostages? He's gonna say where and how do you know, and then we have to confess that we don't much believe in his intel and we think he's a traitor to his country and he should fuck off."

"Then he whips up his .45 and shoots the Skipper, and we shoot him and his aide, and we have our own war right here on base," Canzoneri said.

"We might have to come up with something soon if Lam snoops out a new target for us, say by tomorrow night. They can't have much for us tonight. First they'll have to figure out where to go and look. My guess would be on upstream on the same river."

"How can we go around the colonel?" Sadler asked.

"There may be a way," Murdock said. "Stroh is working

on that right now. The only obvious way is to outrank him. Get a local general to take over the hostage problem so he can authorize choppers for attacks and eventual hostage rescues."

By 2350 most of the SEALs were out of their bunks, or waiting around the SATCOM, which Bradford had turned on to receive. Midnight came and passed. Nothing happened. They looked at the SATCOM set, and somebody yelled at Bradford to check his dish setting for the satellite. He did, and the set gave him a small beep that it was ready.

By a quarter after they had heard nothing from the radio. Half the men went back to bed. At a quarter to one, Murdock motioned to Bradford to turn off the set.

"They must be moving, or running out of a problem, or maybe just trying to get in position tonight to monitor something tomorrow," Murdock said. "Get some sleep."

The rest of them went back to their double-tier bunks. Murdock lay there not able to sleep. Why hadn't they called in? He told Lam to call every night at midnight. Maybe he didn't think he needed to call tonight. Yah, maybe. Still, Murdock couldn't put down a feeling of unease at the situation. Were Lam and Lieutenant Ejercito alive and well, or had they been caught, tortured, and then executed by the Muslim rebels?

9

Jungles of Mindanao
Near Davao, Philippines

A half hour after the chopper took off, Lam and Juan Ejercito lay in the brush watching the rebel Muslims pick up the pieces of the attack on the two buildings. They had left the duffel hidden and hiked back up to check out the blasted rebels.

"We really kicked the shit out of them," Lam said.

The Filipino lieutenant grinned. He had told Lam to call him Juan, it would be easier. "We did. Those twenty-millimeters are astounding."

They had counted twelve different men working around the building. The two motorcycles were totaled. They wouldn't even be good for parts.

"Motorcycles are the elite transportation in here where there are no real roads," Juan said. "Only the top men own them. Which means we may have wiped out some top brass in there."

"Hope so. Are we through here, or what?"

"Thinking of grabbing one of the survivors and doing some gentle questioning."

"Great idea. You see anybody with stripes on his green sleeves?"

"I don't think they use any rank. Just leaders and followers. If you don't know who is who, you don't belong in the group and get yourself shot dead."

"Tough outfit. We wait until dark to snatch one?" Lam asked.

"Best. Then we can take him into the brush, question him, and he won't be missed until morning. By then we'll be halfway to their new GHQ, or whatever location we get out of our friend."

The rebels carried bodies out of the building.

"Laying them out in a row," Lam said. "Must be going to have a mass Muslim funeral."

"Never saw one," Juan said.

They counted as the bodies came to the line. Juan saw the last one. "Twenty-eight," he said. "That will put a big hole in their ranks. Three hours to dark, five or six until I can snatch a live one. Let's take a sleep period. Can you wake up on demand?"

"Not usually."

"I can. Back into the jungle a ways, and watch for snakes. They move around this time of day."

At 2200, Juan roused Lam. "Time, Lam. We'll move up about where we were before, but closer. You'll cover me with the MP-5, but fire only if I'm in big trouble and can't get out by myself. That means at least four of the bastards pointing guns at me. I'll go in with my pistol and knife. Should be enough. No combat vest."

Lam watched the soldier slip through the woods to the cleared area, then come upright and walk toward the old headquarters as if he belonged there. Two men passed him without a glance. It was dark enough that his uniform nearly matched that of the rebels. Here they all had green shirts and pants. There were few lights in the village. Candles and kerosene lamps, Lam guessed. None showed in the burned-out building, only one in the other structure.

Juan headed for it. He was only a dozen yards away when a man came out and hurried toward him. Juan said something and the man stopped. He motioned and as he did, Juan put the five-inch blade of his fighting knife into the man's side so the point gouged in a quarter of an inch. Juan put his arm around the man's shoulders, and they walked quickly toward the brush and the jungle.

Two minutes later they were in the cover and Juan had put a gag around the man's mouth. They hiked farther into the jungle, past a swampy area and to a slight rise. Lam figured they were a mile from the village.

The prisoner looked young. Lam had given up trying to figure these men's ages. He could have been sixteen, but was probably in his late twenties. Lam guessed he was five-five and maybe 120 pounds. A lightweight.

They were in a small rocky clearing. Juan jerked the gag off the man and spoke pleasantly to him a moment in Filipino. Then, with no warning, Juan slugged him hard on his jaw and knocked him down.

"Get up," Juan roared.

The man struggled to his feet feeling his jaw.

"Now we get serious. How many rebels were killed today?"

"Six."

Juan hit him with a jab that splattered his nose and brought a froth of blood that ran down and dripped off his chin. He staggered backward but kept his feet.

"How many?" Juan asked again.

"Twenty-eight."

"That's better. What's your name?"

"Piang Miguel."

"We make a deal, Piang. From now on you tell me the absolute truth and I won't hit you. Agreed?"

"Yes."

"Who rode the motorcycles, your leaders?"

"Yes."

"Were they both killed?"

"Both, yes."

"How many rebels were here before the attack?"

"About forty-five and some women rebels."

"Where did your leaders go to report to their superiors?"

"Down the river almost to the coast. Near the town of Lebak, but inland about ten miles."

"Is that where your leader stays?"

"Sometimes. He moves around a lot. He thinks the government is trying to kill him."

"He's probably right. What's the next camp downstream from here?"

"Small one about ten miles down, then twenty-five miles or so to a big camp."

"Piang, why is it so big?"

"Much training done there. I was there for two months learning how to shoot, to rig bombs, how to kidnap, and fighting with a knife."

"Yet you didn't fight me when I touched my knife to your side."

"I am not a fighter. I am a clerk. I should have been in the office and killed with the others there. I was late getting back."

"How many men at the training camp?"

"Sometimes two hundred. We are gaining in strength. This camp was mostly to recruit from the surrounding area. To get young men to come and fight for independence."

"What's the name of your top leader now?"

"He is called Muhammad Al Hillah."

"Is he often at the training center?"

"Yes, often."

"Good, Piang, you may sit down and relax. We'll be here for a while." Juan Ejercito walked into the woods, circled around, and came up behind the rebel so quietly not even Lam could hear him. Lam didn't watch him. He looked away. A moment later a shot jolted into the stillness of the jungle. A dozen different insects and birds went silent at the sound.

Piang's head slammed forward from the round that shattered the back of his skull and killed him immediately.

"Time we move south," Juan said. "It looks like we have a thirty-five-mile hike ahead of us."

They were about halfway to the second camp, near where they had left the duffel bag, when Juan stopped and turned to Lam.

"Did you disapprove of my execution of the rebel?"

Lam shook his head. "No, not at all. SEALs take no prisoners, and leave no wounded on an operation. Had to be done. We should be almost to that cleared field."

Five minutes later they came to the field and to the spot where they had left the duffel. It was still there. They put on their combat vests, dug out the backpacks, and stowed most of the ammunition and clothes and food into them. Then they changed their minds and left all of the extra clothes.

"Better food than a clean shirt," Lam said. When they finished packing, they had most of the gear. They stashed the duffel again and covered it up, then hiked south along the faint trail. Four miles downstream they came to the village where they had attacked earlier and killed two of the rebels. They skirted it, moving into the jungle, and then worked on past. There was nothing they could do there, and they didn't want the locals to remember them moving south. Twice they saw and smelled smoke from cooking fires. They passed them, but did not see any sign of villages. Just before dusk they heard a strange sound from south on the trail.

"Dirt bike moving fast," Lam said. "Let's take him."

They moved into the trees beside the trail and motioned for fields of fire. They both would fire down-trail when the biker was within twenty feet. They waited.

The sound grew louder, and then the bike came around a slight bend in the trail and headed for them. One rider with helmet and goggles. Both men lifted their MP-5's and in sync leaned around the trees and fired two three-round bursts of the 9mm Parabellum. Eight of the twelve rounds hit the rider. He threw up his hands, and the bike slued to the left into a tree and the rider toppled off the back, sprawling on the ground, never knowing what hit him. Four of the rounds hit his chest, two his neck, and two his head. They pulled the body off the trail into the brush and checked his pockets. There was a folder inside his shirt that had four bullet holes in it, but also a dozen sheets of paper and writing, all in English.

Juan righted the cycle and put down the stand. He examined it, and found no damage other than a scraped front fender. The double seat looked inviting, but the front man would have to drop half the goods in his pack. Juan at once took off his pack and threw out the bulky MREs and three boxes of Parabellum rounds. He put it back on, and they tried both sitting on the machine.

"Yes," Lam said. "We can do this. We have twenty-five

miles and an hour of sunlight left. We should be able to do most of it."

A half hour later, they realized that the average speed on the rough trail was about fifteen miles an hour. They settled for that.

By the time darkness swept in on them in a two-minute stretch, they were ready to find a spot to spend the night.

They rolled the bike well off the trail and found a place on a small rise where they could keep watch on the trail and still have good cover. Not even taking the SATCOM off his back reminded Lam that he was supposed to radio in every night at midnight. He checked his watch. 0200. Too late by then. The next night there would be lots more to tell Murdock. He eased his head onto his pack and went to sleep.

Lam woke up the next morning, and looked down to see a black and orange snake three feet long crawling over his legs.

"Don't move," Juan said from somewhere behind him. "He's just out looking for breakfast and he decided you were too damn big."

The snake took his time, his forked tongue tasting the air as he moved. He soon zeroed in on a clump of grass nearby. The snake moved forward slowly. Lam could not see any movement in the grass. Then, a moment later, the snake struck. Its head came out of the grass holding a six-inch-long ratlike rodent in its jaws. Its fangs were buried in the animal's back and stomach.

"Breakfast," Juan said. "Wait just a minute and he'll slither away and start unhinging his jaws so he can swallow that critter whole."

"Glad I'm not that size," Lam said. "Poisonous?"

"Deadly on anything under a hundred pounds. On us it would be extremely painful and we'd take two days off and let the swelling go down. About the same as your rattle-snake."

"Thanks for waking me up."

"Best to let them move along. I usually don't kill them. They have a right to live the same as I do."

They ate MREs for breakfast, then loaded up and headed down the trail.

"Figure we covered fifteen miles last night," Juan said. "Ten miles ahead we should find some friends."

"We stash the bike at least two miles this side," Lam said. "They probably will have security all over the place here as much for training as for security."

Juan shook his head. "Not two miles. We'll leave it and our packs out four miles. You estimate our distance as we motor along. I've got trouble enough dodging ruts, gullies, and tree roots."

After twenty minutes Lam slapped Juan on the shoulder and he turned off into the jungle, drove the bike as far as he could, then they hid it behind some large trees and piled brush around it.

Lam went back along their trail and wiped it out as best he could, then did the same thing for a hundred yards back down the sometimes damp trail along the increasingly strong river. They left their packs with the bike and worked down the trail on foot.

"You kept the radio?" Juan asked.

"Glued to my skin," Lam said.

A half mile down the trail they smelled cigarette smoke. Almost every Filipino Lam had seen had been smoking. It seemed to be a national craze. Big Tobacco in the U.S. must be chortling.

They went into the brush away from the river and moved through the jungle slower, but safer. The smokers were at a guard post astride the trail. No camouflage, just two big logs that it would take five grown men to move across the trail. The rebels in green shirts and civilian pants sat on the logs. Each one had a rifle. Lam couldn't tell what kind they were, but they were all alike. He guessed they were AK-47's or maybe the new AK-74's. Either one was deadly.

"We could take them all out before they got off a shot," Juan said.

"Easy, Juan. We can come back and get them later. Let's get some intel for Murdock. We want the whole package. Maybe they have the hostages here."

"Yeah, right."

They moved past the guards silently in the jungle, then worked back closer to the trail and kept it in sight as they slogged through the trees, vines, and an occasional swamp.

It was a half hour before they came on more men. This time they had a machine gun set up in a fortified position with sandbags draped around it and making a three-foot protective wall. Juan checked the weapon with binoculars and nodded.

"Yeah, it's a NATO 7.62. Probably one they stole from the Army. Good weapon. I wonder how many they have." The gun was was set up to fire directly down the trail and in an arc of about thirty degrees on each side. Four men were in and around the emplacement.

"Getting more interesting," Lam said. "Like they have something to protect."

"Like six million dollars worth of hostages."

"Hopefully."

The trail went through jungle again, past giant mahogany trees. Far ahead, Lam could see smoke and hear sounds. He couldn't tell what they were.

They faded more into the jungle, wary of some outlying guard posts in the jungle well beyond the trail. The river was on the other side and gave protection there. By this time it was fifty yards across, racing downhill over some rapids, and swirling along darkly. It made an effective barrier from any attack on that side.

Now, for the first time, they could spot huts and small buildings along the trail. The edges of the village. They saw no rebels, and kept moving well inside the protection of the jungle growth.

Another half mile and the trail had become a fifteen-foot-wide road with ditches on each side. Buildings now sprouted all over the area and the place had the appearance of a real town. Slightly farther along they could see down a street, with what looked like businesses, and sidewalks. A whistle sounded, and a group of rebels marched around a corner and headed right at the two watchers. They were six abreast and at least ten deep. Sixty men, led by a sergeant or officer. They came toward the road, then turned left down another street and were gone.

"Damn, this is not a ragtag bunch of rebels," Juan said. "They have the start of a real army here. If they get enough men and equipment, they could take over the whole island and have their independent nation."

"We'll work on that next. What about hostages? You see anywhere that they could be held?"

"Yes. Several of the buildings could be sealed and the people kept inside. They would have enough food here to feed them and keep them healthy for the big payoff."

"There," Lam said. "See that antenna on that three-story building? Looks like the biggest one in town. That could be their radio tower. I wonder how good their radios are."

"Let's find out," Juan said. He took from his vest the small handheld radio he had taken at the checkpoint the day before. He turned it on and they listened. Soon a transmission came in Filipino. Lam looked at him.

"Someone asked a road checkpoint if they had seen anyone. A report has come through that the three men in checkpoint thirty-five have not reported in as required."

"This place looks like there could be two or three thousand people living here. Mostly civilians. How do we attack a place like this?"

Juan waved one hand. "We get intel on where their headquarters are, where their barracks are, any other equipment they have, and then we come in at night and blow up those buildings and hose them down with hot lead."

"Yeah, down and dirty. No air strike here. Looks like we have some work to do."

Juan shook his head. "No, I have some work. First I get a green shirt that will fit me, then I go in and see all that I can and come back. You have a rough sketch of the place by that time in your notebook and I'll fill in the facilities."

"Can you find them all today?"

"I'll try, do all of them I can locate. Should be enough to have a raid tomorrow night."

"You'll watch for any hostages?"

"You bet. That's our primary mission. But while we're

here we can take out a few hundred rebels. The Army will be pleased."

"Let's set up a landmark to meet at." Lam looked at the little town. "See that one building down there about a block away that's painted?"

"Red, of all colors."

"Let's key on that. We can see it down this street, so we meet around here somewhere."

"Good, I'll leave some of my gear, my combat vest for sure. I should wait for dark to get a shirt off one of them, but I can persuade one of them to come through. I'll have to be careful not to get any blood on it or a knife hole in it. That's the toughest part."

They put his combat vest and some equipment under a huge mahogany tree, and covered it all with brush. He slipped down to the trail, and walked casually across it and to the fringe of brush on the other side, then down the trail that led to the first street. No one bothered him. He vanished past the first building, and that was the last Lam saw of him that morning.

Lam went deeper into the jungle, found a spot with some sky showing overhead, and set up the SATCOM. He could do some transmitting on the chance the SEALs had their set on receive just in case he had anything to report. He tried four times sending out a message to Phil One. There was no response. He left the set on receive and waited around it for an hour. Then he turned it off and worked his way down the road along the rest of the town, making a sketch of everything he could see along the road. Marking in the streets that led off it and any buildings he could identify by shape or size.

Well beyond the town he saw where the valley spread out into a huge open plain that looked to be highly cultivated. He saw few buildings, but realized the farmers used all the land for growing, and lived in the jungle where nothing could be grown.

He sketched the rest of the streets and parts of the town he could see, and worked back to the "home" tree, where he had left the SATCOM with the other gear. Once more he tried the SATCOM in his transmission spot, and on the third try he had a response.

"Yes, Scout One, been waiting to hear from you."

He kept the volume low on the speaker and replied.

"We have found what may be one of the major training camps and headquarters of the rebels. A prisoner said there were usually three to four hundred rebel soldiers here. Don't know the name of the town yet, but Juan is inside now scouting out their GHQ, arms storage, barracks, any targets we can hit on a raid. Probably two thousand civilians here as well, so we'll have to be selective. Over."

"Good news. Wait for your call and your position. Colonel is furious with us for hitting the camp without authorization. He has come up with no new intel to give us a new target. We're waiting for him. He doesn't know about you recon guys yet. When he finds out he'll blow sky-high. Stroh working on a general to outrank this man. None on base. He's trying to get a new one assigned here to take over temporarily for the push against the rebels. More later. Make checks on radio every four hours. Out."

Lam stashed the radio and moved down to where he could see the little town better. He wondered what Juan was doing over there. He could get in trouble, get himself killed, and never come back. Lam began making plans about what he would do if that happened. It wouldn't, but he'd rather be ready. What the hell was taking so much time?

10

Lieutenant Juan Ejercito slid behind the first building in the town and looked around. He could see no green-shirted rebels. His own green shirt wasn't quite the same and his pants not right, but he could pass unless some officer called him on it. He had to find the right shirt fast so he could pass as one of them. He walked down the street again casually, as if he knew where he was going. He passed more buildings, saw that some of them were small stores. Down the next block he saw rebels lounging around a store. He walked toward them, then went down an alley so he could come up behind them. Six men, and they were all young. Maybe you didn't live long being a rebel. Some surely didn't yesterday.

He spotted one man about his size at the back of the group, and moved up to him casually. They were all speaking Filipino. Juan cleared his throat and the man looked around.

"Hey, could I borrow a smoke? I just ran out."

The man nodded. "Got to have another one myself." He shook out a cigarette from a pack and took one himself, lit Juan's and then his own.

"Thought something was going to happen today," the rebel said. "I guess not."

"Way it goes. Can I buy you a drink?"

The rebel looked up quickly. "We're not supposed to drink."

Juan chuckled. "New here, huh? Hell, we do lots of things we're not supposed to do. I've got a bottle stashed down the alley here. How about a quick snort?"

The rebel looked around and nodded. "Why not. Nothing else to do."

They wandered down the alley, then Juan pulled the man into an alcove in the alley where nobody could see them from either end. Juan didn't waste time. He had his knife in his hand, and as soon as they were in the alcove, he pushed the sharp blade through the rebel's right belly just under his rib cage, and slanted it upward into his heart. The man's eyes went wide, he tried to scream, but nothing came out as he collapsed into Juan's arms.

Two minutes later, Juan had the man's shirt off and his own discarded. He took the man's soft hat as well, and now he looked as much like the other rebels as was possible. He began his tour of the town. The rebel headquarters was easy to find. He followed green shirts to the spot where most of them were headed. It was a two-story wooden frame building with no windows on the sides and two on the front. It sat alone at the end of a block, with an open market just beyond it.

Juan realized he had no money with him. He couldn't buy anything to eat. He saw some commotion around the headquarters, and he faded against a building and watched. Four men came out and began shouting orders. Two rebels with red tabs on their shoulders appeared and everything stopped. The men walked around looking at the other rebels, who had all come to attention. Juan did as well. Then the two red tabs and three others walked away from the building, and the men around it relaxed. The group came toward Juan. He and two other rebels there came to attention. The four men stopped, and one of the red-tabbed men shouted.

"You three men, follow us." He pointed to Juan and the other two. The first two hurried to the group, and Juan knew he was trapped; he walked up and got in step beside them.

"Where are we going?" Juan whispered to the man beside him.

The rebel shrugged. "Don't matter. Nothing happening."

They went down two blocks, then the four in front went into a building through a door. Juan held to the back and when the rest were inside, he turned and sprinted down the block and around a corner, and ran another block before he stopped. No one chased him.

He decided to be less obvious, and kept to alleys and less traveled streets as he checked out the buildings and places where the rebels were concentrated. He soon had the barracks pegged, and the mess hall. There was a line there, so he stood in it and went through the early lunch line. They had cooked brown rice, a thin noodle soup, and bread. At least it was real food. He wandered the town for another two hours, and decided he had everything he could remember. There had been no sign of any hostages, or any guards around any buildings that might have contained them.

Juan moved to the farthest part of the town, then walked across the road and into the brush and trees and jungle on the far side. Ten minutes later he was back at the "home" tree, and found Lam aiming his MP-5 at the spot where Juan finished his silent approach and stepped out of the last brush.

"Got you," Lam said.

Juan shook his head. "Thought I was sneaking up on you. Where's your sketch of the town? I can fill in some blanks. You talk to your commander yet?"

Lam gave him a report on the radio talk. "We're due for another call in a half hour. We have enough info for a strike on this place, if the commander can get any choppers. His last word was it would be better not to ask for any just yet."

They worked for twenty minutes over the sketches of the town, and put in the approximate locations of the rebel facilities.

"Spread all over the place," Juan said. "Not sure if that was on purpose, or just wherever they could find a building that would fit their needs."

He told Lam about the men with red tabs on their shoulders. "Maybe they do have officers designated that way. Everyone snapped to attention when they came by."

Lam set up the SATCOM antenna, training it on the section of the sky where he had found the satellite before, and adjusted it until he heard the beep from the set.

He raised Murdock on the first call. It was just after 1400.

"Home Plate, we have scored here. Have all the info we need to make a social call. Anytime you get transport. We estimate about three hundred guests, and the rest are locals. Pinpoint work is required. Some eggs may be broken. Over."

"Understand, Scout One. We still have nothing from our friend with the Company. He promised results today. He's burning up phone lines to Manila. Sit tight. Hope to have an action plan for tomorrow. Out."

"Now what?" Juan asked.

"Did anyone follow you?" Lam asked.

"Not that I know of."

"There are some troops in the woods here. We better scat back a ways and discourage them. I'd guess about six, maybe eight. Let's work directly away from the road."

They moved silently, with all of their gear, and stopped on a gentle slope up the side of the hill. They wedged in behind trees and watched below. On one small clearing they saw eight men moving through the jungle area, with rifles at the ready and bayonets attached.

"Hunting us or just on a training mission?"

Lam checked them with his 6 × 30 binoculars and shook his head. "Could be a little of both. Must not be permitted for one of the rebels to wander into the jungle away from the camp. You must have made some guard curious."

"We take them?" Juan asked. "Be a piece of cake."

"Not our mission, Juan. We go for a full-blown hit on the various targets inside the town with the whole platoon. That's what we're here for. If we find something about the hostages, we'll be a step ahead."

They moved twice again, working higher on the slope of the mountain that formed one side of the narrow valley that led upstream. At last the hunters turned and hiked back down the slopes to the road and into their camp.

Lam and Juan stayed at their spot far up the slope and watched the camp below. Lam looked at his watch and waited for the time to make another radio call, at 1800.

Davao, Mindanao

Murdock had Bradford turn on the SATCOM to receive at 1745. Promptly at 1800 the speaker came on.

"Home Plate, this is Scout One. Calling Home Plate."

"Yes, we have you, Scout. What's happening?"

"Juan's targeted and identified a dozen spots where some courtesy calls could be made at your convenience."

"Roger that, Scout. We're still having communication problems here. The old man hasn't noticed that Juan isn't around here. That's good. Don Stroh hasn't come through yet. You suggest a day or night visit?"

"Night would be safest. Lots of weapons around here. No sign of the hostages."

"Hope we're getting closer. I asked for a new target to hit, but the colonel said he didn't have any more intel where the rebels might be, let alone the hostages."

"Any more released?"

"Four more, Japanese. They were driven by car to a town over on the west coast. Doesn't help us much, but it's a pointer."

"Keep us informed, Home Plate. We'll cool it here tonight and see what you can develop tomorrow."

Murdock put down the handset and scowled. "Where in hell is Stroh when you need him?"

He looked up and saw Stroh standing just behind him.

"Any closer and we'd have to get engaged," Stroh said. He had a grin six feet wide. "Finally snagged some politicos who would whip the Army into shape. We have a major general flying in here tonight from Manila. He's been given temporary command of the Mindanao Region. He has complete authority and he's been instructed by his government to give us carte blanche in chasing down the hostages, even if it means fighting the rebels. We're hot to go. You have a target?"

Murdock told him what he'd just heard from Lam.

"Sounds interesting, but how does that get us to the hostages?"

"We take two prisoners. We interrogate them downstream somewhere. They will talk. Someone will know where the hostages are and how we get to them."

A Filipino Army runner with sergeant's stripes on his sleeves came to the door, and Jaybird let him in. They talked a moment and Jaybird pointed to Murdock and Stroh. The Filipino came over at once and saluted.

"Sir, Commander Murdock?"

"Yes."

"Sir, Colonel Alvarez would like to see you at once. No others are required, just you."

Stroh put his hand on Murdock's shoulder. "Don't like the sound of this. I'm going to tag along. If he don't like it, tough shit."

A few minutes later a jeep let the two Americans off in front of the post commander's office, and they went inside. A master sergeant looked at both of them, stared hard at Don Stroh in his summer civilian clothes, then nodded and led them to the colonel's office.

Colonel Alvarez worked on some papers on his desk. When he heard his door close, he looked up.

"I asked to see only Commander Murdock," the colonel growled.

"I understand that, Colonel Alvarez, but I'm along for the ride. Anything you want to say to him you can say while I'm here."

"Mr. Stroh, your CIA credentials don't mean shit in my office. You get out now, or I'll call two military police and have them haul you out by your balls."

Stroh chuckled. "Colonel, I don't think you should do that. First put in a call to Manila and check with Major General Nofrando Domingo."

Colonel Alvarez jolted to his feet at the mention of the name. "What in hell have you been doing?"

"Make the call, Colonel. You'll find it interesting. However, you better hurry. As I remember, the general and his staff are flying here tonight. They may have taken off already."

Alvarez slumped in his chair. "Bastard."

"How long did you think you could get away with protecting the rebels, Colonel?" Murdock asked. "First you send us on a wild-goose chase to a camp you knew was abandoned. The next day you give us three rebels in an

out-of-the-way village that was of no importance. Then you
were livid when we told you that we had found another
rebel camp and attacked it. Since then you've been stalling
and putting us off."

"I did no such thing."

"A little late for alibis, Colonel," Stroh said. "You and
your career are gone. Zippo, poof, like a light winking out
at midnight."

"Just for your information, Colonel, we left two men
along that river," Murdock said. "They have located a rebel
regional headquarters. We knew it was impossible to get
any chopper support through you. But General Domingo
has been ordered by your President to give us full cooperation."

The colonel reached for his phone.

"Afraid not, Alvarez," Stroh barked. "General Domingo
has given me and Major Rodriguez the authority to put you
under house arrest until he arrives. You won't be tipping
off the rebels anymore about anything."

Murdock turned to go, then went back and ripped the
telephone wires out of the wall. "Colonel, how much of
that six million dollars were you supposed to get for your
work here stopping all Army efforts to find the hostages?"

Alvarez glared at Murdock. Stroh went to the door, and
two military policemen came in. Right behind them was a
tall man with gold oak leaves on his shoulders.

"Good, Major Rodriguez," Stroh said. "The colonel here
would like to be shown to his quarters, where he is to be
isolated with no phone or radio use until Major General
Nofrando Domingo arrives later. You are dismissed, Colonel. You're outgunned and outranked."

The colonel left without his unlit cigar, and Stroh
laughed. "Well, now, the old CIA dog does come in handy
sometimes, doesn't he?"

"More than you know this time. We were dead in the
water."

"Well, let's talk about it over dinner. I understand the
officers club here has a wonderful range of foods. I'm buy-
ing. You can pick out the wine."

Murdock looked at his watch. "Fine, but we have to be

back to our SATCOM by 2200. Lam and I need to work
out a schedule for tomorrow, or tomorrow night, whichever
he thinks would be the best."

Dinner was delicious: a rare steak with all the trimmings
and a huge baked potato that Murdock could have made
his dinner by itself.

They hit the SEALs area at 2130; Bradford set up the
radio to receive and they waited.

Promptly at 2200 the call came.

They decided on a nighttime operation for their own
safety and to keep civilian casualties at a minimum.

"We'll find an LZ that your ship can land in and mark
it with flares," said Lam. "We'll keep it four miles downstream from the village so they won't hear it. The jungle
eats up sound around here like magic."

"Roger, Scout One. We'll be on station there at an hour
after dark, or about 2000 tomorrow. Anything else?"

The sound of a rifle shot came over the radio. "Yeah,
Skipper, we're hauling ass. Somebody is moving in with
about twenty men we didn't hear. I must have been sleeping. Got to go. See you tomorrow, I hope."

The radio went dead. There were no more transmissions.

"Now what the bloody hell is that all about?" Murdock
asked. "Lam is our best set of ears. He can hear a mouse
sneeze at fifty yards. Hell, we'll check again later and see
if we can get any signal. I hope to hell that they got away."

11

Murdock and the rest of the SEALs slouched around their quarters. Everyone knew about the general coming in and that they had a target. If they could find it, and if Lam and Juan didn't get themselves shot full of holes before daylight.

Bradford tried the SATCOM call every half hour until midnight; then Murdock told him they would try in the morning.

"Get some sleep," Murdock said. "We still have a mission tomorrow afternoon until we hear differently. My gut feeling is that the two of them will come through the attack."

Stroh lifted his brows. "Did they say upstream or downstream from the second village you hit before?"

Murdock frowned, rubbed his face with his hand, and shook his head. "They didn't say. But with two thousand people, it would have to be downstream. Up there in the boonies where we were, there was nothing to support a population that size."

"So how far down?"

"We need a good detailed map of the area. Wonder if the colonel has any."

"You mean the general. We don't know if he came in tonight or not, but at least we stopped the damn Colonel Alvarez. I bet he was in for some big cash money."

"Damn, I wish those guys would call in."

"Leave the SATCOM on all night. You've got plenty of battery."

"True, and replacements. Let me find Bradford and the set. I'll baby-sit the thing."

"Do we know where the leader of this rebel bunch has his headquarters?" Stroh asked.

"Not a clue. I don't even know his name."

"That I can give you. He's Muhammad Al Hillah. He took a Muslim name and wants to be a hero to his people."

"How many Muslims in Mindanao?"

"Nobody knows for sure. Some say four million, some say less than two million. It's a huge place."

"So this Al Hillah has a big pool to draw from."

"Most of them were fanatics until a couple of years ago when the big peace treaty came. So now Al Hillah has only to work with the true dissidents and rebels who have broken away from the old Separatist Islamic Liberation Front. Complicated, isn't it?"

"Yeah. Give me a good old-fashioned firefight any day." Murdock yawned and looked over at Stroh. "You going to stay up all night and help me watch the radio? They could call at any time."

"Oh, hell, no. I've got to get my beauty rest. I've got some major's digs while he's on leave. You take care." Don waved and hurried out the door.

Murdock took the SATCOM from Bradford and set it up near his bunk, where the antenna could reach through a window and nail the satellite. He let it beep once, then turned it to receive and stretched out on his bunk. If Lam called, he would hear the voice and be on it like a fly on sticky paper.

Near Lebak, Mindanao
On the Moro Gulf

Muhammad Al Hillah sat in his house on the cliffs high above the west coast town of Lebak. It was one of his hideaways where no one could bother him, or even find him. He came here to think, to plan, to make love, and to meditate. He was due to travel over the mountains to the training center at Bunga, a good source for many of his recruits. He stood and stretched to his full five feet eleven. He was sturdy at 190 pounds, and had not gone to fat as many of his fellow Moro fighters had done since the peace treaty in 1996. He had carried on the fight even when most of the others had signed the paper and accepted the benevolence of the central government. Now many of them were regretting it.

He scratched his arm and rubbed his nose. He should be doing something. His skin was lighter than that of many Filipinos, and he had a broad face, deep-set eyes, and a prominent nose. At thirty-eight he was already losing his hair, and his forehead had increased by almost an inch in the past five years. His father had been bald at fifty.

Muhammad worked on a bunch of grapes, and checked a large wall map he'd stolen from the Army. He had it tacked to the wall. It had colored pushpins in it showing each of his camps and strong points, his training camp, and where most of his equipment and materials were hidden.

He should be in the training camp at Bunga. His captain in charge sometimes went overboard in his realistic training. In the long run it would make better soldiers for him. It was a hard trip to Bunga. He and his bodyguard would have to go by motorcycle in a few days. On the trails it would take them most of two days. What he needed was a helicopter.

Muhammad smiled at the thought. He could just see himself in a small Bell chopper lifting off from a clearing and soaring over the trees and mountains, setting down at one camp after the other. He could coordinate his work quicker and better. He shook his head. But where would he keep it and how would he service and maintain it? He knew that helicopters took five times as much maintenance and service as a regular airplane. He had no mechanics who knew helicopters. Sadly, even stealing one from the Army was not a viable plan.

So, what was next? The hostage operation was moving along. So far he had ransomed out eight of the men and women from three different countries for eight hundred thousand U.S. dollars. Already he had a victory. He had heard by radio that the U.S. had sent a crack fighting unit into Davao. They had hit one of his camps well above Bunga. Twenty-eight dead. He hadn't suffered a loss like that since they began the campaign three years ago.

He paused a moment thinking about it. What was the best way to discourage them? The U.S. public went crazy over casualties in a mini-war. Yes. He would inflict six or eight casualties on them the next time they tried to hit one of his camps. The U.S. press would hear about it, and the public pressure would force the President to call the fighting group home. He didn't know what elite group they were. It didn't matter. With the new weapons he had after the three-million-dollar gift from Osama bin Laden, he could stand up against any fighting force. They would be surprised by the larger-caliber guns he had.

He looked out over his mountain stronghold. Misty today. On a clear day he could see six miles to the sea. This was a beautiful spot—but more importantly, it was safe and secure and known only to a handful of his most trusted lieutenants. The troops assigned here never left. They were his permanent elite bodyguard unit.

He looked across the room at a girl who lounged on a round bed. "I'm thirsty," he said. The girl stood at once, smiled, and hurried out the door. Muhammad nodded. She was a pleasant girl who gave him no trouble. She was topless as usual, and that pleased Muhammad. He glanced at his desk and the list of projects to get done today.

One item on his list was not to his liking, but had to be done to insure discipline. A recruit, not much more than seventeen, had decided he didn't like the rebel life after all and had deserted. He had been tracked down, captured, and brought to the stronghold by a roundabout means by a trusted lieutenant. The boy must be dealt with.

Teta brought in the insulated cup filled with his favorite chilled wine. He thanked her, reached out, and stroked her breasts, so young they still had a slight upthrust. Then he waved her away. He took the cup with him as he left the office and went outside. Three of his best soldiers stood at attention next to a rock wall. Directly in front of them knelt the deserter.

Muhammad didn't waste time. He marched to the deserter, lifted his chin, and stared into his eyes.

"You deserted the holy Muslim troops. You have shamed

yourself and your family. For this you must pay."

The youth looked at Muhammad and nodded. Muhammad went behind him, drew the .45 pistol from his holster, and fired one shot into the back of the deserter's head. The youth slammed forward, his arms flying out to the sides as his face scraped in the grass of the yard.

"Send him back to his family for a traditional burial," the rebel leader said. Then he went back into his office. The wine in his cup was almost gone. He needed some more.

Near Camp Bunga

Lam had nearly finished the radio call to Murdock when the first shot slammed past him and hit a tree. He signed off, grabbed the antenna and radio, and bolted out of there.

"Incoming," he bellowed at Juan, who had slid behind a tree when he heard the first shot. He turned his MP-5 and sprayed the whole clip at the direction the fire flashes came from. He jerked out the empty and pushed in a new clip.

"Move to the rear, I'll cover you," Juan yelled. "Go now." He fired again at the single flashes from below and to the right. He had no idea how the patrol had found them. They had only single-shot rifles. That was good. Maybe a squad in training. He fired spaced shots now, three here, then another three. It kept the attackers' heads down.

"I'll cover you now," Lam shouted from forty feet to the side of the hill. As soon as the shots came from Lam, Juan grabbed his combat vest and small pack and surged toward Lam. It was across the face of the hill and not that hard moving. He felt something sting his leg, but kept going. A graze maybe. A few seconds later he dove behind a fallen log and out of the line of fire.

"Where did they come from?" Lam asked.

"You're the ears," Juan said. "First I heard them was that first shot somebody fired too soon. They knew where we were; they should have closed in and cut us to pieces before we knew they were there."

"Thanks for green troops," Lam said. "We better keep moving along the hill. If we don't fire, they won't know where we are. The growth is too thick here for them to spot us."

They ran along the hill, then climbed higher and went along the side of the slope again. Lam figured they were a mile from the first attack and he called a halt.

He held up his hand and listened. Shook his head. "Nobody back there. Hasn't been for the last half mile. They gave up on us. Green as grass in-training troops."

"So what should we do now?" Juan asked.

"Get back in touch with Murdock. Lay out a sked for tomorrow on the town. I'd bet he's left his set on to receive. I didn't tell him where to come."

Lam checked their back trail, listened intently again, then set up the dish antenna so it would pick up the satellite. He closed his eyes and listened again.

"Nobody out there for a mile at least." He turned on the set and made the call.

"Yes, Scout, sounded like you were attacked."

"We were, Home Plate. Some green troops in training, we figured. They should have riddled us like a pair of sat-down ducks. We were lucky. I didn't tell you where this camp is. Figured you'd want to know. It's about twenty-five miles below the one we hit where we had the good firefight."

"Twenty-five miles downstream. Shouldn't be hard to find. Our LZ will be which side of it?"

"Upstream three to four miles on the west bank. Can't really go downstream because the valley flattens out into farmland."

"Roger that. Same time. We have the place. You guys dig a hole somewhere and wait for us. Don't get fancy and try to do anything by yourselves."

"We'll go find an LZ and stay put. I can see a long nap before bedtime."

"Do it and we'll talk to you just before we take off at 1900. Home Plate, out."

"Right, Home Plate. See you there."

Lam folded up the dish antenna and packed it with the SATCOM. "Nothing like modern communications," Lam said. "Let's get out of here and find a good LZ three or four miles upstream from the town."

They found it about 0100. It was maybe five miles from the town, Juan figured, but a great spot. Here a small piece of farmland had been carved out along a tributary that came into the main stream. There was an open space of two or three acres on this side of the river that had been recovered from the encroaching jungles. Now it was dry, but there was a two-foot dike all around the field like in a terrace. Only here there was but one level. It could be flooded from a short canal from upstream. Part of the field was still green. The area nearest the river was harvested, and Lam guessed rice had been the crop.

They moved back away from the LZ to the first lift of a ridgeline, and found a level spot just in back of the top. They could stretch out there and sleep and still get to the ridgeline in seconds to check out the trail along the river and the farmed field.

They relaxed.

"Should we stand guard?" Juan asked.

"Oh, yeah. Take your pick, 0100 to 0300 or 0300 to 0600."

"Hey, I'll take the first shift. You get some sleep. Don't worry, I won't go to sleep. I value my Filipino hide too much for that. They could have a night patrol out roaming around. If I hear them or see them, we'll be fine."

Lam hesitated. Now to 0300 was the most dangerous time for night patrols. He lifted his brows. The guy was an officer in the Army. He should know what he was doing. No complaints so far. Lam changed his mind in a flash.

"Hell, no, Juan. I want the first shift, worst time for night-time raiders. I can hear them better than you can. You get some sleep. I'll wake you up at 0300."

"Either way. Yeah, I am a bit tired." He lay down and propped his head on his pack, and was sleeping by the time Lam found his OP on the ridgeline.

Nothing happened for an hour and a half. Just after 0230 Lam heard movement in the growth below. He hated how the jungle ate up the sounds, but enough noise was there. He tried to count the men, but he couldn't. The moon was out halfway and gave some light in the heavy growth.

Then a man ran across an open space two hundred yards away. The motion caught Lam's eye. He put his binoculars on the spot. At night the glasses magnified the image, and also magnified the light. Not as good as NVGs, but they helped. He saw the next man go across. All had new-looking uniforms. They had field packs and rifles, canteens, but no blanket rolls or shelter halves. A patrol.

Lam watched them for another fifteen minutes as they worked their way slowly closer to the ridge where he crouched. If they came too close, he'd have to wake Juan and haul ass. He watched them through the glasses. The lead man looked tired. He kept moving across the face of the slope instead of going up it. Somebody would yell at him and he'd go up a step, and then to the left again.

Lam's finger gently caressed the MP-5's trigger. He could nail all six of them right there in the opening and nobody would hear a shot. They were too far from the camp and the jungle muffled the sound like a blanket. He moved the sights to the first man. Three-shot bursts from one to the other, right down the line. The fools were no more than two or three feet apart. Bad soldiering.

He eased his finger off the trigger.

No. Not his mission. They would pay, but it would be later tomorrow night when the whole SEAL platoon was there and they were taking down selected targets like bowling pins.

Yes, wait.

Then moments later a new leader took over, and he moved straight up the slope. When he crossed it he would be only a dozen feet from where Lam lay. Lam pulled the MP-5 down so the muzzle aimed at the men. Seventy-five yards away. How long could he wait? He blotted sweat off his forehead. He should wake up Juan.

12

A sharp command came from behind the rebels, and they turned in stride and worked their way back down the slope and in the direction of their camp.

Lam wiped sweat from his forehead. He decided not to wake up Juan right then. He'd tell him about it at 0300.

Nothing else happened the rest of the night. The word about the patrol coming so close was enough to keep Juan alert for the next three hours. Then the pair picked up and hiked over the next hill, and two miles deeper into the untarnished wilderness. At 0700 they stopped and used the SATCOM.

Lam told about their close call the night before, and emphasized the idea that the town might be expecting some kind of an attack since they had found two strangers with automatic weapons on their doorstep.

"They might be ready, but we'll be ready too," Murdock said. "I had an early meeting with General Domingo this morning. Alvarez has been placed under arrest and will probably be charged with treason, misappropriation of funds and equipment, bribery, conduct unbecoming, and all sorts of nasty stuff. General Domingo says we get anything we want. He brought in three forty-sixes. Turned out there were only two here despite what Alvarez said. Now we're ready when we track down the hostages."

"Don't think we'll find them on this shot," Lam said. "We'll have to keep our eyes and ears open about where they might be. Juan says some of the rebels wear red tabs on their shoulders. That may be our only sign who the leaders are."

"Roger that. It's in our briefing. You find a better hole?"

"Right, we're three miles from the river, and snuggled down for a long daytime nap. Next we're going to try out those new MREs they gave us this time. Supposed to be better than what we had before. About it. We're out."

"We'll check again 1900 to keep our ducks in a row. We'll leave the receive button on here in the meantime in case you need to call. Home Plate, out."

"New MREs," Juan said. "Let's try them, right now."

They dug out the large brown plastic envelopes and tore them open. "Mine says menu number one: grilled beef-steak," Lam said. He looked at what was inside. It contained the main meal in a plastic pouch. There was another long plastic pouch that could be used to heat up the entree. "It's called a nonflammable ration heater," Juan said. "You just put some water into it, insert your main meal pouch, seal it, and it heats the food piping hot in a few minutes."

They tried it and it worked. Juan had menu number ten, chili and macaroni. Also in the large MRE pouch were packets of salt and sugar, Taster's Choice coffee, a non-dairy creamer package, a Tootsie Roll, a Jolly Rancher bar, a tiny bottle of Tabasco sauce, a plastic tray and plastic spoon, iced-tea-drink mix, a book of matches, crackers, an envelope of peanut butter, an envelope of jam, and a Hooah! Nutritious Booster Bar.

"How do we heat the water for coffee?" Juan said. They tried putting water in the heating envelope, and it worked. They ate, drank, and decided the Hooah! Bars were the hit of the meal.

"Better than most airline food," Lam said. "You should see some of the junk they try to feed you on those airlines. Our Senior Chief, who picked these up, said that there were twenty-four different menus. He mentioned beef strips in teriyaki sauce, chicken breast strips with salsa, black bean and rice burrito, and boneless pork chop with noodles. How many more do we have?"

They each had two more, and checked what the main

courses were. Two each of chicken breast strips and bone-less pork chops.

"So much for our gourmet food," said Lam. "What are we going to do today?"

"Hide out here, sleep, and sharpen our KA-BARs," Juan said.

"Mine won't get any sharper," Lam said. He jolted up from where he lay on the grassy mat under the trees. He pointed to his left. Lam had heard noises; something moved through the heavy growth. Somebody in Davao had said that there were more then ten thousand kinds of flowering plants and shrubs in the Philippines. Looking at the over-grown lush tropical rain forest now, Lam believed it.

The sound came again, foliage crashing and a grunting sound.

Before Lam could lift his MP-5 a wild pig as big as a German shepherd darted out of some heavy green growth and charged straight at where he lay. An instant later a man jolted through the cover and threw a wooden spear that hit the pig in the side and lanced all the way through. The animal sprawled, then rolled, trying to get rid of the lance. The man was short, no more than four feet tall, and dark with stringy black hair. He took a knife from a belt and slashed the animal's throat. Lam stood and the small man turned, holding the knife pointing at Lam.

"I'm a friend," Lam said. The small man scowled, then wiped the bloody blade on the side of the dead wild pig and pulled out his spear.

"Friends from America," Lam said.

The small black man rolled his eyes and looked at the pig, then back at Lam. Behind Lam, Juan stood and rattled off a dozen words in some strange tongue that Lam figured was Filipino.

The small man relaxed and put down the spear. He grinned.

"You GI. Me go teach GI jungle survival at old Navy base at Subic Bay."

Juan moved up and shook hands with the small man. They squatted near the pig and talked in the other Philippine official language, English.

The small man stood and walked over to Lam. "GI call me Blackie. You come my house, we have feast."

Lam looked at Juan, who nodded. "How better can we spend the day? The food will be good. These guys are the best hunter/gatherers in the world. They roam around the hills, drop down to the lowlands for coconuts, make out like crazy. The government has even set aside a huge reserve for several of the minorities where no logging or trespassing can be done. I've seen these guys work before. They are good. Spears and knives, that's their weapons. They don't trust guns."

"How far?" Lam asked.

Juan translated. "Blackie says two ridges, which could be two miles or ten. My guess about three or four miles. It won't come close to the town. They stay well away from the roads, camps, and guns."

"Hell, why not?" Lam said, and they picked up their gear and walked. The spear had been rammed through the pig from the open mouth and out the tail. Lam carried one end of the lance and Blackie the other. Lam figured the wild pig must weigh about 120 pounds. His shoulder got sore, and he traded off with Juan. Blackie didn't notice; he just kept hiking up the side of the slope and through the growth of evergreen trees, bamboo, and a few banana trees. Blackie stopped at one banana cluster of trees and looked at a three-foot-long stalk with twenty or thirty hands of bananas. He shook his head.

"Too fucking far walk carry," he said. Lam laughed and they moved ahead.

They soon passed through growth of teakwood trees and a sprinkling of towering Philippine mahogany trees. Lam figured they were well over 150 feet tall. The jungle was so green, and up here on the slope it didn't feel all that tropical wet. Lam started to sweat. The average temperature hovered around eighty degrees, Juan had told him. Up here on the slope it was cooler, but not much.

After a half hour of hiking they moved down a slope, and Lam could smell, then soon see small spirals of smoke rising through the trees. They came into a village that was so temporary it had only small lean-tos, with the tops made of nipa palm fronds. Two women and six children ran to meet Blackie as the little caravan arrived. The women grabbed the lance with the pig and hurried it to a large rock, where they began butchering it. At once slabs of the meat were cut out, taken to a small cooking fire, and dropped into two heavy cast-iron skillets.

"Out here these people, who are called Negritos, eat when and where they can," Juan said. "No three squares a day here. It's feast or famine, but with these people, it's usually feast. They can harvest a dozen kinds of fruit from the jungle, including bananas and cassava, which makes tapioca, or the roots can be used to make flour like meal. Down near the coast they can find coconuts, and there are a few deer around and if they get really hungry, monkeys and crocodiles down on the rivers near the coast."

Blackie wore only cut-off jeans. Lam had no idea where he'd gotten them. The two women wore loose fitting dark cloth skirts and no tops. The children, all under ten, wore nothing at all. The kids and women clustered around the pig, and soon it had been cleaned and skinned and the head put in a special iron pot.

Soup later on, Lam thought and grinned. Wild pig-head soup. Not high on his eating list.

Blackie took pride in introducing his two wives to his guests. They spoke no English at all, but Juan talked with them in Filipino.

Blackie said that usually they lived much higher on the mountain and farther from the coast. His wives wanted coconuts, so he'd brought the family here. He would make nighttime trips lower where the coconuts grew, and harvest some to take back to his village.

"How many people at the village?" Lam asked.

Blackie grinned. "How many I know. I speak how many. Yes, maybe thirty. I learn count in Subic Bay but not good. No?"

They all laughed. "You count good, Blackie, good," Lam said. He looked around, and could see almost nothing that would be moved. The lean-tos would stay; the fire pit held only the three cast-iron skillets and pot. There were no bed-rolls, no bundles of clothes, no eating utensils that he could see. It was a camp ready to move at any time.

Then he saw several nets that looked as if they had been woven from some local vine. They had two- or three-inch squares, and he figured they were used for carrying things, like the coconuts that the Negritos had come to harvest. At one side he saw two dozen coconuts that had been husked out of their fibrous shell. The brown inner shell remained.

Blackie picked up one of the coconuts, pierced the eyes with a sharp-pointed stick, and drank the milk. Then he broke it on a rock and dug out the white meat.

"Take just meat when walk home," he said.

Lam thought Blackie and the others might even dry the coconut meat before they carried it back to their main camp. They were efficient, self-sufficient, answering to nobody, beholden to no one, man or government. Now there was a lifestyle.

A curious monkey swung from trees high overhead. Blackie looked at him, judged the distance, and put down his spear.

"Eat monkey too," he said. "Monkey taste good."

"How old are you, Blackie?" Juan asked.

The short man built furrows in his forehead and twisted up his face. "At Subic Bay, Navy Chief Chief call me twenty-five. Not know for sure. Now, maybe fifty, fifty-five. Blackie no count good now."

The women shouted at the children, and three of them ran into the rain forest and came back quickly with a dozen green shiny leaves as big as dinner plates. They laid them on a log that had been flattened somewhat by cutting with a knife. The pork slabs were placed on each of the leaves, and topped with a mixture of fruits that one of the women had been preparing.

"Chow," Blackie said. He grinned. "Blackie remember chow call good from Navy."

They sat in front of the log and ate. The pork was well done and different from anything Lam had ever tasted. It wasn't like pork, or beef. It had been butchered and cooked before most of the blood had been drained out of the animal and while it was still warm. That made a difference in the taste. It was good, but Lam didn't think he'd want to make it a permanent part of his diet. The fruit was marvelous. He recognized the bananas, but that was all. Whatever it was, he liked it.

Lam checked his watch. "Chogie time. We need to get back to the LZ." Lam looked around for a minute. "Be damned if I'm certain how we got here."

Juan chuckled. "I made a small wager with Blackie that he'd have to take us back partway and point us down to the river. He said no problem. As soon as you finish your pork. It's not polite in a primitive society to leave any food that has been given to you."

Lam looked down at his leaf and scooped up the last of the pork and chewed it down.

It was a little over an hour later that they settled in at their former hideout three miles from the river. The time was almost 1400. Plenty of time. Lam set up the radio, and this time he showed Juan how to do it.

"Home Plate, this is Scout."

A response came back immediately. "Yes, Scout. We're in our final prep here for our jump over there. A little longer flight this time, but still well within the range of the forty-six. We're going to leave the bird on the ground this time with six Army security guards while we make our hike."

"Good thinking, Home Plate. We're at our safe spot and will move down to the LZ in about two hours. Any changes?"

"None right now. We'll talk later just before we pull out. Take care and we'll see you soon."

Juan closed down the radio, folded the antenna, and put it in its pouch on the SATCOM.

Lam leaned back on the soft greenery and looked at Juan. "I better say it, Juan. I've been thinking about Colonel Alvarez. He did pick you to come on this mission, you and the sergeant."

Juan nodded. "I know where you're going with that. But you can rest easy. I was rammed down Alvarez's throat. He didn't want me to come. He had a captain from his headquarters he had picked and primed. Then somebody said it should be a man who had been in contact and combat with the rebels. My CO pushed me for the spot and I won out. I have no loyalty to the colonel. I didn't even like him. He's getting what he deserved. No, I won't sabotage the fight tonight. I could have done that yesterday on my recon. If I was his man, I'd have acted before now. I'm not. I'm clean."

"I believe you, Juan. I just had to ask, in case Murdock nails me."

"No problem, Lam. Hey, I've been in the Army for eight years, I know how the military works. Cover your ass. Hell, yes. When are we heading for the river?"

13

The big CH-46 let down easily on the harvested rice field to the west of the river and settled on its wheels. The six Filipino Army guards stormed out the side doors and took up positions to protect the ship. The SEALs raced out behind them and charged forward along the river until they hit the jungle growth and cover.

"About time you blokes got here," Lam said after he stepped from behind a large mahogany tree.

"Got stuck in a beauty of a traffic jam on the freeway," Jaybird cracked.

Murdock called the men around him. "Any changes in the plans, Lam?"

"No, sir. All about the same. We haven't been any closer to the town than this since we left yesterday. Don't see what they could do even if they think there is some opposition out here."

"Good. Our timing is a little off. Won't be full dark for another half hour, but we can move down toward the town. Lieutenant Ejercito, how do you feel about a 2100 attack time, or should we push it back to 2400?"

"Would be fewer civilians out at midnight, Commander, and fewer rebels on guard duty. Still, it's going to take us some time to hit all the targets. If we get pinned down on one . . ."

"Okay, then let's keep the sked we have. Five miles to target, Lam?"

"Right, Skipper."

"Time now is 1934. Let's take a hike and get in position,

then decide on our attack time. Juan, can we split into two teams for the hits? Can Lam point out some of the targets to us?"

"He knows where they are on the map, Commander. He has seen only two of them. But he's a smart man, I think he could do it."

"Lam?"

"We have eight separate targets. I know three and can find the other one. Juan gets four."

"Good. Lam, you'll be with Alpha Squad, and Juan, you go with Bravo. Let's take a hike."

Moving down the trail beside the river with Lam out in front by three hundred yards, they took almost an hour to cover the five miles. They headed up the slope of the ridge to the left near the town to take a good look. They could spot some of the targets by the lights.

"Must have a generator for some of the troops," Murdock said. "You didn't see any power poles or lines in there, did you, Juan?"

"No, sir. Before we saw some lamps, but no electr   ones like this. Maybe new, maybe they just use them for defense."

"Any limits on type of arms?" Jaybird asked.

"No EAR unless absolutely necessary. We want to punish these guys. We don't even need to occupy the buildings. Just waste them with the twenties and anybody who comes running out or to the defense. We should be able to take down each site and move on to the next one. We'll all keep in touch with the Motorolas. If one squad runs into trouble, tell us where you are and how we can help. The twenties should do the job on most buildings. Shoot through doors and windows. If the door isn't open, one contact round will blow it halfway across the building. Questions?"

"Targets are only the green-uniformed guys?" Ostercamp asked.

"You may return fire at anyone shooting at you no matter what clothes he's wearing. The uniformed rebels are our main targets."

"What kind of return fire?" Senior Chief Sadler asked.

"After the first attack, they will be ready. We expect

some machine-gun fire, and automatic rifles and sub guns. We don't think they have anything heavier. We'll have to wait and find out."

By that time the sudden night had closed in, and they worked their way slowly down the slope to the jungle at the edge of the road. Juan led Bravo Squad downstream along the road to be closer to his targets. Lam kept Alpha Squad at the first road they had seen into the town, the one with the red building.

"Ready, Bravo," Juan said on the Motorola.

"Let's do it," Murdock said. "Move out, hit the targets, vanish into the jungle across the road by squads, and return to LZ. Move."

Juan took the jungle-cammy-clad squad down the narrow street into the town. It had mostly wooden buildings and a few made of stone and rock. They jogged in fifty yards without seeing a person; then two men idling on a corner ran into a building. Another fifty yards ahead they came toward the three-story headquarters building. The SEALs spread out and DeWitt came on the Motorola.

"Let's do it. Twenties first. Open fire."

The sharp sound of the 20mm rounds being fired cracked into the jungle stillness, followed almost at once by the blasting sound of the twenties going off inside and on the outside of the building. Eight of the heavy rounds punched inside windows and exploded, bringing screams and wails. Green-clad men rushed out the front door with their weapons ready, but were cut down by machine-gun and sniper fire as the SEALs poured it on.

Six men rushed from the darkness toward the dimly lit exterior of the building, and were splattered by a contact 20mm round that exploded in the middle of them. Only one man could crawl away from the murderous shrapnel.

Colt Franklin put two 40mm white phosphorus grenades into the building. One smashed through a second-story window and exploded in white death and fire, setting the whole room ablaze. The second round bounded off a wall, went off next to it, and set the wall on fire and rained furiously burning bits of white phosphorus into a machine-gun bunker just to the right of the doorway. The two men there, preparing to fire the weapon, were splattered with the burning particles and ran into the night screaming and slapping at the sticky material that couldn't be put out and bored through cloth, leather, skin, and bone until it burned itself up.

"Hold your fire except for green shirts," DeWitt said into his lip mike. Two men bailed out a smashed window on the first floor, and were promptly dropped with sniper fire. A machine gun chattered from the far corner of the building. Hot lead slammed into the ground and overhead. DeWitt put a 20mm round on the corner of the building and silenced the MG.

Another burst of firing broke out in the third floor of the structure. Then all went silent. A siren wailed somewhere in the distance. They could hear gunfire. Alpha Squad was busy upstream.

Ed DeWitt watched the building. If it was the headquarters of the rebels, there weren't many men inside. Maybe too late at night. How long could he wait here watching the place?

"Twenties, one more round each in windows. Canzoneri and I on the first floor. Jefferson and Mahanani second and third in that order. Let's fire, now."

The four big twenties roared into the night, and the resulting blasts inside the building were muted, but nevertheless had a sharp cracking roar. After a minute no one else exited the structure.

"Juan, next objective," DeWitt said.

Juan moved them rapidly down a full block to a building that showed a dozen lights through windows. Two guards in green uniforms stood at the front door. Both had submachine guns held in front of them and ready. They had been looking at the headquarters and then the other way at sounds of more small arms.

Juan and the SEALs paused at the corner of a wooden building.

"This is a supply depot for them," Juan said. "I didn't get inside, but there are all sorts of military supplies and I'd guess ammo as well."

Two windows showed on the near side, one in front.

"Twenties, you've got numbers, front-to-back marching order. First two twenties the side windows, last two those front windows. Three rounds each. Fire when ready."

The four guns went off almost at the same time, and the resulting explosions from inside were softer than usual. After the second salvo of rounds, they could see fire gushing inside. The last rounds brought secondary explosions, and half a dozen men ran out the front door. Khai and Fernandez blasted them before they were ten feet from the door.

They watched a moment as another explosion wracked the place and hundreds of small-arms rounds began cooking off in the fire.

"Haul ass," DeWitt barked, and Bravo Squad ran up the street behind Juan, who led them. They stopped after about fifty yards. They could still see the building behind them. Now flames licked through the roof; the building would be a total loss, including everything inside it.

"What's next?" DeWitt asked.

"Barracks," Juan said. "With all this action it's certain that they will be empty. The men probably were routed out and are on guard around the place."

"Show us," DeWitt said.

They passed two long blocks of buildings later, part wood, part bamboo, and nipa-leaf-thatched. Juan stopped behind a wooden structure and pointed around the corner.

"The only building over there with two stories and lots of windows. No guards out front. No lights on inside. There should be lights this time of evening."

DeWitt pulled up the NVGs and studied the layout. "Men prone facing outward on these two sides of the building," DeWitt said. "All four twenties to laser sightings on the front of the barracks from one end to the other. First two guns left, last two to right. Everyone fire at the front and side of the building when the twenties go."

They fired. The lasers worked on two rounds, with airbursts directly over the prone figures. The other two twenty-rounds exploded on the side of the building flashing hot shrapnel to the side and rear.

A dozen rebels jumped up and ran to the side away from

the attack. The SEAL gunners trailed them, bringing down half of them.

"Another airburst for us all," DeWitt said. The rounds went off almost before the sound of the shots came. They were all airbursts this time, and riddled the men left on the ground.

"Franklin, that roof looks tinder dry. See if you can lob a couple of forties on it," DeWitt said. DeWitt and the rest of Bravo Squad had heard the progress of Alpha Squad on the radio. They tried not to pay any attention to it, intent on their own situation.

Franklin fired his first 40mm round from the launcher under his Colt M-4A1. It landed long, and they didn't see the spray of white phosphorus. He adjusted, and the second round splattered all over the roof. Now they saw it was made of wooden shingles, and within seconds the shingles caught fire from the furiously burning WP.

"Next?" DeWitt asked Juan, who ran beside him. They had put a half block between them and the barracks.

"Down a short ways," Juan said. "Lots of men around it. Looked like a clinic or maybe a hospital."

"No," DeWitt said at once. "We don't do hospitals. We're done. Get us out of here, now."

Murdock came on the radio. "Right call, DeWitt. Get your men back to the jungle beyond the road. We have one more target here and we'll meet you."

"You heard me," DeWitt said. "Get us back to the jungle the safest way. We don't want to go by any of the targets."

Murdock heard that conversation as well, and looked back at his own problem. Lam had not been sure of the third target. It was supposed to be the red building, but now they couldn't find it. The few streets looked identical. They saw the fires burning downstream, and knew it wasn't in that direction. Lam squinted into the night, then grinned.

"Okay, down this way about fifty yards and we should be there. Everything looks different in here."

They came up on the red building slowly. They saw no one on the street. Murdock had guessed that there would be armed patrols running all over the place by now. Good. The rebels weren't a real army yet. They must be short on discipline and command. Two vitals for any military operation.

The SEALs lay fifty yards from the red building and watched it. Two guards with the green shirts and pants of the rebel cause stood outside. Both had weapons at the ready.

No lights showed in the one window they could see. Murdock had asked before, and Stroh had said there were no 20mm rounds with WP. They sure would come in handy. Murdock wondered if the small size of the round compared to the 40mm grenades was the problem. Maybe they couldn't pack enough WP into such a small size to be of much value.

"Bradford, you and I'll put twenties through that window and see what happens. Give me a ready." A second later, Bradford did. "Fire," Murdock said. The two rounds went off almost together. One hit the front of the building; the other went through the glass. The front round killed both guards and blew a hole in the wall as it exploded. The second round blasted inside.

They waited. Nothing happened. No men came out. The place didn't burn. "Lam," Murdock said. "Try three rounds of WP on that one. Now."

Lam fired. The first one was short, the second hit just in front of the wooden structure, and the third dropped on the roof. In the first glow of the WP they could see that the roof was partly nipa leaves, and the fronds burst into fire at once.

"Out of here," Murdock said. "Lam, which way, and let's chogie at double time."

Lam led them back on the street and two long blocks to the road. They charged across it and into the brush and greenery of the rain forest. Once they were fifty yards into the jungle, Murdock called a halt.

"DeWitt, are you and your men in the green?"

"Yeah, we're out, probably still downstream from you. We're getting ready to move. We took some return fire, and I don't know when it happened, but we've got one man shot up pretty bad. He says he can walk, but Mahanani said no way. How deep are you in the brush?"

"Fifty yards. Work the road. We haven't seen any kind of resistance. We'll get close to the road and wait."

Murdock moved his squad back so they could see the road and offer defensive fire if needed.

Three minutes later, Lam lifted his head and turned his head so his ear was toward the trail. "Coming," Lam said. "Not sure who. Somebody. Making too much noise."

"DeWitt, are you on the road?"

"No, having trouble getting Ostercamp moved. He's worse than we thought. We're just past the road in the edge of the jungle."

"Still coming," Lam said. "My guess about twenty armed men with all their equipment jingling."

In the soft Philippine moonlight, Murdock soon saw the men approaching. They were soldiers in a column of fours with their weapons at port and ready. They were less than forty yards away.

"Open fire," Murdock said. He had no idea what a 20mm round would do at point-blank range, but he was going to find out.

14

Eight SEALs opened fire on the formation. The first three 20mm rounds slammed into the unsuspecting rebels, exploding instantly, shredding the green-uniformed men into masses of bloody corpses.

"Hold fire on the twenties," Murdock shouted into his mike. The remnants of the rebel formation charged away down the road and into the jungle to escape the SEALs' continuing small-arms fire. Murdock had switched his Bull Pup to 5.56-round and kept firing. Five or six of the men might have escaped. The rest were down and dead or dying. Screams of agony cascaded over the SEALs from the wounded on the roadway forty yards in front of them.

"Leave them," Murdock barked in his radio. He tried to listen through the cries.

"Murdock, that you?" DeWitt called on the radio.

"Small firefight. How is Ostercamp?"

"Not good. We're carrying him. He's a load. Ten minutes to the end of the town where you should be."

"Roger that. I'm sending Lam to run up to the chopper and move him as close as possible to us here. Keep coming. We've got some carrying help here."

Murdock looked at Lam. "Leave your vest and your Colt. Trade with Jaybird for his MP-5. Five miles to the chopper. You can do that in forty minutes. Be sure to call out your ID before you bust in on those Filipino Army guys. Pick out a new LZ on your run up there. Close as you can come to us here. We'll be on the trail, but moving slow with Ostercamp. Go."

Jaybird had run up with his weapon, and traded and took Lam's combat vest as well.

"Howard and Jaybird, go back down-trail and find DeWitt and help with Ostercamp. Go."

Five minutes later, Jaybird came on the radio. "Found Bravo Squad. We're about three hundred yards downstream from you and moving."

Ten minutes later the platoon was together again. Mahanani talked to Murdock.

"He's hit bad in the chest. Bleeding too much. I stopped most of it, but we've got to get him to a hospital soon as we can."

"Lam's going for the chopper," Murdock said. "This time we didn't leave a Motorola with the chopper pilot."

"Howard took him when he got there," Mahanani said. "He's a good man. I'll take Ostercamp again. We're going pickaback so far. Best way so far. You and Sadler and Bradford can spell us off. We better move now."

They went down to the trail and hiked along at the speed of the one carrying Ostercamp. Murdock put out Jaybird as lead scout, and DeWitt served as rear guard back twenty yards. Murdock figured they were making about three miles an hour.

Lam dug down the last mile and tried to go faster. He'd spotted a good LZ about a mile from where he'd left the other SEALs. Now all he had to do was identify and contact. He checked his watch. He'd been gone for almost thirty-five minutes. Seven minutes to a mile, so he should be almost there.

Then he was there. He paused behind a huge mahogany tree and whistled, then called out. "Hey, Army. SEALs here. Don't shoot. Coming in. Okay?"

"Okay, SEALs, come on in."

After that it took only thirty seconds to get the Army men in the chopper, the blades whirling, and the engines warmed up. The pilot was told about the wounded man.

Lam tried the Motorola. "Skipper, we're taking off in about ten seconds. See you there in nine or ten minutes."

"Read you, Lam, soft and breaking up, but read you."

"Straight down the river and the new LZ is on the same side," Lam told the pilot.

"This kid shot up bad?" the pilot asked.

"Yeah, chest, lots of blood. He needs a good doctor, fast."

They lifted off, and only a few minutes later Lam pointed down.

"That's it. No rebels around there when I came past."

The Army men hovered at the two open doors, their submachine guns ready. Wheels touched, and the Army men and Lam jumped to the ground and sprinted away from the bird. Lam headed down the trail. He found the platoon two hundred yards away. Murdock had Ostercamp on his back as he plodded forward.

Howard came up and relieved him.

"Hey, Commander, you look fucked out, my turn," Howard said. Murdock made the transfer, took a deep breath, and looked at the troops. "The rest of you, double time up to the chopper and get everyone on board. I want to stay here for rear guard. Go."

A hundred yards from the clearing, Bradford took over the packhorse duties, and then gently laid Ostercamp on the floor of the forty-six.

Murdock counted heads. "Let's fly, Captain," he shouted. The bird lifted off with no enemy fire, and Murdock collapsed against the thin skin of the helicopter.

"Pilot says forty minutes to the airfield," DeWitt said. Mahanani worked on Ostercamp. He had the bleeding stopped, and now put two blankets from the chopper on him.

"Keep his head up," the medic said. "We don't want him to go into shock. Stay with us, Ostercamp. I've never lost a patient yet, and you sure as hell ain't going to be my first."

Ostercamp gave him a thin grin, and closed his eyes. "Damn, but that hurts."

Mahanani injected another ampoule of morphine into Ostercamp's arm, and Ostercamp nodded.

Later, DeWitt came back and touched the medic's sleeve. "Pilot says we're twenty minutes out. How's he doing?"

"Can't tell. He's breathing ragged, so he's got some lung damage. Don't know about internal bleeding. Missed his gut, I think, but no way of knowing if the slug broke up inside. He's conscious and talking, which is good. He's gonna make it, j.g. I don't let none of my guys cash in. Not on my fucking watch."

DeWitt slapped him on the back and went back to the cabin up front.

Murdock had checked. There were no other wounded. One was too damn many. Ostercamp would be out of action.

"Did you see those fucking twenties hit that formation?" Bradford asked. "I saw one hit and it blew this rebel into twenty pieces. No lie. One round must have taken out twenty of them, and they got three rounds. Then we pulled back to the five-five-six. Damn. Those twenties are just plain murder against a formation of troops."

"What were the shitheads doing in formation after their home base was attacked?" Jaybird asked. "They were a bunch of stupid assholes who will never make that mistake again."

The power changed and the rotors slowed a little as the big bird made a gentle turn and then settled down on the pad at the airfield. The pilot had called, and an ambulance waited twenty feet away. By the time the wheels touched the ground, a gurney had been rolled up and four medics and doctors waited. Mahanani and Howard picked up Ostercamp's 210-pound body and gently put him on the rolling stretcher.

DeWitt took over the platoon, and Murdock went in the ambulance. He'd shucked out of his combat vest and given it and his Bull Pup to Lam.

The ambulance used siren and lights as it streaked through the night traffic to a civilian hospital on the edge of Davao. At the emergency entrance, they tried to keep Murdock out, but one look at his worried and determined countenance and they let him go in.

He stood outside the emergency mini-operating room as two residents and two doctors worked over Ostercamp. They did some preliminary work, hung some fluids and stabilized him, and rolled him to an elevator to take him to surgery.

Two hours later, Murdock stood as a pair of doctors came into the waiting room outside the operating rooms.

"Commander?"

"Yes, about Ostercamp?"

"The young man is out of danger. He took a round high in his chest and it cut through his left lung, but we've repaired that and removed the bullet. It didn't shatter, so we got it all. There's some more minor damage, but the internal bleeding was minimal and his lung will heal as good as new. He won't be going on any long hikes or swimming for at least three months."

Murdock shook the man's hand, then looked down at his own dirty hands and jungle-filthy clothes. Couldn't be helped.

"Thanks, Doctor. He's an important man in our operation. We thank you."

When Murdock walked out of the hospital, a young Filipino Air Force man came up to him.

"Commander Murdock?" Blake nodded. "I'm here to drive you back to your quarters, courtesy of General Domingo."

"Thanks. Tell the general that I really appreciate it, and that our wounded man is going to be all right."

By the time the airman had driven Murdock back to the barracks/meeting room, most of the SEALs had showered and hit their bunks. He had no idea what time it was. When he looked at his watch, he was surprised that it was only 0135.

DeWitt hurried over, a question on his tired face.

"Yeah, Ostercamp's going to make it. Should recover fully." Murdock told DeWitt what the doctor had told him.

"Good, but for three months I want a temporary replacement," DeWitt said. "A warm body to fill in the slot. We need him for training. Of course that's after we get back to the States. By then I may need half a new squad, or maybe the squad will need a new squad leader."

"You can't give up on me now, hotshot," Murdock said.

"Just my out-of-gas brain talking," DeWitt said. "We

hurt them bad out there tonight, but we're not a bit closer
to finding the hostages."

"Our best hope now is that General Domingo can tie
down some good intel on the camps. For sixty people it
would have to be a big camp. I was hoping that one we hit
was it."

Murdock yawned. He shook his head and looked at the
showers in the latrine area. Yes. Now. Tomorrow he would
talk to General Domingo about the hostages. Maybe he had
some new information or ideas where they could be hiding
the hostages.

The next morning at 0830, General Domingo put in a call
for Murdock. He went to the general's office with DeWitt,
Senior Chief Sadler, Jaybird, and Juan. The general
frowned a moment as he looked at the team.

"I understand you do much of your planning and attack
workups by committee. I've never seen enlisted men on
this level before, but if it works for you, fine. Now, I've
had a sketchy report about your mission last night. Could
you fill me in with the particulars?"

Murdock motioned to Lieutenant Juan Ejercito. He
gulped once and then gave a precise report about their recon, the attack itself, and the approximate number of casualties inflicted on the rebels.

"Pardon me, Lieutenant, but you say you believe that you
killed or wounded over one hundred rebels?"

"Yes, sir. Some of them were undoubtedly raw recruits,
but they had weapons and fired at us. We think we closed
down for all practical purposes the training camp there at
the town, which we hear is called Bunga."

"Any contact with the hostages?"

"No, sir, we found nothing to indicate they were there
on the recon I made through the town, or when we attacked.
We believe the hostages are not being held at Bunga."

Murdock spoke up. "Sir, we didn't do a house-by-hut
search, but if they had hostages there, we believe there
would have been a good-sized guard force around them.
We saw no such force, and the buildings we burned were
manned and guarded by only a few of the rebels."

The general nodded and sipped at a cup of coffee. He put it down, then smiled. "Gentlemen, would you like some coffee?" They all declined, and he took another drink. "Lately I've been living on the stuff." The general turned to the Filipino lieutenant.

"Ejercito, you were named to be liaison with the SEALs by the colonel. I checked that out, meaning I went over your record with a magnifying glass. Your CO was right. I liked what I saw. And since your CO had to fight to get you on this detail, I like it even more. You'll stay. Can't say the same for Master Sergeant Estrada. He's been shipped back to his outfit and reduced in rank. We found several questionable contacts with people associated with the rebels. I'll send you a new man." The general looked at the SEALs. "None of you seem surprised."

"Estrada was in my squad, General," DeWitt said. "I found no fault with him in camp or in the fighting. He performed well."

"But when might he betray you or a mission?" the general asked. He went on. "We have what we think is a significant break. Some of our agents working the far west coast of the island have been contacted by a family whose son was executed for trying to leave the rebel cause. They were bitter and had a lot to say that their son had told them. He had been on the hostage guard detail. The parents of the dead boy, who was just past seventeen, told us where the hostages were held for a time and where they were moved."

The general went to the large-scale wall map and pointed. He indicated a section that seemed to be in an area where there were no roads.

"The west coast. The closest town of any size is Lebak. This area is well north of that and from what we can tell, up this river that runs down from the range of mountains that make up the western part of the island. From what our source says, there are about fifty guards at this location. It was well prepared in advance, with soldiers carrying heavy loads on packboards hiking up the trails from the seacoast and from the short distance up the river that could be navigated by flat-bottomed boats.

"Evidently they had built the housing for the hostages, provided food and bunks and clothing for those who needed it. It is from there that those who have been released were taken to Lebak, and sent by boat here to Davao, where they could catch air transportation home."

"When can we go in, General?" Murdock asked.

"Probably the sooner the better. If we take the time to set up a military maneuver in the area, the rebels will hear about it and might scatter the hostages."

"General, sir. How far from here to Lebak?" Jaybird asked.

The general pointed to one of his aides.

"Straight across the mountains, it's about a hundred and twenty-five miles," a captain with pilot wings on his shirt said. "To the camp itself we think it's about a hundred and ten miles. That's at a different angle. The distance from Lebak to the suspected hostage area is thirty miles up the coast road and then about six miles on a trail up the side of the mountains. This road up is supposed to be good enough for a jeep."

Jaybird turned to Murdock. "Sir, that's well within the turnaround range of the forty-six. There and back to Davao with no added fuel."

"How many hostages can we get into a CH-46?" the general asked.

Jaybird nodded. "Sir, we can put twenty-five combat troops in the bird, so thirty civilians wouldn't be unreasonable. I understand there are only fifty-two hostages now."

"Yes, that was right yesterday," said the general. "Amsterdam came through with some more cash and three more of the Dutch tourists are now free. So we're dealing with forty-nine, if they are all alive."

"Sir, it's not yet 1000," Murdock said. "We can be ready for a mission tonight. We'd need to leave here about 1910 for a 2000 landing. Do we have any intel about possible landing zones in the area?"

"None. We could send a Super Saber over there to check out LZs, but that would only alert them that we know where they are."

"If there's no LZs, we can always rope down," Murdock

said. "Then, after we capture the compound, we'll find an LZ tonight or in the morning with daylight. We'll tell the birds which. How much circling time would they have, Jaybird, before they need to fly back to Davao?"

Jaybird scowled for a moment, then nodded. "Two-hundred-fifty-mile round trip off a four-hundred-and-twenty-mile range. That leaves them another hour to cruise around before heading back."

"What about long-range radio?" Murdock asked. "We have only five-mile-range units."

"You can talk to the chopper, he can relay," the general said.

"But when the chopper goes back to Davao, how do we contact him to come back and get us?" DeWitt asked.

The general frowned for a moment. "We can put a portable radio in the chopper for you to take with you. It's on the same band as the chopper and can communicate over two hundred miles. You pick it up as you exit the chopper and you'll be able to talk directly with us here at Davao, or with the chopper."

"Good, that covers one problem," Murdock said.

An aide came in and handed the general a slip of paper. He read it. "Gentlemen, your new man to replace Sergeant Estrada has been selected. He's Sergeant Pablo Kalibo, one of our best. He's checked in at your compound."

"We should get cracking on our attack plan," Murdock said.

"Good, Commander. There are a few other elements you need to know about. You can have anything on the base that we can furnish you as before. We'll have the longer-range radios on the choppers to communicate here with the base. The other item may surprise you, but it's a firm decision and set in concrete and there is no way to change it. I'll be going on the strike with you."

15

Murdock turned toward the general. "But sir, this is a highly dangerous field operation. My men train year-round to climb ropes and swim and run twenty miles a day."

"Commander, last week I ran a marathon, three hours and twenty-two minutes. Every morning before breakfast I do a hundred sit-ups and then a hundred push-ups. I might not be in as good a shape as your men, but I can handle my end of things. Commander, I was an enlisted man for six years. I came up through the ranks. I fought the old bunch of guerrillas for five years. I've been bloodied more times than I can remember. My younger brother and his wife died in a rebel terrorist bombing three years ago. I was sent here to help end this reign of terror, and I fully intend to go and help you."

Murdock and the others in the room were silent.

"One more thing. I won't have any insignia on. I know that you men function as a team and there is no rank in the field. The two leaders do everything every other grunt does. I can do that. I'm coming, or you're not going. Clear enough?"

Murdock grinned and held out his hand. "Welcome on board, sir. What will we call you?"

"Domingo has worked for forty-two years; in the field I'll be Domingo. I'd like an hour to fire some of your weapons." He looked at one of his aides. "Captain, take one of the SEALs and get the weapons and ammo, and come back

136

and pick me up here. We're due on the range in fifteen minutes."

"Jaybird, go," Murdock said. The two men left the room quickly.

"I'll check on ammo and see what we need," Senior Chief Sadler said. He hurried out.

"Not much we can plan on this one, General. We'll go in, find an LZ as near the place as we can, then hike in and take the compound down. We won't be able to use our hot weapons because of the hostages. This will be a surgical strike, not a broadsword bash. If there are only fifty defenders, we should have no trouble. My big worry is that they will use the hostages as shields."

"We go in silent," DeWitt said. "We go in with knives and the two EARs, and try to take down all the awake guards around the hostages before we fire a shot."

"Great minds," Murdock said. "So, if we can control the hostages from their quarters and fire out, we'll have the war half won."

"Then we mop them up and call in the choppers," DeWitt said. "They will be back in Davao by then, so we'll have a fifty-minute wait."

"Worst possible?" Murdock said.

"If they have enough guards inside the hostage area to hold it and we have to try to take it down from the outside."

"Right, and if they threaten to execute a hostage every five minutes unless we withdraw, and they shoot the first one," Lieutenant Juan Ejercito said.

"Don't even suggest that," Murdock said.

"What's this EAR weapon?" the general asked.

DeWitt explained it to the general.

"It doesn't harm them in any way?" General Domingo asked.

"Not that we can tell. Maybe a headache or two, but nothing serious or lasting."

"I must admit that as an old infantryman, I'm amazed at what I hear about this twenty-millimeter rifle. It actually shoots a twenty and you can get airbursts with it?"

Murdock went through it for him. Then he looked at his watch. "Sir, we better get back to the men and get set up for tonight. We'll need extra chow and some late chow, and probably some new ammo. Who will our contact man be?"

"Major Ramos will handle that for you," the general said. "My car should be here. I'll be in your quarters without any insignia and in jungle cammies to get outfitted with gear at 1800."

The SEALs jumped to attention as the general walked out the door. Murdock looked at DeWitt. "I just hope to Christ that we don't come out of this mission with a wounded or dead general."

Juan shook his head. "Hey, he's a legend in the Army. One of the top rebel fighters of all time. He can do it all. I was pleased when he was sent over here to take command."

Murdock nodded. "I hope he's that good and that we don't have any bad luck on this one. It could get a little grim."

Back in the barracks/general room, the SEALs took the news of an assault with a few cheers and a lot of calm professionalism. This was their job, they'd do it.

When Jaybird came in an hour later, he was all smiles. "Hey, that bloody general can shoot. He's a natural. Took to the Bull Pup and the EAR after one quick run-through. We're not going to have any trouble with him."

"Trouble?" Vinnie Van Dyke asked. "What does he mean, trouble with the general?"

"Oh, yeah, I forgot to tell you guys. General Domingo is coming along with us on this mission. He'll be fitting into Ostercamp's slot. Don't worry, he's a combat man who's been fighting the rebels and guerrillas around here for ten years. Probably has as many kills as most of us. He came up through the ranks from private."

"No rank in the field?" Bradford asked.

"Oh, damn right," DeWitt said. "He understands that. You won't see any stars on his shoulders when he's with us."

They finished prep for the mission, then went for an early chow that had been arranged.

"Nice to have a genuine general on your side," Fernandez said. "He lifts a brow and things get done."

Just after 1800 Domingo arrived. He had walked over from his office. He wore jungle cammies and a soft hat; all had been well used. On his hip he had a .45 automatic in a battered holster.

Jaybird had dug into their replacement supplies and laid out a complete setup for Domingo. As soon as he came in he held up one hand. All conversation stopped.

"Men, my name is Domingo. I've had some experience fighting these rebels over the years. I'll be going with you. Call me Domingo. I'll fit in wherever I can. Thanks."

Jaybird motioned, and Domingo looked at the gear. He grinned. "Oh, yes, I dreamed of a setup and weapons like this a million times. Now I can use it."

Jaybird had him outfitted in a half hour and familiar with all the gear. He loved the radio.

"What weapon do you want to carry, Domingo?" Jaybird asked. The small pleasure of using the man's name and not rank seeped through.

Domingo grinned. "Whatever weapon the wounded man had. I'll fill his slot."

Jaybird grinned. "Ostercamp had the H & K NATO 7.62-round machine gun. You better talk to the j.g., Mr. DeWitt, about your weapon. It's his call."

The new Filipino sergeant was outfitted as well with equipment that Sergeant Estrada had used.

By 1900 the SEALs were on the tarmac in front of the hangar where the forty-six sat warming up its engines. Murdock had a chance to talk to Domingo.

"General, on this mission I won't use your rank again. We do need a little chat. Out here in the field we have no rank, but I'm still in charge. On this mission, you answer to me. I'll listen to your ideas as I will the rest of the men's, but the final decision in everything is up to me. Do you agree?"

"Absolutely, Murdock."

"For this mission, in the field, I outrank you. I don't think we'll have any problems. You've done your share of rebel chasing, so we'll get along fine."

They shook hands, and Murdock went out to talk to the chopper pilot. He was a captain, and his nameplate said he was Samar. Murdock told the captain their destination, and indicated that he should drop them off, and then turn around and fly home.

"I want you on a five-minute alert the rest of the night and all day tomorrow back here at the field. Better sleep in your flight suit. When it's time to come out, we'll have to get out of there fast."

"Understood, Commander. We have no set LZ?"

"Right, we don't want to alert them that they will have company. We'll check out the area. It's in the mountains, or on the slope of a mountain, which won't help. If there's any danger to the bird, we'll do a rope drop keeping you thirty feet off the deck."

"Sounds like good insurance. I'm ready for you to load. Oh, I won't be taking a door gunner or a crew chief on this run. Saving some weight. Besides, my chief is down sick."

The chopper took off precisely at 1910 and turned west toward the mountains. The southern part of Mindanao had mountains just behind Davao, Murdock had learned, then a fairly wide plain in the middle and a ridge of mountains near the west coast. Those were the ones they would drop in on.

Murdock wished he could come up with some kind of a strategy or a plan, but there was nothing they could do until they were on the ground and could determine the layout of the place and where the strengths and weaknesses were. They had about forty-five minutes of flying. It was nap time for most of the SEALs. The three Filipinos sat rigid, unable to relax.

Murdock dozed once, came alert, and checked his watch. They were more than halfway there. He went up to the pilot.

"You know these ridges over here, Captain Samar. Any places where you can find a good LZ?"

"Not usually. More likely a little opening in one of the valleys between the ridges. Like the ones we're coming up on now. See how they peak and then run down the other side? No real level spots except if the valley below is wide enough and some stream has gouged out a flat place here and there."

They were shouting to hear each other over the noise of the helicopter. Looking down, Murdock saw some flashes.

"Gunshots from down there?" he asked.

"Yes, some wild-eyed rebel with an AK-47 trying to be a hero," Samar said. "Those rounds could hurt us if they hit us, but not much chance of that. They routinely fire at our Air Force planes. That's partly how we know where the areas are the rebels control."

"We need to go up a little higher?"

"Not on my flight plan. We're still two thousand feet over those rifles, and that's straight up. Seven hundred yards is a long shot for a rifle against a little target like we are."

They flew for another five minutes, and Captain Samar said it would be about ten minutes before they would start looking for an LZ.

The impact of the rifle round came like a bright star. The bullet grazed the canopy and made a long crack in the Plexiglas. At the same time three more rounds hit the chopper and the pilot scowled.

"Damn, somebody has our range," the pilot said. He jerked the bird to the left and down to get away from the bullets. Murdock almost fell when the pilot jolted the helicopter to the left.

"Anything vital hit?" Murdock asked.

"Should know in about two minutes. Worst problem could be an oil line. Not very well protected on this model. I'm moving lower toward that ridge up there. See the one in the moonlight? It has a lot of trees, mostly pine in here, but sometimes there are landing spots. Probably should check out the bird on the ground if I can."

They came in lower and slowed, and then Samar saw an open place. It was an area of slab rock twenty yards square where nothing would grow. The pilot grinned and pointed at it.

The CH-46 was dropping down now closer to the ground and heading for the rock sheet.

They were ten feet off the ground and over the rock when the engine quit, the rotors wound down, and the big bird dropped straight to the rock slab below.

"Hold on!" Murdock bellowed; then they hit. The landing gear smashed flat, the body of the bird slammed hard into the rock, and they all heard sheet metal crumpling. The craft slued sideways and the rotors slammed into the rocks and shattered.

To Murdock it seemed five minutes before the huge metal box stopped smashing and falling and tipping. Then it all quieted.

"Get out the doors, now," Murdock brayed. "Might catch fire. Move, move, move."

He grabbed Captain Samar, who seemed dazed, unstrapped his belts, and pulled him back toward the doors. The craft lay on its side. One door was facing the rock slab; the other side door was straight overhead. The big ramp door on the back had bounced open and yawned to one side.

"Out the ramp," DeWitt barked, and the men struggled to sit up, then stand and move toward the opening. Murdock had to help the pilot. They were the last ones out, and Murdock saw that DeWitt had moved the men off the rock into the fringes of trees twenty yards away. He struggled that way with the captain.

Bradford and Howard ran out to help them.

They stared back at the bird. "Casualty report," Murdock snapped. "Alpha Squad, any injuries?"

"Sprained ankle," Lam said, "but I can walk on it, no sweat."

"Twisted shoulder, but not bad," Ching said.

"Bravo Squad?"

DeWitt spoke up. "Murdock, we've got one broken arm and a batch of bruises and scrapes. We'll live. Khai has the busted left arm down by his wrist. Mahanani is working a splint on it now."

"Everyone has his equipment and weapon?" Murdock asked.

"Oh, shit," Howard said. He raced back to the wounded forty-six, and slipped inside.

"Thought for sure it'd be burning by now," Captain Samar said. "Must be fuel and oil leaking all over the place. That hot engine could spark it."

"Howard, get out of there," Murdock screamed.

The big black man slipped past the ramp and ran full tilt for the woods. Five seconds later the whole forty-six blew up like a Roman candle in July. The explosion slammed Howard forward and drove him to the ground. He covered his face with both big hands, then when the first force of the blast was past, he stood and hurried to the rest of the platoon. He carried three rifles and a combat harness and the big first-aid kit from the chopper.

"All right," Murdock said, staring at the shadowy faces in the darkness. "Anybody else want to try to be a fucking dead hero?" He looked around, but nobody said a word.

"We've got a situation here. Captain. How far do you think we're from the last ridge to the coast?"

"Six, maybe eight miles. About three ridges over."

"This is our situation. Oh, Domingo, you okay?"

"A little shook up but fit for duty, Commander."

"Good. Juan and Kalibo?"

Both said they were shaken up, but okay.

"We're eight miles from our target. We lost our transport and our only way to contact Davao. The portable radio we were going to bring with us is now melted into a puddle of cooling metal. No help will be coming from Davao. Samar here won't be overdue for another hour and a half back at Davao. I don't know about the Air Force's search and rescue. Will they send out a bird on our course, Captain?"

"Not until daylight."

"So we do it on our own. No bullshit now. Can everyone hike up and down these fucking hills?" There was a chorus of *Hooo-yas*. "If somebody can't hike we've got to know now, so you can stay with the burned-out hulk here so the S & R can find you. Sound off."

Silence. A night bird off somewhere wailed out a mating call.

"Okay. Captain Samar, what was our compass heading for the hostages?"

He sang out with the azimuth reading.

"Get on it, Lam. You're point. Samar, you were shaky coming away from the chopper. Can you hike these hills?"

"Yes, sir. I can make it for eight miles."

"Kalibo and Domingo. You both ready to move?"

Their two voices answered, and Murdock nodded.

"Okay, Lam, head out. Bravo behind you and Alpha will bring up the rear. We're in single file at five yards. If anyone doesn't have at least one long gun, sing out."

Silence.

"We should have seven Bull Pups and two EARs. Lam, stay five yards in front of Bravo. Let's chogie out of here."

Murdock thought the jungle would be thinner up on the higher slopes of the hills. Now he decided the higher the slope, the more rain and the more vegetation. It was hard going as they hiked down the side of the ridge, across a small stream, and up the far side.

Khai fell on the way up the next hill, and screeched in pain.

"Man behind Khai, take his weapon," Murdock said into the radio.

"Got it," Jefferson said. "I'll help him now that he knows he needs it."

Mahanani found Khai's bruised and swollen leg, and wrapped it a dozen times with tape. He gave Khai some pain pills, and they kept hiking.

Lam was just over the top of the ridge when he stopped, and used the radio. "Murdock, you and the locals better take a look at this."

"What do you have?" Murdock asked on the net.

"I don't have the foggiest, Skipper. Not too sure I want to go down the other side. From what I can see from here, there seem to be about twenty fires down in the small valley below and then one large fire that lights up half the jungle. Come on up and take a look."

16

Mindanao jungle
Philippines

Murdock, DeWitt, Juan, Domingo, Lam, and Kalibo lay on the crest of the ridge and stared down at the fires burning three hundred yards down the hill in a small valley.

"Cooking fires," Juan said.

"So it could be a company of regulars down there eating their late supper," Lam said.

"Could be," DeWitt said. "What's the big fire for?"

"Domingo?" Murdock asked.

"Can't tell. Cooking fires, for sure, but we're too far into the brush here for regulars, as regular as rebels ever get. Why would they be in here? Not reasonable."

"This is one of the areas the government has set aside for the aborigines," Juan said. "There are more than sixty different groups of ancient and original people of these islands. A lot of them want to maintain their original culture. Lam met some of the Negritos, the pygmy tribe. There are dozens of others, like the Tasadays, here in northern Mindanao. They are Stone Age people who knew nothing of iron or steel or modern man until they were first discovered in 1971."

"You think these could be some such tribe?" Murdock asked.

"I'll go see," Lam said. He looked at Juan, who grinned and stood.

"I'm with you, Lam." The two faded into the jungle

growth below the ridgeline and worked their way down toward the fires.

"Why the big fire?" Lam asked Juan.

"Looks like a ceremony of some kind. A wedding, a death, a change of leader. Maybe they killed a couple of big deer and a wild pig or two and decided to celebrate. I did a paper on our aborigines when I was in college. We toured six different tribes."

"Friendly ones?"

"Mostly. We did get chased out of one place by all the men in the area."

They worked closer. When they were fifty yards from the closest fire, they stopped and Lam used his binoculars.

"Yeah, natives. But what tribe?"

He passed the glasses to Juan, who studied one fire, then another.

"Oh, boy, we could have some trouble. These are Tasadays, I'm almost sure. The most primitive of the tribes out here. They use stone knives, clay pots, and woven reed baskets. No metal is allowed. I have no idea what reaction they might have if we barged into their camp."

"Can we go around them?"

"An extra four or five miles. See that cliff over there in the moonlight? It could be one that we can't climb up. But there could be one trail up it if you know where to look. The Tasadays would. If they would help us."

"We wait for daylight?"

"That's a long time. But going in at night might really spook them."

"Could you strip down to just your pants and shoes and go in and talk to them?"

"I'm not sure what language skills this tribe might have. Theirs is unlike any other. I could do some sign language, but even my presence there would be shocking to them."

"Let's give it to the decider," Lam said. They worked their way back up the hill.

"So that's the situation, Murdock," Juan said. "Going around them is an option, but we'd have to scout that ridge across from them. Some of these ridges are almost unclimbable."

"Do they have weapons?" Domingo asked.

"Yes, sir," Lam said. "I saw spears with some kind of stone points that looked sharp. And bows and arrows. They could be a deadly force."

Murdock considered it a moment. "Any more ideas?" he asked.

The rest of them shook their heads.

"Okay, Lam, Juan, and DeWitt. Do a recon around this right-hand end of their camp. Get over that small valley and check out the hills on the other side. If we can we'll swing around them, go up the mountain, and still have a shot at getting to the rebel camp before daylight. Report in every five minutes by radio, and don't in any way contact or be seen by the natives."

"That's a roger," DeWitt said. The three stood and walked down the hill, angling to the right around the camp below. As they went, chanting began in the camp and Murdock shook his head. He had no idea what the natives were doing down there.

In the recon party, Juan stopped when he heard the chanting. He motioned the other two to come to him. "That chanting is part of a ritual of some kind. I've heard something similar in some of the other abo groups. All the more reason we shouldn't go through them. They could be hopped up on something, maybe even drunk on some homemade wine. Lots of fruit out here, and wine can be a problem."

They worked ahead.

"Let's slant around the camp and check out the ridge," Juan said. "We'll come look over the camp closer on the way back. I want to see if I can figure out what the celebration is about."

The three moved silently through the jungle's lush growth. Once they kicked out a wild pig that went charging into the greenery with a few snorts.

"Glad that wasn't an abo, or we'd be pincushions by now," Juan said. "This bunch tends to be on the ferocious side when they get riled."

Five minutes later they were past the camp and working

toward the green mountain ahead of them. It looked much taller and steeper than it had from across the small valley. When they started up the first rise, they found a clearing where they could check out the top of the ridge.

"Oh, boy," Lam said as he stared at the slopes above them through his night vision goggles. "We're not climbing up there without some ropes and pitons." He passed the goggles to DeWitt, who groaned.

DeWitt saw the face of the cliff, which looked like it was bare rock and soared almost straight up for over three hundred feet.

Juan took his turn with the glasses and looked to each side of the cliff. "Let's try upstream," he said. "We might have a better chance there."

They moved a mile through the heavy growth near the small stream and checked the mountain all the way. The rocky out-thrust continued for half the distance, then narrowed, but was still a hundred feet of sharply sloping rock that they couldn't get up.

"Downstream," DeWitt said. He checked in on the radio with Murdock, reporting their bad news.

"Keep looking," Murdock said. "We need to be a long way from this little valley by sunup."

They worked as high on the slope as they could as they passed the abos' camp. They were less than fifty yards away, and Juan motioned for a stop so he could check the camp out. He looked through the NVGs, then the field glasses, and waved to move ahead. When they were a hundred yards past the last of the small fires still burning, he stopped.

"Strange bunch back there. They were in the middle of some kind of ceremony or service. Not sure what it was. I did see a few skulls set on poles. Not a friendly sight. I counted about fifty of them, so I'm not sure it is the Tasaday tribe. I remember the last figures on them showed only about thirty. I still have no idea what the ceremony is. Could be some kind of fertility rite, or maybe a peace offering to the god of thunder. One of the Stone Age tribes I visited was scared shitless of thunder."

They kept looking up at the cliff, and it seemed to be

the same as before. The trio worked down almost a mile, and the rock wall remained stalwart and tall.

DeWitt checked in with Murdock and told him the findings.

"Keep going," Murdock said. "The damn cliff can't go on forever. We might have to make a four-or-five-mile detour. It will be better than getting roasted in a pot by our Stone Age friends out here."

After another mile of plowing through the vines and undergrowth and going around fallen trees, they found a cleared place so they could see the top of the ridge.

"Yes, the rock is almost all gone and the trees and vines have taken over," Juan said. He used the NVGs. "Yeah, we can get up the slope here all the way to the top of the ridge."

Murdock sounded pleased on the radio.

"Good, stay put and we'll meet you there. You're on the right-hand side of the creek going downstream?"

"That's a roger, Skipper."

"Hang tight, we should be there in about twenty to thirty."

The three sat on a log waiting. Juan looked upstream and shook his head. "Still wonder what tribe that is and what ceremony it was. I could do an addition to my paper on the abos."

After a ten-minute wait, Lam lifted up and looked upstream. "Thought I heard something."

"Could have been a night call from a bird," Juan said. "We have a few thousand different species on the islands."

"Yeah, probably."

Twice more Lam lifted up and tried to hear something, but shook his head and settled down to wait.

The Motorola came on in their ears.

"Juan, we've got a situation here," Murdock said. "You better come back up here. We've got abo men all around us, with their bows and arrows and spears, and they are screaming at us."

The three took off running. Juan led the way through the vines, trees, plants, and orchids that grew wild everywhere.

It took them twenty minutes to cover the two miles. Juan had been talking to Murdock as he ran.

"Don't for any reason fire a weapon. That would freak them out and you'd be a dartboard full of spears. Don't shoot any of them. Kill one and the federal penalty is fifty years in the jailhouse." Juan caught his breath, and then ran again. "Stay calm and don't let them see that you're upset. How many of you are surrounded?"

"All of us. We were going past a hundred yards out and they heard us, trapped us like wild game."

"That's how they make their living. Stay calm. We're almost there."

Juan moved his party up cautiously the last fifty yards. The abos were so busy with their captives that they'd let down their guard. Juan watched the situation. The SEALs were standing, weapons at their sides, abos surrounding them all with bows and arrows or spears.

"Stay here, I'm going out," said Juan. "Try to communicate with them." He worked forward silently, then only ten yards from the nearest abo, let out a long wailing cry. The abos turned, surprised, nervous, holding up their weapons.

Juan gave the cry again, but different this time. It was shorter and more strident. The abos talked among themselves, their prisoners forgotten for the moment.

The third time he gave the cry, Juan stepped out into the clearing. He was bare to the waist, had no hat or weapons with him. When he ended the cry, he gave two signs with his hands, then bowed low and came up slowly.

Juan watched the abos. Some were still talking. From the back came one man, slightly taller than the rest of them. Most stood no more than five feet. This man wore a colorful headpiece made of bird feathers and crowned with orchids. He had a cape made of some native vines and fibers. In his left hand he carried a machete, probably a relic of some World War II Japanese Army camp.

The abo chief stopped just outside his ring of warriors, brandished the machete at Juan, who put his hands together in front of him and bowed again.

"I don't know if this is working," Juan said to his lip

mike. "I'm using some old inter-tribe rituals I learned. I hope he knows them."

The warriors wore only loincloths that looked to Juan like they were made from soft leather. A stiff belt held up the garment, and their bodies had been painted with bright red and yellows.

Juan took in all of this at a glance. Not a war party. He didn't know what the celebration was.

"Your game," Murdock said on the radio. "All our weapons are on lock/safety."

Juan came up from his deep bow, glad his head was still firmly attached to his shoulders, and took two slow steps toward the chief. He stood there, arms folded, the machete gleaming in his left hand.

Juan used the sign for "friend" that he had learned from three different tribes. It was almost the same for each one. Now he used it again and again, changing it slightly, until the old chief's face brightened. Then he frowned. He walked closer to Juan, pointed to Juan's pants and boots, then at those of the closest SEAL, and shouted something.

Juan nodded and made another sign, then another. The old chief frowned, then looked frightened.

"Peace, we come in peace," Juan said in English. Then he said the same thing in Filipino, and the chief's head came up. He chattered two or three words, and Juan relaxed.

The old one knew the Filipino language. At least a little of it. Juan began to talk in that language, and a moment later the chief bellowed out what could only be a command. He bent and stabbed the machete into the dirt, and all the warriors laid their weapons on the ground and sat beside them.

"I'm feeling better already," Murdock said into his mike.

"We're not out of here yet," Juan said. "There are customs and courtesies that must be observed. Remember, these are Stone Age people. The machete is not a weapon, it's a symbol of command."

Juan took two steps closer to the old chief, who made some motions, and both men sat down facing each other four feet apart. Their feet almost touched.

As they talked, Juan soon learned what words he could use that the old chief would understand. The chief said he had been captured when he was a boy and taken to a mission school where they'd taught him modern ways and to speak the Filipino language. When he was twelve, he stole the machete, wounded a guard, escaped, and traveled back to his people. He hated the modern ways, and had kept his tribe pure and free from them.

"We wish only to pass," said Juan. "There are bad men near the coast we must deal with."

The old chief's eye lit up. "Two men go to coast to get coconuts. Last time one was killed by boom-boom. From ten coconut palms away he was killed."

"Those are the men we hunt," Juan said. "It is not your hunt, it is ours, and we should be going."

"Must stay for ceremony. The rite of the virgins. Must stay. Come." They stood.

"We just got sucked into watching a ceremony," Juan said in his mike. "Bring everything. We're no longer a big danger to them. But be cautious. Any little thing could bring an outburst of anger and violence."

"You heard the man," Murdock said to his mike. "We go see the pretty, then get back on the road."

The warriors picked up their weapons and scurried to fires and small lean-tos, and then assembled near the large fire at the end of the village.

Juan figured the entire village was there, including children. Everyone sat cross-legged in rough rows in a semicircle around the fire. It had burned down now, but still gave off a lot of light and heat.

The SEALs were positioned in back of the warriors. They sat cross-legged in rows. The women and children were on the other side of an aisle. The chief had vanished; now he came out wearing a jacket that had been covered with orchids of every size and color. He still wore the headdress, and now carried a white cane.

A small stone platform had been crafted in front of the fire. The stones looked to Juan as if they had been chiseled into precise shapes and fitted together without mortar and wedged into place.

The chief stood on the platform and waved the white cane. The chanting began and continued in a higher or lower tone as the chief seemed to direct it with the cane.

Then he stepped aside and a drummer began to beat a slow rhythm. Three young women came to the small area in front of the platform and began dancing to the music. Most of the women in the tribe were bare to the waist, but these three wore blouses Juan figured were made of soft animal skins. As the beat picked up in tempo, the dancing became faster as well, and soon the three young women had flung off their blouses and were topless.

Now their dancing took on an erotic tone and it went faster and faster, and one after another the girls dropped their short skirts and danced naked in the soft moonlight mixed with the firelight.

Suddenly the drum stopped and the dancers froze in the positions they were in; then on a single drumbeat they turned and ran off into the darkness.

The ceremony was over. Juan sat near the chief, who did some explaining.

"We are alone here. In the old days we would raid neighboring tribes and steal women. Others did the same to us. It was a way of bringing fresh blood into our society. Without it we would wither and die. For ten years we have had no fresh blood. Now we will. The three virgins you saw dancing are ready tonight to become with child. The three will approach your men, each select one or two and mate with them. The mating should last all night.

"I can't allow your men to leave until this life-giving act is done. I know you will understand."

"Let me talk to my chief."

Murdock laughed when he heard what the old chief had said.

"Impossible. We have to be on that ridge overlooking the hostage center before daylight."

Juan shook his head. "It's too far now for us to get there. Besides, if we refuse to mate with the three virgins, there would be huge trouble. It's an honor the chief is giving us, and in his society, there is not the slightest chance that such an honor can be refused. If we try to walk away now, there could be considerable bloodshed. Those arrows and spears are deadly, and we would have no warning."

Murdock scowled. He called Jaybird, Sadler, DeWitt, and Domingo together and Juan went over the situation.

"Hot damn, pussy tonight," Jaybird yelped.

Domingo looked at Juan. "I have heard of strange customs for some of these Stone Age tribes. This one seems slightly more advanced than some of them. Commander, I don't see how we can risk the chance of losing some men by refusing this honor."

DeWitt grumbled, and at last looked up. "Afraid I'm with the overnighting here," he said.

Sadler shrugged. "Makes not a lot of difference to me. But I'd as soon not kill any of these people, and that's what it would come to. I'll vote to stay."

Murdock looked at Juan. "Tell the chief we accept this honor and we will stay. Can we ask for volunteers for this?"

"Afraid not, Commander. Each of you has been assigned a small fire to sit beside. The ladies will circulate, find the ones they like, and vanish into the jungle. In the morning, the chief will give us a guide to show us the quickest and easiest way to get to the far ridge overlooking the sea."

"Done," Murdock said.

The SEALs and the three Filipinos sat beside the fires, gently stoking them with wood to keep them burning. Murdock saw the girls, still naked, making the rounds of the fires. None of the girls came as far as he was, and he breathed a sigh of relief when Juan said on the Motorola that the exercise was concluded, the choices had been made, and the rest of the men were free to take their gear and find a sleeping area. They did not bunk down together, and no one was sure which men had been chosen.

In the morning all the SEALs were up at daylight and took time out to eat MREs. All men were present, and nobody was sure who had been selected the night before.

"I still say that Jaybird has an unusually big grin," Ching said.

Jaybird just grinned wider.

Juan went to see the chief, and a few minutes later the chief came and bowed and presented Murdock with a carved walking stick five feet long. Murdock hesitated, then took the KA-BAR from his leg sheath and presented it handle-first to the chief. The old man stared at it and hesitated. Murdock took the knife and picked up a vine from the ground, and sliced it in half with a gentle stroke.

The chief's eyes went wide. Murdock cut a branch off a shrub and whittled it down to a toothpick.

"Sharp," Juan said in the chief's language.

This time when Murdock offered the chief the handle of the knife, he took it and bowed deeply.

Two warriors stood by, waiting. Juan said the chief told him neither of them spoke any Filipino but they knew the best route to the sea. Juan and the chief both bowed again.

"Let's roll," Juan said. He motioned to the two warriors, who ran ahead, then settled down to a walk, and they moved out of the village. At the far side of the village and only a dozen feet from the trail, the three former virgins from the previous night stood, topless, wearing the short palm-leaf skirts. They laughed and smiled and waved at the platoon as the men walked past. Murdock watched each of the SEALs, but he couldn't figure out which three had the largest smiles.

17

The two Tasaday guides had no secret trail up the face of the cliffs, and took the party around to the point where the recon had shown that going up was possible. There was even a semblance of a trail that had been used before up the sharp incline, through the trees and vines and occasional small pond where rainwater gathered.

The hiking was tough going up the hill, and almost as bad coming down on the other side. The pilot was hurting, and Murdock hiked directly behind him and could see that he was slowing them down. He was trying, and that was all Murdock could ask. This wasn't his job, he had been crashed into it.

Just as they started up the other side of the next ridge, Lam came on the net.

"Quiet, everyone. I hear a chopper." They all stopped moving and hardly breathed, but Lam soon reported that the sound had faded.

"We're well off the compass line to the target," Lam said. "The chopper pilot probably is working that line first; then he'll start moving to each side, and eventually should find the burned-out forty-six there in plain sight on the rock slab. Which doesn't help us one hell of a lot."

"If they see no survivors, they might shut down the S & R," Canzoneri said. "Kind of figures."

They hiked again. Murdock called a halt after they had been on the trail for two hours. Juan and one of the guides vanished into the jungle, and five minutes later came back with a stalk of over one hundred bananas and an armload of mangoes.

"These funny round suckers good to eat?" Jaybird chirped.

"You've led a sheltered life, Jaybird," Lam said. "Dig in, take a bite, you'll love them."

"This and some pork chops for dinner and you could damn well live off the land out here," Khai said. "The only trouble is, how do you peel a banana with one hand?"

"With your teeth," Bradford said. "Pretend you're a chipmunk."

Ten minutes later the stalk of bananas had been seriously depleted. The men then took two or three each and pushed them into their combat vests wherever there was a spot open.

Murdock had talked to Lam. "Slow these boys down a little, Lam. The captain is having a hard time. We don't want to have to carry him the rest of the way."

They slowed.

Before a half hour was up they had scaled the next ridge, and Lam hit the radio. "My boys up here indicate this is the last one before we come to the ridge that looks out on the sea. We're making progress."

He paused. "Oh, yeah, chopper incoming. We should be able to see this one."

They did. Through the trees and lush growth, they caught sight of it as it turned and headed the other way.

"He's making S turns on a search," Lam said. "What we need is something that we can use to make a quick fire. Everything is so damn green and wet. What will burn in here?"

Juan came on. "Kalibo and I will find burnable material and bundle it and bring it with us. Then a match or a lighter and we have a fire. We add green pine branches to make smoke. It will lift through the trees and should get the pilot's attention."

There was a small rocky place near the top of the ridge where Lam kept them for ten minutes. The helicopter didn't return.

Murdock called Lam and suggested they move down the

slope. Halfway down Lam heard the chopper coming again. Juan lit a match to the bundle and put on small pine boughs, and seconds later he had smoke drifting upward through the canopy of tree leaves. They added more pine boughs until the smoke was intense, but the chopper sound faded.

"Next time," Lam said, and Juan and Kalibo put out the fire by stomping on it. There was little chance of a jungle fire in this rain forest.

Murdock and the pilot, Captain Samar, went to the head of the line, just in back of the scouts, and set the pace. It went slower now, but the pilot was holding up better. The bananas had helped.

Just after noon, they worked up the last ridge. Murdock looked over the top, saw the calm waters of the Moro Gulf, and called a halt. The SEALs flaked out in the softness of the vines and relaxed.

Juan came up and made signs to the guides.

"Shouldn't we give them something?" Murdock asked.

Juan shook his head. "Can't, because then they would have to give you something of equal or more value. They have nothing to give. A bow will be enough."

Murdock bowed to the two guides; they bowed back, then bowed to Juan. They turned and headed back toward their camp at once.

Murdock lay on the rim of the ridge looking down. The water was five or six miles away across some hills and a narrow plain along the coast. He saw one small stream going down from this side of the mountain, but didn't think that could be the one that was partly navigable. Lam used his binoculars and looked to the south. He grunted and passed the glasses to Murdock, who scanned the way the lead scout pointed.

"Oh, yes," Murdock said. "The river. Good-sized. Might get some big canoes up that thing or the flat-bottomed boats that look like big canoes.

"We'll take an hour's break here, then move to the south along the reverse slope of this ridge," Murdock said to the net.

Murdock called Jaybird, Sadler, DeWitt, Lam, Domingo, and Juan together.

"We've spotted a river to the south that looks like it could be the one that leads up the valley toward the cliffside hostage keep. It's now about 1300. Any suggestions?"

"We still planning on a night attack?" DeWitt asked.

"Unless someone has a better idea," Murdock said.

"So we need to move down the ridge until we can find the fucking place," Jaybird said.

Murdock nodded.

"We find it, then recon the compound and pick out any weak points, check the guard force, and look for an attack point," Lam said.

"Yes, but will that need to wait for darkness?" Domingo asked.

"Be better to get there in the daylight," Lam said. "Get a better feel of a place that way. Motorola will get the info back to you quickly."

"Still a silent hit for as long as possible," DeWitt said. "If there are obvious guard posts, do we take them out with the EAR and risk hitting the hostages?"

"Yes," Sadler said. "We can wait for the sleepers to wake up if we hit any, or we can carry them to the choppers. Big question is, how do we communicate with the Air Force to get a lift out of here?"

"There are telephones at Lebak," General Domingo said. "After we capture the place and free the hostages, I'll run up there and call the base."

"It's thirty miles, Domingo," Murdock said.

"I'm a marathoner, Commander. No sweat. I'll take Lam along for company. We might even find a motorboat along there someplace or a fishing boat."

"Fine with me," Lam said.

"So, our commo problem is solved. What's next?"

"Wait for intel from our recon squad and then work out our attack plan," Juan said. "I'd like to go down with Lam on the recon."

"Done." Murdock looked around. "Anything else?" There were no more comments. "Eat your bananas. Juan says he can get all we want." He looked at his watch. "We leave in thirty-five minutes." The planning session was heard by all on the Motorolas.

An hour later, the SEALs and friends looked across the ridge and downslope five hundred yards at a frame and stone house that had been built on a flat area at the end of a gentle slope. The flat place was still five or six miles up a winding road from the valley below.

Part of the land around the house had been used to build a large dormitory-type building. It looked temporary, and was made of pine logs with a nipa-thatched roof and woven leaf panels for the walls. It was one story and covered a big area.

"Plenty of room for sixty people," Sadler said after taking his turn with the binoculars. The jungle growth came within twenty feet of the buildings. So far they had seen no sign of any guards or rebels.

"The rebel guards have to be there," Lam said. "Our job is to find them. I'd like to take an EAR along just in case we get in a firefight."

"Done," Murdock said.

"We're moving," Lam said. He switched weapons with Bill Bradford, who had carried two guns, and waved. He and Juan vanished in the jungle growth at once, and hard as Murdock tried, he could not see a single branch or palm frond move to indicate where the pair was.

"We wait," Murdock said. He studied the area, then went on the net. "DeWitt, I want you to take your squad and move south along the ridge one hundred yards. We need a pincers movement here, or at least two attack points. Take an EAR with you. Alpha will remain here or go another thirty yards south, and we'll all hike down the slope and get in an attack position before we hear from Lam."

"I heard that," Lam said.

"We'll stay back twenty yards from the compound if we don't run into any security down there. They could have some trip wires to set off alarms, but they must feel too secure for that. Your objective will be the buildings to the left of the house and the garage or whatever it is. Alpha will try to get into the hostage barracks and secure that, then take down the house. Comments."

"We can move down and get in position," DeWitt said. "Oh, yes. Now I see guards. Six just came out of the two buildings which may be guard housing. Both look like garages, but one may be a caretaker's house. They are our targets. My estimation is that there are no hostages in there so they're legitimate targets for our twenties."

"Agreed," Murdock said. "Yes, I have the guards. They seem to be spreading out, three going to the front and three to the back. Ideal targets for the EARs. If we agree, coordinate with Lam to use the EARs both at once on the three guards."

"Roger that. Should we be moving out now?" Ed DeWitt asked.

"Let's do it," Murdock said. "Remember, stay back twenty to thirty yards from the target and get fields of fire if possible. No firing into the hostage barracks."

"Got it. We're moving."

"Alpha Squad. On me, single file. Let's chogie."

Halfway down the slope, Murdock stopped and called Lam.

"Nothing so far, Skipper. You saw the six guards. Three in back. My suggestion. We take down the hostage barracks first. There's a back door I didn't see before. It's fifteen feet from the jungle cover. Suggest that Alpha come to that door and we take down the hostage area, then work the main house."

"Agree. DeWitt, you copy?"

"Right, we're in reserve until you take the hostages. Then when you go for the house, give us the word and we use twenties on the rebels' sleeping quarters and attack with our teeth bared."

"You got it. Watch the twenties. Interior bursts would be best. No more than three rounds."

"Should do it."

"Alpha, we can't do any more here," Lam said. "Come on down."

Murdock had held his men at the halfway point. Now he clicked the mike twice, and Alpha Squad moved on down the hill. Murdock was in front with his Bull Pup set on 5.56mm rounds. He paused at the thinning foliage and looked ahead. One of the guards walked a post within ten feet of where Murdock lay. He let him go. He and Alpha

Squad were thirty feet from the hostages' door. He let the guard get farther away, then saw that he would meet another guard at the center of the clearing.

"Take them with the EAR," Murdock said. Almost at once two whooshing sounds came. The two guards Murdock could see went down in a heap of flailing arms and legs and lay still.

"Two guards down," Lam said on the net.

"Third guard down," DeWitt said.

"Let's move, Alpha," Murdock said. He lifted up and ran hard for the rear door of what he hoped was the hostage compound.

18

Murdock sprinted once he was out of the vines and trees, and skidded to a stop beside the door handle on the rear entrance to the hostage barracks. He waited for three more SEALs to come beside him; then he turned the knob slowly.

Not locked.

He edged the door outward an inch so he could look inside. It was surprisingly light. He saw rows of double-decked bunks; then he saw people. He nudged the door another inch. He couldn't spot any guards inside. He opened the door a foot and slipped through. Nearest him was a man wearing shorts and a T-shirt. He looked about sixty. He looked up and scowled. Murdock gave him a thumbs-up sign, and he looked confused.

Four more SEALs edged past the door and inside; then a man from near the front of the barracks ran back. He was thin, white-haired, and wore glasses.

"Who are you, and thank God you're here," he said. "I'm Philpot, English."

"We're Americans. Where are the rebel guards?"

"Out front mostly. Come in here just to bring us food, what there is of it."

Now all nine of the SEALs and friends were inside. Two ran to the front door. One guarded the rear.

Murdock estimated the number of people on bunks and standing around.

"This can't be all of you. Where are the rest?"

"They loaded up two trucks early this morning and took them away," Philpot said. "Told us they wanted to split us up. We still have thirty-one here, and there are eighteen at another camp. Don't know where it is."

The sound of gunfire came from outside, and Murdock recognized the blast of the 20mm rounds. Then the small arms. Ching and Lampedusa edged the front door open and looked outside.

"Skipper, okay to fire out of here? We've got some targets."

"Go," Murdock said.

Lam fired from the ground level, and Ching used his Colt carbine over the top. They found six rebel guards slipping out a back door of their sleeping area and moving into firing positions to contest those weapons still in the jungle.

Lam and Ching reduced their number to two, who fled in back of the building and to the other side. A man came out of the rock house and charged toward an ancient jeep that was parked behind it. Lam punctured his back with four 5.56 slugs and jolted him into the Philippine dirt. He rolled over once, tried to get up, then fell and didn't move again.

"How many guards?" Murdock asked the Englishman.

"Fifteen, maybe twenty. Some went with the other hostages."

"Have they hurt any of you?"

"Not so far, but they're getting impatient."

"Who's in the big house?"

"The guard officers. Just three of them."

"Murdock, we aren't taking any return fire. Time we charge up and clear the guards' place?" It was DeWitt.

"Move when you're ready. Only about ten to fifteen guards, did you copy that?"

"Yes, copied."

Murdock looked back at the Englishman. "How do we get to the main house?"

"Front door, then to a side door about thirty feet over to the right."

"Ching, back door cover, Bradford, stay at the front door for protection. The rest of you on me. We're out the front door and thirty feet to the right. We go in a rush. Ready?"

Murdock looked out the front door, saw no green-clad

rebels, burst out, and sprinted for the house to the right. He heard some firing out an upstairs window; then he was at the door and pulled it open. No shots came through. Lam was beside him.

"I'm right," Murdock said as he pushed the panel fully open and charged inside, diving to the right. Behind him came Lam, who dove to the left. They took no fire.

Murdock saw they were in a utility room, with closets and a small table. One door led off and it was closed. Both SEALs came to their feet as the other members of Alpha charged into the room.

Murdock and Lam did the diving entry again through the second door, and took some rounds from across the room. Lam lifted up over a small chair and cut down the shooter with a bust of three rounds.

There was no more firing from the room. The living room was furnished part Western and part Filipino. The SEALs ran down a short hall, clearing two rooms, then looked at the stairway. It was open on one side of the living room with a landing on top and an open door.

Lam held up a fragger. Murdock nodded. Lam threw the grenade, and 4.2 seconds later it exploded on the top stairs landing. Lam, Domingo, and Van Dyke charged up the stairs. Murdock was behind them. Two rooms. Two SEALs charged into each room. Murdock and Domingo took the one on the left. Domingo went first and dove right. Before Murdock made it out of his dive, Domingo had rattled off two three-round bursts. Two guerrillas had brought up rifles, but didn't have time to fire them before they died.

"Clear left," Murdock said.

"Clear right," Domingo said. They looked out the windows. The high ground gave them a different view. Beyond the jeep and the guards' quarters, they saw a narrow roadway heading downhill. Near it was a sedan, maybe a Honda or Toyota. Near the sedan lay three rebels in a bunker designed to protect them from down the hill. Murdock punched out the small window, aimed the Bull Pup out it, and put a 20mm round in the center of the bunker. When the smoke and dust settled, the three rebels sprawled lifeless.

"DeWitt, how are you doing over there?"

"We've cleared one building and have a wounded prisoner. He should be able to talk. We think the next building is empty. We're going in there now."

"Second building clear," Mahanani said on the net.

"Check the rest of the grounds. We took out the guards at the far back aiming downhill. One jeep and one sedan should be operational. Juan, get to that prisoner. We need to know where they've taken the rest of the hostages."

"Roger," Juan said, and ran out of the house and across to the rebel guards' quarters.

"Check out all these second-story windows and see what else we can find," Murdock told the rest of his squad.

He motioned to Domingo. "Glad you're aboard. Those two rebels with guns up might have nailed me before I could get to them. Thanks."

Domingo grinned. "I haven't had this much fun for six years. Damn, I forgot the surge of emotion that comes in combat. We still need to get to Lebak, right?"

"Absolutely."

"That sedan might be our best bet. I could take it, a driver, and another gunner and get to that town in an hour or so, depending on this dirt road along the coast over there."

"Go check it out, Domingo. Take Franklin for your driver. You hear that, Franklin? Go check out the sedan at the front of the place."

"Will do, Skipper."

Murdock and the rest of Alpha looked out the windows, but could spot no more rebels. Murdock went down to the hostages.

He got their attention, then talked to the Englishman. "How many of these people speak or understand English?"

"Half. We have interpreters for the others."

"Listen up, people. We're with the United States Navy and we're here to get you back into circulation. We hope to have helicopters here before dark and take you back to Davao. There you will able to get air transport."

Half the people cheered; the others were told of the news and they wept and then cheered.

"We're not sure how long it will be. We're driving a car to the nearest town, where one of our men will contact the Philippine Air Force and they will be sending helicopters here. Once loaded up, it's only a forty-five-minute flight to Davao."

He waited until all the translations were made. Then he looked at them again.

"Any questions?"

"Did some of the rebels outside die?" one woman asked.

"Yes," Murdock said, and looked around. There were no more questions.

"Have you been fed enough lately?" Murdock asked.

There were a chorus of boos and nos.

"I'll have some men look over the kitchen and see what we can serve you." He turned and used the Motorola. "Mahanani, Howard, and Jaybird. You guys are on KP. See what kind of a meal you can get up for these people out of the supplies. Must be some here. Do it now."

"Sedan looks workable," Franklin said on the net. "Low on gas, but we siphoned all that was in the jeep and found a five-gallon can in the shed. Should be plenty."

"Good. General, your ears on?"

"Yes, sir, Commander."

"Let me know when you're ready to move out. Sooner the better. You have your shooter and driver?"

"Roger that, Commander. If Canzoneri wants to take a ride."

"I'm running for the sedan, Skipper," Canzoneri said.

"Take one of the Bull Pups and a sniper rifle. Get the right tools, men."

Juan called on the radio. "Murdock, you better come over to the rebel quarters. Our rebel doesn't want to talk."

Murdock told the hostages they were free to roam around the grounds, but to stay close. "There could still be some rebel snipers around." Most of the hostages elected to stay inside.

The Englishman Murdock had first talked to came up. "Sir," said Philpot, "I was with the 82nd Grenadiers for forty years. Done a bit of bash-and-shoot myself. Like to come with you if you don't mind."

"It's an interrogation, Mr. Philpot. Might be better if you stayed here."

"That's Colonel Philpot, Commander. You must be at least a commander for the Navy to give you this role. I can pay my way with action if it comes to that."

Murdock nodded, and led the way out the front of the barracks to the rebel quarters. It was now one large room. Some walls had been taken out. A dozen bunks were at one side, and on the other a table and chairs. A rebel guard, bare to the waist and tied by arms and legs, sat in one of the sturdy chairs.

"Commander, we're loaded and ready to travel," Domingo said on the net. "One tire's a little low on air, but that should be no problem. We'll hope to get to town in an hour or an hour and a half. I'll make the calls and set up the flights and should be back here by the time the choppers arrive. How many hostages?"

"Thirty-one. One chopper could do it. Two would be better. We won't be going back. They took the rest of the hostages somewhere. We're trying to find out where. You should go back to Davao with the hostages."

"We'll see about that, Commander, when the time comes. We're moving. Take care."

Murdock looked back at the rebel prisoner. He was young, eighteen, maybe a year more. Juan slapped him with his open palm using a full swing. The man's head jolted to one side and came back slowly.

Juan spoke in Filipino, and the man in the chair scowled but said nothing. Juan saw Murdock come in, and walked over.

"Sir, this isn't going to be pretty. I'm sure it isn't in your SEAL book on how to treat prisoners. Might be better if you were outside."

"Carry on, Juan. SEALs seldom take prisoners; we never leave them alive. Do what you have to. We need to know where those other hostages are."

Juan went back to the prisoner and asked him another question. When the man refused to talk, Juan took a knife and made a slice down the man's cheek. Blood flowed down the cut and dripped on his legs. With the cut, the man bellowed in pain. Juan ignored him and asked the same question again. This time the sharp point of the knife hovered a quarter of an inch from the young man's right eye.

"I say, now, that could produce some results," Philpot said.

The rebel Filipino tried to draw back from the point. Juan moved it with him, momentarily grazing the eye but not damaging it.

The man jabbered off four sentences.

Juan countered with another question.

The rebel closed his eyes.

Juan moved the knife and sliced down his other cheek. Another bellow of pain.

When the rebel opened his eyes again, he saw the blade even closer to his right eye, the point small and deadly.

He talked again, and this time he relaxed. Tears seeped from his eyes and his voice went strangely hoarse.

Juan let the knife down and turned.

"He says they left early this morning before daylight. They herded about twenty people into the big truck and drove away. The best he knows is that they would go back nearer to Lebak. He heard something about an Eagle's Nest. He said the lieutenant in charge here told the men he would be going to the Eagle's Nest."

"Where is that?"

"He said he didn't know. Somewhere high. Somewhere on the ridges over the sea."

"Is he lying?"

"I don't think so, but he's still holding back. I need to persuade him more."

"I've heard that cutting off fingers is counterproductive," Murdock said.

"I've heard that too." Juan grinned. "But I'm not sure I believe it."

"Find out how far down or up the coast the Eagle's Nest is. That would be helpful. I'm going to check the kitchen. KP crew, how are you doing?"

The Motorola talked back. "Not a hell of a lot here to

work with," Jaybird said. "No beans, no flour, no potatoes. How can I make a dinner without potatoes?"

Mahanani came on. "Hey, Skipper. We've got a whole truckload of fruit here. We can make a good fruit salad. Then there are some other staples. Lots of bread and cans of tuna. Yeah, tuna fish sandwiches. Lots of coffee. We'll find something else. Take about half an hour. Where do these people eat?"

"Don't know. I'll find out. Mr. Philpot. Where have you folks been eating your meals?"

"Tables in the hostage room," he said. "Nothing fancy. The women set them up the first day we were here."

Murdock relayed the message to the kitchen.

"Ed, see if you can find any more gasoline. We might be able to use that jeep down there. Check it out."

"Can do, Skipper."

Murdock grabbed Fernandez and they toured the whole complex again, looking for any hidden rebels, and anything that might help them find the missing hostages. They found DeWitt with two five-gallon cans of gasoline. He poured one can into the jeep fuel tank and the rig started. Somebody had tuned the engine.

"Can haul five men and a driver on here," DeWitt said.

"Take it on a test run," Murdock said. "Go down the road here to the beach and see if you can figure from the big truck tire marks in the dirt which way the rig turned. Help us know which way they went."

DeWitt drove, and Jefferson went along as shotgun as they gunned the vintage rig down the narrow road toward the beach five miles away.

Murdock checked the kitchen in the big house. Mahanani had just mixed up the tuna fish, and Murdock tested the first sandwich. "Needs minced onion, pickle relish, and chopped almonds," Murdock said.

"Sure, Skipper, and throw in the champagne and baked Alaska for dessert."

Murdock finished the angle-cut sandwich and nodded. "Yeah, that's good. You can make my sandwiches anytime, Mahanani."

Outside, Murdock tried to raise the general on the Motorola. Either he was too far already, or the hills cut down on the signal. Now all they could do was wait. Transport. They were dead in the water without any air transport.

19

Beach Road
To Lebak, Mindanao

Guns Franklin tooled the old Toyota along the dirt and gravel road down the mountain, taking it easy, stopping for a washout halfway down where mountain-caught water must have come roaring down after a hard rain. He eased the front wheels into the foot-deep gully on the road, gunned them up the far side, and let the rear wheels come across slowly. Once past that, there were three more miles to the beach road. It ran along the surf and had been black-topped once, but didn't look like it had been resurfaced for ten years.

"Not much traffic out this way, so they don't bother fixing the road," Domingo said.

There was no traffic at all. An occasional shack of boards and woven panels showed on the beach side at the end of dirt trails off the road. They saw no people.

After five miles the road was a little better, and that let Franklin gun the eight-year-old Toyota up to thirty miles an hour. They had just come down a short hill to a wash that was a hundred yards wide, and had started up the slope on the other side, when something cracked the windshield and slanted off into the brush and trees at the side of the road.

"Incoming," General Domingo barked. "From the left. Stop and bail out the right-hand-side doors."

Canzoneri, in the backseat, had his window open and the muzzle of the Bull Pup pushed out toward the mountain.

172

When the round hit the car he automatically pumped three three-round bursts into the trees on the other side of the road. Then he bailed out and dove into the shallow ditch on the beach side of the road with the car between him and the shooters.

A dozen more rounds slammed into the Toyota, and the three men ducked as low as they could go.

"Sounds like two or three of them," Franklin said. He held his sniper rifle in his hands and jacked a shell into the chamber.

General Domingo took over as if he was shot at every day.

"Franklin, you worm down the ditch past the rig and see if you can get a sighting on the shooters. Canzoneri and I'll go up the other way. Everyone have a radio?"

He saw their nods. "Let's move. If you get a target, fire away."

Franklin crawled, toes and elbows, with his head down and the Colt 4A1 across his forearms. He went twenty feet, then pulled his floppy green hat low and eased up so he could peer over the roadway at the jungle growth.

The best spot for an ambush was a splash of trees about a hundred yards off the road with some rocky places in front. It would make cover for a dozen gunmen. He watched that area, and a minute later saw a glint of sunlight off metal. Franklin concentrated on the spot and saw a flash again. He lifted the Colt up and fired three three-round bursts into the greenery where he'd seen the flashes. At once he dropped down. The dirt over his head splattered on him as half a dozen rounds came back at him. He crawled ten feet on down the ditch, which became a little deeper, and waited.

From up the road he heard gunfire, and then the sound of a 20mm round going off. He darted up for a look, and came right back down. Shrapnel still flew in the same copse of trees he had fired at. There was no return fire. They waited ten minutes.

"Think we nailed all of them?" Franklin asked on the net.

"If we didn't we scared them to death," Canzoneri said.

"I'm going up and take a look," Domingo said.

"No," Franklin barked. "Pardon me, General, but I'm senior SEAL here and I'm in command. Right here I outrank you. I'm moving back up to your position in a series of short runs. If there's anybody there, they will try for me. If they do, put another twenty in the spot they fire from. You ready?"

"Ready," Domingo said.

Franklin had never had a death wish. This was about as fucking close to it as he had come. His call. He sucked it up, surged out of the ditch, and ran toward the Toyota ten yards and dove into the sandy ditch.

No shots. He did another dash and was behind the Toyota. He opened the door and looked inside. It didn't look hit too bad. If the engine was okay and the tires didn't get flattened . . .

He made another dash, twenty yards this time, and saw the other two in the ditch. He dove into the dirt just behind them.

"So far, so good," Franklin said.

"Yeah, you got to play hero," Canzoneri said. "Now my turn. See that old log right over there? Like they had to bulldoze it aside to put down the road? I'm going over there. Put some cover fire into the trees for me. Then, from there I go to that brushy patch, and should have cover the rest of the way to that bunch of ambush trees. Ready?"

The other two nodded. "Oh, General," Canzoneri said, "use the 5.56 on that slammer you have. I don't want to get caught in a shrapnel bath up there." Then he darted across the road as the two men fired into the trees. Canzoneri slid feet-first behind the three-foot-thick log like a quarterback trying to avoid being tackled. He came up and peered over the log. Nothing came from the spot of trees.

He made two more dashes, then used the Motorola and called off the covering fire. He was in the right bunch of trees a moment later, and found three dead bodies. One with a small round through the forehead, the other two cut up by shrapnel from the twenties.

"All down and out here, three of them. I'll bring their

AK-47's and a pair of sub guns. Nothing else of value. No radio so nobody knows we're coming."

"I'm checking the Toyota," Franklin said. "Hope to hell they didn't shoot up the engine or the gas tank."

Five minutes later, Franklin reported the rig was ready to travel. "One round cut a spark plug wire in half, but I pasted it back together again, good as new. We moving on down the road, or what?"

"Faster we get to Lebak, the quicker we get the hostages out of here," Domingo said. He grinned. "Just a suggestion."

"Let's motor," Canzoneri said.

They rolled along at over thirty miles per hour now, and the passing lush green of the island reminded Canzoneri of Hawaii. They saw two dirt roads leading off the blacktop going up toward the mountains, but didn't see any houses or buildings up that way.

"Why is this area so undeveloped, isolated?" Franklin asked.

"We have lots of undeveloped areas," Domingo said. "The loggers haven't got into this area yet. It might be a federal preserve of some kind, I'm not sure. I didn't realize there were so few people on this side of the island."

"Well, we just passed the ten-mile mark from where we hit the main road," Franklin said. "All is A-okay so far."

"Makes me nervous when you say that," Canzoneri said. "Why were the rebels back there on an outpost and why did they fire at us before they could possibly know who we were?"

"Orders," Franklin said. "They were told no one would be driving the Toyota down this road. If anyone did, shoot them."

"So, hotshot, are there any more surprises up this road. Like a block, or a tank, or some more shooters?"

"Probably," Domingo said. "We better keep a sharp eye."

Another mile down the track and right along the surf, they came around a corner and found a two-foot-thick log stretched across the road. There was no room on either end to drive around it, even by going into the shallow ditch. They stopped fifty yards away and studied it. Plenty of cover around for snipers. Was it an active block, or just a delaying tactic without any shooters involved?

"Ease up on it," Canzoneri said.

The Toyota crawled forward, all three men evaluating everything they could see of the brush, vines, trees, and jungle that came down almost to the road on the mountainside.

"Could be booby-trapped," Franklin said. He put on the emergency brake, shifted into neutral, and opened the car door. No shots came. He checked both sides of the log where it lay on the tarmac, and shrugged. He ran back, jumped in the Toyota, and backed up, then came at the left end of the log.

"Bumper height," he said. "See the crown on the road? If I can push it enough to get it to roll, this end will keep rolling down and right off the side of the road without moving the other end more than two or three feet."

The car spun its wheels a moment when the bumper touched the log. The other two men got out and pushed as the Toyota's bumper shoved ahead with all the horsepower the little car had.

The log rocked, then rocked again. Both men pushed from the side near the end, and on the third try, the big log rolled over and then the top end rolled faster, and soon it was off the road and in the ditch.

"Yeah, let's chogie," Franklin shouted.

They drove along the scenic roadway with the crashing surf on one side and the emerald green on the other for four miles before they came up a slight grade and saw a roadblock ahead. It was more than a quarter of a mile away, but Franklin knew what it was.

"Hold off four hundred yards," Domingo said. "I want to try this laser sighting." He stepped out of the car and sighted on the truck that had been parked across both lanes of the road. To one side was a sedan, and they saw six or eight soldiers standing around waiting for them.

Domingo fired, then aimed and fired again. Both rounds were airbursts over the truck and car. The soldiers there melted to the ground, splattered with shrapnel from the two airbursts. One man ran behind the truck, which had had its fabric bow roof ripped to shreds. Domingo sighted in on the cab of the big truck. The fuel tank should be right under it. He fired the contact round and it hit on the cab door, blew it off, and exploded inside the cab. A moment later a secondary explosion rocked the quiet beach land as the gasoline tank detonated with a roar spraying burning fuel over the sedan and the last two rebels still alive. Domingo watched it burn for a minute. "I've got to get a thousand of these for my troops. We could wipe out every rebel stronghold in the whole Mindanao Island."

They drove slowly up to the truck's hulk. The burning sedan had been blasted halfway into the ditch. A gentle nudge by the Toyota bumper, and it continued into the shallow depression and left room for Franklin to drive through. They saw six bodies in the wreckage and no survivors. Franklin floored the sedan, and they raced down the road away from the smoking ruins.

"Why all this firepower, these roadblocks?" Franklin asked. He looked at Domingo.

"Do you know where the head man rebel has his headquarters?" Canzoneri asked Domingo.

"Not for sure. It's a big secret even from most of the rebels. But I'm getting suspicious. He brought the hostages here. He has an ambush set up, then a log across a public road, then a military-type roadblock with rebel soldiers. This could be rebel country. He might own the countryside and the town. He could have his GHQ there in Lebak."

"If so we're really fucked," Franklin said. "How will we get a phone line out to anywhere?"

"We can't fight our way into town," Domingo said. "If we need to do that, we'd be stopped short by a larger force. I've heard the rebels have bought heavier weapons lately. If it looks like the rebels control the town, we'll have to recon, and maybe walk in and con somebody who has the phone system, or take over the building or at least one phone line. I'm sure they have phone service over here; maybe it's microwave or satellite."

"How big is Lebak?" Canzoneri asked.

"Never been there," Domingo said. "Don't see how it could be very big. No industry, no farming, no logging.

What, maybe four or five hundred people? A little fishing, maybe."

"This odometer is in miles and it shows we have done just over seventeen so far," Franklin said. "If that town is twenty-five to thirty, we have a ways to go."

"My guess is that with the increased amount of security and guards, the rebel leader's GHQ must be nearby, but maybe not all the way to town."

"So, the security should pick up the closer we come to the GHQ, and then once we break through that it would be less on the way into town?"

"That's what I'm thinking. Why else all this security out here in the wilderness?"

"So our job is to get through the last of the roadblocks and masses of rebels. Then we should be free to roll into Lebak?" Franklin asked.

"We hope," Domingo said. "Let's see what new surprises the rebels have for us."

It came from the rear, and they didn't know it was there until a machine gun mounted on a jeep chattered a dozen rounds at them, breaking out the rear window and puncturing one tire. Domingo had the Bull Pup up in a second, aimed out the blown-out rear glass, and fired a contact round at the jeep. The round hit the radiator, and exploded on contact, smashing the little rig off the road, rolling it three times, and sending the two live rebels in the vehicle flying through the air.

The Toyota slid across the road and wound up sideways in the wrong lane. Franklin shut it down.

"Casualty report," Franklin said.

"Got some glass in the back of my head, but nothing serious," Canzoneri said.

"Fine here," Domingo said. "I love this twenty-millimeter."

Franklin jerked open the door and checked the tire.

"Blown to hell," he said. "Do we have a spare?"

"A car this old damn well better have one," Canzoneri said. "Usually older cars have lousy rubber."

They found the spare in the trunk, along with two sub-machine guns and a box of ammo. It took Franklin twelve minutes to change the tire with the bumper jack.

"I used to have contests changing tires," he said. "I almost always won."

Domingo had scraped most of the shattered glass from the rear seat of the car by the time they drove away from the wrecked jeep. They didn't look for survivors.

At twenty miles from the hostage house, they found roads that went off from the highway every mile or so, usually one into the mountains and then one to the beach. All were plain dirt roads, some that had been graded up, some just tracks in the jungle and coastal grasses.

A few houses began to appear.

"If we don't find a lot of rebel uniforms in town, how do we play it?" Franklin asked.

"If the rebels don't control the town, there should be a police station. We'll start there. If the town is under police control, we'll have no trouble phoning out. I'll use their phone."

"Damn big 'if,' " Franklin said.

Canzoneri, in the front seat, growled. "We have some trouble up ahead. Looks like another roadblock. This one has a truck in the middle of the road and a swing-up bar across the traffic lane."

"Only two uniforms, they look different," Franklin said.

"Could be Filipino Army men," Domingo said. "Let's ease up and stop and see what the situation is."

"Too dangerous," Franklin said. "I'm keeping one of them in my sights. Canzoneri, you aim for the second one. If it isn't what it seems to be, we blast them and race on through."

"I'm not sure of those uniforms," Domingo said. "Not even sure that my Army would post any men out here. And if we did, why a roadblock?"

When the car came to within a hundred yards of the block, one soldier held up a submachine gun in both hands for them to stop. He was on the driver's side. Another armed man stood on the passenger's side. Both stood waiting.

Franklin stopped the car five feet from the guards, who swung up their weapons.

"Step out of the car, please," one guard said in English. The other guard said something in Filipino.

Domingo frowned and said something back in Filipino.

"Not our men," Domingo shouted. Franklin felt the first round from the guard's submachine gun hit the Toyota.

20

Franklin jerked his Colt carbine up over the car's windowsill and slammed three rounds into the chest of the surprised guard, who had fired into the door panel evidently as a warning shot. Domingo had out his .45 pistol, and fired three times so fast they sounded like one round. The rebel on the passenger's side caught one in the chest, one in his throat, and the third one on his forehead, jolting him backward like he'd been yanked to the rear by a rope.

"Charge!" Canzoneri said, looking out the window for a new target. He found none. The thin pole across the single lane of the roadway that was left open shattered against the front of the Toyota just below the hood ornament and splintered away on both sides.

They were through. There appeared to be no one beside the two guards at the block.

"What the hell next?" Franklin asked. "How far are we from the real town?"

"More buildings along here, looks like some houses too," Canzoneri said.

"Looks like this could be the start of the town, the old barangay," Domingo said. "Several families would settle an area together and give it its name. The practice is still around, but often now used in sections of a larger city. This has that feel. Like several of these barangays merge and you have a small town."

"I can see more buildings ahead," Franklin said. "Looks like a real town with wooden buildings and even some telephone poles."

"Watch for rebels in their green uniforms," Domingo said. "If the police are controlling the town, then there probably won't be any rebels carrying guns. Most Filipinos don't own guns."

Franklin slowed. Now they could see children playing in the yards. There were no real streets yet, just some roads wandering off toward the sea.

"Should we turn in here and not be so obvious?" Franklin asked.

"Not yet," Domingo said. "Up there at those two-story buildings would be a good spot to give it a try."

Two men standing near a small house with a corrugated metal roofed stared at them as they drove past. No wave, no friendly smiles.

"Probably think we're rebels," Domingo said. He dropped the magazine out of his .45, and pushed three fresh rounds into it, filling it up. Now he had eight shots again.

The buildings were looking more Western now, but some nipa huts with their thatched roofs were still mixed in.

"Next street to the right," Domingo said. It was more of an order this time. Franklin grinned. "Aye aye," he said.

The street had wooden-frame buildings on both sides. The street was dirt, and looked like it had been freshly watered to keep down the dust. Halfway along the street Franklin saw a two-story building with a Philippine flag flying over it. A telephone pole nearby trailed lines into the building that could be both telephone and electrical.

"That one?" Franklin asked.

"Ah, yes, the flag. That's either the city hall or the police station or maybe the post office," Domingo said. "Worth a try. Keep your weapons out of sight and stay in the car. My turf now, okay?"

"Yes. We'll sit tight," Canzoneri said.

"I'm leaving the rifle here, just my .45 on my hip. I doubt if I'll have any trouble. If I can, I'll use one of their phones. If I'm not out in ten minutes, bring your weapons and come in softly and gently. It may just be trouble with the phone lines."

Franklin eased the Toyota to a stop in front of the building. He saw only four other cars in the street. General Domingo slid out of the car and walked directly to the front door of the building. It had four windows showing on the street, but they weren't big enough that the SEALs could see inside.

Domingo turned the knob and walked inside with a military manner. It was the police station. He saw only two uniformed men behind a long counter across the front. A woman not in uniform sat behind a pair of telephones. She looked up.

"Yes, how may I help you?"

"I'd like to speak with the police commander."

"I'm sorry, he's not here this week. We do have a lieutenant who you can talk to. What is your name, please?"

"Captain Nofrando Domingo. I'm a policeman from another area. It's quite urgent."

The woman chattered at one of the uniformed men. She spoke in Filipino, which Domingo understood. She said, "He says he's a policeman, so be careful."

The man stood and came to the counter. He held out his hand. "Lieutenant Rosales, temporarily in charge here. Will you come into the office where we can talk?"

Domingo had scanned the small area. Nothing seemed out of order or dangerous. A filled gun cabinet on the wall with a glass front had a keyhole on the door. It could be locked.

"Yes, of course."

They went into a room to the left and the lieutenant closed the door. Domingo saw the office had another door leading back into the other areas of the building.

Rosales sat in a chair behind a clean-topped desk and smiled.

"Now, what's the business that you have?"

"First, jurisdiction. In my charts there is no major policing presence here in Lebak. Most matters are handled by the police in Kiamba or Cotatabo."

"Progress, Captain Domingo. We were granted jurisdiction here only two months ago. It's not unusual that you had not been informed. Where are you stationed?"

"I'm usually at Buayan. Here on a special mission for the President. You may have heard about it. It's called the further integration of our aboriginal people."

"Yes, that's moving along nicely for us. We've contacted two of the tribes up in the hills."

"Good. I can make a good report then. I need to call Davao. I trust your microwave units are working properly?"

"Davao? I'd think you would report to Manila."

"Usually. The Vice President is handling most of this and he's in Davao for another day. So I need to get your report to him quickly."

"I'll check to see if the lines are available," the lieutenant said, starting to stand.

"I can do that myself, Lieutenant. Please stand and face the wall and lace your fingers on top of your head."

"What? You are joking."

Domingo drew the .45 in one practiced move and centered the muzzle on the lieutenant's chest. "Now would be a good time to move, Lieutenant. Face to the wall, hands on top of your head, and lean in and touch your forehead to the wall. Now, or I'll shoot you dead."

Slowly the man complied. Domingo went behind the desk, picked up the phone. He dialed information. "Yes, operator, I need the number for the Davao Air Base in Davao. Yes, in Davao." He waited. A moment later he wrote the number down on a pad of paper on the desk.

"Could you dial it for me, operator? My phone isn't working well." He paused. "Yes, thank you." He waited for it to ring. The policeman edged toward the door. "Not another inch, or you're dead, you rebel. Stay right there.

"Yes, I want the base commander," Domingo said into the phone. It took a few moments; as he waited, a knock came on the door.

"No, no messages, wait outside," Domingo called loudly.

"This is Colonel Romano," said the voice on the phone.

"Colonel, Nofrando Domingo. We need two CH-46's to fly at once to a rock house on the west coast about thirty miles north of Lebak. Get them off for a round trip within ten minutes. You'll have thirty-one return passengers." He paused, listening.

"Yes, I'm fine, the other bird did go down. No casualties. Get those birds over there as quickly as possible."

He hung up, and had started to turn when a shot blasted into the room from the room's back door and he felt a searing, knife-sharp pain in his right shoulder. He dropped the .45 and grabbed his arm.

"Now, Mr. Domingo, or should I say General Domingo, we have a bit of a turn of events, no?" Rosales said. "I have some questions for you. Thanks, Pepe. I can handle the general for now. Check out those other two men in the Toyota out front."

Just as he said it, the door to the front of the office burst open and Franklin stormed in, the Colt Carbine out in front. He saw the man holding the pistol near the back door and before the rebel could move, Franklin took him down with three rounds in the chest. The sound of the three cartridges going off filled the room with a bouncing thundering sound that kept going from wall to wall.

Right behind Franklin came Canzoneri, and just as Franklin shot, Canzoneri put a single round in Lieutenant Rosales's chest where his heart was supposed to be. He went down like a brain-shot steer in a slaughterhouse.

When the sound faded, Domingo bent and grabbed his .45 off the deck. Canzoneri looked at the general's right shoulder, and used a kerchief from around his neck as a bandage and a wad of tissue from a box on the desk for a pad, wrapping the entry wound tightly to stop the bleeding.

"Just a tad late, guys," Domingo said. "When did you figure them for ringers?"

"When the woman out front listened to your talk on the telephone," Franklin said. "The woman had a tap on the line at the desk. The other one vanished out the back and we tied her up, then came in, as you say, a tad too late."

"You get through to the air base?" asked Canzoneri.

"Yes, the base commander said he'd get two CH-46's on the way within fifteen minutes. So, we should have those thirty-one hostages on their way to Davao soon."

"Now how do we find the other eighteen?" Franklin asked.

"I was hoping we could ask one of these two, but looks like we're too late."

"What about the broad outside?" Canzoneri said. "She can still talk. Should I bring her in here?"

Domingo nodded.

She was young, twenty-eight maybe, Franklin figured. Her skin was a shade lighter than Domingo's. She said her name was Rosa.

"Why all these Mexican names?" Canzoneri asked.

"The Philippines was a colony of Spain for over three hundred years," Domingo said. "They decreed that every person in the country must have a Spanish name. All the Spanish names you see today are holdovers from the Spanish reign."

Domingo turned back to Rosa.

"Now, young lady. You are a rebel, we know that. You have conspired against your homeland. Your two friends here are dead, you can see their bodies. I am trying to be civilized about this, but I do have a short temper. Do not irritate me. Some questions. Where is your home?"

"Here, Lebak."

"Are you married?"

"Yes. I have two children."

"Is your husband a rebel?"

"Yes."

"Where is he?"

"Away with the People's Army."

"Who is the leader of the People's Army?"

"I don't know. None of my friends know."

"What is the Eagle's Nest?"

She flinched when he said the words, and he looked at her closely. "You recognized the name. What is it and where is it?"

Rosa looked straight ahead and didn't say a word.

"Tie her hands behind her back," Domingo said. Franklin did.

"Canzoneri, lock the front door and any back doors. Stand guard out near the front door." He hurried out.

Domingo slapped Rosa gently on each cheek. "Rosa, do you want me to knock you off the chair with a hard slap?"

"No."

"Then answer. What is the Eagle's Nest and where is it?"

"It's where the leader of the Army lives. I don't know where it is."

"You're lying, Rosa. Your husband is there as one of the leader's personal bodyguards. Where is it?"

Rosa stared straight ahead.

Domingo swung his right hand, palm open, and slapped her so hard it knocked her off the chair. She hit the wooden floor hard, and not having her hands to break her fall, she hit on her shoulder and the side of her head.

Domingo nodded at Franklin. He lifted her back on the chair.

He repeated the question. She shook her head. He hit her again, knocking her off the other side of the chair.

When Franklin picked her up, she was crying.

"Strip her to the waist," Domingo ordered. It wasn't a request; it was a general talking to a yeoman second. Franklin used his knife to slice the buttons off a colored blouse, then cut the bra straps and cut the blouse to get it off without untying her hands, then threw the clothing on the floor. At first she tried to hunch her shoulders to hide her breasts.

"Now, we get down to the interesting forms of interrogation," Domingo said. Rosa screeched at him in Filipino. He shouted back at her in the same tongue.

She stopped the words, and began screaming. Domingo took her blouse and jammed it into her mouth.

"Rosa, what would your husband do if he found you had only one breast?" Domingo held out his hand, and Franklin gave him his own carefully honed KA-BAR fighting knife. Domingo grabbed one of her breasts and drew a thin blood-line across the top. He let it go. Rosa looked down at the blood, spat out the gagging blouse, and screamed again. Domingo slapped her quickly twice and she stopped.

"Young lady, I was fighting Moros and other guerrillas when you were a child. I've cut off men's genitals and sent them back to their wives. I've cut all sorts of pieces off prisoners urging them to cooperate on sharing information. I can do the same thing to you. One last time. What is the Eagle's Nest and where is it?"

Rosa sobbed silently for a moment, then stared hard at him.

"It is where our leader lives, his retreat. It is on the mountain about ten miles north of here and up in the hills overlooking the sea. Some say it is six miles from the waves."

"Now, that wasn't so hard, was it, Rosa? Is that where they took the last eighteen hostages this morning?"

"I don't know."

General Domingo stared hard at her. "I believe you," he said. "Now, how many rebels in town?"

"Only eight."

"Where are they?"

"Some in stores, offices."

"Call them all. Tell them there is a special meeting here in ten minutes. Have them come here."

Franklin handed her the blouse. He untied her hands, and she shrugged into it. It was cut so much that it didn't cover her.

"I have another blouse," Rosa said.

Domingo motioned them away. Franklin went out the door with her and watched her put on the new blouse. She didn't turn her back as she slipped it on. Franklin let her go to her desk; then he checked it and found a knife and two small handguns. He took them all.

"Make the calls, now," Franklin said. "Don't warn them in any way, or I'll shoot you, just the way I killed that man in the office."

"Speak in English," Domingo said.

She made the calls, took no arguments, gave no reasons, just told them to be at the police station in ten minutes.

Canzoneri had checked out the rest of the building. There was a small jail in back, three cells, and in each was a real police officer. He let them out and told them what was happening. They said they would help. Two officers stood on one side of the main door. They locked both rear doors. When the first rebel came in he was dressed in a summer suit, and went down hard when one of the policemen slammed the butt of his pistol down on the man's head.

The next three were held under guns, put on the floor,

and tied. When the fifth one came in, he was suspicious and already had a revolver in his hand. He saw the men on the floor and lifted the weapon, but Domingo put two .45 slugs into his chest and he went down and died a minute later.

The next three came in quickly, and were put on the floor and tied. One of the policemen seemed to be in charge. He had sergeant's stripes, and grinned when the last rebel was down.

"They steamed in here three days ago and took over," the man said. "Oh, I'm Sergeant Esteban. I'm in charge here. Not a lot to do, but the rebels wanted a town, I guess."

"The Eagle's Nest," Domingo said.

"Yes, a rich man's estate high up on the edge of the mountain about ten miles north of town. I'm not sure who owns it now. He comes in sometimes for supplies. We get everything in here by boat. We built a pier, but it isn't long enough for big boats."

"Now all we have to do is decide what we do next," General Domingo said. "How do we get word to Murdock? How do we get back through those roadblocks? They will be waiting for us now."

He went over to Rosa. She sat at her desk, not moving, not looking at anyone. "Rosa, how many guards does your leader have at his Eagle's Nest?"

"Fifty, my husband told me that."

"Figures," Domingo said. Then he grinned. He took out the piece of paper and dialed the phone number. A short time later he spoke to the air base commander.

"Colonel Romano. Did those choppers take off on time?"

"Yes, sir, General Domingo. Armed and ready. They won't have any trouble finding that rock house."

"Good. Now I want you to radio them to divert one to Lebak, down here thirty miles south of the rock house right on the coast. Also, radio the pilot to tell Commander Murdock that we believe the missing eighteen hostages are at the Eagle's Nest, about twenty miles south of him high on the mountain cliffs."

"Yes, sir. I have that information."

"Now, I want you to send here to Lebak two more CH-

46's with ten Rangers on each one combat ready with triple regular ammunition. Get them into the air within a half hour. Got that?"

"Yes, sir. We have relayed the radio messages. The diverting chopper says he'll be at Lebak in approximately thirty minutes. The other two birds won't be there quite that fast."

"Thanks, Colonel. Oh, if you need me, you can call here at this number." He gave the number of the police station and hung up.

"Well, Sergeant. Looks like you need to get your jail cleaned up. Two bodies in the office over there. I could use some first aid and a doctor for my shoulder, and you have jail cells for these rebels. Get them moving. Rosa goes in a cell too."

"Eagle's Nest?" Canzoneri asked.

"Yeah, but first we have to find it, then figure out how to take it when they have fifty guns up there," Franklin said.

"Only fifty?" Canzoneri asked. "Hell, piece of cake."

21

Rock House
Mindanao West Coast

Murdock had done everything he could think of. Juan had continued to question the prisoner until he died, but had learned nothing more.

"Happens," Juan said.

Murdock ignored it. He checked with the hostages again, and all were excited about being rescued and at last getting on with their travels. Now it would be straight home for most of them. They had loved the tuna sandwiches and fruit, and Jaybird had another meal for them made from some canned meat he'd found in a storage closet. He soon found flour and potatoes, and relaxed and got ready to fix another meal for the hostages.

They had complete security. If any of the rebels had survived and run into the jungle, they were heading somewhere else and not trying to attack the compound. Murdock found a radio in one of the upstairs bedrooms and caught up on the news. The government was still pressing the rebels trying to get the hostages released, informed sources in Manila reported.

Murdock laughed. They had no more casualties. The pilot of the chopper was feeling better. Khai's broken arm wasn't so good, and Mahanani said it might have to be rebroken if it had started to heal crooked.

It was after 1300, and Murdock was starting to wonder if the general and his team had had any trouble getting to

Lebak. If they had, he and the platoon might have a few days to sit here waiting for a chopper.

He was in the backyard of the place, trying to figure out if a forty-six could land in the area, when he heard the familiar whirling and churning sound of a helicopter.

Half the SEALs appeared as if by magic when the bird came closer. Then it was right overhead. Murdock grabbed a red flare off his shoulder and lit it and tossed it in the middle of the open space behind the hostage structure.

The pilot circled the area again, then came in upwind and gently settled the giant windmill to the ground. A cheer went up from a dozen hostages who had crowded out the door when they heard the helicopter coming in.

The pilot let the bird run, and came out to talk with Murdock.

"Commander, I'm Captain Jonas Virac. I have some messages for you. First the general and your two men are fine and safe. They are in Lebak. One of our birds was rerouted to Lebak. The general says that they think they know where the rest of the hostages are. In the Eagle's Nest, which is about twenty miles south of you and ten miles north of Lebak.

"We are supposed to take the thirty-one hostages and transport them ASAP to Davao. You will remain here for transport by the bird that is now in Lebak. Any questions?"

"Your chopper pilot Captain Samar is a little shaken up, but in good shape. We were shot down by a sniper on the ground. He'll go back with you on this run."

"Good, we've been worried about him. Commander, we can leave as soon as you get the people loaded on board. We have doors on the sides so we can close them and not lose anybody."

Murdock went into the hostage area and began sending the people two at a time out to the helicopter.

"Take anything with you that you have. I don't know about luggage, but I haven't seen any."

"The damn rebels stole everything we owned," one woman yelled.

"There will be thirty-two of you and it will be close quarters, but even if you have to stand up, the flight is only for a little over forty minutes. Please help us all you can, and we'll get you all out of here and home safely."

The loading took almost twenty minutes. One little lady had to be carried, and they put in a small chair for her to sit in during the trip. The thirty-two fit in snugly, but some of them found places to sit down.

"Commander, we're buttoned up. I may be back, not sure. All hell broke lose back at the base when we found out that other bird was overdue and unreported and that the general was on board. Then the S & R guys found the burned-out hulk and we didn't know what to think."

"All's well."

"Oh, the bird that went to Lebak will probably be up to get you shortly and transport you down there. That will be the staging area for a shot at the Eagle's Nest. Good luck, Commander."

The CH-46's rotors spun faster, and it lifted off smoothly, gained altitude, and turned gently so it wouldn't upset any of the very important cargo it carried.

Murdock waved, then looked to the south. How long would it be before the forty-six from Lebak came to haul them out south so they could look for the next eighteen hostages?

Murdock was heading back to the main house when he heard the shots. Rifle shots from a distance. He sprinted for the corner of the rock and wood house.

"Anyone hit by those shots?" he asked on the net.

Jaybird shouted a warning into the mike. "More incoming," he said, and then Murdock heard the new shots. A submachine gun chattered off a dozen rounds.

"Where are those shots coming from?" Murdock asked.

"From the south side of the compound, in back of the guards' quarters," Jaybird said. "May be two shooters. We've got one man down. I think it's Train. I'm into the woods to circle those bastards."

"Take another man with you," Murdock said.

"Nobody here. I'm gone."

Murdock ran toward the guards' barracks. He was shielded from the shooters. He paused at the side of the place and peered around the corner. He saw Tran "Train"

Khai sprawled near a chair that had tipped over. The chair was in a patch of shade. He watched closely. Train wasn't moving.

"Anybody else see where those shots came from?" Murdock asked. For the first time he realized he didn't have his weapon. He'd been too quick to decide this was a secure area.

"Yeah, to the south somewhere," Van Dyke said. "Heard them, but didn't see any flashes. They must be deep inside the bush out there."

"Two of them?" Murdock asked.

"My guess. Or one guy and two weapons."

"Everybody go to ground and stay out of sight. Can anybody see Train?"

"Yeah, I have him," Howard said. "He's down and I don't see him moving."

"Who has weapons?" Murdock asked. Four men sounded off. "I want you to give me some cover. Fire into the brush to the south. Jaybird, get behind a big tree for a minute."

"Roger that," Jaybird said.

"Cover me, now," Murdock said. He waited for the first shots, then charged around the corner of the guard building and raced the forty feet to where Train lay. He scooped him up like a sack of wheat and pounded back the way he had come and around the corner.

Murdock put Train on the ground and looked for the hit. He didn't find it at first. Then he looked closer, pulled open his shirt, and there it was, one small turning-purple hole right over his heart. He'd died in the microsecond that the bullet hit him.

"Cease fire," Murdock said. "Tran is gone. Took one round in the heart. Every man with a weapon, now, and stay under cover. Get the bastards, Jaybird."

Jaybird came out from behind the large mahogany tree and worked forward. He moved like a ghost, not making a sound, edging under, around, and through the growth, not fighting it, accepting it and passing it by. He stopped to listen. Nothing. He worked ahead again toward the spot he had picked out as most likely to hold the snipers.

Again he stopped. He listened, but heard nothing. He

worked ahead for twenty yards and stopped. This time he heard whispering. Two of them. He angled to the right, worming his way through heavy growth flat on his belly, his H & K MP-5 sub gun cradled on his forearms. Jaybird stopped and listened. More whispers. Then a clicking sound. A fresh magazine sliding home into the receiver.

Jaybird headed directly for the whispers now. He figured he was still twenty feet away. Then he edged around a tree trunk and saw them. Both had settled down behind a mahogany tree that had fallen long ago and was three feet thick. They must have lifted up and fired over the trunk, then dropped down.

Jaybird was behind the log. He sighted in on single-shot and drove one 9mm Parabellum through the side of the farthest man's skull. He jolted to the side. The other man fell to the ground and began to squirm away. Jaybird watched him, pushed the lever to three rounds, and sprayed the rebel with twelve rounds. Jaybird waited a minute, then moved in and checked the weapons. A sub gun and an AK-47. He took them and extra magazines and hiked back to the compound.

"Scratch two in the first race," Jaybird said on the net. "Two down and dirty. Is Train really gone?"

"Afraid so, Jaybird," Murdock said. "A heart shot. Nothing we can do."

"Fuck!"

"You can say that again," Van Dyke said.

"Fuck again," Jaybird said.

It was almost a half hour later before they heard the sound of the chopper coming in. They had raided the big house for all the good food they could find. Mahanani found a bottle of whiskey that he confiscated for "medical purposes only" and put in his pack. Four men covered the south area in a defensive line as the bird landed in the backyard. General Domingo was the first one out of the craft, and he grinned.

"Got us some airpower," he said. "You get our guests off all right?"

"No problem, General. Only we had a sniper attack by

two of the guards we flushed out when we came. They caught one man in the open and he's KIA."

"Sorry, Murdock. I know how close you men become. A damn shame. You track down the snipers?"

"Jaybird did and they paid the price. You know where the other hostages are?"

"It's a probable. Maybe the leader of the rebels too. I've got twenty Army Rangers coming in and two more birds. We're going to have a shot at this place bright and early in the morning."

"Why not tonight?"

"We're not sure where we're going, and we don't want to tip him off with a recon flight. We can talk about it. We'll get you and your men out of here and in some quarters in Lebak, and take him at dawn."

"We need to get Tran on his way back to the States."

"Yes, we'll do that as soon as we get to Lebak. A chopper will take him to Davao. I'll have the Army provide a casket and do preliminary work, then get him on a flight to the States as quickly as possible."

"I'll need to call San Diego in California and tell my CO. He'll notify the family."

Senior Chief Sadler had the men police the area. When they were done, no one could prove that the SEALs had been there, except for the line of corpses by the barracks. They left the two in the jungle where they had fallen. The men put Train on the chopper first, then the rest filed on, looking more serious than usual.

Murdock gave the general a thumbs-up, and the general spoke to the first lieutenant flying the chopper and it lifted off, on its way down the coast as the afternoon shadows began to lengthen.

The first thing Murdock did when they landed at Lebak was go to the police station and use their telephone. It took fifteen minutes to get the right operator and get through to San Diego.

Commander Dean Masciareli was not pleased to take the call. He knew it was Murdock.

"This better be damn important, Murdock. It's two A.M. here."

"We lost a man today, Tran Khai. One bullet right through his heart. He's on his way home. Somebody has to tell his folks. This is an open mission, so you can tell his mother exactly what is going on, how we just rescued thirty-one hostages. The boy's a hero and should get a medal. I'll leave that up to you."

Masciareli scowled, then let out a long sigh. "Yeah, Murdock, I'll make the phone call, and somebody nearest his home will send out a chaplain to tell them. Least we can do. You done there?"

"No, sir. We still have eighteen hostages we need to find. But we think we know where they are. We're eating a lot of bananas."

"Fine, let me know when you close that operation. I'll call the CNO, but this should be an open newsworthy mission. Then I'll call the closest base to Khai's family. Out."

Murdock snorted and hung up the phone. Yeah, out. That's how he felt at that minute. Another KIA. That was ten or eleven? Christ, he couldn't even remember. He had the number back in Coronado.

By the time Murdock came out of the police station and walked two blocks over to their barracks, the next two choppers from Davao had landed. The ten Filipino Army Rangers who charged out of each bird looked fit and combat ready. They bunked with the SEALs in a warehouse where cots of all kinds had been hurriedly set up by the local police.

The men filed through a local restaurant for a late lunch, and were served large portions of adobo. It was a dark, saucy stew of chicken and pork, flavored with vinegar and soy sauce, garlic, and chunks of liver. There were stacks of rolls and butter, coffee, and a big fruit salad served family-style in huge stainless-steel bowls.

"Better than MREs," Ching said.

General Domingo had been busy. He called Murdock, a lieutenant from the Rangers, and Murdock's brain trust of DeWitt, Sadler, Jaybird, and Lam to a conference at the end of the warehouse.

"I've found two men who know the Eagle's Nest," Domingo said. "It was built about ten years ago by a reclusive millionaire. He lived there for two months, then his wife died and he left the place and sold it. We're not sure who owns it now, but we do have a sketch of the place, the road, the buildings, and something of the inside of the main house.

"It may have been changed a lot by now. We do know that there has been a large barracks and mess hall built to serve the fifty guards that the leader has up there. He never comes into town. He sends someone for whatever he needs. The guards up there are not rotated. They are his permanent private guard team. Which means they know the landscape, the weak points, and the spots where someone could try to get in. That makes it a lot tougher."

"Where might he have the hostages?" Lam asked.

"Our guess is in the barracks building. Part of it could be used for the eighteen."

"What about access?" the Ranger lieutenant named Quezon asked.

"There's a good road up from the highway on the coast. It's about six miles, the locals say. There are no trails or any other easy access from the sides or back. In back of the place there is a four-hundred-foot vertical wall that geologists have had trouble explaining. So it's possible to get someone in from both sides."

"What kind of a schedule are we talking about?" Murdock asked.

"Sooner the better for the hostages," Domingo said. He had on a different shirt now, one with gold stars on the shoulders. Murdock had grinned at him when he saw the Rangers two hours ago. "General, you're back in command. You have more men than I do."

"We'll work it together. But with my men here, I better wear the stars."

"I'm wondering how long it would take to hike up on each side of the place and hit it from both sides," Murdock said. "The road is out as access. He must have it well defended."

Juan spoke up. "General Domingo, I like the idea of hitting them from the sides. It will take a little more time, but if we took off from here by truck and came within a mile of the road up the mountain, then jumped off and one half of us went straight up the mountain, and the other half hiked a mile the other side of the Eagle's Nest road . . ."

Heads nodded all the way around.

"Seems to be a consensus," General Domingo said.

"We'll take the far side," Murdock said.

"No," Domingo said. "You've been in the field for three days. I'll take the fresh troops the extra two miles. What's your ETA on the attack site, Murdock?"

"Up that hill six miles?" Murdock scowled. "Jaybird?"

"Two hours, sir."

"Should work," Lieutenant Quezon said.

Domingo rubbed his face. "We won't be able to use the twenties until we're sure where the hostages are. However, we can use the EAR. Commander, I'd like to have you attach one of your men with an EAR to Lieutenant Quezon's unit."

"Done. We'll need communications with all parties. We'll send six Motorolas to the Rangers to use for coordination."

"Range of the radios?" Quezon asked.

"Five to six miles, depending on the line of sight," Jaybird answered.

"What advance planning do we need to take care of?" General Domingo asked.

"Not much else we can do, General, until we see the layout," DeWitt said. The others nodded.

"Agreed. Juan, can you find transport for us? A big stake truck or five or six vans. Tell the owners it's a temporary confiscation. I'll have a portable radio that I can use to contact the three aircraft. I don't want to use the choppers to take us down the road so we won't alert anyone."

"Roadblocks," Jaybird said.

"Two of them between here and ten miles," Domingo said, looking at Jaybird. "Did you talk to Franklin?"

"Yes, sir. He said one about a mile out of town, and the other one was more than seven or eight miles away from here."

"So we could have two of them, if they have been reestablished. We put the twenties in the lead cars, side by side down the roadway. If the blocks are there, the twenties can do the job and we crash on through just at dusk. Get to our objective and hike up the hill. The transport will return to Lebak."

"Anything more about the target?" Murdock asked.

"Reports say the jungle comes within a dozen feet of the buildings in many places," Domingo said. "There is an open area we can land a chopper in. There are four buildings there: garage for three cars; big house; one large building that might be for machinery or recreation, we're not sure; and the barracks."

"Suggestion," Murdock said. "We put one EAR and two twenties with the Rangers. Then we both get into position, say a hundred yards from the site, and do any last-minute planning by radio. We'll hit them tonight. We can take out the guards outside with the EAR. Then work a couple of EAR shots into the main house and one into the garage and the building we're not sure of. If we put to sleep some hostages, it won't hurt them. When the EAR shots are done, we move in and try not to shoot each other."

"The leader up there must know that something is happening," Juan said. "Roadblocks blown apart, choppers flying over. A runner or a man on a bicycle could have gone to the mountain by now and told him who we are and how many men we have. What I'm saying is that the rebels could be on a fifty-percent alert."

"The safety and welfare of the hostages has to be our first concern," Sadler said. They all nodded.

There was a pause. General Domingo looked around. "All right. We're done here. It will be dark in two hours. Get your men ready and we'll move out at that time. A half hour to our point of departure and then we hike. Two hours for the hike and positioning. We'll keep track of each other by radio as we move." He paused. "Any chance that the rebels could monitor the Motorolas?"

Jaybird shook his head. "No, sir. Not unless they have a greatly sophisticated scanner that checks all frequencies. Doubtful."

They broke up and went to an early chow at the same restaurant they went to before. Domingo said the Philippine

Army was picking up the tab. The food was good, different this time, roast pork with lots of vegetables and ice cream for dessert.

An hour later they left the village in two large trucks, and drove past the first roadblock, which had been burned out and not replaced. The second one came up soon, and they could see a new truck across the road. It was just dusk and the roadblock truck turned on its lights shining down the road. "Twenties," Murdock said. "Two only, Lam and I." They fired.

The truck erupted in flames and rolled off the road.

"Clear ahead," Murdock said, and the trucks raced ahead and rolled past the former roadblock, which showed two bodies near the truck.

Five minutes later they stopped where Domingo decided was about a mile from the road that led up to the Eagle's Nest. They had been driving with lights out, and now the trucks stopped side by side on the roadway. Murdock's radio came on and they all listened.

"Murdock, not sure what to make of this, but there is a lot of firing up front there about where that next roadblock should be."

"Hear it. My guess is that they're green troops shooting at shadows and ghosts of their ancestors. They are now in a combat situation, maybe for the first time, and getting nervous."

"Should we send up a patrol and check it out?" Domingo asked.

"No," Murdock said. "Let them have their fun. Then they won't spot your troops going across the road as you move on north of them."

"Yes. Let's dismount, troops, and get ready to move out."

22

Near Lebak
Mindanao Philippines

Murdock lined up his men in the usual marching order, with Lam out in front by twenty yards. Even that close, it was hard to see him sometimes in the gloom of the rain forest. Murdock was behind him, then Alpha Squad with Juan attached, and then Bravo Squad. Lieutenant (j.g.) DeWitt acted as rear guard. They went single file at five-yard intervals. The Philippine sergeant went with the general. Murdock had assigned Bill Bradford to go with the general's platoon with the Bull Pup and twelve rounds of 20mm. Miguel Fernandez took one of the EAR weapons and joined the Filipino platoon.

The narrow plain here next to the Moro Gulf was about two miles wide; then the mountains rose up in a series of gentle ridges, each one higher than the last. Murdock didn't know how high they were, but the highest peak in Mindanao and in the Philippines was Mount Apo at over 9,600 feet. These hills were far lower than that, but dirty to climb.

The rain-forest jungle was unrelenting as they worked their way up one ridge after another one. Now and then they could spot the splash of lights above them that they knew must be the target, the Eagle's Nest.

Murdock called a halt after an hour. He went on the net. "General, we're taking a break, figure about halfway up. How is it going?"

"We're about the same place. Tough going at night. We should surprise them. Your two men are doing well."

"Reception is good. This is as far apart as we will be. I'll check later when we turn toward the target."

They went back to the climb. It was tougher now, over the roots and vines and around the branches and trees. There were all kinds of trees here they didn't have names for except the huge towering mahogany. They came to the top of a ridge, and ahead and to the left they could see the Eagle's Nest. It was still above them on the next slope below the ridgeline. This was their last one. Now they could swing to the left and approach the target.

Murdock talked with Lam and they moved in that direction. There were still some slopes to climb, but not all the way up the ridge. That was progress.

Murdock called in the change in direction to the general. "Figure about twenty minutes to be in position," Murdock said.

"We're not quite that far along," General Domingo said. "Hold your attack position until we contact you."

"Roger that, General," Murdock said, and moved quicker before he lost Lam in the darkness.

It took twenty-five minutes before Lam stopped, and Murdock almost stepped on him.

"Here we are," Lam whispered. They were fifty yards from the blazing lights.

"We're fifty yards out and holding," Murdock said on the net.

"Give us ten minutes and we'll be there," Domingo said.

"I didn't figure on all these lights," Lam said.

"Might help us," Murdock said. "We use the EAR to take out the guards and anyone we can see. Then when someone investigates, they are lit up like in a shooting gallery."

"Right. And if we need to douse those lights we can do it with a few rounds later."

"Wish we knew where the hostages are. Then we could put about six twenties into the barracks and wipe out half of their guard force."

"We might do it yet. After we hit the guards with the EAR, a recon might be worthwhile."

"You trying to get yourself killed, Lampedusa?" Murdock asked. He grinned. "Yeah, a recon might be good. But if we do one, I'm going with you."

They waited.

The radio earpieces chirped.

"In place, fifty yards out, and setting up fields of fire," General Domingo said.

"Right. We're in position. We have a small exposed part here where we have excellent fire lanes. So far we've seen only one guard. He's near the main house. Haven't seen any roving guards. Must be some. Suggest we wait for twenty and check."

"That's a roger, Commander."

"General, do your troops have any silencers on their weapons?"

"No."

"We're thinking of a recon after we use the EAR. Lam and I would go in and locate the hostages. Take out any guards who saw us with silenced rounds, then ID the guards' barracks for a batch of twenties. You approve?"

"Let's use the twenties when ready and see what reaction we get," Domingo said.

"Roger."

They waited the rest of the twenty minutes.

"I see one guard working the perimeter fence," Lam said.

"Another guard on our side walks behind the house and the new barracks building," one of the Filipino Rangers said.

Five minutes later they had six guards' positions tied down and knew their routes.

"We'll do the three we can see here on command," General Domingo said. "Murdock, you have your man do the guards on that side. Not more than twenty seconds and we should have all of them. That's with ten seconds between shots."

"Roger that, General. Our EAR is up to power. Whenever you're ready."

"Ready, EAR weapons, aim, and . . . fire," Domingo said.

Kenneth Ching took out the guard beside the front of the barracks first, then moved his sights to the roving guard who had just turned from the widest spot on the perimeter fence and started back to the big house. He never made it, crumpling and lying still in the warm night air. Chin nailed the third guard when he ran over to look at the fallen body of the first one.

"Three down," Ching said.

"Three more hit the dirt," Fernandez said.

"What about the big house and the windows in the barracks?" Domingo asked.

"Rather do a quick recon," Murdock said. "We're home free so far. We'll take silenced weapons and take a look, then get out of the way when you want to use the EAR or the twenties."

"Go," Domingo said.

Murdock and Lam had already arranged to trade weapons, and both headed for the compound with their MP-5's with silencers attached. They moved without a sound, paused at the edge of the lighted area, then carried the MP-5's by the top handles and walked across the lighted area to the edge of the first big building.

They would each check different buildings. Lam ran thorough the shadows to the door on the biggest building. He turned the knob and opened it slowly. Inside, night lights showed a barracks with double bunks, and military gear all over the place. No sign of hostages. He slipped out and closed the door without a sound.

Murdock checked the second large building. One guard had been near the door. He lay sleeping, his rifle a few feet away. Murdock opened the door gently, saw night lights in back, and behind a heavy wire fence partitioning off the far end of the building were bunks and civilian clothes. He ran in and made sure. Eighteen bunks, but only six women in them. He ran soundlessly back to the door, slipped out, and looked for Lam. He didn't see him.

"Lam," he said on the radio. "Let's get out of the lights. Six hostages are in the second big building. We've got to check the garage. Might be more hostages in there. Let's ramble."

They ran to the garage and found the door open. They looked inside, but it was totally dark. Murdock pulled out his penlight, held it at arm's distance from his body, and shone it around. A gun blasted from almost in front of him, but the round went under Murdock's hand where the shooter figured the body would be.

Lam fired two three-round silent bursts into the muzzle flash area, and they heard a soft moan, then a scream and silence. Murdock shone the narrow beam of light ahead and on the floor, and found a rebel lying there with four bullets in his chest and face. They checked the rest of the garage. Two vehicles, some gasoline drums, but no hostages.

"Let's chogie," Murdock said.

They ran to the fence where they had come in, and jogged back to their positions just outside the floodlighted zone.

"We have the hostages pinpointed," Murdock told the net. "General Domingo, there are six women hostages in the big building. We cleared the garage. No guards, no hostages. They must have moved the other twelve. Guessing there aren't any in the big house. We've moving up to twenty-five yards off the fence and are ready. Suggest six EAR rounds into the main house and the barracks. There are at least forty men in there. Let's put EAR rounds through the windows of the house and barracks until we run out of power. Okay?"

"Yes, let's do it. Then after the EARs, we do the twenties into the barracks and the main house?" Domingo asked.

"That's a roger, General. Open fire with the EARs now."

He heard the whoosh of the EAR round, then ten seconds later a second. Glass smashed at the main house and at the barracks as the blasts of super-accelerated sound smashed inside the buildings. Murdock still didn't understand exactly how they worked, but they sure did.

"Let's do the twenties now," Murdock said. The four twenties fired at the barracks windows, and quickly they heard the rounds exploding inside. Moments later a few half-dressed guards struggled out of the barracks, and the SEALs pounded them with searing streams of hot lead. Murdock heard firing from the other side as the general blasted the big house with the high-explosive 20mm rounds.

Counterfire came from behind the garage area, and two

twenty-rounds there silenced those weapons.

"Cease fire on the twenties," Murdock called. The weapons were silenced, with only an occasional shot coming from the compound.

Suddenly four rebels raced toward the hostages' building. A 20mm round fired from Murdock's left, and the round exploded just in front of the running men, cutting them all down into rag dolls bleeding on the grass.

All was quiet. "My men are going in the big house and clean up," Domingo said. "Murdock, hold fire. We're at the fence now and going over. We'll work the big house first and clear it, then the garage, just to make sure, and the barracks last. We're at the door and going in."

Murdock and his men waited. They saw lights blink on in the big house. Murdock had heard it had fourteen rooms. The second-story lights snapped off and he heard rifle and submachine-gun fire. Then all was silent.

"Watch for any stragglers," Murdock said. "If there are any, the sniper rifle is cleared to fire if the target is for sure a rebel."

They saw none during the next five minutes.

It took an eternity to clear fourteen rooms. At last the earpieces came on.

"Big house cleared. We found six men and four local women. The men are dead. One woman is wounded. The women say there are no guards in the hostage building. We'll move on to the barracks. We have two wounded, one serious. If we clear the area, we may call for a night evac."

"Roger, still holding, covering."

Murdock and the SEALs saw the Rangers move up on the barracks. Firing came from inside. The Rangers went flat against the outside of the building and threw grenades through the broken windows. Then two men forced open the doors and jumped to one side.

The rangers sprayed the inside with submachine-gun fire, then charged inside. Murdock heard only three shots; then lights flared inside the barracks and two more shots sounded.

"Barracks clear," Domingo said on the Motorola. "We have four prisoners for interrogation."

"We'll move up and take over the hostage building," Murdock said. They were halfway there across the sixty-foot-wide grassy area inside the fence when they saw a section of the lawn near the fence move aside. Two men in rebel green uniforms came out of the ground and sprinted for the fence, and were in the jungle before the SEALs could get off a shot.

"Lam and I, after them," Murdock said on the net. "The rest of you occupy the hostage area. Go."

Lam and Murdock charged into the jungle near where the two men had vanished. Just inside the curtain of green, they stopped and listened. Sounds to the left, crashing brush.

They ran that way, dodging around the trees, over vines and brush and a dozen flowering plants. Lam took the lead. He stopped again. For a moment there was no sound; then the steps came again, and the sound of trees and growth being slapped to the side during passage.

They were soon off the flat area near the Eagle's Nest and charging along the side of the slope that towered over them.

"Gaining," Lam said. They had their regular weapons again, Murdock his Bull Pup and Lam his Colt 4A1. They jogged through the growth toward the sounds. Lam knelt down again, listening.

No sounds.

He waited. A sound to the left. He pointed that way. Another to the right. They were being attacked. Lam made a down motion, and both dropped to the ground, slid behind trees, and waited.

Nothing happened for five minutes. Then Lam made some sounds, clanked his Carbine barrel against his KA-BAR and then cleared his throat.

Lam had indicated he would take the left. Murdock stared to the right into the jungle, desperately trying to see anything that looked like a green-clad man. The two men charged from different directions. Murdock blasted with the 5.56 Bull Pup on full auto, and saw his rounds nearly slice a man's form in half. He slammed to the ground six feet from Murdock and never moved.

The second man started to charge, then dodged behind a tree just as Lam fired. The rounds missed. Neither man had fired a shot at the SEALs.

Again a wait. Often in combat the man with the most patience will win, Murdock knew. They waited another five minutes; then Murdock put a dozen rounds into and around the tree that Lam pointed to as the other man's shelter. The rounds brought no response. Murdock crawled to the side behind cover of a log and some huge trees. Two minutes later he used the radio.

"The tree is bare, he's slipped away. We lost him."

They took the dead rebel's submachine gun and ammo belt and walked back to the compound.

A hundred yards away, the lone survivor of the Eagle's Nest heard the retreat of the two attackers and gave a sigh of relief. He had escaped them, he always would. He had no idea how the men had been able to attack him. He had double the guards out, and the roadblocks on the highway. He had not been told that both had been destroyed today.

Muhammad Al Hillah, the leader of all the Muslim rebels in Mindanao, leaned against a tree and sucked in air. He was out of shape. Only the tunnel had saved him. If it hadn't been for that he would be dead or captured. Better dead than captured. He knew how the Army tortured prisoners to get information.

Now he had his fallback position, his number-two camp that almost none of the guards at the Eagle's Nest knew about. Maybe one. He hoped that man had been killed in the fighting. Now he had a long walk. He couldn't risk using the road. It would be a hike through the jungles to his new camp. He could go down near the road and walk along the flat country. That would be easier. He had many miles to go. Down past Lebak at least ten miles.

Muhammad shrugged. The night was young, he was strong, and he had his submachine gun. At Lebak he would grab any car he found and use it, without the owner's approval. The quicker he could get to the secret camp, the better.

He still had negotiating power. He still had those twelve

hostages and more than a million dollars in a solid Filipino bank in Davao under another name. Yes, he was down a little now, but with his men in the secret camp, he would survive, and he would win. It was just a matter of time.

23

Murdock and Lam came back to the compound at the Eagle's Nest just as the mop-up finished. There were thirty-eight dead in the barracks, on the grounds, and in the house. The four prisoners had been questioned, and the most promising was questioned again by Juan.

The session had been brutal and direct. By the time Juan had sliced off the man's second finger he'd told them all he knew, including where the hostages had been taken.

General Domingo called for two helicopters to come pick up the SEALs and Rangers and move them back to Lebak, where they would evaluate the rebel's information and plan the next attack.

"Twelve hostages are still out there," General Domingo said. "Our job is to go out and find them."

The night landings, one at a time by the choppers, were tricky in the small LZ in back of the big house, but they came in. First loaded were the six women hostages, most in their forties and fifties. Then the SEALs went into the same bird and it took off. General Domingo and the Rangers followed in the second forty-six.

When they landed at Lebak, they learned that the general had arranged for the hostages to stay in the town's only hotel and eat there as well.

"Ladies, you will be flown by helicopter to Davao in the morning," Murdock told them.

"That's where our tour started from," one of the ladies said as they were being driven from the improvised landing pad to the hotel.

"My name is Sadie Benjamin and I'm from Oregon. My first trip to the Philippines, and after this, it's gonna be my last."

"Sadie, you're a spoilsport," a little lady with blue-tinted white hair said. "Why, we haven't even been to Manila yet. I'm going there and the tour company is going to pay for it."

Murdock led them into the small hotel, and the manager met them at the front desk. Murdock waved and hurried back out the door.

He rode back to the landing pad, and met the CH-46 as it landed with the Rangers and General Domingo.

Mahanani had treated the wounded Ranger as best he could at the Eagle's Nest. Now the Ranger was driven in a sedan to the only doctor in town. The rifle bullet had gone in his chest and hadn't come out. There was considerable bleeding. Mahanani said he thought the slug must have shattered and had caused a lot of damage. The hospital corpsman gave the Ranger two shots of morphine and got the outside bleeding stopped, but he wondered about internal bleeding.

General Domingo stayed with the wounded Ranger, while Murdock got the men into bunks for the rest of the night. He kept Jaybird, Lam, Sadler, Juan, and DeWitt up to talk over what they had found out. The rebel had given them all he knew. The second hidden camp was south of Lebak about ten miles. It also was in the jungle off the road toward the mountains, but not up so high. The man guessed there were no more than ten or fifteen men there, but they had some of the new weapons. They included RPGs (rocket-powered grenades), a fifty-caliber machine gun, and an armored personnel carrier that they had captured months ago from the Army.

"Some heavy hitters there," Jaybird squawked. "Where they get that kind of firepower?"

"Good old bin Laden," Sadler said. "He dropped three million dollars on them. Buy a lot of firepower with that."

"So how do we counter it?" Murdock asked.

"If we can't take out the equipment and the firepower, we take out the men who run the weapons," Lam said.

"Without men the fucking fifty-caliber don't shoot up nobody."

"Amen to that, brother," DeWitt said.

"This time they'll be on the alert for anyone and everyone," Murdock said. "And I'd bet my grandma's petticoat that they will use the hostages as shields."

General Domingo came into the warehouse they had turned into a barracks. He carried his hat and he slapped it against his leg.

"We lost him. Ranger Carlos Flores died on the doctor's table. The bullet shattered into his lung and collapsed it and caused all sorts of hell. The doctor said Flores died of internal bleeding and there was no way he could stop it with a dike."

"Sorry," Murdock said. "Should be a medal for his family."

"There will be. These are all volunteers I've got." He shook his head, trying to get out of the downcast mood. He checked around the small operations table. "Any ideas where we're going next?"

"Looks like we wait until daylight," Sadler said. "Then we take both choppers up with ten sets of eyes and do a recon on any structures east of the highway and about ten miles south of Lebak."

"What if he has a wilderness camp tucked in under a double canopy down there in the jungle?" DeWitt asked. "If he's down there, there's no way we could spot him."

"Not a chance this man would have a primitive camp," General Domingo said. "We learned his name. He's Muhammad Al Hillah. I remember him. He was in the Army for three or four years. He was one of my sublieutenants. Always was a bit out of kilter. Something just not quite straight and true. He was a perfectionist. He also was the most creature-comfort guy I'd ever seen. He had to have the latest and best of everything. Roughing it for him was going from his air-conditioned sedan to his air-conditioned quarters."

"He's a good tactician, good basic military mind, but he's also an idealist. Right now he's trying to create the Muslim state of Mindanao, and he's been doing all he can to bring it about. We got the name of the man from the second prisoner Juan persuaded."

"You think an air recon will work?" Lam asked.

"Yes," Domingo said at once. "It's all we have. We use both choppers with the best recon eyes we have. We'll take off at daylight. Now let's see about getting these men down for some sleep. We'll get a re-issue of ammunition and supplies in the morning. I'm calling Davao for two more choppers to be landing here with first light. Then we'll get the hostages on their way to Davao, and send Ranger Flores back to that town as well." He nodded at them and headed for the door. "See you in the morning."

Morning came too early for Murdock. He groaned as he slid out of the bunk and pulled on his pants. He was dressed two minutes later, with his combat harness, and took his Bull Pup as he went to the door. Sadler was rousting out the spotters they would take: Jaybird, Lam, Bradford, and Mahanani. DeWitt would be along, three SEALs in each chopper along with three Rangers.

It was just coming light as the six SEALs hiked two blocks to the improvised landing pad on a vacant area across from the city hall. General Domingo was already there with his team. He assigned three Rangers to the second chopper, accepted the three SEALs, and walked over for a conference with Murdock.

"About ten miles down, as that prisoner told us, really could be anywhere from three to fifteen. We'll look sharp for any buildings and when we find one, even a house, we'll buzz it and if needed, land and investigate. Just the idea that we might land should be enough to bring out some kind of attack from them. There will be some farmers in there, I think. I don't know what else. Let's take a look. Oh, I have one of the Motorolas for commo."

Murdock nodded and climbed into the forty-six. He wondered how old it was. Did they buy it new or was it a retread from a U.S. surplus sale?

Five minutes later they had slowed to a crawl in the sky as they cruised over the jungle growth of the heavy rain area just off the highway south. They had seen only one building so far, a cabin in a small clearing that wouldn't hold six people, let alone the hostages and a guard force.

The pilot did a gentle S-turn search pattern, so they had a good look at the area, some of it from two or three angles. A series of plowed fields showed with two terraces to extend the arable land farther up the slope of the mountain. At the far side of them were half a dozen buildings, but most were small, and some had nipa-thatched roofs and woven-reed sidewalls.

"Don't think so," Murdock said as the other chopper circled the buildings.

"Right, too small, too much in the open."

They searched another five miles, working slowly along the widening plain, but found nothing.

At the ten-mile mark they found a road that angled off the main highway and arrowed into the jungle growth up the side of the first ridge.

"Could be interesting," Murdock said. They followed the road, which often vanished under the canopy of trees. Twice they saw buildings along the road, but they too were too small. They came to the end of the road, found only more trees and the mountain extending upward, and retraced their pattern to the road.

Back at the highway, they moved south again, and checked out two more roads into the jungle and up the side of the steep ridge. Nothing.

By noon they had found no trace of any setup that looked as if it could be a hostage camp. They went back to Lebak, ate at an improvised chow hall, and met again over the planning table.

"What else did the rebel say when you questioned him?" Murdock asked Juan.

"Most of it I've told you. He said their leader talked to them every day to keep up their morale, to keep them fired up. He said one day Muhammad told them he was just like they were. While he wasn't afraid to die for Allah, he'd just as soon serve him alive for another fifty years or so. Then he told them he could go to ground if he needed to. He didn't always have to perch in the trees watching his enemies."

Murdock frowned. "Go to ground? What could he mean by that?"

"I asked the rebel. He said he had no idea. Nobody in his group could figure it out. Their leader often said things they didn't understand. They had learned not to question him about them."

"To go into hiding," Jaybird said.

"Yeah, but more than that," Lam said. "He said he could come down out of the trees. That would be the Eagle's Nest. Then he said he could go to ground. What the hell?"

DeWitt grinned. "Hey, go to ground means he's hiding. What did a lot of guys do during World War II? They went underground. Some of them literally in caves."

"General Domingo," Sadler said. "Are there any caves around this area? Would some of the locals know?"

The general said they should. He nodded at Lieutenant Quezon. "Take ten men and canvas the town. Find out about local caves. Bring anybody back here who knows where caves are that are big enough to hold a couple dozen people."

The young officer saluted and hurried outside.

For no good reason, Murdock thought about Don Stroh. He had really come through for them this time with his underhanded, back-room, devious methods to get Colonel Alvarez sacked. Great job. It was that or dump the whole project. Murdock should check in with Stroh, tell him about Tran. He could use the SATCOM.

"Bradford," Murdock bellowed. The big guy who did marine oil paintings in his spare time looked up from his bunk and came jogging over.

"Yes, sir, Skipper."

"Where the hell is our SATCOM? Why didn't we have it when we hit the hill out there in that forty-six?"

"SATCOM, sir? You didn't tell me to bring it. No specific instructions."

Murdock covered his face and nodded. "Yeah, yeah. Okay. I figured by now you knew that the SATCOM was like a part of your skin. You never go anywhere without it, unless specifically instructed. Like on a training swim. Otherwise, you keep that motherfucker in your hand, on your back, or in your pack at all goddamn times. Do you read me, Mr. Bradford?"

"Yes, sir. I . . ." He stopped.

"That's all, sailor. I'll try to have one brought out here on the next chopper run to Davao."

Ten minutes later, General Domingo sent a radio message through their chopper to find the SATCOM in the SEALs gear and have it on the next helicopter flight to Lebak.

Lieutenant Quezon and three of the men came jogging into the warehouse.

"Sir, we've found two men who know about the caves. They're working in their business and say they can't leave it right now. They told us the caves are about eight miles south, up against the mountain at the end of a road. The road isn't good. The caves themselves are large, maybe five hundred feet deep and twenty feet high to the rocky ceiling. Both are dry and were used in ancient days for dwellings. Some say there are extremely old drawings on the walls.

"The men say as far as they know no one is using them now for anything. At one time they were used for storing things. During the war the Japanese stored ammunition and explosives in them. But one of the men thinks all of that has long since been hauled away."

General Domingo left with the three Rangers. "I'll bring one of them back as a guide," he said. "Get the troops resupplied with whatever they need. We'll be flying out in a half hour."

"Be damned," Lam said. "No wonder we didn't see anything. A cave. Cut fresh greenery every day and use it for camouflage to cover the front of the cave, and nobody could find it in a year."

"Now that we know it's there, we take out the camo with two contact twenty rounds, and then blow about a dozen more into the cave and let them explode inside," Jaybird said. "If it has a rock ceiling, the shrapnel is going to ricochet all over the place."

They checked their ammo supply, filled pouches, and then added some extra, cleaned weapons and monitored the charging batteries on the EARs.

Senior Chief Sadler reported to Murdock. "Skipper, the platoon is resupplied and ready to rumble. The men are asking about chow. Yep, they are hungry again."

When the general came back, he had with him a small truck filled with boxes of sandwiches, big urns of coffee, and baskets of fruit.

"We eat and then we fly," he said.

A small Filipino man, who looked like he could be seventy-five, came with the general, and now stood to one side watching everything. He munched on a sandwich, his eyes wide looking at the weapons.

Lam walked over and talked to him.

"Yes, the cave. I remember when the Japanese made us carry boxes of shells and weapons up the road to the caves. We worked at it for two weeks. One cave was full of guns and explosives. The officers lived in the other smaller cave."

"When was that?" Lam asked.

"Back during the big war, in 1942."

"That was fifty-nine years ago," Lam said.

The old man smiled. "It doesn't seem like that long ago." He shook his head. "Things change so much. Now the Japanese are our friends."

Twenty minutes later they loaded in the helicopters and took off. The dirt road they flew up from the highway was one they had been along before. They'd come back that time finding nothing that looked like a rebel camp. This time the old Filipino stood beside the pilot directing him. They went up almost to the edge of the slope, then turned back.

"Yes, there, there. See where those branches have been cut and put over the entrance? I can see it. Yes, still there. Now find a place to land."

The landing place was a half mile down on the road where the trees had been cut away. Both birds landed, and the men charged out and into the jungle cover.

"Can they see us from the caves?" Murdock asked the old man.

"Oh, yes, can see the whole valley out here. Good binoculars I bet they have."

"Let's get moving," Murdock said. He marched his men through the cover of the trees, and was closely followed by the Rangers. Less than a minute after they left the choppers, the SEALs heard a heavy fifty-caliber machine gun thundering away ahead of them. The men dove for the sides of the road.

But the rounds weren't coming at the men. Behind them Murdock saw the big explosive fifty-caliber rounds drilling into the helicopter closest to the mountain. The rotors were still going as the rounds chopped them up, splintered them, and riddled the cabin and engine. Then the chopper exploded in a huge fireball.

The second chopper lifted off at once and darted away from the danger. It made it away safely.

Murdock screamed at the gunner, then moved to where he had an open shot at the end of the road. He aimed a 20mm round at the cliff where he thought the cave mouth might be, and fired. He saw the round hit and explode, and then he fired again. He put three rounds into what he thought was the entrance to the cave. There was no more fire from the fifty. But it had no target. Murdock and the rest of the men jogged forward toward the cave. Now they knew for sure that this cave must be the spot where the hostages were being kept. Murdock set his jaw when he realized they had just seen some of the results of Osama bin Laden's generosity. His cash must have been used to buy the fifty-caliber machine gun. As they jogged forward, Murdock wondered what other heavy weapons that Muhammad might have were now set up and ready to use defending the cave.

24

"Let's all get off the road," Murdock said into his radio. "They should have concentrations of fire mapped out. The road would be one. Split into two groups. SEALs to the right, Rangers to the left. Stay off the road fifty yards and move up through the cover. Don't make any noise or let the cover move to give yourself away. Let's split, now."

They moved slower through the woods. Murdock brought up his three Bull Pups. He'd sent two with the Rangers.

Murdock called a halt when his unit was a hundred yards from the face of the slope where the cave was.

"General, let's talk. Strategy?"

"I'd say we hit the cave entrance with four rounds of twenty, then do two shots from the EAR and move up and recon and see what they have left."

"If they have a heavy plank door over the cave entrance, it could bounce the EAR beam off at an angle and not hurt them at all," Murdock said.

"We should find out about that when the twenties wash away all of their camouflage. Worth a try. We don't have enough men to assault a fort like that."

"Agreed. You have two twenties. Let's have each of the five guns put two rounds on the cave entrance and see what happens."

Before they could shoot, two RPG's flashed out of the brush near the face of the cliff and raced out a hundred yards, but fell and exploded harmlessly between the two units near the road.

"Fire when ready," Murdock said, and he heard the report of the heavy rifle rounds leaving the weapons, then the stuttering explosions of the twenties against the face of the cliff. He hoped some went inside.

Murdock found a spot where he could look through the jungle at the cliff. He saw one section where the growth had been blown aside, and he thought he could see the edge of a hole, maybe the entrance to the cave. He used his own Bull Pup again, and put a round on the spot with the laser sighting. The airburst shattered a whole section of cut branches shielding the opening. Now they could see half of the cave opening.

Murdock had charged through the jungle for fifteen yards as soon as he saw results of the shot. He was safely behind two tree trucks when the machine-gun slugs riddled the area he had fired from.

"Casualty report," Murdock barked into the net.

Both squads checked in with no casualties. "Two more rounds each Bull Pup," Murdock said. "Fire and then move your ass at least twenty yards. First find a spot where you can see through the trees to the cave entrance. Then fire. Go."

The weapons fired with spaces between as the men found fields of fire. When the ten rounds ended, Murdock moved again to where he could see the cave. The entrance was void of any cover now. It was a black hole that looked at least ten or twelve feet high. He saw a sandbagged machine gun that had been placed in front of the opening. One rebel had fallen half over the sandbags and wasn't moving.

"General, how about some EARs into that opening?"

"Agree. Two shots each at ten-second spacing. EARs fire when ready."

The shooters had to move to a spot where they could get a clear area to fire through at the cave mouth. Then the whooshing sounds came, and Murdock watched the opening for some reaction. He saw no men there, and none appeared after the rounds went inside.

This time there was no return fire.

"We've got to go in there," Murdock said. "Ideas, General?"

"Let's each send up one squad with the EAR and Bull Pups for a probe. You're right, we have to go inside."

"Moving now up this side, we'll check with you at the cliff face. Alpha and Juan, let's go. Whoever has the EAR come with us. Now." Murdock moved to the head of the squad, and they worked silently up the slope toward the cliff face. It was only eighty yards now and they moved slowly, not disturbing any of the lower growth. The canopy overhead was thirty feet above them, but grew lower as they climbed.

"General, we're about forty yards from the cliff face."

"Roger that, we're a little closer. Haven't seen any action at the cave mouth. The EARs must have done their job."

"We don't know how far they penetrated into the cave, so be alert," Murdock said.

They came to a rocky ledge that was in plain sight of the cave opening. They had to cross it. Murdock studied the cave opening again. Two rebels were draped over the machine gun and its sandbags. Both looked to have massive, bloody wounds. He could see no one else.

He grouped the squad behind him. "Okay, we go over all at once. If anybody is there, he can't get all of us. Ready? Let's go, now." Alpha Squad and Juan charged across the ten yards of rocky shale, and dove into the jungle cover on the other side. Everyone made it, and there was no fire from the cave mouth.

Murdock told the general about it.

"Good, they must be back well inside if any are alive or awake," General Domingo said. "We're near the face and moving toward the opening."

A minute or two later the SEALs were there and could see the Rangers moving up with each man covering for the next. The SEALs did the same routine, and Lam came up to the gun mount first.

"Two KIA here, Skipper," he said. "The weapon is out of action as well. I can't see anything or any bodies in the cave."

"Hold there at the side," Murdock said.

Two minutes later the Alpha Squad men and Juan clustered against the wall next to the mouth of the cave. The general's Rangers were on the other side.

"Scout," Murdock said. "We'll send in Lam."

"Roger that," the general said.

"Ten or fifteen yards, talking all the time," Murdock said to Lam. The scout lifted away from the wall, and holding his Bull Pup at port arms, he edged around the side of the opening and darted inside.

"Okay, I'm in. Nothing so far. No lights. No bodies. Yes, now I have two men on the ground. Looks like the EAR got them. Weapons are by their sides. No visible wounds."

There was a moment of dead air. "Oh, shit, now we get to it. About a dozen rebels, looks like a twenty came in here and then went off. Body parts all over the place. Hold it." The radio went silent.

"Yes, faint but I can hear it. I'd say it's a generator and that could mean lights back a ways. I'm using my flash. I'm maybe thirty yards inside now. Suggest some backup. One squad up here, one in reserve."

"General?" Murdock asked.

"I'll send in a squad. One of the men has a Motorola."

Murdock saw the ten Rangers led by a sergeant come to the cave mouth and charge inside.

"Hi, guys, glad you could make it," Lam said when the Rangers got up to him. "Use your lights if you have them."

The air was quiet for a while.

Lam peered ahead in the cave. The ceiling was way up there. The cave widened out now to almost forty feet. He could still hear the pounding of the engine. Must be enough air in there so the carbon monoxide wouldn't be a problem, he decided. Lam stabbed the short light into the darkness ahead, then swung it side to side. It didn't help that much, and a moment later he stumbled over a body. He checked it. Sleeping. He bound the man's feet and hands with plastic cinch straps and moved on. The cave made a turn, and ahead he could see lights. At the same time he heard the magnified sound of a sub gun chattering off a dozen rounds. He dove to the stone floor and rolled to the side.

"Contact. We've made contact with some live rebels who

have a working sub gun. It's around a bend in the tunnel.
What now, oh, wise leaders?"

"Back off to the corner and wait," Murdock said. "We're
coming in." Both squads outside pulled out flashlights and
ran for the cave entrance.

"Look sharp," Murdock said. "Some bodies up here,
don't stumble over them."

"We're with you," General Domingo said.

At the bend in the cave, Murdock found Lam, and edged
around the wall with him and looked from ground level
down the void toward the faint lights. Murdock could hear
the engine chugging along now.

"No idea how many of them down there, Cap," Lam said.
"The guy on the MG had his sights set too high."

"Good. I need an EAR up here," Murdock said. He
waited a minute, and Ching slid into the rocky floor beside
him. "We want one round down the cave. Then when it
fades, the three of us are going down there full bore. Gonna
try out my new flash, a Maglite two-cell. Throws a good
beam so we won't be surprised. Your round should knock
out any rebels down there for a long way. It might not go
around corners, but we'll see what happens."

Ching checked his weapon. "Up to charge," he said.

"Fire."

The whooshing sounded louder inside the cave. They
heard it jolt down the tube, and then there was nothing. The
only sound came from the engine Murdock figured ran a
generator.

"Let's chogie," Murdock said. "General, we'll recon and
report back. Hold the fort."

Murdock swung the light from side to side in the cave.
It widened again to fifty feet. Here and there he saw the
remnants of old ammo boxes. This Maglite was twenty
times as bright as his penlight. He kept it moving, just in
case there was a live one down there with a gun.

A hundred feet down the tunnel they found a man with
a sub gun. He slept. They tied him hand and foot and
moved on.

"He was a lookout," Lam said. The next ones they found
were a squad lined up across the tunnel, all with AK-74's,

the new ones, which must have been furnished by bin Laden. The six rebels lay sleeping, and the three SEALs tied them hand and foot.

They were closer to the generator now, the sound louder, insistent. They stopped and lay on the rocky floor. Murdock reported what he had found. He suggested to the general that he keep three men at the cave mouth as a rear guard, and the rest come up around the bend in the tunnel to a six-man squad taking a nap.

"We'll move on forward. Can hear the generator better, so it should be close. Wonder if they have a fresh-air outlet for the exhaust."

The three moved ahead. Twenty yards farther they came to a small mess setup, with gas stoves, food cabinets, even two tables with chairs. No cooks.

Another twenty yards and they found another bend in the cave, again to the left. The three edged up to the turn, where they could see around it. At the first use of the flashlight around the bend, they took incoming small-arms fire from at least three weapons.

They pulled back.

"An EAR round?" Ching asked.

Murdock scowled. "If there are any hostages, they should be close. That engine is next door here somewhere."

"Better packing out some sleeping hostages than it is getting the shit shot out of us from those three weapons out front," Ching said.

"Oh, yeah," Murdock said. "Oh, yeah. Give them a round, Ching."

He fired one round with the whoosher, and they waited a full minute; then Murdock waved the flash around the corner, but had no response. "I'll charge across the cave here and see if I get any response," Murdock said. He came to his knees and surged across the fifty feet to the other side. No response.

"Let's move forward," Murdock said.

They found the three shooters behind sandbagged positions forty feet up the cave. Now all three men were sleeping. The SEALs used the plastic ties, then stared into the darkness beyond.

"Why keep the generator running if they don't have some lights on?" Lam asked. "We saw some lights before, but now they all seem to be off."

"Good question, any answers?" Ching asked.

"To keep some equipment turned on," Lam said.

"To keep a radio net open," Murdock said.

"Or to keep a timer running on a booby trap, a bomb," Lam said.

"Let's move faster," Murdock said. "We should find somebody here. They've had time to set up bombs all around this damn cave."

They jogged forward for fifty feet and came to a dead stop.

Just ahead, behind a chain-link fence, they saw people moving.

"Are you the tourists, the hostages?" Murdock called.

"Yes, some of us are here," a man called. They ran up to the fence but didn't touch it. It was ten feet high and with posts set in concrete into the rock floor.

"How many of you?" Murdock asked, shining the light around.

"Six. They took six men out of here late last night. We don't know where they are." The man looked about sixty, with white hair and a stubble beard. He held his hand in front of his eyes. "Damn rebels said something about a bomb. Don't know what they meant."

Lam tossed his KA-BAR against the fence. It fell to the floor.

"Not electrified," Lam said. "I'll find a gate or an opening."

"Did some men come past here recently?" Murdock asked.

"Yep, about a dozen. Looked dazed and not happy. Went on down the cave. Don't know where they were heading."

Murdock frowned. "Didn't the old man say something about there being two caves here? The large one and a smaller one."

The two with him nodded.

"So where did the rebels go?" Lam and Ching shrugged.

"Lam, stay with the group here, get them out of there if

you can. Ching and I are heading on down the cave. Chance there's a connection between this cave and the other one. Sounds like something the Japanese would do in the last war."

The two SEALs jogged down the cave. Now, in Murdock's light, they saw it was getting smaller. Twenty feet farther and they came to the end.

Murdock used his light all around the end of the cave, and found it to one side almost hidden.

"A tunnel," Murdock said. "Tall enough to stand in. Our rebel friends have gone through it, and either to the outside or to the other tunnel and back to daylight. Let's get back to the captives."

When they came to the chain-link fence partitioning off a section of the cave, they saw that Lam had found a gate and released the hostages. They stood around waiting, two men and four women.

"General, we have six hostages," Murdock radioed. "The rest of the rebels have gone through a tunnel into the second cave. Tell your men at the mouth of this one to watch for any movement out there. We're coming back with the hostages."

"You didn't tell him about the bomb?" Lam said.

"We don't know for sure. If we find the generator, make sure that nobody turns it off. That could be a break to make circuit and set off the charges, wherever they are."

"A bomb?" General Domingo asked.

"Forgot we were live full-time on the radio, General. Chance the generator is powering some equipment or maybe a timer on a bomb. We're not sure. Get everyone out of the tunnel on double time. Don't spare the horses, as we used to say in Nebraska. Move them, now."

Murdock turned to the hostages. "We're going to walk out of here now. Does anyone have trouble walking?"

They all said no, and Lam led them forward. He paused once to let them catch up, then continued.

"With any luck we'll be out of here in about ten minutes," Lam said.

They came to the first bend in the tunnel and headed toward the next one. The explosion came as a grinding, blasting sound, tearing through the tunnel that amplified it. The hostages looked behind, then hurried forward. The jolt of hot air and smoke hit them a moment later and knocked down two of them. Then the surge of air was past and they coughed in the smoke.

"Bomb must have been in the hostages area," Murdock said. He helped one of the men stand and held his shoulder as they walked forward.

"Everyone all right back there?" General Domingo asked.

"A little shook up, but everyone is moving. Another five minutes."

"The rest of us are out and I've sent a security force to protect the helicopter. I still can't believe we lost that first one. The old man was in that one and said he'd wait for us."

"Moving as fast as we can. Just hope there aren't any more bombs. You might have your men scout around the entrance to see if they can find any wires or any explosives."

"Will do, Commander. Good idea."

They kept walking forward. One of the women tripped over something. Murdock helped her up and as he did, his flashlight shone on a rebel body, torn apart, that the woman had tripped on. She gave a low cry and fainted. Murdock caught her, picked her up, and carried her in his arms as they kept moving forward.

Fifty yards down the cave, where the last turn came, Ching took the still-unconscious woman and Murdock ran on ahead.

"Better clear your men out of the entrance," Murdock said on the Motorola. "I'll give it one last check before the hostages get there."

Murdock hurried forward. He was less than fifty feet from the light at the entrance when the bomb went off.

25

The blast knocked Murdock down, and for a minute or two he didn't know where he was or what had happened. He lay on the cold stone floor gagging and coughing. His eyes were glued shut with dust, and for a moment he thought he was blind. Slowly he realized that it had been a bomb near the entrance. He couldn't hear a thing. He shook his head and wiped gently at his eyes. He shook the dirt and dust off his cammy shirt and wiped at his eyes with it. Slowly he could see faint light.

Light, there should be lots of light near the mouth of the cave. He had been only twenty feet from the outside. His head hurt like it had been stomped by a herd of elephants. He blinked, wiped his eyes again, and felt the pain of the dust in them. Slowly he wiped them again and tried to look at the light. Yes, there was some still coming in the mouth of the cave. A hole near where the top had been. Rubble, rocks, dirt everywhere.

"Hello inside," a voice called. Then a shadow at the hole. "Are you all right in there? We're digging out this hole for you to make it larger. Can you answer me?"

Murdock looked at the hole and the shadow and wanted to yell back, but his voice didn't work well. He was choked up with the dust. He croaked out some words, but he couldn't hear them. At least his hearing was coming back a little. Next, maybe, his voice. He tired to stand, made it on the second try, and slowly worked his way toward the hole. It was a mountain of shattered rocks and dirt. He climbed and climbed, and when his strength had almost given out, he pushed one hand through the opening. Someone grabbed it.

"Hello, we have a live one here," Jaybird bellowed out. "Hang tight there, man, we're going to get you out of there in a few minutes."

More than fifty yards behind the entrance, the six hostages and the two SEALs had all been knocked down by the force of the blast. They were still spitting dust out of their mouths and coughing and wheezing in the dusty air.

Lam was on his feet first. He brushed off his uniform, then began helping the people up.

"Yes, the other bomb, but we're okay. Everyone is fine here, right? Nobody broke anything. Good. Now, we'll all get up and walk on up to the mouth of the cave. You bet we're going to get out. We have two platoons outside who will move half the mountain if they have to, in order to get us out. We all ready to move?"

"Yeah, ready," Ching said. He picked up the woman he had been carrying. She had revived and was asking questions. Ching didn't bother to answer them; he just carried her forward. The rest of them walked carefully in the tiny twin beams of the pencil flashlights.

Murdock sat beside the hole and slowly pulled himself together. Somebody was talking on the other side of the hole.

"Water," he said, and then said it again. He reached out through the hole and grabbed a hand and pulled the person closer. "Water," he croaked, and Jaybird understood him. He gave him his canteen, and Murdock took a mouthful and washed his mouth and spat. Then he swallowed some, then some more. He tried talking again.

"Who's out there?" he asked.

"Skipper, it's Jaybird. We're moving rocks and dirt here to make the hole bigger. Glad they didn't use one more quarter-pound on that entranceway, or we'd be looking for a bulldozer. You okay, Skipper?"

"Could be better. I'll move some of these damn rocks."

Murdock began to pull away rocks from his side of the opening. Five minutes later, when Lam and Ching brought up the hostages, the hole was big enough to sit in and slide through. The hostages went first, then Murdock and Lam, with Ching bringing up the rear. Lam looked up at the brilliant blue sky.

"Oh, yes, daylight, what a wonderful invention."

Murdock clambered down the pile of smashed rocks and dirt from the top of the cave opening, and sat down under a tree. He washed his mouth out again and blew his nose half a dozen times. The air still didn't seem clear. The headache wouldn't go away. Mahanani looked him over and gave him some pills for the headache, then went to look at the hostages.

General Domingo came up.

"Glad you made it, Murdock. You must have been close to the front when it went off. We gave up trying to find the charges. They must have hidden them well. Now, a few matters. We didn't see anyone coming out of the mountain. The other cave mouth must be highly concealed. We have six hostages here, so we're still six short.

"We have eight or ten prisoners inside we need to go in and untie and walk out. Juan will work with them until we find out where the rest of the hostages were taken. The next cave would be too easy. I'm sure that Al Hillah had a better backup plan than that.

"I've sent the hostages down to the chopper. One of my men will go with each one to assist. Once they are at Lebak, we'll arrange to fly them to Davao, then on their way. I still can't believe we lost that helicopter." He frowned.

Murdock thought of it at the same time. "Right, we never did find that fifty-caliber MG inside the cave. They must have taken it with them. I hope they don't mount that on the armored personnel carrier one of the rebels said they have. Why haven't we seen it before now?"

Domingo grinned. "Yes, Commander, you must be feeling better. Glad that blast didn't shatter you into pieces. I've got to get some things done."

DeWitt had taken over the platoon, and they were moving most of the rocks from the opening. "We still have to get the prisoners out of there after they wake up," DeWitt said. "The general and I figured it would be easier to let them wake up than to carry them out."

Mahanani hovered around Murdock like a bantam hen. "Wondering if you had a concussion in there when that beauty blew," the hospital corpsman said. "If that headache doesn't go away, we'll see if there's a doctor in Lebak."

"Get out of here and get to work," Murdock growled.

Mahanani grinned. "Yeah, now that sounds more like my Skipper."

The helicopter took off shortly, and in fifteen minutes it was back. General Domingo sent all of the SEALs back on the next trip, and said he'd keep his men there and bring out the prisoners as they woke up. He borrowed Murdock's two-cell Maglite.

Back in their warehouse home in Lebak, the men settled into their bunks and cleaned their weapons. Mahanani brought two-ounce shots of the liberated whiskey and gave them to Murdock and Lam and Ching.

"Medicinal purposes only," Mahanani said. Murdock downed his in one long pull, shook his head, and then frowned.

"Now, all we have to do is find out where that damned Muhammad went and rescue the other six hostages," said Murdock. "Any ideas?"

Lam shook his head. "Hard telling. Where can he go? He's lost the rock house up on the ridge. We busted that, and next he went to his own lair, the Eagle's Nest. We kicked his ass there. Next he fell back to the cave with the built-in generator and bombs. What has he left? He's going to need supplies, food if nothing else. Hell, maybe he checked into the local hotel and ordered up room service."

They kicked around where he might go. The villages were out. They didn't have enough food to feed him, and there were no defenses. There wasn't any place he could fall back to.

Murdock shook his head. "I don't know, maybe that bomb shook up my brains more than usual, but I keep thinking that Lam might have something there. Lebak here is the only place he could come where he might fit in and not be noticed at least for a while. He could buy or steal food here for his men."

"I told you guys this man is brilliant," Jaybird yelped. "I've known it all along."

The rest of them thought it over and heads began to nod.

Murdock grinned. "So, after you guys get washed up and your weapons cleaned, I want you to go in twos all over this small town and talk to people and see if they have noticed anything unusual, like ten or fifteen people suddenly showing up in a house or a store or an old warehouse. Git on your horses and move. Maybe when you get back, we'll have figured out some chow for you."

Murdock went outside to see the men on their rounds. That was when he saw a CH-46 drop into the LZ and power down. He went over and talked with the pilot.

"We have some more hostages for you to take to Davao," Murdock said, "but General Domingo will tell you about that. You bring anything for me?"

"How about a radio," the pilot said, and handed Murdock a SATCOM complete with antenna.

"Oh, yes, we've been needing that. Thanks."

Murdock took the SATCOM back to the warehouse, and set it up and called Don Stroh on his special frequency. He connected on the second call.

"Hey, Mr. Banana out there, how is it peeling?" Stroh asked.

"By the bunch. We just liberated six more hostages, but we're short on the final six. Trying to get a sighting on where they might be. So far no more problems. You know we lost Train Khai."

"Yes, I heard from your CO in Coronado. At least on this one we don't have to make up a death story. You guys have been all over the international press, TV, newspapers, everything. The rescue mission is in the clear and you'll have a scrapbook of clippings by the time you get home."

"I didn't know that, Stroh. Then maybe we can get another dozen Bull Pups and six more EAR guns."

Stroh laughed. "Probably not, but I'll try. I'm still here in Davao. The brass here wouldn't let me come to Lebak. I could have grabbed a forty-six, but decided against it. They don't even have a five-star hotel there, as I understand."

"You're right there, Stroh. Just wanted to check in. We have our SATCOM back. It was lost for a spell. You take care. Don't call us, we'll call you."

They signed off. Murdock went outside the quarters looking for any of his men. Jaybird and Lam came in, but were empty-handed.

"Nobody we talked to had seen anyone or anything unusual. They all asked at once if we meant the rebels, and we said yes. The rebels are not well liked in this town."

Murdock called the general on the Motorola, but he was too far away to be reached.

A short time later the bird that was at the cave came back with six of the Rangers and three prisoners who were awake and with their hands tied behind their backs. Juan was along, and he and the rebels vanished into a shed behind the warehouse.

"Looks like it's question-and-answer time," Jaybird said. "I want to go watch."

Murdock shrugged. "You might pick up some pointers on how to torture a prisoner for longer periods of time without killing him."

Jaybird lifted his brows. "Hey, maybe I'll watch the next time."

It was almost dark when the forty-six landed with the final group of prisoners and General Domingo and the rest of his men. They tied the prisoners, pushed them into the shed, and locked the doors.

Later, Juan came out and shook his head. "So far we have learned nothing about where Muhammad might have gone. We were told he had that armored personnel carrier, and we know he has that fifty-caliber MG. We just don't know where he is."

Domingo scowled and nodded. "Let's take a fresh look at it in the morning. Not much else we can do tonight."

Murdock told the general about their idea that Muhammad had retreated right into Lebak.

"He could be hiding in a dozen buildings around here," Murdock said. The general agreed.

"I'll put my men on a four-hour shift shaking down this

town," he said. "If he's here, or if anyone knows anything about him, we'll find out."

By 2200 the Rangers hadn't turned up any evidence of the rebel leader, his men, or his equipment. Everyone called it a day and hit the sack. Breakfast would be at 0600.

After breakfast at the improvised mess hall, Murdock went to the structure behind their warehouse and checked on the interrogation. Juan had a knack for it, knowing which of the ten prisoners to question in depth and which ones to dismiss. The lot had been narrowed down to two men. Juan thought both of them knew more than they were saying.

He concentrated on one. "We know where your mother and your wife and twin daughters live," Juan said. The man looked over with a frown, but said nothing. He sat tied to a chair, his hands behind his back.

"I will release you as soon as you tell me where Muhammad has gone. You know. I can see it in your eyes, and the eyes never lie. This is the big picture. You either tell me where Muhammad has gone to, or you die where you sit. Quite simple really. You tell me, and I release you and you can walk out the door a free man, with civilian clothes, and go back to your mother and family right here in Lebak."

The man turned, his face a mask of terror.

"Don't hurt my family."

"Tell us where the evil rebel, Muhammad, has gone."

"He would kill me."

"He won't have the chance. He will never know. Besides, his power is shattered. He has lost the rock house, the Eagle's Nest, and even the hidden cave. Now he is hiding like a snake in the jungle. He has no men, no power. He is a sniveling coward, using men like you to promote himself for his own ends."

"No, he says we will be better off."

"What has he given you besides the misery of being a rebel, of being shot at and chased and interrogated? What has he done for you?"

The man started to cry. He looked at Juan and back at the second man, who also sat tied to a chair. The man had blood dripping down his cheeks and off his chest. He had been tortured for an hour before Juan left him and moved to this man.

"I'm not sure where he is. There was a place we were to run to if we lost the fight at the caves. He said the big machine gun would stop anything the Army could throw at us. It didn't."

"Where is the hiding spot?" Juan asked.

The man took a deep breath and let it out slowly. "He said go to the church here in Lebak and ask for asylum. The priest there could not deny us entry."

Juan thought about it a moment, then nodded. "Yes, that sounds like something this infidel would do." Juan pointed to two Rangers. "Keep him here, as he is. We'll see if he's telling the truth."

He and Murdock left the building and ran back to the warehouse, where General Domingo studied a map of the area. He glowered at the news of where Muhammad might be.

"We'll take all our men," he said. "We move up from all four sides of the church and the small rectory. Then I'll go knock on the door and talk to the priest."

Murdock called his men up, told them to come fully equipped with weapons and combat vests, and they marched out in patrol order.

The Catholic church sat on a lot of its own with no other buildings around it. The rectory perched beside it. Since this was a poor village town, the church was modest, a wooden structure painted white with a gleaming cross over the two-story building.

SEALs took the south and west sides of the church, finding hiding places and cover up to fifty yards from the structure. Rangers covered the other two sides. When all were in place, General Domingo walked up to the church and knocked on the door. No one answered. He checked his watch, then opened the door and walked inside. He was alone.

Murdock's men were closest to the church door. "If we hear any shots, even one, we're charging that door. Alpha

Squad on the front door, Bravo take the side and back doors."

They listened, but heard nothing.

Inside the church, the general took off his floppy hat and looked around. No people. Only some candles burning at the altar.

"Hello," he called. A moment later he called again.

A small priest in his clerical dress came from a door near the front, saw the general, and hurried up.

"I'm so glad you came. They were here all night, but are gone now. They ate everything in the rectory and made me go get more food. There were seven rebels and six hostages. They said if I told anyone they were here, they would shoot me."

"When did they leave, Father?"

"At daybreak. They hurried out the door and toward the river. I watched them. They went north along the highway. I couldn't see them far."

"North?" Domingo thought about it a moment, nodded, and thanked the priest, then hurried outside.

Murdock relaxed when he saw the general. Domingo called the troops together and told them what the priest had said.

Juan frowned and spoke up at once. "I need to do more work on our rebel captive."

"We haven't heard anything about the APC," Murdock said. "We should check with the townspeople to see if they have seen the armored carrier anywhere. If he has it, that might be a last resort."

Domingo motioned for Juan to go back to the warehouse. The general nodded. "Yes, Commander. A good idea. We'll use all of our men to canvass the whole damn town. We can do it in two hours. Officers, assign your men to the areas and let's get asking questions."

The survey wasn't total, but Murdock figured they talked to people in at least eighty percent of the buildings and houses. An hour later one of the Rangers came on his Motorola.

"We have a sighting of the APC," he said. "A man saw it come out of a garage building just before daylight and

drive toward the highway. You can still see where the
treads tore up the street."

Five minutes later Domingo and the others looked at the
track marks on the soft dirt street, and followed them to the
highway. The driver had angled into his turn before he hit
the blacktop, giving away the direction he would go on the
hard surface. He had turned north.

"Back to the helicopters," Domingo barked. They all
jogged three blocks to the improvised LZ.

"Once that machine turns off the hard-surface road, we'll
be able to see the marks the tracks make and follow him.
Everyone with full combat gear and ready to take off in
five minutes,"

Murdock's men were ready. They loaded in one of the
two helicopters waiting. Soon the Rangers arrived and
crowded into the other bird, and they both took off.

The choppers flew low and slow. One bird watched the
surf side of the highway; the other chopper did the same
on the mountain side. They worked out two miles, retraced
the area to be sure it was clear of any tread tracks, and
moved on down the highway. Twice more they doubled
back to check their work. By the time they were about six
miles out from the town, Domingo used his Motorola.

"We have a turn. Plain as day the tracks come off the
road and go up a narrow dirt lane."

"Here we should get cautious, General," Murdock said.
"Remember those RPGs they have and the fifty. How about
some altitude and a high-level survey first to see what we
can find. Must be some buildings up here."

"Yes, Commander. I agree. I was getting too anxious.
Let's go up to two thousand feet and see what we can find.
There should be some buildings here somewhere." The
birds circled as they climbed, and Domingo used binoculars
as he tracked the vehicle below.

Murdock said the rebels should have known better.
Someone on the ground fired an RPG at the choppers at
their two-thousand-foot altitude. Not a chance the grenade
would get that high. Even before it reached its zenith and
turned down, Murdock had put two rounds of 20mm into

the area where the smoke trail showed that the rocket had been fired from.

He had shot out the side door, and had no idea if he hit the rebel below.

"At least we know we're on the right track," Murdock said. They circled another five hundred feet higher, remembering the fifty-caliber weapon somewhere below. The plain here was three miles wide before the mountains lifted up in a gentle series of hills.

"I've still got the tracks," Domingo said. "They turn off the road and leave a highway of broken shrubs and plants through the small growth of trees. But I don't see any buildings. Yes, there, just ahead. Looks like an old ranch house that the jungle has taken over. Could be some livable places inside."

"Incoming," Murdock bellowed. He pushed his Bull Pup out the forty-six's door and got off one round at the wisps of blue smoke coming from a small clearing below.

"Got to be the fifty MG," Murdock said. "Get us the hell out of here," Murdock bellowed at the pilot. "He's got a mile range with that fucker."

The chopper jolted to the left and then the right as it dropped quickly to get out of any firing pattern.

The bird Domingo was in had tried the same maneuver, but the other way. "We're hit," Domingo shouted into the Motorola.

26

"We're not hit too bad, and the pilot says he can fly to the left and down, but not with much maneuverability. Must have hit some of the control wires. We're maintaining control, looking for a cleared spot. Down to a hundred feet and out of range of the MG. Murdock, are you all right?"

"Not hit, and we have a good sighting on the spot where the tracked rig stopped. We'll go treetop level and the MG won't be able to get on us. I want to rip a dozen rounds of twenty into that area and see if we can discourage the MG and maybe cut up the APC or some of the men."

"We're almost down, Murdock. Figure we're about a half mile from the tracks and that dirt road. We'll assemble and move your direction. Don't mistake us for the rebels."

"That's a roger, General. We're treetop now and coming in from the other direction. He won't even hear us until we're almost on him. I have three twenties shooting out the left-hand door."

Murdock moved to the floor and got into firing position. The other two twenties were aimed over his head.

"Almost there," he shouted. "We'll get there and bank away and give us a broadside. Coming up. Banking, now."

All three weapons fired one round into the area where they could see the sandbagged position of the fifty-caliber MG; then they were away and hugging the treetops again. They heard the fifty-caliber fire, but none of the rounds came close.

"Once more from a different angle," Murdock yelled at the crew chief, who told the pilot.

The second run at the position was better, and they could see the machine gun set up on a tripod and the men trying to turn it to bring it to play on the chopper's sound. They banked, and all three fired at the machine gun. They saw the twenties hit, and this time there was no answering fire.

They pulled away, and Murdock told the pilot to find the other chopper and set down near it. He did. The SEALs poured out of the bird and Murdock put them on double time, tracking the Rangers on their way to the showdown with Muhammad.

The SEALs caught the Rangers as they had taken cover in the jungle along the narrow road. Murdock used the Motorola and put his men in the jungle cover.

"We had one round of fire from in front," Domingo told Murdock on the radio. "I sent a three-man patrol up there to flush him out. One of them has a radio. No word."

They waited five minutes, then moved ahead cautiously. The Rangers were out front. The radio crackled. "Hey, we've been under attack. Somebody shooting arrows. Yeah, Jose took one in the shoulder and it hurts like hell. We can't hear them, can't see them. Who the hell shoots arrows anymore?"

"The Negritos?" Juan said.

"Maybe coconut hunters," Lam said.

"Talk to them in Filipino," Juan said. "Tell them that we are not chasing them, we're looking for the bad men with long guns."

The radio was silent for a while.

"Would it help if we told them we know one of their chiefs?" Lam asked. "What was that little guy's name we ate wild pig with?"

"Could help. Tell them we know Blackie and his band," Juan said.

There was some talk on the radio that was not aimed at the mike. Soon the voice came on the radio again.

"Okay, all clear here now. I told him that we knew Blackie, and he said the chief with the funny talk was known to them. They are here to collect coconuts and take them back into the hills."

"Let's move up," General Domingo said.

The Ranger scout out front with a Motorola moved slowly, watching everything he could in the dense jungle growth. Twice he stopped and listened, then moved ahead. He was halfway across the open plain when a submachine gun chattered directly in front of him, and only the dense growth saved him. He jolted into the moist ground cover and waited. The weapon fired again at close to the same place, but six feet over, missing him. He lifted up, but couldn't see the shooter.

"I can't dig this guy out," the scout said.

"How about an EAR?" Murdock suggested. "Enough of the shock wave should get through the brush and growth to knock out the shooter."

Domingo agreed, and moved his man with the borrowed EAR to the front. He crawled up to the scout. They whispered a moment, then the Ranger fired the EAR where he was instructed.

"Move up cautiously," Domingo ordered. The two men crawled and wormed their way twenty feet forward, and found one rebel sleeping at the switch, his weapon at his side. They bound him hand and foot, took his sub gun, and the scout moved out again.

"EAR worked good," the scout said. "I'm moving forward."

Five minutes later the Rangers passed the sleeping rebel and worked ahead through the jungle.

The Ranger scout came on the air. "General, I've got a sandbagged machine-gun position dead ahead. Not over forty yards. Lots of jungle between us, but I can see him. Behind that it looks like the outline of a building of some kind, but it's been entirely overgrown with jungle vines and trees."

"Hold there," General Domingo said. Murdock moved forward as well with Lam. They all converged at the point man about the same time. Domingo had brought an EAR gunner with him.

"That should be the hideout right behind the MG," Domingo said. "We can't use the EAR unless we want to carry everyone out."

"Sir," Lam said. "I can move over there about thirty

yards so I'll be shooting at the MG nest, and the rest of the power will go out in the jungle, not inside the building."

Domingo looked at Murdock. "Are they that directional?"

"From what we've seen before, General, I think it would work the way Lam said."

"Move out," the general told Lam. "Lieutenant Quezon, bring up the rest of the men. Extreme quiet. Not a sound. DeWitt, bring up the SEALs too. No sound. We're about thirty yards from the old building."

Murdock used his binoculars on the vine-encased building, but couldn't see much inside. It was like looking inside a tree. At last he spotted something moving deep in the structure. Yes, there were men in there. It would be worth the risk. Only, where were the hostages?

Lam radioed that he was in position. The rest of the troops had not arrived yet. Then Murdock growled deep in his throat. As he watched, six civilians were marched out into the open just in back of the machine-gun nest. They were in plain sight, some even with shafts of sunlight slanting off them. Four women and two men. The rebels darted back into the old building.

"Hold fire, Lam," Murdock said. The general nodded. "What the hell can we do now?"

General Domingo contacted his men and told them to hold in place.

Lam whispered into his mike. "Skipper. Remember how tight the focus is on these things, maybe only four feet wide at a hundred yards? I'm at a different angle from you. I can still see into the old building, and I have an eight-foot slice of space between the backs of the hostages and the inside of the building. Plenty of space to get off some shots without harming the hostages."

Murdock grinned. He looked at the general.

"Yes, Lam, take your shots," the general said. "Do it now. Do four shots in forty seconds. Quezon and DeWitt, bring up the troops. We need the best snipers we have up closer."

"Every man behind a thick tree," Murdock said. "After that first EAR shot, all hell is going to break loose from that machine gun. Hold fire for a minute, Lam. We need to get situated."

The men found thick trees and stood behind them.

"Fire when ready, Lam," Murdock said.

Murdock watched around his tree. He concentrated on the machine-gun crew less than forty yards away. The gunner's head jolted toward the whooshing sound; then he pivoted the machine gun in that direction. Murdock had a clear shot. He aimed the Bull Pup on 5.56 on single-shot, and before the machine gunner could pull the trigger, a deadly slug jolted into his chest and knocked him off the gun. The second gunner rolled him out of the way and got behind the automatic weapon. Murdock's second shot nailed him in the throat.

Lam's second EAR shot blasted into the structure behind them.

Murdock leaned out. "Hostages, run to either side of the gun emplacement. Get lost in the jungle. Go now before those inside recover."

One man translated, and the hostages scuttered away, walking, running, and semi-jogging. There were no shots from inside the building. Murdock sent twelve rounds into the machine-gun nest, and saw the third man there half stand, then dive over the side of the parapet but not quite make it. He didn't move.

"Let's go in," Murdock said. Lam stood and rushed forward. The EAR was around his back and his Colt M-4A1 in his hands. Murdock charged across the forty yards with General Domingo and his scout right beside him. They darted into the vine-covered structure and saw the whole place go dark.

"Like a tunnel in here," Lam said. He held up his hand, and everyone stopped moving. They could hear nothing. Then what could only be a door banged shut. Lam saw in the dark better, and he ran forward, past a green wall, around some old furniture that was molding and falling apart, and through what could have been a grand living room. Then he was at an outside door that perched half-open on long-rusted hinges. Lam pushed it all the way open and jumped behind the wall.

Six hot lead messengers blasted through the open space. Lam turned his head to hear better out the door, and heard someone crashing through the jungle.

"Left side clear," Lam said. "Skipper, we've got one live one, maybe as many as three, heading out through the jungle."

Murdock slid to a stop beside him.

"What the hell are we waiting for?"

They ran into the heavy, green, moist growth for ten yards, and Lam stopped, listening. General Domingo had not been close enough to go with them. Lam pointed to the left and they moved that way, slipping through the growth, making as little noise as possible. Twenty yards forward and Lam stopped again, with Murdock right behind him. Lam listened.

"They're heading for the road," Lam said.

"What good will that do them?" Murdock asked.

The roar of a diesel engine came suddenly from somewhere directly ahead.

"The damn armored personnel carrier," Murdock said.

"Shit. Our twenties ain't gonna put a dent in that baby. What is it, one of ours they stole?"

"Probably one we sold to the Philippine Army and the rebels snatched it. What kind of main gun does it have?"

"Jaybird would know," Lam said.

"Wrong," their earpieces reported. "Jaybird doesn't know. Not enough input. The U.S. has two or three types. Could have anything on it up to a forty-millimeter front gun. We've seen them before."

"Yeah, the tracks," Murdock said grinning. "And Lam and I both have two quarter-pound chunks of TNAZ."

"Let's go get it," Lam said.

They plowed through, past, and over the jungle growth. They sensed that the machine was moving away from them, but not quickly. It couldn't knock down the big trees. Evidently it had been driven in as close as they could get it to the old ranch house and parked.

"So, they must have a track back out of the heavy stuff," Murdock said. "We find the track we can run it down. In this stuff they can't make more than maybe ten miles an hour."

It took them five minutes to catch up to the APC enough to find the wagon-wide track through the less-dense jungle. It had bulled its way in past some good-sized trees, and around them, flattening many smaller ones. Now going out was easy.

"Tracks," Lam said, and took off on a sprint toward the sound of the diesel engine and the clanking of the tracks. They could see ahead fifty yards, and the rig wasn't in sight.

At the end of the fifty, they slowed and looked around a bend in the trail. The vehicle, resembling a mini-tank, sat thirty yards down the trail, stopped for the moment. The heavy gun was aimed away from them, and they couldn't estimate how large it was.

"Don't want to know the size of that shooter," Lam said. "Want him to keep it pointed the other way."

"Any rear portholes or firing slots on these things?" Murdock asked.

"Don't know, but we'll find out." Lam took off down the smashed-flat trail directly at the APC. He took out a quarter-pound of TNAZ and popped a timer/detonator in the soft puttylike explosive that was fifteen percent stronger than C-4 plastic.

Murdock did the same as they jogged forward. The big machine started to move ahead again, and they could see no firing slots in the rear. The APC could hold up to eight combat troops. Murdock hoped there weren't that many inside this one.

The armored vehicle stopped suddenly, and a side door slid back and four armed rebels charged out of it. Murdock and Lam fired from the hip as they charged, one on each side of the cleared path, and dove into the jungle growth. The troops ahead fired on the run.

Murdock hit the ground, rolled, came up with the Bull Pup on the 20mm barrel, and fired one shot. He didn't have time to laser it. The contact round hit a tree beside the APC and shattered the area with shrapnel. Lam got off a pair of three-round bursts and one rebel, not quite to cover, lifted higher, threw his weapon away, and staggered backward, then crumpled to the ground.

Murdock took more time, lasered a round on the side of the APC, and had an airburst right over it. He heard some screams, and the rig jolted forward. Murdock fired two contact rounds with the twenty, but both rounds exploded on the hard shell of the armored rig and did little damage. He wondered if the side door was still open. He lasered a round on the trunk of a tree just at the side of the vehicle, and watched it explode as the APC ground past.

Murdock took some return fire from at least one of the rebels still alive where they had run into the brush and vines. He sent another contact round into a tree at about where he had seen the rebels last, and watched it explode and shatter the area with deadly shards of metal.

"Can't see him," Lam said on the radio.

"He's on my side," Murdock said. "You're free over there. Charge through the cover and try to catch that APC. I'll move up and clear this area one way or the other and catch you."

"Need any help out there?" Jaybird asked on the radio.

"Lots of it, but you're too slow and too far away," Lam said. He carried the ready-made bomb as he ran, making sure he hadn't activated the detonator/timer when he rolled in the carpet of green growth.

Lam's shout came over the radio a moment later.

"Look out, Murdock. He's turned around and has his big gun pointing back our way, at you. Find a big tree to get behind it."

Just as he finished talking, the long gun on the APC fired.

"That's bigger than a damned forty," Lam said, and he kept on charging through the heavy growth in cover as he moved to cut off the APC.

27

Murdock heard Lam's shout on the radio, looked up, saw the big gun swinging around on the APC, and dove into the woods and scrambled for the largest tree he could see. He had just straightened up behind a mid-sized mahogany tree when the blast of the cannon went off. The round slammed into the tops of trees in front of his protection and detonated. Shrapnel blasted down into the greenery like jet-propelled hail, shredding shrubs and vines, stripping all the leaves off others, some of the steel fragments jolting into the trunk of the tree he stood behind.

"Got to be a forty at least," Murdock told his radio.

"I'm moving up beside him in the cover," Lam said. "Got to find a blind spot and get this joy-putty on his tracks. If we can get him dead in the water, we've got him."

"Yeah, maybe," Murdock said just before the APC gunner got off a second round that blasted into the trees again, this time detonating thirty yards behind Murdock, all of the shrapnel cascaded away from the SEAL.

"No fun getting shot at with one of those bastards," Murdock said. "I can't move ahead any, no trees big enough."

"Almost there," Lam said, panting now. "Give me another two minutes. He's still stopped. Growth is thick here almost to the tracks. I'm on my belly working forward. Yeah, another minute."

Murdock leaned around the tree, but he couldn't see the APC. Too much jungle growth. For the first time he saw some coconut palms. They must grow in certain areas and not others. He knew they had to be in the lowlands. Probably because of somewhat warmer days.

Another round slammed overhead and exploded in the trees behind Murdock. Now he had some idea what the troops must feel like when they came under fire from the SEALs' twenties.

Ahead, Lam squirmed another six feet and paused. Tougher going on your belly in this jungle. He just hoped he didn't come cheek-to-jowl-to-fang with any of the poisonous snakes they said were local residents. He could see the vehicle ahead. Slightly to the left. He had to get there before it moved. He worked forward, and then he was there. The tracks were over his head. He pushed the chunk of powerful plastic explosive into the roller just where it picked up the track, and set the timer for fifteen seconds. Then he activated it and wormed back, lifted up, and ran through the jungle for fifty feet before he dove to the ground.

The explosion came moments later. A cracking, roaring that, even through the shield of jungle, jolted Lam where he lay. He turned and worked slowly back toward the APC, his Colt Carbine in his hands and ready to fire.

"Remember that thing has doors on both sides," Murdock said on the Motorola. "If anyone inside goes out the far door, you won't see him and neither will I."

Lam stopped and listened. For a moment he heard some chatter, evidently in Filipino. Then nothing. Nobody came toward him through the jungle. He edged closer until he could see through the last fringe of growth at the APC. It sat slightly askew. The near track had been blown apart and the roller assembly shattered, with most of it missing. The rig wasn't going to move.

"Nobody out this side," Lam said on the net.

"I've moved out so I can see the APC," Murdock said. "Yes, the side door on this side is open. I don't see any bodies. My bet that whoever was inside is gone."

"I'll move around and drop a fragger in the can and clear it," Lam said.

He slid out of the jungle to the mashed-down trail, edged around the back of the armor on the mini-tank, and flipped a fragger into the open door. It went off in 4.2 seconds. And Lam charged into the opening the second the hot steel stopped flying.

"Nobody home," Lam said. He ran into the edge of the jungle on the far side and looked for a sign. At once he found boot prints of two different sizes.

"Come on up, Skipper. We have two boot sizes in the brush and motoring. Looks like we have a footrace. Want to play?"

"Be there in twenty seconds," Murdock said. He left the growth, hit the beaten-down trail of the heavy tracks, and ran up to where Lam stood behind the armored vehicle.

"Heard them a minute ago," said Lam. "My guess, they're heading for the road and to get into town and melt into the community. Then be damn hard to find them."

Lam led out on the trail. Murdock was glad Lam was there. He himself could track the men through the jungle, but it would take him twice as long as it would for Lam. He watched for a bent-over plant, a scuffed vine, a torn-off branch, and always for boot prints in the soft mulch of the jungle floor.

They moved ahead in a straight line for fifty yards; then Lam stopped and listened.

He shook his head, and moved on. The trail bent to the left, then into a more open area where there once might have been a plowed field, but which was now reclaimed by the jungle growth. The difference was no tall trees. They went across the area quickly, but when they were near the far side, a rifle shot snarled in the stillness and Lam lunged to one side and curled behind a clump of vines.

"Missed me," Lam said. They waited a half minute, then rushed the last twenty yards into the deeper jungle growth. Lam stopped and listened. This time he nodded and pointed to the left again.

"Ambush," he whispered. And they both went to ground. Lam pointed to the left at a forty-five-degree angle and then to the right at another forty-five degrees. He mouthed the word "twenty," and Murdock nodded. He sighted in on a tree about forty feet away on the left and fired a 20mm shot without the laser. The round detonated and sprayed shrapnel over a wide area. Lam had crawled behind a tree, and even there he felt hot steel fragments hit the brush around him.

As soon as he fired to the left, Murdock swung to the right and fired a second contact round on a preselected tree there, and it went off with a crack and the singing sound of shrapnel.

When the hot steel stopped slicing through the air, Murdock and Lam each lifted up and charged to the spots where the rounds had exploded.

"I have one KIA," Lam said into his mike. "He has an AK-74, the new one, but no red tabs on his shoulder, and he doesn't look old enough to be Muhammad."

"No body here," Murdock said. "But I do have a small blood trail. Come take a gander."

Lam grinned when he saw the drops of fresh blood, and moved out at once, following them. He went quickly for a while, then slowed. Two shots blasted into the silence of the jungle. Lam swore and slid behind a tree. "Careful, Murdock, I picked up a round in my right leg. Feels like a broken bone. Put a couple twenties out front of me about fifty feet."

Murdock did, and the rounds went off with chilling force. Murdock moved up to Lam and looked at his leg. It was bleeding.

"Go, go," Lam said. "I can tie up the fucking leg. Go up there and bring back the bastard's hide."

Murdock moved up silently, from large tree to small tree, then a spurt toward the tree he had fired at with the twenty. Under the tree he found a pack that had been discarded. Also some brass from a rifle. He listened, and could hear someone ahead. Murdock checked for the blood trail. He found it, but the splatters were larger now, another hit with the twenty. He jolted from cover to cover now, moving quickly.

He stopped behind a large mahogany tree and listened. When he looked around the tree, three shots blasted from not twenty feet ahead of him. They missed. Murdock jerked two fraggers off his combat vest, pulled both pins, and threw them both as quickly as he could. The explosions came seconds apart. One hand grenade had landed shorter than the other, and after the last blast had quieted, he could hear a moaning and a high keening.

Murdock took it slow now, checked his cover from one tree to the next. He moved off the direct line and came in from the side of the spot where the hand grenades had shredded leaves off trees and vines.

A man lay against a downed log, his submachine gun aimed over the log at his own back trail. Murdock crept up slowly, with no sound whatsoever. He tested each step. The muzzle of his Bull Pup on 5.56 trained on the side of the rebel at all times. When he was ten feet away and with no jungle growth between them, Murdock called out.

"You're covered, Muhammad. Don't move even a finger, or you're a dead man."

The man jumped when the voice came, then steadied and turned his head, his face distorted with fury and pain.

"Motherfucker SEALs," he said. "We were fine before you assholes came into my territory."

"We're here. Let the sub gun drop over the edge of the log, now."

"If I don't are you going to shoot me?"

"Absolutely."

Muhammad must have known he didn't have a chance, Murdock figured. Muhammad swung the submachine gun to bring it around to train on Murdock. He got it only half-way before three rounds from the 5.56 barrel jolted into his back and neck. He flinched, then tried to continue the gun on around. Six more rounds splashed through his flesh and bone, the last three into his skull.

Murdock knew there was no reason to check the body. He sighed and slumped down on the ground next to a tree, and let the Bull Pup rest over his legs. "Lam, how you doing?"

"Fine here, hurts like hell. What happened up there? I heard the firing."

"He's down and dead. He even has the red tabs on his shoulders. Can't be sure, but I'd bet this is Muhammad. General Domingo, do you copy?"

"Copy that, Murdock. Sending in some men to bring out

the bodies. We'll make a certain ID. Muhammad has some scars I know about from before. Good work. We're also sending in two men to help Lam out. Mahanani has gone to find him and take care of his leg."

"I'll wait here, almost a straight line toward the road from the APC. You copy?"

"Roger that," Mahanani said. "I'm almost there."

Two hours later in Lebak, they wrapped it up. The last man killed was Muhammad. Positive ID was made. Lam's leg was set and a metal splint put on it to keep it immobile until the doctors at Davao could look at it. The hostages had been flown to Davao already, and another chopper would take the SEALs to the same city, where Stroh was already working out transportation for their homeward trip.

"Yeah, yeah, that's all fine and dandy," Jaybird said. "But where in hell is the food? I haven't eaten since breakfast and I'm fucking starved."

The mess call came a half hour later, and Jaybird grinned.

28

Three days after the final shoot-out in Mindanao, the Third Platoon of SEAL Team Seven was back in quarters in Coronado. It was a Thursday morning when Murdock came over the quarterdeck, paid his respects to Master Chief Petty Officer Gordon MacKenzie, and made it safely into his small office.

When they hit the North Island airfield, Murdock had sent Senior Chief Sadler with the uninjured men directly to the base. He took Lam and DeWitt straight to Balboa Naval Hospital in San Diego's Balboa Park to check their gunshot wounds. The hospital treated them, checked Lam's broken leg through the splints, and decided it didn't need any further medical attention. Told him to stay off it for two weeks, then to come back for a walking cast.

Murdock and DeWitt went to check on Ostercamp. He had been flown to Balboa the day after he was shot. The wound in his upper chest was not as serious as they had feared in Davao, but he was kept in the hospital for observation and would be there another week.

"Nothing strenuous for three months," the doctor on the floor said. "Then he can begin gradual workouts. I understand he's a SEAL."

"He is, Doctor. We want him back in top shape before he's operational with us."

Then the two headed home.

Now, in the office, Murdock looked at his personnel

chart. He needed two replacements. One would be permanent, one would be temporary for at least five months, and on call after that as a filler for the platoon.

A half hour after Murdock began reviewing replacement candidate files, which MacKenzie had already put on his desk, the phone rang. It was his CO, Commander Masciareli.

"Murdock, I want to see you this second. Get your ass into my office."

"Yes, sir," Murdock said. He hadn't sorted through the stack of paper on his desk, but he knew what it had to be about. Bradford. His trouble with the law.

Three minutes later, Murdock stood stiffly at attention in front of the commander. Dean Masciareli was so furious that his face had turned red and sweat beaded his forehead.

"What the hell were you thinking, taking that man on a mission when the San Diego Police and the district attorney had a warrant for his arrest?"

"I was following Navy procedure. You tell me a dozen times a day that I have to go through the chain of command. I had no orders from you about Bradford. I had nothing that would allow one of my men to be detained. What I did have were orders from you and from the Chief of Naval Operations and the President of the United States ordering my platoon to leave the country. I followed my orders from you to the letter."

Masciareli frowned. "By God, I never thought about it that way. You're right. The person who phoned you the day you left had no authority from the Navy to contact you. He should have gone through Navy channels. He didn't, so it's his fault and I'll back you all the way."

Masciareli sat down, motioned for Murdock to sit. He looked at a sheaf of papers in his hand. "You haven't seen the charges. The more I go over them the flakier they look. All they have are the words of this one witness, who is the main one facing charges of counterfeiting old-master paintings."

"Sir, have you seen any of Bradford's paintings?"

"No."

"I have. I bought two of them. They are good marine

subjects, and fairly well done. But Bradford is by no stretch good enough to fake an old-master painting."

"Not what the warrant and charges say. They indicate that Bradford is the seller of the paintings to some person up the coast somewhere. He's charged with concealing a felony, aiding and abetting a felon, and selling illegal goods.

"I've scheduled a meeting at 1600 with a Navy lawyer who's a friend of mine, an assistant DA, and a San Diego Police detective. I want you and Bradford there. Before that, you and I need to talk to Bradford and find out exactly what's been going on."

"Bradford will be across the quarterdeck at 0800. I'll bring him right over here and we'll get to the bottom of this."

Back in his office, Murdock tried to puzzle it out. Bradford simply wasn't the kind of man to take part in an art scam. Not a chance. Murdock had started on the top of the stack of paperwork MacKenzie had left him when Bradford knocked on the door.

"Senior Chief said you wanted to see me, sir."

"Right, we need to go over to the commander's office. He says there's a warrant for your arrest for being part of an operation that sells fake old-master paintings."

"Oh, damn," Bradford said.

"Then you do know something about it?"

"Yes, sir. But I had no part in it."

"That's what we have to dig into. There's a meeting at 1600 with a Navy lawyer, an assistant district attorney, and a San Diego Police detective. Before then we need to have all of our answers, and we want to know everything you do about this situation. Hold it until we get to the commander's office."

Murdock stood up to go as the phone rang. He hesitated, then picked it up.

"Missed you this morning for breakfast," a familiar female voice said. "Can I count on you for lunch at your place?"

"Hey, wondered where you were." Murdock motioned Bradford out of his office. "Yeah, you're late. I've been home almost twenty hours now. What happened?"

Ardith Manchester laughed softly, and Murdock felt that surge of delight at simply hearing her voice. "I knew you were coming, I wasn't sure when you'd arrive. You've been all over the newspapers. This is the first time, since this one was not covert at all. Your platoon has been hailed as heroes in a dozen different countries."

"Good, but that and a five-dollar bill will get you a double latte at a coffee shop. Great to hear that you're in town. Lunch at home for sure. I'm in the middle of a big brouhaha with one of my men and the San Diego Police. Trying to get to the bottom of it. Call you later about lunch for sure. Got to go."

"See you then. I have a surprise for you."

"Can't wait."

They hung up, and Murdock hustled Bradford straight over to the commander's office. They were shown directly in.

"What the hell is going on, Bradford? I've got cops and district attorneys all over me. Take it from the start and tell us what this is all about."

Bradford gulped once, then twice. "You say there's a warrant for my arrest? I don't see how."

He told them about his painting, how he'd teamed up with the other artists and rented this run-down building almost a year ago. He told them about the other artists in the group.

"Yeah, yeah. But what about this girl Xenia? Doesn't she have a last name?"

"No last name. A lot of artists do that. She's good. She sells some. I've been selling some, but we hadn't been making the nut on the rent and utilities. I guess she had been paying the rest of the tab. I didn't know that. I didn't ask where the extra money came from."

"Now you know," Masciareli said. "You sleeping with her?"

"I don't see how that—"

"Bradford, it will come out, so you might as well get used to it," Murdock said.

"Yes, I'm sleeping with her. She's good at her painting, and I'm learning from her work."

"You knew she was faking the old masters?"

"Not until two weeks before we left for the Philippines. That's the first I knew about it. I never sold any of her paintings, never arranged to sell them. I don't even know that guy in Santa Barbara who evidently is the middleman on the scheme."

"Then you swear that you didn't know about this until two weeks before we left for the Philippines, that you never acted as her agent to sell or place any of the paintings, and that you never received any kind of compensation in relation to these fake old-master paintings that she created?" Masciareli asked.

"Correct," Bradford said. "Absolutely true. I don't know how they could charge me with anything like this."

"The charges were made by Xenia," Murdock said.

Bradford scowled, shook his head. "Not a chance. You're joking. Why would she make up a lot of bullshit like that?"

"Why?" Masciareli asked. "To spread the blame. To give the cops another victim they could prosecute. To make her a little less guilty-looking. Lots of reasons. Maybe she was mad because you wouldn't marry her. Maybe she wanted a baby and you said no. Who knows how a woman thinks?"

"Is she out on bail?" Murdock asked.

"Yes, and restricted to the county area."

"I want to talk to her," Bradford said.

"Not a good idea," Murdock said. "But I'm going to. She should be at that studio?" he asked Bradford.

"She lives there."

"Okay, Bradford," Masciareli said. "Let's go over it again from the top. Everything that happened since you started there with the other painters. I want it all. We'll have a lawyer here this afternoon. He's Navy, but since this is a civilian warrant, the Navy can have no part in the case. He's here as a personal favor to me, to see what we can do before you get arrested. If what you say is true, he may be able to help us blow enough holes in the girl's testimony to get your charges reduced or maybe withdrawn. No guarantees."

Murdock stood. "I'm going to see that girl. When is the attorney going to be here?"

"Fourteen-hundred. Be careful with the girl. Tell her nothing about what Bradford just told us. Tread carefully."

"I'll be back for the 1400 meet." Murdock picked up his floppy hat and hurried out to his office. Senior Chief Sadler was running the show at Third Platoon. J.G. DeWitt had been sent on a three-day leave to let his arm heal. Lam was back at Balboa, where his leg was being checked over again. They might need to take the cast off and reset the bone.

"Make it an easy day, Senior Chief," Murdock said. "A five-mile training run this morning, and a five-mile swim this afternoon, then early release at 1600. Bradford will not be here. He's in a meeting."

"Heard about the charges," Sadler said. "Sound phony as hell to me."

"Yes, to me too. I'll be back tomorrow, Senior Chief. You've got the con."

It took Murdock almost forty minutes to get out of Coronado, across the sweeping bridge into San Diego, and then downtown to the studio. He'd been there twice to showings, and remembered where it was. The door was locked, so he pounded on it until he heard someone coming.

"Yes, yes, what do you want?" A woman's voice. There was no glass in the door. It opened slightly, then all the way.

Xenia stood there with two artist's brushes in her hand. The smock she wore had smudges of a dozen different shades of paint, and there was one small spot of blue on her cheek.

"Oh, it's you. I remember you from the showing. Bill's friend."

"Bill Bradford's commanding officer. We need to talk."

"My lawyer told me not to talk to anyone."

"I'm not Bradford's lawyer. I'm not anyone's lawyer. I want to know why you're trying to ruin the life of a fine young man when you know that you're lying right through your fucking teeth."

She stepped back a bit, then smiled. "You SEALs always

talk so colorfully. How do you know that it isn't Bill who's lying?"

"Because I know Bill. He and I have put our lives on the line for each other a dozen times. We're bonded in a way you never could be, that you couldn't even understand. You shit on my friend like this, you shit on me and I don't like it."

She took another step back. "Commander, are you threatening me?"

"Hell, no. If I threaten you, young lady, you damn well will know it for sure. I could snuff you right here and get away with it. Nobody would ever know. And you'd be dead and rotting in some garbage dump. I'm not threatening you. In fact, I'm trying to help you."

"Help, oh, shit, yes, you're a big help."

"If you maintain that Bill was your sales agent, we can shoot that down in the first hearing. Then the judge and a jury will go twice as hard on you, and there could even be additional charges brought against you. Whoever your lawyer is must know this. Remind him about it before the preliminary hearing. You must have some feelings for Bill since you've been sleeping with him. Why drag him down to your level?"

"I have my reasons."

"He wouldn't marry you, would he?"

She turned and flounced away, looked back at Murdock, and threw both slim artist's brushes at him. "Fuck, no, he wouldn't marry me. I pleaded with him. He said not quite yet. Too dangerous a job, he had. He said people shot at him, tried to kill him. I said, sure, sure, show me some newspaper clippings. So, he was my contact man for the old masters that we 'found.' Nothing on paper, all verbal. Lots of cell-phone calls to Santa Barbara. Easy to trace. Check it out. Yes, that stupid son of a bitch wouldn't marry me." She grabbed a painting off an easel and threw it at Murdock, then ran up the stairs to her studio.

Murdock figured the room above would have a lock on the door and it would be a good one. At least he had talked to her. Maybe planted some doubts in her mind. Now to see what the DA and the cops said. He didn't see how they

could have anything more than the girl's word against
Bradford. That wouldn't hold up in court. Trouble was,
Murdock didn't want this to get to court. No way it should
get that far.

Time to get home for lunch with Ardith. Murdock began
to grin; it spread across his face, and was still there when
he pulled to a stop in front of his apartment in Coronado.
He ran up the steps to the second-floor unit and barged in
the door.

Ardith Manchester had heard the car stop and had seen
him coming. She stood waiting for him.

Murdock stopped just inside the door and stared at her.
She was tall and slender, with long blond hair, a face with
high cheekbones and perfect eyes, so beautiful it made him
wince and wonder at his luck. She was a lawyer working
in Washington, D.C., for her father, the senior senator from
Oregon. She was so smart and quick and just plain nice
that it made him gulp in a quick breath.

"Hi there, sailor."

"Hi, beautiful lady. I thought you said something about
lunch."

"Maybe just dessert." She hugged him and put her head
on his shoulder, pressing against him hard so he wouldn't
leave her again.

"I have a whole envelope full of *Washington Post* clippings about our daring SEALs, the hostage busters."

Murdock grinned again. "Yeah, for once we're out of the
closet. Feels kind of good." He looked around. "You mentioned dessert?"

She unwound herself from him, caught his hand, and led
him toward the bedroom.

"It's in here," she said. "I'm it."

29

Murdock was five minutes late getting to the meeting at Commander Masciareli's office at 1400. A Navy lieutenant commander was there looking worried. Melvin Price was tall, with a wide body that looked like it was all muscle and tendons. He carried himself like a pro linebacker, and his nose had been broken more than once. He had a flat-top haircut, white-sides, thin lips, nervous blue eyes, and the demeanor of a caged lion.

"What the hell do we have here, Bradford?" Price barked.

"Sir, it's a total fabrication. I have never done any of the things that she charged me with or that are in the warrant."

Price read part of the papers in front of him and looked up. "She says here that everything you did was verbal, that there will be no records."

"That also means she has no possible way to prove that he did do anything that she says he did," Murdock said. "It's merely her word against his."

"Who are you?" Price demanded.

"Lieutenant Commander Blake Murdock, Commander. I'm Bradford's CO. These charges are totally ridiculous. It's a case of a spurned woman flailing out in desperation to get her own charges reduced."

Price frowned. "Could be, but the DA isn't going to jump at that explanation. Bradford, can I see some of your work?"

Bradford opened a large portfolio case and took out three of his unmounted marine oil paintings. One was of a pair of seagulls on a fishing boat at the wharf. Another one was the waves breaking over the Ocean Beach Jetty. A third showed a pair of Navy SEALs paddling for shore in a rubber duck.

The lawyer stood and walked up and down in front of the paintings. "Yes, not bad. They are not old-master quality, but the quality of your paintings is not at issue here."

"Sir, I have my telephone bills for the past six months showing all of my long-distance calls. There are a total of five, all going to my parents' home. I also have my bank statements for the same period showing my savings and checking balances. All miserably low."

The lawyer brushed the records aside. "Means nothing. You could have a dozen other accounts around town under your own or other names. You could use a pay phone to call in orders to Santa Barbara."

"Commander, doesn't the DA have to have some proof of the charges before they can make an arrest?" asked Murdock.

"Not necessarily, if they have enough suspicion and think they can prove the charge later. Depends on the DA, and the cops. In this case, I'd think they must have some solid evidence that what the woman says is true. Otherwise, why go to court with a case that they know they will lose?"

"Exactly my point, Commander. The woman has said all of the transactions were verbal, nothing written. What possible proof could she have of what she says? Bradford denies categorically that he knew anything about her counterfeiting until two weeks before we went to the Philippines. Just because he knew about it is not criminal. There was no conspiracy, no intent to harm or mislead, nothing of a criminal nature whatsoever."

Lieutenant Commander Price chuckled. "Murdock, are you sure you weren't a lawyer in some former life? You make some good points. But until we know what the police have, we don't have much to work with. I'll be at the meeting this afternoon at 1600, but not in any official capacity. I'll be an observer, and if I have any suggestions I'll make them in whispers to Commander Masciareli. This is a civilian matter; the Navy can have no part in it whatsoever.

The Naval Criminal Investigation Service has no jurisdiction. And despite what you may have seen on television, the JAG lawyers have no say here as well. All I can do is advise you when we see what they show."

"One other thing, Bradford. Did Xenia ask you to marry her?" Murdock asked.

"Oh, yes, every other week for the past two months. She wanted three kids in three years, and then she'd become a world-renowned painter. She got part of her wish. A lot of people around the world who bought her fake old masters are certainly going to hear about her."

The meeting broke up then, and the linebacker lawyer and Bradford and Murdock went to have coffee until time for the meeting at 1600.

Murdock kept digging. "Did you ever meet any of her friends from Santa Barbara?"

"Don't think so." Bradford stopped. "Yes, once, a rather large man with a huge nose who always made jokes about his proboscis. Yeah, he could have been the one. Had on a suit he must have paid fifteen hundred dollars for, and shoes almost as expensive. I thought he was a rich buyer. He could have been the one making the forty-thousand-dollar sales of her fakes."

"Don't mention that unless they ask you."

Price sipped his coffee and stared over the rim of the cup at Bradford. "Something has me puzzled. They say they have a warrant. All they need to do is show it at any military gate in the country, and the PD can march right into any facility and arrest the person named on the warrant. The Navy is without power or jurisdiction. So why didn't they arrive this morning when they knew Bradford would be here?"

"How would they know?" Bradford asked.

"That's right, you've been away. Your platoon has been front-page news with pictures every day and on every newscast on radio and TV for the past week. This was not a covert SEAL deal, so Navy PAO blasted it for all it was worth. They even released a picture of the platoon to the press. Those Public Affairs Office guys knew a good thing when they saw it. Great PR for the Navy. Now, were the cops a little afraid to charge into this base and grab a hero?"

Murdock began to smile for the first time since he had left Ardith. "Along with that, they may be doing some second-guessing about Xenia's statements about Bradford?" he said.

"Right," Price said. "So they come in with what they have and request, that is, *request,* a meeting to talk over the situation face-to-face. Sounds tremendously flaky to me, like they almost want to get out of a bad situation."

"What about Bradford? Has his name been mentioned in the news about Xenia's arrest?"

"Curiously, no. He hasn't been arrested, so maybe the press can't get to it yet."

Bill Bradford shrugged his six-two frame and 215 pounds and sat up a little straighter in the chair. The frown that had been on his face since early morning had started to make a slow and gradual withdrawal.

The 1600 meeting took place in Commander Masciareli's conference room, where they had been earlier. There were pads and pens at each of the seven chairs, a tray of chilled soft drinks, along with glasses and ice cubes. Murdock, Bradford, and Price arrived ten minutes early, and found three tight-lipped civilians already at the table.

Introductions were quick. Ramona Jefferson, assistant district attorney, looked about twenty-eight, wearing her Thursday blue suit, man's white shirt, and necktie. Sergeant Walter Jones, SDPD detective and arresting officer on Xenia, was in his forties, balding, twenty pounds overweight, and in a suit ten days out of the cleaners, rumpled and tired. Lieutenant Williams had no first name. He was lead detective on the case and shadow-thin, with a narrow face, heavy black brows, glasses, and nearly invisible hearing aids in both ears. There were no FBI men present. Had they given up on Bradford? Murdock wondered.

Commander Masciareli sat at the head of the table where he usually did, and directed the meeting. "Lieutenant Williams, do you want to get this started?"

The cop cleared his throat, stood, and looked at Bradford. "Mr. Bradford. We are here due to the statements of record of one Xenia, no last name, who has accused you of being a part of the swindle of art patrons in the creation and sale of fake old-master oil paintings. You have seen her charges. It is our position that before we move ahead with this case we need to hear from you and let you have your say."

Murdock stood. "Just a moment, Lieutenant Williams. Is Mr. Bradford under arrest?"

The detective took a breath, frowned, and then shook his head. "Not at the present time. But that isn't saying that he won't be when this meeting ends."

"I haven't heard him being read his rights," Price said. "If this is even an informal session, shouldn't he have his lawyer present?"

"Commander Price," Williams said. "He hasn't been arrested, so we have no need to read him his rights. The same with a lawyer. That would be true once he had been arrested. This is simply a fact-finding meeting with interested parties." He paused. "Mr. Bradford?"

"I don't care what Xenia says, I had nothing to do with her painting or selling fake old masters. Hell, I just wish I could paint that well, then I could do a lot better on my work. I only learned about her old masters when she let me look at a painting she was working on in her studio two weeks before we left for the Philippines. I knew at once what it was and what she was doing. We talked about it. I did not feel that I needed to run to the authorities, like if someone was threatening to kill a person.

"That was two weeks before we shipped out. I never knew she sold her paintings to the man in Santa Barbara until that night. I never had anything to do with the painting or selling of the paintings. It came as a total shock to me that she was doing this. We both knew it was against the law. Fraud, I would imagine it would be. That's about it."

Murdock looked at the woman. "Miss Jefferson, doesn't the district attorney's office insist on a good deal of evidence against a person before they issue an arrest warrant?"

"Yes."

"I don't see how you could possibly have such evidence against my squad member," Murdock said. "Do you?"

"When the warrant was first issued, we had what we believed was enough evidence for the document." She looked at Bradford, then back at Murdock. "Since that time, the police have done considerable backgrounding on Xenia, and we have talked to the other artists working and displaying their art at the showroom. We have determined that one of the others in fact did know that Xenia was copying old masters and selling them through a contact in Santa Barbara. They told us yesterday that they were sure that Mr. Bradford did not even know about this trade, and they were absolutely positive that he had nothing to do with the painting or selling of the pictures."

"We tracked down Xenia when she lived in Sedona, Arizona," Detective Jones said. "This morning we received back information that Xenia had two outstanding warrants in Sedona. One for defrauding an innkeeper. She skipped out on over a thousand dollars in back rent. The second was for copying and selling old-master paintings."

The assistant district attorney stood. "Gentlemen, we are withdrawing the arrest warrant, and clearing any record there may have been of it. We find Mr. Bradford has committed no crime and he is free to go."

"HoooRah!" Bill Bradford bellowed.

The three civilians turned and walked quickly out of the room.

The Navy men stood and grinned, and all shook Bradford's hand. Then Price frowned. "Bradford, that picture of the two seagulls and the fishing boat. Is that for sale?"

"Oh, you bet. All of my paintings are for sale."

"How much is that one?"

"Unmounted, it's a hundred and twenty-five. But for you I'll put it in a good frame and you can pick it up here at the commander's office, if that's all right with him."

Price took out his billfold and counted out 130 dollars. "Forget the frame, Bradford, I'll take it as is. I have exactly the right spot for it in my den and it needs a special frame."

Price went to his car, and Murdock and Bradford walked back to the Third Platoon office. Bradford grinned.

"Hey, you look happy," Murdock said.

"Haven't felt this good since I sold my first painting," he said. "Have a hundred and thirty to go on the rent. Now we need another painter to fill in the slot. Doesn't look like Xenia's gonna be there for a while."

"I'd say three to five," Murdock said.

"When's the fish fry?" Bradford asked.

"Fish fry?"

"Sure, we have one after every hairy mission."

"No fishing right now, let's make it a hamburger burn, Saturday night. I'll get the Senior Chief organizing it. Bring your own burgers. I've got everything else."

"Lots of beer, Skipper, I feel like lots of beer."

In the office, Murdock snorted when he saw DeWitt behind the desk.

"Couldn't stay away?"

"Hell, somebody has to mind the store. We've got a killer schedule set up for tomorrow. Senior Chief is putting together the hamburger feed cookout at your place for Saturday night, and then we have six replacement candidates coming in Monday for interviews. I wouldn't miss that."

DeWitt moved, and Murdock dropped into the chair. "Is that all? Nothing important going on? Like how is the arm doing? What is Milly up to, and when are you going to have your first kid?"

DeWitt looked up sharply. "Milly been talking to you?"

"No, just probing. Ardith's here. Maybe we can get together Sunday at your place and do something."

"Yeah, sounds good. Whatever happened to those new rebreathers we were going to get in from England with the computer that automatically feeds the right air mixture into the system? The ones we can dive as deep as we want with and still have the right mix. Did we order them?"

"Give Stroh a call. That's his baby."

"Yeah, I will," Ed said. "Senior Chief, get in here, we got work to do."

Murdock settled back. Yes, the good old home base. Now if Don Stroh and the CIA just gave him two months of easy time to train and work in two new men, he'd be happy. The phone rang. He picked it up.

"Third Platoon, Murdock."

"How did it go with Bradford?" Ardith asked.

"Let me tell you about that," Murdock said. He kicked his feet up on the desk and leaned back in the chair and grinned. Oh, yeah, it didn't get much better than this.

SEAL TALK

MILITARY GLOSSARY

Aalvin: Small U.S. two-man submarine.

Admin: Short for administration.

Aegis: Advanced Naval air defense radar system.

AH-1W Super Cobra: Has M179 undernose turret with 20mm Gatling gun.

AK-47: 7.63-round Russian Kalashnikov automatic rifle. Most widely used assault rifle in the world.

AK-74: New, improved version of the Kalashnikov. Fires the 5.45mm round. Has 30-round magazine. Rate of fire: 600 rounds per minute. Many slight variations made for many different nations.

AN/PRC-117D: Radio, also called SATCOM. Works with Milstar satellite in 22,300-mile equatorial orbit for instant worldwide radio, voice, or video communications. Size: 15 inches high, 3 inches wide, 3 inches deep. Weighs 15 pounds. Microphone and voice output. Has encrypter, capable of burst transmissions of less than a second.

AN/PUS-7: Night Vision Goggles. Weighs 1.5 pounds.

ANVIS-6: Night Vision Goggles on air crewmen's helmets.

APC: Armored Personnel Carrier.

ASROC: Nuclear-tipped antisubmarine rocket torpedoes launched by Navy ships.

Assault Vest: Combat vest with full loadouts of ammo, gear.

ASW: Anti-Submarine Warfare.

Attack Board: Molded plastic with two handgrips with bubble compass on it. Also depth gauge and Cyalume chemical lights with twist knob to regulate amount of light. Used for underwater guidance on long swim.

Aurora: Air Force recon plane. Can circle at 90,000 feet. Can't be seen or heard from ground. Used for thermal imaging.

AWACS: Airborne Warning And Control System. Radar units in high-flying aircraft to scan for planes at any altitude out to 200 miles. Controls air-to-air engagements with enemy forces. Planes have a mass of communication and electronic equipment.

Balaclavas: Headgear worn by some SEALs.

Bent Spear: Less serious nuclear violation of safety.

BKA, Bundeskriminant: Germany's federal investigation unit.

Black Talon: Lethal hollow-point ammunition made by Winchester. Outlawed some places.

Blivet: A collapsible fuel container. SEALs sometimes use it.

BLU-43B: Antipersonnel mine used by SEALs.

BLU-96: A fuel-air explosive bomb. It disperses a fuel oil into the air, then explodes the cloud. Many times more powerful than conventional bombs because it doesn't carry its own chemical oxidizers.

BMP-1: Soviet armored fighting vehicle (AFV), low, boxy, crew of 3 and 8 combat troops. Has tracks and a 73mm cannon. Also an AT-3 Sagger antitank missile and coaxial machine gun.

Body Armor: Far too heavy for SEAL use in the water.

Bogey: Pilots' word for an unidentified aircraft.

Boghammar Boat: Long, narrow, low dagger boat; high-speed patrol craft. Swedish make. Iran had 40 of them in 1993.

Boomer: A nuclear-powered missile submarine.

Bought It: A man has been killed. Also "bought the farm."

Bow Cat: The bow catapult on a carrier to launch jets.

Broken Arrow: Any accident with nuclear weapons, or any incident of nuclear material lost, shot down, crashed, stolen, hijacked.

Browning 9mm High Power: A Belgium 9mm pistol, 13 rounds in magazine. First made 1935.

Buddy Line: 6 feet long, ties 2 SEALs together in the water for control and help if needed.

BUD/S: Coronado, California, nickname for SEAL training facility for six months' course.

Bull Pup. Still in testing; new soldier's rifle. SEALs have a dozen of them for regular use. Army gets them in 2005. Has a 5.56 kinetic round, 30-shot clip. Also 20mm high-explosive round and 5-shot magazine. Twenties can be fused for proximity airbursts with use of video camera, laser range-finder, and laser targeting. Fuses by number of turns the round needs to reach laser spot. Max range: 1200 yards. Twenty round can also detonate on contact, and has delay fuse. Weapon weighs 14 pounds. SEALs love it. Can in effect "shoot around corners" with the airburst feature.

BUPERS: BUreau of PERSonnel.

C-2A Greyhound: 2-engine turboprop cargo plane that lands on carriers. Also called COD, Carrier Onboard Delivery. Two pilots and engineer. Rear fuselage loading ramp. Cruise speed 300 mph, range 1,000 miles. Will hold 39 combat troops. Lands on CVN carriers at sea.

C-4: Plastic explosive. A claylike explosive that can be molded and shaped. It will burn. Fairly stable.

C-6 Plastique: Plastic explosive. Developed from C-4 and C-5. Is often used in bombs with radio detonator or digital timer.

C-9 Nightingale: Douglas DC-9 fitted as a medical-evacuation transport plane.

C-130 Hercules: Air Force transporter for long haul. 4 engines.

C-141 Starlifter: Airlift transport for cargo, paratroops, evac for long distances. Top speed 566 mph. Range with payload 2,935 miles. Ceiling 41,600 feet.

Caltrops: Small four-pointed spikes used to flatten tires. Used in the Crusades to disable horses.

Camel Back: Used with drinking tube for 70 ounces of water attached to vest.

Cammies: Working camouflaged wear for SEALs. Two different patterns and colors. Jungle and desert.

Cannon Fodder: Old term for soldiers in line of fire destined to die in the grand scheme of warfare.

Capped: Killed, shot, or otherwise snuffed.

CAR-15: The Colt M-4Al. Sliding-stock carbine with grenade launcher under barrel. Knight sound-suppressor. Can have AN/PAQ-4 laser aiming light under the carrying handle. .223 round. 20- or 30-round magazine. Rate of fire: 700 to 1,000 rounds per minute.

Cascade Radiation: U-235 triggers secondary radiation in other dense materials.

Cast Off: Leave a dock, port, land. Get lost. Navy: long, then short signal of horn, whistle, or light.

Castle Keep: The main tower in any castle.

Caving Ladder: Roll-up ladder that can be let down to climb.

CH-46E: Sea Knight chopper. Twin rotors, transport. Can carry 25 combat troops. Has a crew of 3. Cruise speed 154 mph. Range 420 miles.

CH-53D Sea Stallion: Big chopper. Not used much anymore.

Chaff: A small cloud of thin pieces of metal, such as tinsel, that can be picked up by enemy radar and that can attract a radar-guided missile away from the plane to hit the chaff.

Charlie-Mike: Code words for continue the mission.

Chief to Chief: Bad conduct by EM handled by chiefs so no record shows or is passed up the chain of command.

Chocolate Mountains: Land training center for SEALs near these mountains in the California desert.

Christians In Action: SEAL talk for not-always-friendly CIA.

CIA: Central Intelligence Agency.

CIC: Combat Information Center. The place on a ship where communications and control areas are situated to open and control combat fire.

CINC: Commander IN Chief.

CINCLANT: Navy Commander IN Chief, atLANTtic.

CINCPAC: Commander-IN-Chief, PACific.

Class of 1978: Not a single man finished BUD/S training in this class. All-time record.

Claymore: An antipersonnel mine carried by SEALs on many of their missions.

Cluster Bombs: A canister bomb that explodes and spreads small bomblets over a great area. Used against parked aircraft, massed troops, and unarmored vehicles.

CNO: Chief of Naval Operations.

CO-2 Poisoning: During deep dives. Abort dive at once and surface.

COD: Carrier Onboard Delivery plane.

Cold Pack Rations: Food carried by SEALs' to use if needed.

Combat Harness: American Body Armor nylon-mesh special-operations vest. 6 2-magazine pouches for drum-fed belts, other pouches for other weapons, waterproof pouch for Motorola.

CONUS: The Continental United States.

Corfams: Dress shoes for SEALs.

Covert Action Staff: A CIA group that handles all covert action by the SEALs.

CQB: Close Quarters Battle house. Training facility near Nyland in the desert training area. Also called the Kill House.

CQB: Close Quarters Battle. A fight that's up close, hand-to-hand, whites-of-his-eyes, blood all over you.

CRRC Bundle: Roll it off plane, sub, boat. The assault boat for 8 SEALs. Also the IBS, Inflatable Boat Small.

Cutting Charge: Lead-sheathed explosive. Triangular strip of high-velocity explosive sheathed in metal. Point of the triangle focuses a shaped-charge effect. Cuts a pencil-line-wide hole to slice a steel girder in half.

CVN: A U.S. aircraft carrier with nuclear power. Largest that we have in fleet.

CYA: Cover Your Ass, protect yourself from friendlies or officers above you and JAG people.

Damfino: Damned if I know. SEAL talk.

DDS: Dry Dock Shelter. A clamshell unit on subs to deliver SEALs and SDVs to a mission.

DEFCON: DEFense CONdition. How serious is the threat?

Delta Forces: Army special forces, much like SEALs.

Desert Cammies: Three-color, desert tan and pale green with streaks of pink. For use on land.

DIA: Defense Intelligence Agency.

Dilos Class Patrol Boat: Greek, 29 feet long, 75 tons displacement.

Dirty Shirt Mess: Officers can eat there in flying suits on board a carrier.

DNS: Doppler Navigation System.

Draegr LAR V: Rebreather that SEALs use. No bubbles.

DREC: Digitally Reconnoiterable Electronic Component. Top-secret computer chip from NSA that lets it decipher any U.S. military electronic code.

E-2C Hawkeye: Navy, carrier-based, Airborne Early Warning craft for long-range early warning and threat-assessment and fighter-direction. Has a 24-foot saucer-like rotodome over the wing. Crew 5, max speed 326 knots, ceiling 30,800 feet, radius 175 nautical miles with 4 hours on station.

E-3A Skywarrior: Old electronic intelligence craft. Replaced by the newer ES-3A.

E-4B NEACP: Called Kneecap. National Emergency Airborne Command Post. A greatly modified Boeing 747 used as a communications base for the President of the United States and other high-ranking officials in an emergency and in wartime.

E & E: SEAL talk for escape and evasion.

EA-6B Prowler: Navy plane with electronic countermeasures. Crew of 4, max speed 566 knots, ceiling 41,200 feet, range with max load 955 nautical miles.

EAR: Enhanced Acoustic Rifle. Fires not bullets, but a high-impact blast of sound that puts the target down and unconscious for up to six hours. Leaves him with almost no aftereffects. Used as a non-lethal weapon. The sound blast will bounce around inside a building, vehicle, or ship and knock out anyone who is within range. Ten shots before the weapon must be electrically charged. Range: about 200 yards.

Easy: The only easy day was yesterday. SEAL talk.

ELINT: ELectronic INTelligence. Often from satellite in orbit, picture-taker, or other electronic communications.

EOD: Navy experts in nuclear material and radioactivity who do Explosive Ordnance Disposal.

Equatorial Satellite Pointing Guide: To aim antenna for radio to pick up satellite signals.

ES-3A: Electronic Intelligence (ELINT) intercept craft. The platform for the battle group Passive Horizon Extension System. Stays up for long patrol periods, has comprehensive set of sensors, lands and takes off from a carrier. Has 63 antennas.

ETA: Estimated Time of Arrival.

Executive Order 12333: By President Reagan authorizing Special Warfare units such as the SEALs.

Exfil: Exfiltrate, to get out of an area.

F/A-18 Hornet: Carrier-based interceptor that can change from air-to-air to air-to-ground attack mode while in flight.

Fitrep: Fitness Report.

Flashbang Grenade: Non-lethal grenade that gives off a series of piercing explosive sounds and a series of brilliant strobe-type lights to disable an enemy.

Flotation Bag: To hold equipment, ammo, gear on a wet operation.

Fort Fumble: SEALs' name for the Pentagon.

Forty-mm Rifle Grenade: The M576 multipurpose round, contains 20 large lead balls. SEALs use on Colt M-4A1.

Four-Striper: A Navy captain.

Fox Three: In air warfare, a code phrase showing that a Navy F-14 has launched a Phoenix air-to-air missile.

FUBAR: SEAL talk. Fucked Up Beyond All Repair.

Full Helmet Masks: For high-altitude jumps. Oxygen in mask.

G-3: German-made assault rifle.

Gloves: SEALs wear sage-green, fire-resistant Nomex flight gloves.

GMT: Greenwich Mean Time. Where it's all measured from.

GPS: Global Positioning System. A program with satellites around Earth to pinpoint precisely aircraft, ships, vehicles, and ground troops. Position information is to a plus or minus ten feet. Also can give speed of a plane or ship to one quarter of a mile per hour.

GPSL: A radio antenna with floating wire that pops to the surface. Antenna picks up positioning from the closest 4 global positioning satellites and gives an exact position within 10 feet.

Green Tape: Green sticky ordnance tape that has a hundred uses for a SEAL.

GSG-9: Flashbang grenade developed by Germans. A cardboard tube filled with 5 separate charges timed to burst in rapid succession. Blinding and giving concussion to enemy, leaving targets stunned, easy to kill or capture. Usually non-lethal.

GSG9: Grenzschutzgruppe Nine. Germany's best special warfare unit, counterterrorist group.

Gulfstream II (VCII): Large executive jet used by services for transport of small groups quickly. Crew of 3 and 18 passengers. Cruises at 581 mph. Maximum range 4,275 miles.

H & K 21A1: Machine gun with 7.62 NATO round. Replaces the older, more fragile M-60 E3. Fires 900 rounds per minute. Range 1,100 meters. All types of NATO rounds, ball, incendiary, tracer.

H & K G-11: Automatic rifle, new type. 4.7mm caseless ammunition. 50-round magazine. The bullet is in a sleeve of solid propellant with a special thin plastic coating around it. Fires 600 rounds per minute. Single-shot, three-round burst, or fully automatic.

H & K MP-5SD: 9mm submachine gun with integral silenced barrel, single-shot, three-shot, or fully automatic. Rate 800 rds/min.

H & K P9S: Heckler & Koch's 9mm Parabellum double-action semiauto pistol with 9-round magazine.

H & K PSG1: 7.62 NATO round. High-precision, bolt-action, sniping rifle. 5- to 20-round magazine. Roller lock delayed blowback breech system. Fully adjustable stock. 6 × 42 telescopic sights. Sound suppressor.

HAHO: High Altitude jump, High Opening. From 30,000 feet, open chute for glide up to 15 miles to ground. Up to 75 minutes in glide. To enter enemy territory or enemy position unheard.

Half-Track: Military vehicle with tracked rear drive and wheels in front, usually armed and armored.

HALO: High Altitude jump, Low Opening. From 30,000 feet. Free fall in 2 minutes to 2,000 feet and open chute. Little forward movement. Get to ground quickly, silently.

Hamburgers: Often called sliders on a Navy carrier.

Handi-Talkie: Small, handheld personal radio. Short range.

HELO: SEAL talk for helicopter.

Herky Bird: C-130 Hercules transport. Most-flown military transport in the world. For cargo or passengers, paratroops, aerial refueling, search and rescue, communications, and as a gunship. Has flown from a Navy carrier deck without use of catapult. Four turboprop engines, max speed 325 knots, range at max payload 2,356 miles.

Hezbollah: Lebanese Shiite Moslem militia. Party of God.

HMMWU: The Humvee, U.S. light utility truck, replaced the honored Jeep. Multipurpose wheeled vehicle, 4 × 4, automatic transmission, power steering. Engine: Detroit Diesel 150-hp diesel V-8 air-cooled. Top speed 65 mph. Range 300 miles.

Hotels: SEAL talk for hostages.

Humint: Human Intelligence. Acquired on the ground; a person as opposed to satellite or photo recon.

Hydra-Shock: Lethal hollow-point ammunition made by Federal Cartridge Company. Outlawed in some areas.

Hypothermia: Danger to SEALs. A drop in body temperature that can be fatal.

IBS: Inflatable Boat Small. 12 × 6 feet. Carries 8 men and 1,000 pounds of weapons and gear. Hard to sink. Quiet motor. Used for silent beach, bay, lake landings.

IR Beacon: Infrared beacon. For silent nighttime signaling.

IR Goggles: "Sees" heat instead of light.

Islamic Jihad: Arab holy war.

Isothermal layer: A colder layer of ocean water that deflects sonar rays. Submarines can hide below it, but then are also blind to what's going on above them since their sonar will not penetrate the layer.

IV Pack: Intravenous fluid that you can drink if out of water.

JAG: Judge Advocate General. The Navy's legal investigating arm that is independent of any Navy command.

JNA: Yugoslav National Army.

JP-4: Normal military jet fuel.

JSOC: Joint Special Operations Command.

JSOCCOMCENT: Joint Special Operations Command Center in the Pentagon.

KA-BAR: SEALs' combat, fighting knife.

KATN: Kick Ass and Take Names. SEAL talk, get the mission in gear.

KH-11: Spy satellite, takes pictures of ground, IR photos, etc.

KIA: Killed In Action.

KISS: Keep It Simple, Stupid. SEAL talk for streamlined operations.

Klick: A kilometer of distance. Often used as a mile. From Vietnam era, but still widely used in military.

Krytrons: Complicated, intricate timers used in making nuclear explosive detonators.

KV-57: Encoder for messages, scrambles.

LT: Short for lieutenant in SEAL talk.

Laser Pistol: The SIW pinpoint of ruby light emitted on any pistol for aiming. Usually a silenced weapon.

Left Behind: In 30 years SEALs have seldom left behind a dead comrade, never a wounded one. Never been taken prisoner.

Let's Get the Hell out of Dodge: SEAL talk for leaving a place, bugging out, hauling ass.

Liaison: Close-connection, cooperating person from one unit or service to another. Military liaison.

Light Sticks: Chemical units that make light after twisting to release chemicals that phosphoresce.

Loot & Shoot: SEAL talk for getting into action on a mission.

LZ: Landing Zone.

M1-8: Russian chopper.

M1A1 M-14: Match rifle upgraded for SEAL snipers.

M-3 Submachine gun: WWII grease gun, .45-caliber. Cheap. Introduced in 1942.

M-16: Automatic U.S. rifle. 5.56 round. Magazine 20 or 30, rate of fire 700 to 950 rds/min. Can attach M203 40mm grenade launcher under barrel.

M-18 Claymore: Antipersonnel mine. A slab of C-4 with 200 small ball bearings. Set off electrically or by trip wire. Can be positioned and aimed. Sprays out a cloud of balls. Kill zone 50 meters.

M60 Machine Gun: Can use 100-round ammo box snapped onto the gun's receiver. Not used much now by SEALs.

M-60E3: Lightweight handheld machine gun. Not used now by the SEALs.

M61A1: The usual 20mm cannon used on many American fighter planes.

M61(j): Machine Pistol. Yugoslav make.

M662: A red flare for signaling.

M-86: Pursuit Deterrent Munitions. Various types of mines, grenades, trip-wire explosives, and other devices in antipersonnel use.

M-203: A 40mm grenade launcher fitted under an M-16 or the M-4A1 Commando. Can fire a variety of grenade types up to 200 yards.

MagSafe: Lethal ammunition that fragments in human body and does not exit. Favored by some police units to cut down on second kill from regular ammunition exiting a body.

Make a Peek: A quick look, usually out of the water, to check your position or tactical situation.

Mark 23 Mod O: Special operations offensive handgun system. Double-action, 12-round magazine. Ambidextrous safety and mag-release catches. Knight screw-on suppressor. Snap-on laser for sighting. .45-caliber. Weighs 4 pounds loaded. 9.5 inches long; with silencer, 16.5 inches long.

Mark II Knife: Navy-issue combat knife.

Mark VIII SDV: Swimmer Delivery Vehicle. A bus, SEAL talk. 21 feet long, beam and draft 4 feet, 6 knots for 6 hours.

Master-at-Arms: Military police commander on board a ship.

MAVRIC Lance: A nuclear alert for stolen nukes or radioactive goods.

MC-130 Combat Talon: A specially equipped Hercules for covert missions in enemy or unfriendly territory.

McMillan M87R: Bolt-action sniper rifle. .50-caliber. 53 inches long. Bipod, fixed 5- or 10-round magazine. Bulbous muzzle brake on end of barrel. Deadly up to a mile. All types .50-caliber ammo.

MGS: Modified Grooming Standards. So SEALs don't all look like military, to enable them to do undercover work in mufti.

MH-53J: Chopper, updated CH053 from Nam days. 200 mph, called the Pave Low III.

MH-60K Black Hawk: Navy chopper. Forward infrared system for low-level night flight. Radar for terra-follow/avoidance. Crew of 3, takes 12 troops. Top speed 225 mph. Ceiling 4,000 feet. Range radius 230 miles. Arms: 2 12.7mm machine guns.

MIDEASTFOR: Middle East Force.

MiG: Russian-built fighter, many versions, used in many nations around the world.

Mike Boat: Liberty boat off a large ship.

Mike-Mike: Short for mm, millimeter, as in 9 mike-mike.

Milstar: Communications satellite for pickup and bouncing from SATCOM and other radio transmitters. Used by SEALs.

Minigun: In choppers. Can fire 2,000 rounds per minute. Gatling gun-type.

Mitrajez M80: Machine gun from Yugoslavia.

MI-15: British domestic intelligence agency.

MI-16: British foreign intelligence and espionage.

Mocha: Food energy bar SEALs carry in vest pockets.

Mossberg: Pump-action, pistol-grip, 5-round magazine. SEALs use it for close-in work.

Motorola Radio: Personal radio, short range, lip mike, earpiece, belt pack.

MRE: Meals Ready to Eat. Field rations used by most of U.S. Armed Forces and the SEALs as well. Long-lasting.

MSPF: Maritime Special Purpose Force.

Mugger: MUGR, Miniature Underwater Global locator device. Sends up antenna for pickup on positioning satellites. Works under water or above. Gives location within 10 feet.

Mujahideen: A soldier of Allah in Muslim nations.

NAVAIR: NAVy AIR command.

NAVSPECWARGRUP-ONE: Naval Special Warfare

Group One based in Coronado, CA. SEALs are in this command.

NAVSPECWARGRUP-TWO: Naval Special Warfare Group Two based at Norfolk.

NCIS: Naval Criminal Investigative Service. A civilian operation not reporting to any Navy authority to make it more responsible and responsive. Replaces the old NIS, Naval Investigation Service, that did report to the closest admiral.

NEST: Nuclear Energy Search Team. Non-military unit that reports at once to any spill, problem, or Broken Arrow to determine the extent of the radiation problem.

NEWBIE: A new man, officer, or commander of an established military unit.

NKSF: North Korean Special Forces.

NLA: Iranian National Liberation Army. About 4,500 men in South Iraq, helped by Iraq for possible use against Iran.

Nomex: The type of material used for flight suits and hoods.

NPIC: National Photographic Interpretation Center in D.C.

NRO: National Reconnaissance Office. To run and coordinate satellite development and operations for the intelligence community.

NSA: National Security Agency.

NSC: National Security Council. Meets in Situation Room, support facility in the Executive Office Building in D.C. Main security group in the nation.

NSVHURAWN: Iranian Marines.

NUCFLASH: An alert for any nuclear problem.

NVG One Eye: Litton single-eyepiece Night Vision Goggles. Prevents NVG blindness in both eyes if a flare goes off. Scope shows green-tinted field at night.

NVGs: Night Vision Goggles. One eye or two. Give good night vision in the dark with a greenish view.

OAS: Obstacle Avoidance Sonar. Used on many low-flying attack aircraft.

OIC: Officer In Charge.

Oil Tanker: One is: 885 feet long, 140 feet abeam, 121,000 tons, 13 cargo tanks that hold 35.8 million gallons of fuel, oil, or gas. 24 in the crew. This is a regular-sized tanker. Not a supertanker.

OOD: Officer Of the Deck.

Orion P-3: Navy's long-range patrol and antisub aircraft. Some adapted to ELINT roles. Crew of 10. Max speed loaded 473 mph. Ceiling 28,300 feet. Arms: internal weapons bay and 10 external weapons stations for a mix of torpedoes, mines, rockets, and bombs.

Passive Sonar: Listening for engine noise of a ship or sub. It doesn't give away the hunter's presence as an active sonar would.

Pave Low III: A Navy chopper.

PBR: Patrol Boat River. U.S. has many shapes, sizes, and with various types of armament.

PC-170: Patrol Coastal-Class 170-foot SEAL delivery vehicle. Powered by 4 3,350 hp diesel engines, beam of 25 feet and draft of 7.8 feet. Top speed 35 knots, range 2,000 nautical miles. Fixed swimmer platform on stern. Crew of 4 officers and 24 EM, carries 8 SEALs.

Plank Owners: Original men in the start-up of a new military unit.

Polycarbonate material: Bullet-proof glass.

PRF: People's Revolutionary Front. Fictional group in *NUCFLASH*, a SEAL Team Seven book.

Prowl & Growl: SEAL talk for moving into a combat mission.

Quitting Bell: In BUD/S training. Ring it and you quit the SEAL unit. Helmets of men who quit the class are lined up below the bell in Coronado. (Recently they have stopped ringing the bell. Dropouts simply place their helmets below the bell and go.)

RAF: Red Army Faction. A once-powerful German terrorist group, not so active now.

Remington 200: Sniper Rifle. Not used by SEALs now.

Remington 700: Sniper rifle with Starlight Scope. Can extend night vision to 400 meters.

RIB: Rigid Inflatable Boat. 3 sizes, one 10 meters, 40 knots.

Ring Knocker: An Annapolis graduate with the ring.

RIO: Radar Intercept Officer. The officer who sits in the backseat of an F-14 Tomcat off a carrier. The job: find enemy targets in the air and on the sea.

Roger That: A yes, an affirmative, a go answer to a command or statement.

RPG: Rocket Propelled Grenade. Quick and easy, shoulder-fired. Favorite weapon of terrorists, insurgents.

SAS: British Special Air Service. Commandos. Special warfare men. Best that Britain has. Works with SEALs.

SATCOM: Satellite-based communications system for instant contact with anyone anywhere in the world. SEALs rely on it.

SAW: Squad's Automatic Weapon. Usually a machine gun or automatic rifle.

SBS: Special Boat Squadron. On-site Navy unit that transports SEALs to many of their missions. Located across the street from the SEALs' Coronado, CA, headquarters.

SD3: Sound-suppression system on the H & K MP5 weapon.

SDV: Swimmer Delivery Vehicle. SEALs use a variety of them.

Seahawk SH-60: Navy chopper for ASW and SAR. Top speed 180 knots, ceiling 13,800 feet, range 503 miles, arms: 2 Mark 46 torpedoes.

SEAL Headgear: Boonie hat, wool balaclava, green scarf, watch cap, bandanna roll.

Second in Command: Also 2IC for short in SEAL talk.

SERE: Survival, Evasion, Resistance, and Escape training.

Shipped for Six: Enlisted for six more years in the Navy.

Shit City: Coronado SEALs' name for Norfolk.

Show Colors: In combat put U.S. flag or other identification on back for easy identification by friendly air or ground units.

Sierra Charlie: SEAL talk for everything on schedule.

Simunition: Canadian product for training that uses paint balls instead of lead for bullets.

Sixteen-Man Platoon: Basic SEAL combat force. Up from 14 men a few years ago.

Sked: SEAL talk for schedule.

Sonobuoy: Small underwater device that detects sounds and transmits them by radio to plane or ship.

Space Blanket: Green foil blanket to keep troops warm. Vacuum-packed and folded to a cigarette-sized package.

Sprayers and Prayers: Not the SEAL way. These men spray bullets all over the place hoping for hits. SEALs do more aimed firing for sure kills.

SS-19: Russian ICBM missile.

STABO: Use harness and lines under chopper to get down to the ground.

STAR: Surface To Air Recovery operation.

Starflash Round: Shotgun round that shoots out sparkling fireballs that ricochet wildly around a room, confusing and terrifying the occupants. Non-lethal.

Stasi: Old-time East German secret police.

Stick: British terminology: 2 4-man SAS teams. 8 men.

Stokes: A kind of Navy stretcher. Open coffin shaped of wire mesh and white canvas for emergency patient transport.

STOL: Short TakeOff and Landing. Aircraft with high-lift wings and vectored-thrust engines to produce extremely short takeoffs and landings.

Sub Gun: Submachine gun, often the suppressed H & K MP5.

Suits: Civilians, usually government officials wearing suits.

Sweat: The more SEALs sweat in peacetime, the less they bleed in war.

Sykes-Fairbairn: A commando fighting knife.

Syrette: Small syringe for field administration often filled with morphine. Can be self-administered.

Tango: SEAL talk for a terrorist.

TDY: Temporary duty assigned outside of normal job designation.

Terr: Another term for terrorist. Shorthand SEAL talk.

Tetrahedral reflectors: Show up on multimode radar like tiny suns.

Thermal Imager: Device to detect warmth, as a human body, at night or through light cover.

Thermal Tape: ID for night-vision-goggle user to see. Used on friendlies.

TNAZ: Trinittroaze Tidine. Explosive to replace C-4. 15% stronger than C-4 and 20% lighter.

TO&E: Table showing Organization and Equipment of a military unit.

Top SEAL Tribute: "You sweet motherfucker, don't you never die!"

Trailing Array: A group of antennas for sonar pickup trailed out of a submarine.

Train: For contact in smoke, no light, fog, etc. Men directly behind each other. Right hand on weapon, left hand on shoulder of man ahead. Squeeze shoulder to signal.

Trident: SEALs' emblem. An eagle with talons clutching a Revolutionary War pistol, and Neptune's trident both superimposed on the Navy's traditional anchor.

TRW: A camera's digital record that is sent by SATCOM.

TT33: Tokarev, a Russian pistol.

UAZ: A Soviet 1-ton truck.

UBA Mark XV: Underwater life support with computer to regulate the rebreather's gas mixture.

UGS: Unmanned Ground Sensors. Can be used to explode booby traps and claymore mines.

UNODIR: Unless otherwise directed. The unit will start the operation unless they are told not to.

VBSS: Orders to "visit, board, search, and seize."

Wadi: A gully or ravine, usually in a desert.

White Shirt: Man responsible for safety on carrier deck as he leads around civilians and personnel unfamiliar with the flight deck.

WIA: Wounded In Action.

Zodiac: Also called an IBS, Inflatable Boat Small. 15 × 6 feet, weighs 265 pounds. The "rubber duck" can carry 8 fully equipped SEALs. Can do 18 knots with a range of 65 nautical miles.

Zulu: Means Greenwich Mean Time, GMT. Used in all formal military communications.

MARINE SNIPER

Charles Henderson

The incredible story of the remarkable Marine, Carlos Hathcock, continues—with harrowing new stories of a man who rose to greatness not for personal gain or glory, but for duty and honor. This is a rare inside look at the U.S. Marine's most challenging missions—and the man who made military history.

❏ 0-425-18172-3/$14.00